The Danvers Jewels And Sir Charles Danvers

By

Mary Cholmondeley

The Danvers Jewels And
Sir Charles Danvers
by Mary Cholmondeley

Copyright © 2023

ISBN: 978-93-60463-96-0
Published by

DOUBLE 9 BOOKS

2/13-B, Ansari Road
Daryaganj, New Delhi – 110002
info@double9books.com
www.double9books.com
Tel. 011-40042856

ABOUT THE AUTHOR

English novelist Mary Cholmondeley was born on June 8, 1859, and died on July 15, 1925. Her best-selling book Red Pottage parodied narrow-minded country living and religious hypocrisy. In 1918, a silent film version of it was created. Mary Cholmondeley was the third of Rev. Richard Hugh Cholmondeley's (1827–1910) eight children, and his wife Emily Beaumont's (1831–1893) children were born at Hodnet near Market Drayton in Shropshire. Her niece, Stella Benson, was a writer, and her great-uncle, Reginald Heber, was a bishop who wrote hymns. The American novelist Mark Twain was hosted by his uncle, Reginald Cholmondeley of Condover Hall, during his trips to England. Mary's family narrative, Under One Roof (1918), includes excerpts from her sister Hester's poems and diaries, which she composed and maintained before her death in 1892. Following short stays at Leaton, Shropshire, and Farnborough, Warwickshire, the family moved back to Hodnet in 1874 when her father succeeded his father as rector. Despite having asthma, she spent a large portion of the first thirty years of her life supporting her father in his parish work and her ailing mother in running the home. From a young age, she would tell stories to amuse her siblings.

CONTENTS

THE DANVERS JEWELS

CHAPTER I

I was on the point of leaving India and returning to England when he sent for me. At least, to be accurate—and I am always accurate—I was not quite on the point, but nearly, for I was going to start by the mail on the following day. I had been up to Government House to take my leave a few days before, but Sir John had been too ill to see me, or at least he had said he was. And now he was much worse—dying, it seemed, from all accounts; and he had sent down a native servant in the noon-day heat with a note, written in his shaking old hand, begging me to come up as soon as it became cooler. He said he had a commission which he was anxious I should do for him in England.

Of course I went. It was not very convenient, because I had to borrow one of our fellows' traps, as I had sold my own, and none of them had the confidence in my driving which I had myself. I was also obliged to leave the packing of my collection of Malay *krises* and Indian *kookeries* to my bearer.

I wondered as I drove along why Sir John had sent for me. Worse, was he? Dying? And without a friend. Poor old man! He had done pretty well in this world, but I was afraid he would not be up to much once he was out of it; and now it seemed he was going. I felt sorry for him. I felt more sorry when I saw him—when the tall, long-faced A.D.C. took me into his room and left us. Yes, Sir John was certainly going. There was no mistake about it. It was written in every line of his drawn fever-worn face, and in his wide fever-lit eyes, and in the clutch of his long yellow hands upon his tussore silk dressing-gown. He looked a very sick bad old man as he lay there on his low couch, placed so as to court the air from without, cooled by its passage through damped grass screens, and to receive the full strength of the punka, pulled by an invisible hand outside.

"You go to England to-morrow?" he asked, sharply.

It was written even in the change of his voice, which was harsh, as of old, but with all the strength gone out of it.

"By to-morrow's mail," I said. I should have liked to say something more—something sympathetic about his being ill and not likely to get better; but he had always treated me discourteously when he was well, and I could not open out all at once now that he was ill.

"Look here, Middleton," he went on; "I am dying, and I know it. I don't suppose you imagined I had sent for you to bid you a last farewell before departing to my long home. I am not in such a hurry to depart as all that, I can tell you; but there is something I want done—that I want you to do for me. I meant to have done it myself, but I am down now, and I must trust somebody. I know better than to trust a clever man. An honest fool—But I am digressing from the case in point. I have never trusted anybody all my life, so you may feel honored. I have a small parcel which I want you to take to England for me. Here it is."

His long lean hands went searching in his dressing-gown, and presently produced an old brown bag, held together at the neck by a string.

"See here!" he said; and he pushed the glasses and papers aside from the table near him and undid the string. Then he craned forward to look about him, laying a spasmodic clutch on the bag. "I'm watched! I know I'm watched!" he said in a whisper, his pale eyes turning slowly in their sockets. "I shall be killed for them if I keep them much longer, and I won't be hurried into my grave. I'll take my own time."

"There is no one here," I said, "and no one in sight except Cathcart, smoking in the veranda, and I can only see his legs, so he can't see us."

He seemed to recover himself, and laughed. I had never liked his laugh, especially when, as had often happened, it had been directed against myself; but I liked it still less now.

"See here!" he repeated, chuckling; and he turned the bag inside out upon the table.

Such jewels I had never seen. They fell like cut flame upon the marble table—green and red and burning white. A large diamond rolled and fell upon the floor. I picked it up and put it back among the confused blaze of precious stones, too much astonished for a moment to speak.

"Beautiful! aren't they?" the old man chuckled, passing his wasted hands over them. "You won't match that necklace in any jeweller's in England. I tore it off an old she-devil of a Rhanee's neck after the Mutiny, and got a bite in the arm for my trouble. But she'll tell no tales. He! he! he! I don't mind saying now how I got them. I am a humble Christian, now I am so near heaven—eh, Middleton? He! he! You don't like to contradict me. Look at those emeralds. The hasp is broken, but it makes a pretty bracelet. I don't think I'll tell you how the hasp got broken—little accident as the lady who wore it gave it to me. Rather brown, isn't it, on one side? but it will come off. No, you need not be afraid of touching it, it isn't wet. He! he! And this crescent. Look at those diamonds. A duchess would be proud of them. I had them from a private soldier. I gave him two rupees for them. Dear me! how the sight of them brings back old times. But I won't leave them out any longer. We must put them away—put them away." And the glittering mass was gathered up and shovelled back into the old brown bag. He looked into it once with hungry eyes, and then he pulled the string and pushed it over to me. "Take it," he said. "Put it away now. Put it away," he repeated, as I hesitated.

I put the bag into my pocket. He gave a long sigh as he watched it disappear.

"Now what you have got to do with that bag," he said, a moment afterwards, "is to take it to Ralph Danvers, the second son of Sir George Danvers, of Stoke Moreton, in D——shire. Sir George has got two sons. I have never seen him or his sons, but I don't mean the eldest to have them. He is a spendthrift. They are all for Ralph, who is a steady fellow, and going to marry a nice girl—at least, I suppose she is a nice girl. Girls who are going to be married always *are* nice. Those jewels will sweeten matrimony for Mr. Ralph, and if she is like other women it will need sweetening. There, now you have got them, and that is what you have got to do with them. There is the address written on this card. With my compliments, you perceive. He! he! I don't suppose they will remember who I am."

"Have you no relations?" I asked; for I am always strongly of opinion that property should be bequeathed to relatives, especially near relatives, rather than to entire strangers.

"None," he replied, "not even poor relations. I have no deserving nephew or Scotch cousin. If I had, they would be here at this moment smoothing the pillow of the departing saint, and wondering how much they would get. You may make your mind easy on that score."

"Then who is this Ralph whom you have never seen, and to whom you are leaving so much?" I asked, with my usual desire for information.

He glared at me for a moment, and then he turned his face away.

"D——n it! What does it matter, now I'm dying?" he said. And then he added, hoarsely, "I knew his mother."

I could not speak, but involuntarily I put out my hand and took his leaden one and held it. He scowled at me, and then the words came out, as if in spite of himself—

The Danvers Jewels And Sir Charles Danvers | 9

"She—if she had married me, who knows what might—But she married Danvers. She called her second son Ralph. My first name is Ralph." Then, with a sudden change of tone, pulling away his hand, "There! now you know all about it! Edifying, isn't it? These death-bed scenes always have an element of interest, haven't they? *Good*-evening"—ringing the bell at his elbow—"I can't say I hope we shall meet again. It would be impolite. No, don't let me keep you. Good-bye again."

"Good-bye, Sir John," I said, taking his impatient hand and shaking it gently; "God bless you."

"Thankee," grinned the old man, with a sardonic chuckle; "if anything could do me good that will, I'm sure. Good-bye."

As I breakfasted next morning, previously to my departure, I could not help reflecting on the different position in which I was now returning to England, as a colonel on long leave, to that in which I had left it many—I do not care to think how many—years ago, the youngest ensign in the regiment.

It was curious to remember that in my youth I had always been considered the fool of the family; most unjustly so considered when I look back at my quick promotion owing to casualties, and at my long and prosperous career in India, which I cannot but regard as the result of high principles and abilities, to say the least of it, of not the meanest order. On the point of returning to England, the trust Sir John had with his usual shrewdness reposed in me was an additional proof, if proof were needed, of the confidence I had inspired in him—a confidence which seemed to have ripened suddenly at the end of his life, after many years of hardly concealed mockery and derision. Just as I was finishing my reflections and my breakfast, Dickson, one of the last joined subalterns, came in.

"This is very awful," he said, so gravely that I turned to look at him.

"What is awful?"

"Don't you know?" he replied. "Haven't you heard about—Sir John—last night?"

"Dead?" I asked.

He nodded; and then he said—

"Murdered in the night! Cathcart heard a noise and went in, and stumbled over him on the floor. As he came in he saw the lamp knocked over, and a figure rush out through the veranda. The moon was bright, and he saw a man run across a clear space in the moonlight—a tall, slightly built man in native dress, but not a native, Cathcart said; that he would take his oath on, by his build. He roused the house, but the man got clean off, of course."

"And Sir John?"

"Sir John was quite dead when Cathcart got back to him. He found him lying on his face. His arms were spread out, and his dressing-gown was torn, as if he had struggled hard. His pockets had been turned inside out, his writing-table drawers forced open, the whole room had been ransacked; yet the old man's gold watch had not been touched, and some money in one of the drawers had not been taken. What on earth is the meaning of it all?" said young Dickson, below his breath. "What was the thief after?"

In a moment the truth flashed across my brain. I put two and two together as quickly as most men, I fancy. *The jewels!* Some one had got wind of the jewels, which at that moment were reposing on my own person in their old brown bag. Sir John had been only just in time.

"What was he looking for?" continued Dickson, walking up and down. "The old man must have had some paper or other about him that he wanted to get hold of. But what? Cathcart says that nothing whatever has been taken, as far as he can see at present."

I was perfectly silent. It is not every man who would have been so in my place, but I was. I know when to hold my tongue, thank Heaven!

Presently the others came in, all full of the same subject, and then suddenly I remembered that it was getting late; and there was a bustle and a leave-taking, and I had to post off before I could hear more. Not, however, that there was much more to hear, for everything seemed to be in the greatest confusion, and every species of conjecture was afloat as to the real criminal, and the motive for the crime. I had not much time to think of anything during the first day on board; yet, busy as I was in arranging and rearranging my things, poor old Sir John never seemed quite absent from my mind. His image, as I had last seen him, constantly rose before me, and the hoarse whisper was forever sounding in my ears, "I'm watched! I know I'm watched!" I could not get him out of my head. I was unable to sleep the first night I was on board, and, as the long hours wore on, I always seemed to see the pale searching eyes of the dead man; and above the manifold noises of the steamer, and the perpetual lapping of the calm water against my ear, came the whisper, "I'm watched! I know I'm watched!"

CHAPTER II

I was all right next day. I suppose I had had what women call *nerves*. I never knew what nerves meant before, because no two women I ever met seemed to have the same kind. If it is slamming a door that upsets one woman's nerves, it may be coming in on tiptoe that will upset another's. You never can tell. But I am sure it was nerves with me that first night; I know I have never felt so queer since. Oh yes I have, though—once. I was forgetting; but I have not come to that yet.

We had a splendid passage home. Most of the passengers were in good spirits at the thought of seeing England again, and even the children were not so troublesome as I have known them. I soon made friends with some of the nicest people, for I generally make friends easily. I do not know how I do it, but I always seem to know what people really are at first sight. I always was rather a judge of character.

There was one man on board whom I took a great fancy to from the first. He was a young American, travelling about, as Americans do, to see the world. I forget where he had come from—though I believe he told me—or why he was going to London; but a nicer young fellow I never met. He was rather simple and unsophisticated, and with less knowledge of the world than any man I ever knew; but he did not mind owning to it, and was as grateful as possible for any little hints which, as an older man who had not gone through life with his eyes shut, I was of course able to give him. He was of a shy disposition I could see, and wanted drawing out; but he soon took to me, and in a surprisingly short time we became friends. He was in the next cabin to mine, and evidently wished so much to have been with me, that I tried to get another man to exchange; but he was grumpy about it, and I had to give it up, much to young Carr's disappointment. Indeed, he was quite silent and morose for a whole day about it, poor fellow. He was a tall handsome young man, slightly built, with the kind of sallow complexion that women admire, and I wondered at his preferring my company to that of the womankind on board, who were certainly very civil to him. One evening when I was rallying him on the subject, as we were leaning over the side (for though it was December it was hot enough in the Red Sea to lounge on deck), he told me that he was engaged to be married to a beautiful young American girl. I forget her name, but I remember he told it me—Dulcima Something—but it is of no consequence. I quite understood then. I always can enter into the feelings of others so entirely. I know when I was engaged myself once, long ago, I did not seem to care to talk to any one but her. She did not feel the same about it, which perhaps accounted for her marrying some one else, which was quite a blow to me at the time. But still I could fully enter into young Carr's feelings, especially when he went on to expatiate on her perfections. Nothing, he averred, was too good for her. At last he dropped his voice, and, after looking about him in the dusk, to make sure he was not overheard, he said:

"I have picked up a few stones for her on my travels; a few sapphires of considerable value. I don't care to have it generally known that I have jewels about me, but I don't mind telling *you*."

"My dear fellow," I replied, laying my hand on his shoulder, and sinking my voice to a whisper, "not a soul on board this vessel suspects it, but so have I."

It was too dark for me see his face, but I felt that he was much impressed by what I had told him.

"Then *you* will know where I had better keep mine," he said, a moment later, with his impulsive boyish confidence. "How fortunate I told you about them. Some are of considerable value, and—and I don't know where to put them that they will be absolutely safe. I never carried about jewels with me before, and I am nervous about *losing* them, you understand." And he nodded significantly at me. "Now where would you advise me to keep them?"

"On you," I said, significantly.

"But where?"

He was simpler than even I could have believed.

"My dear boy," I said, hardly able to refrain from laughing, "do as I do; put them in a bag with a string to it. Put the string round your neck, and wear that bag under your clothes night and day."

"At night as well?" he asked, anxiously.

"Of course. You are just as likely to *lose* them, as you call it, in the night as in the day."

"I'm very much obliged to you," he replied. "I will take your advice this very night. I say," he added, suddenly, "you would not care to see them, would you? I would not have any one else catch sight of them for a good deal, but I would show you them in a moment. Every one else is on deck just now, if you would like to come down into my cabin."

I hardly know one stone from another, and never could tell a diamond from paste; but he seemed so anxious to show me what he had, that I did not like to refuse.

"By all means," I said. And we went below.

It was very dark in Carr's cabin, and after he had let me in he locked the door carefully before he struck a light. He looked quite pale in the light of the lamp after the red dusk of the warm evening on deck.

"I don't want to have other fellows coming in," he said in a whisper, nodding at the door.

He stood looking at me for a moment as if irresolute, and then he suddenly seemed to arrive at some decision, for he pulled a small parcel out of his pocket and began to open it.

They really were not much to look at, though I would not have told him so for worlds. There were a few sapphires—one of a considerable size, but uncut—and some handsome turquoises, but not of perfect color. He turned them over with evident admiration.

"They will look lovely, set in gold, as a bracelet on *her* arm," he said, softly. He was very much in love, poor fellow! And then he added, humbly, "But I dare say they are nothing to yours."

I chuckled to myself at the thought of his astonishment when he should actually behold them; but I only said, "Would you like to see them, and judge for yourself?"

"Oh! if it is not giving you too much trouble," he exclaimed, gratefully, with shining eyes. "It's very kind of you. I did not like to ask. Have you got them with you?"

I nodded, and proceeded to unbutton my coat.

At that moment a voice was heard shouting down the companion-ladder: "Carr! I say, Carr, you are wanted!" and in another moment some one was hammering on the door.

Carr sprang to his feet, looking positively savage.

"Carr!" shouted the voice again. "Come out, I say; you are wanted!"

"Button up your coat," he whispered, scowling suddenly; and with an oath he opened the door.

Poor Carr! He was quite put out, I could see, though he recovered himself in a moment, and went off laughing with the man, who had been sent for him to take his part in a rehearsal which had been suddenly resolved on; for theatricals had been brewing for some time, and he had promised to act in them. I had not been asked to join, so I saw no more of him that night. The following morning, as I was taking an early turn on the deck, he joined me, and said, with a smile, as he linked his arm in mine, "I was put out last night, wasn't I?"

"But you got over it in a moment," I replied. "I quite admired you; and, after all, you know—some other time."

"No," he said, smiling still, "not some other time. I don't think I will see them—thanks all the same. They might put me out of conceit with what I have picked up for my little girl, which are the best I can afford."

He seemed to have lost all interest in the subject, for he began to talk of England, and of London, about which he appeared to have that kind of vague half-and-half knowledge which so often proves misleading to young men newly launched into town life. When he found out, as he soon did, that I was, to a certain extent, familiar with the metropolis, he began to question me minutely, and ended by making me promise to dine with him at the Criterion, of which he had actually never heard, and go with him afterwards to the best of the theatres the day after we arrived in London.

He wanted me to go with him the very evening we arrived, but on that point I was firm. My sister Jane, who was living with a hen canary (called Bob, after me, before its sex was known) in a small house in Kensington, would naturally be hurt if I did not spend my first evening in England with her, after an absence of so many years.

Carr was much interested to hear that I had a sister, and asked innumerable questions about her. Was she young and lovely, or was she getting on? Did she live all by herself, and was I going to stay with her for long? Was not Kensington—was that the name of the street?—rather out of the world? etc.

I was pleased with the interest he took in any particulars about myself and my relations. People so seldom care to hear about the concerns of others. Indeed, I have noticed, as I advance in life, such a general want of interest on the part of my acquaintance in the minutiæ of my personal affairs that of late I have almost ceased to speak of them at any length. Carr, however, who was of what I should call a truly domestic turn of character, showed such genuine pleasure in hearing about myself and my relations, that I asked him to call in London in order to make Jane's acquaintance, and accordingly gave him her address, which he took down at once in his note-book with evident satisfaction.

Our passage was long, but it proved most uneventful; and except for an occasional dance, and the theatricals before-mentioned, it would have been dull in the extreme. The theatricals certainly were a great success, mainly owing to the splendid acting of young Carr, who became afterwards a more special object of favor even than he was before. It was bitterly cold when we landed early in January at Southampton, and my native land seemed to have retired from view behind a thick veil of fog. We had a wretched journey up to London, packed as tight as sardines in a tin, much to the disgust of Carr, who accompanied me to town, and who, with his usual thoughtfulness, had in vain endeavored to keep the carriage to ourselves, by liberal tips to guards and porters. When we at last arrived in London he insisted on getting me a cab and seeing my luggage onto it, before he looked after his own at all. It was only when I had given the cabman my sister's address that he finally took his leave, and disappeared among the throng of people who were jostling each other near the luggage-vans.

Curiously enough, when I arrived at my destination an odd thing happened. I got out at the green door of 23, Suburban Residences, and when the maid opened it, walked straight past her into the drawing-room.

"Well, Jane!" I cried.

A pale middle-aged woman rose as I came in, and I stood aghast. It was not my sister. It was soon explained. She was a little pettish about it, poor woman! It seemed my sister had quite recently changed her house, and the present occupant had been put to some slight inconvenience before by people calling and leaving parcels after her departure. She gave me Jane's new address, which was only in the next street, and I apologized and made my bow at once. My going to the wrong house was such a slight occurrence that I almost forgot it at the time, until I was reminded of it by a very sad event which happened afterwards.

Jane was delighted to see me. It seemed she had written to inform me of her change of address, but the letter did not reach me before I started for England with the Danvers jewels, about which I have been asked to write this account. Considering this *is* an account of the jewels, it is wonderful how seldom I have had occasion to mention them so far; but you may rest assured that all this time they were safe in their bag under my waiscoat; and knowing I had them there all right, I did not trouble my head much about them. I never was a person to worry about things.

Still I had no wish to be inconvenienced by a hard packet of little knobs against my chest any longer than was necessary, and I wrote the same evening to Sir George Danvers, stating the bare facts of the case, and asking what steps he or his second son wished me to take to put the legacy in the possession of its owner. I had no notion of trusting a packet of such immense value to the newly organized Parcels Post. With jewels I consider you cannot be too cautious. Indeed, I told Jane so at the time, and she quite agreed with me.

CHAPTER III

I did not much like the arrangement of Jane's new house when I came to stay in it. The way the two bedrooms, hers and mine, were shut off from the rest of the house by a door, barred and locked at night for fear of burglars, was, I thought, unpleasant, especially as, once in my room for the night, there was no possibility of getting out of it, the key of the door of the passage not being even allowed to remain in the lock, but retiring with Jane, the canary cage, and other valuables, into her own apartment. I remonstrated, but I soon found that Jane had not remained unmarried for nothing. She was decided on the point. The outer door would be locked as usual, and the key would be deposited under the pin-cushion in her room, as usual; and it was so.

The next morning, as Jane and I went out for a stroll before luncheon, we had to pass the house to which I had driven by mistake the day before. To our astonishment, there was a crowd before the door, and a policeman with his back to it was guarding the entrance. The blinds were all drawn down. The image of the pale lonely woman, sitting by her little fire, whom I had disturbed the day before, came suddenly back to me with a strange qualm.

"What is it?" I hurriedly asked a baker's boy, who was standing at an area railing, rubbing his chin against the loaf he was waiting to deliver. The boy grinned.

"It's murder!" he said, with relish. "Burgilars in the night. I've supplied her reg'lar these two months. One quartern best white, one half-quartern brown every morning, French rolls occasional; but it's all up now." And he went off whistling a tune which all bakers' boys whistled about that time, called "My Grandfather's Timepiece," or something similar.

A second policeman came up the street at this moment, and from him I learned all the little there was to know. The poor lady had not been murdered, it seemed, but, being subject to heart complaint, had died in the night of an acute attack, evidently brought on by fright. The maid, the only other person in the house, sleeping as maids-of-all-work only can, had heard nothing, and awoke in the morning to find her mistress dead in her bed, with the window and door open. "Strangely enough," the policeman added, "although nothing in the house had been touched, the lock of an unused bedroom had been forced, and the room evidently searched."

Poor Jane was quite overcome. She seemed convinced that it was only by a special intervention of Providence that she had changed her house, and that her successor had been sacrificed instead of herself.

"It might have been me!" she said over and over again that afternoon.

Wishing to give a turn to her thoughts, I began to talk about Sir John's legacy, in which she had evinced the greatest interest the night before, and, greatly to her delight, showed her the jewels. I had not looked at them since Sir John had given them to me, and I was myself astonished at their magnificence, as I spread them out on the table under the gas-lamp. Jane exhausted herself in admiration; but as I was putting them away again, saying it was time for me to be dressing and going to meet Carr, who was to join me at the Criterion, she begged me on no account to take them with me, affirming that it would be much safer to leave them at home. I was firm, but she was firmer; and in the end I allowed her to lock them up in the tea-caddy, where her small stock of ready money reposed.

I met Carr as we had arranged, and we had a very pleasant evening. Poor Carr, who had seen the papers, had hardly expected that I should turn up, knowing the catastrophe of the previous night had taken place at the house I was going to, and was much relieved to hear that my sister had moved, and had thus been spared all the horror of the event.

The dinner was good, the play better. I should have come home feeling that I had enjoyed myself thoroughly, if it had not been for a little adventure with our cab-driver that very nearly proved serious. We got a hansom directly we came out of the theatre, but instead of taking us to the direction we gave him, after we had driven for some distance I began to make out that the cabman was going wrong, and Carr shouted to him to stop; but thereupon he lashed up his horse, and away we went like the wind, up one street, and down another, till I had lost all idea where we were. Carr, who was young and active, did all he could; but the cabman, who, I am afraid, must have been intoxicated, took not the slightest notice, and continued driving madly, Heaven knows where. At last, after getting into a very dingy neighborhood, we turned up a crooked dark street, unlit by any lamp, a street so narrow that I thought every moment the cab would be overturned. In another moment I saw two men rush out of a door-way. One seized the horse, which was much blown by this time, and brought it violently to a stand-still, while the other flew at the cab, and catching Carr by the collar, proceeded to drag him out by main force. I suppose Carr did his best, but being only an American, he certainly made a very poor fight of it; and while

I was laying into the man who had got hold of him, I was suddenly caught by the legs myself from the other side of the cab. I turned on my assailant, saw a heavy stick levelled at me, caught at it, missed it, beheld a series of fireworks, and remembered nothing more.

The first thing I heard on beginning to come to myself was a series of subdued but evidently heart-felt oaths; and I became sensible of an airy feeling, unpleasant in the extreme, proceeding from an open condition of coat and waistcoat quite unsuited to the time of year. A low chorus of muffled whispering was going on round me. As I groaned, involuntarily, it stopped.

"He's coming to!" I heard Carr say. "Go and fetch some brandy." And I felt myself turned right side uppermost, and my hands were rubbed, while Carr, in a voice of the greatest anxiety, asked me how I felt. I was soon able to sit up, and to become aware that I had a splitting headache, and was staring at a tallow-candle stuck in a bottle. Having got so far I got a little farther, and on looking round found myself reclining on a sack in a corner of a disreputable-looking room, dingy with dirt, and faithful to the memory of bad tobacco. Then I suddenly remembered what had occurred. Carr saw that I did so, and instantly poured forth an account of how we had been rescued from a condition of great peril by the man to whom the house we were in belonged, to whom he hardly knew how to express his gratitude, and who was now gone for some brandy for me. He told me a great deal about it, but I was so dizzy that I forgot most of what he said, and it was not until our deliverer returned with the brandy that I became thoroughly aware of what was going forward. I could not help thinking, as I thanked the honest fellow who had come to our assistance, how easily one may be deceived by appearances, for a more forbidding-looking face, under its fur cap, I never saw. That of his son, who presently returned with a four-wheeler which Carr had sent for, was not more prepossessing. In fact, they were two as villanous-looking men as I had ever seen. After recompensing both with all our spare cash, we got ourselves hoisted stiffly into the cab, and Carr good-naturedly insisted on seeing me home, though he owned to feeling, as he put it, "rather knocked up by his knocking down." We were both far too exhausted to speak much, until Carr gave a start and a gasp and said, "By Jove!"

"What?" I inquired.

"They are gone!" he said, tremulously—"my sapphires. They are gone! Stolen! I had them in a bag round my neck, as you told me. They must have been taken from me when I was knocked down. I say," he added, quickly, "how about yours? Have you got them all right?"

Involuntarily I raised my hand to my throat. A horrid qualm passed over me.

"Thank Heaven!" I replied, with a sigh of relief. "They are safe at home with Jane. What a mercy! I might have lost them."

"*Might!*" said Carr. "You would have lost them to a dead certainty; mine *are* gone!" And he stamped, and clinched his fists, and looked positively furious.

Poor Carr! I felt for him. He took the loss of his stones so to heart; and I am sure it was only natural. I parted from him at my own door, and was glad on going in to find Jane had stayed up for me. I soon figured in her eyes as the hero of a thrilling adventure, while her clever hands applied sticking-plaster *ad libitum*. We were both so full of the events of the evening, and the letter which I was to write to the *Times* about it the next day, that it never entered the heads of either of us, on retiring to bed, to remove Sir John's jewels from the tea-caddy into which they had been temporarily popped in the afternoon.

CHAPTER IV

I really think adventures, like misfortunes, never come single. Would you believe it? Our house was broken into that very night. Nothing serious came of it, wonderful to relate, owing to Jane's extraordinary presence of mind. She had been unable to sleep after my thrilling account of the cab accident, and had consoled herself by reading Baxter's "Saint's Rest" by her night-light, for the canary became restless and liable to sudden bursts of song if a candle were lighted. While so engaged she became aware of a subdued grating sound, which had continued for some time before she began to speculate upon it. While she was speculating it ceased, and after a short interval she distinctly heard a stealthy step upon the stair, and the handle of the passage door before-mentioned was gently, very gently turned.

Jane has some of that quickness of perception which has been of such use to myself through life. In a moment she had grasped the situation. Some one was in the house. In another moment she was hanging out of her bedroom window, springing the policeman's rattle which she had had by her for years with a view to an emergency of this kind, and at the same time—for she was a capable woman—blowing a piercing strain on a cabman's whistle.

To make a long story short, her extraordinary presence of mind was the saving of us. With her own eyes she saw two dark figures fly up our area steps and disappear round the corner, and when a policeman appeared on the scene half an hour later, he confirmed the fact that the house had been broken into, by showing us how an entrance had been effected through the kitchen window.

There was of course no more sleep for us that night, and the remainder of it was passed by Jane in examining the house from top to bottom every half hour or so, owing to a rooted conviction on her part that a burglar might still be lurking on the premises, concealed in the cellaret, or the jam cupboard, or behind the drawing-room curtains.

By that morning's post I heard, as I expected I should do, from Sir George Danvers, but the contents of the letter surprised me. He wrote most cordially, thanking me for my kindness in undertaking such a heavy responsibility (I am sure I never felt it to be so) for an entire stranger, and ended by sending me a pressing invitation to come down to Stoke Moreton that very day, that he and his son, whose future wife was also staying with them, might have the pleasure of making the acquaintance of one to whom they were so much indebted. He added that his eldest son Charles was also going down from London by a certain train that day, and that he had told him to be on the lookout for me at the station in case I was able to come at such short notice. I made up my mind to go, sent Sir George a telegram to that effect, and proceeded to fish up the jewels out of the tea-caddy.

Jane, who had never ceased for one instant to comment on the event of the night, positively shrieked when she saw me shaking the bag free from tea-leaves.

"Good gracious! the burglars," she exclaimed. "Why, they might have taken them if they had only known."

Of course they had *not* known, as I had been particularly secret about them; but I wished all the same that I had not left them there all night, as Jane would insist, and continue insisting, that they had been exposed to great danger. I argued the matter with her at first; but women, I find, are impervious as a rule to masculine argument, and it is a mistake to reason with them. It is, in fact, putting the sexes for the moment on an equality to which the weaker one is unaccustomed, and consequently unsuited.

A few hours later I was rolling swiftly towards Stoke Moreton in a comfortable smoking carriage, only occupied by myself and Mr. Charles Danvers, a handsome young fellow with a pale face and that peculiar tired manner which (though, as I soon found, natural to him) is so often affected by the young men of the day.

"And so Ralph has come in for a legacy in diamonds," he said, listlessly, when we had exchanged the usual civilities, and had become, to a certain degree, acquainted. "Dear me! how these good steady young men prosper in the world. When last I heard from him he had prevailed upon the one perfect woman in the universe to consent to marry him, and his aunt (by-the-way, you will meet her there, too—Lady Mary Cunningham) had murmured something vague but gratifying about testamentary intentions. A week later Providence fills his brimming cup with a legacy of jewels, estimated at——" Charles opened his light sleepy eyes wide and looked inquiringly at me. "What are they estimated at?" he asked, as I did not answer.

I really had no idea, but I shrugged my shoulders and looked wise.

The Danvers Jewels And Sir Charles Danvers | 23

"Estimated at a fabulous sum," he said, closing his eyes again. "Ah! had they been mine, with what joyful alacrity should I have ascertained their exact money value. And mine they ought to have been, if the sacred law of primogeniture (that special Providence which watches over the interests of eldest sons) had been duly observed. Sir John had not the pleasure of my acquaintance, but I fear he must have heard some reports—no doubt entirely without foundation—respecting my career, which had induced him to pass me over in this manner. What a moral! My father and my aunt Mary are always delicately pointing out the difference between Ralph and myself. I wish I were a good young man, like Ralph. It seems to pay best in the long-run; but I may as well inform you, Colonel Middleton, of the painful fact that I am the black sheep of the family."

"Oh, come, come!" I remarked, uneasily.

"I should not have alluded to the subject if you were not likely to become fully aware of it on your arrival, so I will be beforehand with my relations. I was brought up in the way I should go," he continued, with the utmost unconcern, as if commenting on something that did not affect him in the least; "but I did not walk in it, partly owing to the uncongenial companionship that it involved, especially that of my aunt Mary, who took up so much room herself in the narrow path that she effectually kept me out of it. From my earliest youth, also, I took extreme interest in the parable of the Prodigal, and as soon as it became possible I exemplified it myself. I may even say that I acted the part in a manner that did credit to a beginner; but the wind-up was ruined by the lamentable inability of others, who shall be nameless, to throw themselves into the spirit of the piece. At various intervals," he continued, always as if speaking of some one else, "I have returned home, but I regret to say that on each occasion my reception was not in any way what I could have wished. The flavor of a fatted calf is absolutely unknown to me; and so far from meeting me half-way, I have in extreme cases, when impelled homeward by urgent pecuniary considerations, found myself obliged to walk up from the station."

"Dear me! I hope it is not far," I said.

"A mere matter of three miles or so uphill," he resumed; "nothing to a healthy Christian, though trying to the trembling legs of the ungodly after a long course of husks. There, now I think you are quite *au fait* as to our family history. I always pity a stranger who comes to a house ignorant of little domestic details of this kind; he is apt to make mistakes." "Oh, pray don't mention it,"—as I murmured some words of thanks—"no trouble, I assure you; trouble is a thing I don't take. By-the-way, are you aware we are going straight into a nest of private theatricals at Stoke Moreton? To-night is the last rehearsal; perhaps I had better look over my part. I took it once years ago, but I don't remember a word of it." And after much rummaging in a magnificent silver-mounted travelling-bag, the Prodigal pulled out a paper book and carelessly turned over the leaves.

I did not interrupt his studies, save by a few passing comments on the weather, the state of the country, and my own health, which, I am sorry to say, is not what it was; but as I only received monosyllabic answers, we had no more conversation worth mentioning till we reached Stoke Moreton.

CHAPTER V

Stoke Moreton is a fine old Elizabethan house standing on rising ground. As we drove up the straight wide approach between two rows of ancient fantastically clipped hollies, I was impressed by the stately dignity of the place, which was not lessened as we drew up before a great arched door-way, and were ushered into a long hall supported by massive pillars of carved white stone. A roaring log-fire in the immense fireplace threw a ruddy glow over the long array of armor and gleaming weapons which lined the walls, and made the pale winter twilight outside look bleak indeed. Charles, emerging slim and graceful out of an exquisite ulster, sauntered up to the fire, and asked where Sir George Danvers was. As he stood inside the wide fireplace, leaning against one of the pillars which supported the towering white stone chimney-piece, covered with heraldic designs and coats of arms, he looked a worthier representative of an ancient race than I fear he really was.

"So they have put the stage at that end, in front of the pillars," he remarked, nodding at a wooden erection. "Quite right. I could not have placed it better myself. What, Brown? Sir George is in the drawing-room, is he? and tea, as I perceive, is going in at this moment. Come, Colonel Middleton." And we followed the butler to the drawing-room.

I am not a person who easily becomes confused, but I must own I did get confused with the large party into the midst of which we were now ushered. I soon made out Sir George Danvers, a delicate, but irascible-looking old gentleman, who received me with dignified cordiality, but returned Charles's greeting with a certain formality and coldness which I was pained to see, family affection being, in my opinion, the chief blessing of a truly happy home. Charles I already knew, and with the second son, Ralph, a ruddy, smiling young man with any amount of white teeth, I had no difficulty; but after that I became hopelessly involved. I was introduced to an elderly lady whom I addressed for the rest of the evening as Lady Danvers, until Charles casually mentioned that his mother was dead, and that, until the Deceased Wife's Sister Bill was passed, he did not anticipate that his aunt Mary would take upon herself the position of step-mother to her orphaned nephews. The severe elderly lady, then, who beamed so sweetly upon Ralph, and regarded Charles with such manifest coldness, was their aunt Lady Mary Cunningham. She had known Sir John slightly in her youth, she said, as she graciously made room for me on her sofa, and she expressed a very proper degree of regret at his sudden death, considering that he had not been a personal friend in any way.

"We all have our faults, Colonel Middleton," said Lady Mary, with a gentle sigh, which dislodged a little colony of crumbs from the front of her dress. "Sir John, like the rest of us, was not exempt, though I have no doubt the softening influence of age would have done much, since I knew him, to smooth acerbities of character which were unfortunately strongly marked in his early life."

She had evidently not known Sir John in his later years.

As she continued to talk in this strain I endeavored to make out which of the young ladies present was the one to whom Ralph was engaged. I was undecided as to which it was of the two to whom I had already been introduced. Girls always seem to me so very much alike, especially pretty girls; and these were both of them pretty. I do not mean that they resembled each other in the least, for one was dark and one was fair; but which was Miss Aurelia Grant, Ralph's *fiancée*, and which was Miss Evelyn Derrick, a cousin of the family, I could not make out until later in the evening, when I distinctly saw Ralph kiss the fair one in the picture-gallery, and I instantly came to the conclusion that she was the one to whom he was engaged.

I asked Charles if I were not right, as we stood in front of the hall-fire before the rest of the party had assembled for dinner, and he told me that I had indeed hit the nail on the head in this instance, though for his own part he never laid much stress himself on such an occurrence, having found it prove misleading in the extreme to draw any conclusion from it. He further informed me that Miss Derrick was the young lady with dark hair who had poured out tea, and whom he had favored with some of his conversation afterwards.

I admired Ralph's taste, as did Charles, who had never seen his future sister-in-law before. Aurelia Grant was a charming little creature, with a curly head and a dimple, and a pink-and-white complexion, and a suspicion of an Irish accent when she became excited.

Charles said he admired her complexion most because it was so thoroughly well done, and the coloring was so true to nature.

I did not quite catch his meaning, but it certainly was a beautiful complexion; and then she was so bright and lively, and showed such pretty little teeth when she smiled! She was quite delightful. I did not wonder at Ralph's being so much in love with her, and Charles agreed with me.

"There is nothing like a good complexion," he remarked, gravely. "One may be led away to like a pale girl with a mind for a time, but for permanent domestic happiness give me a good complexion, and—a dimple," he added, as if it were an after-thought. "I feel I could not bestow my best affections on a woman without a dimple. Yes, indeed! Ralph has chosen well."

Now I do not agree with Charles there, as I have always considered that a woman *should* have a certain amount of mind; just enough, in fact, to enable her to appreciate a superior one. I said as much to Charles; but he only laughed, and said it was a subject on which opinion had always varied.

"How did he meet her?" I inquired.

"On the Rigi, last summer," said Charles. "I am thinking of going there myself next year. Lovely orphan sat by Lady Mary at *table d'hôte*. Read tracts presented by Lady Mary. Made acquaintance. Lovely orphan's travelling companion or governess discovered to be live sister of defunct travelling companion or governess of Lady Mary. Result, warm friendship. Ralph, like a dutiful nephew, appears on the scene. Fortnight of fine weather. Interesting expeditions. Romantic attachment, cemented by diamond and pearl ring from Hunt & Roskell's. There is the whole story for you."

Evelyn Derrick joined us as he finished speaking. She was a tall graceful girl, gentle and dignified in manner, with a pale refined face. She was pretty in a way, but not to compare to Aurelia. Evelyn had an anxious look about her, too. Now I do not approve of a girl looking grave; she ought to be bright and happy, with a smile for every one. It is all very well for us men, who have the work of the world to do, to look grave at times, but with women it is different; and a woman always looks her best when she smiles—at least, I think so.

Then Aurelia came down, perfectly dazzling in white satin; then Sir George, then Ralph, giving an arm to Lady Mary, who suffered from rheumatism in her foot. Then came the gong, and there was a rustle down of more people, young and old, friends of the family who had come to act, or to see their sons and daughters act. As I never could get even their names right, I shall not attempt to give any account of them, especially as they are not of importance in any way.

After dinner, on entering the drawing-room, I found that great excitement prevailed among the ladies respecting Sir John's jewels. About his sad fate and costly legacy they all seemed fully informed. I had myself almost forgotten the reason of my visit in my interest in my new surroundings, not having even as yet given up the jewels to Sir George Danvers or Ralph; but, at the urgent request of all the ladies at once, Ralph begged me to bring them down, to be seen and admired then and there, before the rehearsal began.

"They will all be yours, you know," Ralph said to Aurelia. "You shall wear them on your wedding-day."

"You are always talking about being married," said Aurelia, with a little pout. "I wish you would try and think of something else to say. I was quite looking forward to it myself until I came here, and now I am quite, *quite* tired of it beforehand."

Ralph laughed delightedly, and Sir George reminding me that every one was dying of anxiety, himself included, I ran up-stairs to take the brown bag from around my neck, and in a few minutes returned with it in my hand. They were all waiting for me, Lady Mary drawn up in an arm-chair beside an ebony table, on which a small space near her had been cleared, Charles alone holding rather aloof, sipping his coffee with his back to the fire.

"Don't jostle," he said, as they all crowded round me. "Evelyn, let me beg of you not to elbow forward in that unbecoming manner. Observe how Aunt Mary restrains herself. Take time, Middleton! your coffee is getting cold. Won't you drink it first?"

As he finished speaking I turned the contents of the bag upon the table. The jewels in the bright lamp-light seemed to blaze and burn into the ebony of the table. There was a general gasp, a silence, and then a chorus of admiration. Charles came up behind me and looked over my shoulder.

"Good gracious!" said Lady Mary, solemnly. "Ralph, you are a rich man. Why, mine are nothing to them!" and she touched a diamond and emerald necklace on her own neck. "I never knew poor Sir John had so much good in him."

"Oh, Ralph, Ralph!" cried Aurelia, clasping her little hands with a deep sigh. "And will they really be my very own?"

Ralph assured her that they would, and that she should act in them the following night if she liked.

I think there was not a woman present who did not envy Aurelia as Ralph took up a flashing diamond crescent and held it against her fair hair. I saw Evelyn turn away and begin to tear up a small piece of paper in her hand. Women are very jealous of each other, especially the nice, by which I mean the pretty, ones. I was sorry to see jealousy so plainly marked in such a charming looking girl as Evelyn; but women are all the same about jewels.

Aurelia blushed and sparkled, and pouted when the clasp caught in her hair, and shook her little head impatiently, and was altogether enchanting.

After the first burst of admiration had subsided, General Marston, an old Indian officer, who had been somewhat in the rear, came up, and looked long at the glittering mass upon the table.

"Are you aware," he said at last to Ralph, pointing to the crescent, "that those diamonds are of enormous value? I have not seen such stones in any shop in London. I dare not say what that one crescent alone is worth, or that emerald bracelet. Jewels of such value as this are a grave responsibility." He stood, shaking his head a little and turning the crescent in his hand. "Wonderful!" he said. "Wonderful! Do not tear up that piece of rice-paper, Miss Derrick," he added, taking it from her. "The crescent was wrapped in it, and I will put it round it again. All these stones want polishing, and many of them resetting. They ought not to be tumbled together in this way in a bag, with nothing to prevent them scratching each other. See, Ralph, here is a clasp broken; and here are some loose stones; and this star has no clasp at all. You must take them up to some trustworthy jeweller, and have them thoroughly looked over."

"I suppose the second son was specially mentioned, Middleton?" said Charles, as I drew back to let the rest handle and admire.

"Of course!" said Lady Mary, sharply; "and a very fortunate thing, too."

"Very—for Ralph," he replied. "It is really providential that I am what I am. Why, I might have ruined the dear boy's prospects if I had paid my tailor's bill, and lived in the country among the buttercups and daisies. Ah! my dear aunt, I see you are about to remark how all things here below work together for good!"

"I was not going to remark anything of the kind," retorted Lady Mary, drawing herself up; "but," she added, spitefully, "I do not feel the less rejoiced at Ralph's good fortune and prosperity when I see, as I so often do, the ungodly flourishing like a green bay-tree."

"Of course," said Charles, shaking his head, "if that is your own experience, I bow before it; but for my own part, I must confess I have not found it so. Flourish like a green bay-tree! No, Aunt Mary, it is a fallacy; they don't: I am sure I only wish they did. But I see the rehearsal is beginning. May I give you an arm to the hall?"

The offer was entirely disregarded, and it was with the help of mine that Lady Mary retired from an unequal combat, which she never seemed able to resist provoking anew, and in which she was invariably worsted, causing her, as I could see, to regard Charles with the concentrated bitterness of which a severely good woman alone is capable.

I soon perceived that Charles was on the same amicable terms with his father; that they rarely spoke, and that it was evidently only with a view to keeping up appearances that he was ever invited to the paternal roof at all. Between the brothers, however, in spite of so much to estrange them, a certain kindliness of feeling seemed to exist, which was hardly to have been expected under the circumstances.

The rehearsal now began, and Sir George Danvers, who had remained behind to put by the jewels, and lock them up in his strong-box among his papers, came and sat down by me, again thanking me for taking charge of them, though I assured him it had been very little trouble.

"Not much trouble, perhaps, but a great responsibility," he said, courteously.

"A soldier, Sir George," I replied, with a slight smile, "becomes early inured to the gravest responsibility. It is the air we breathe; it is taken as a matter of course."

He looked keenly at me, and was silent, as if considering something — perhaps what I had said.

I was delighted to find the play was one of those which I had seen acted during our passage home. There is nothing I like so much as knowing a play beforehand, because then one can always whisper to one's companion what is coming next. The stage, with all its adjustments, had been carefully arranged, the foot-lights were lighted, the piece began. All went well till nearly the end of the first act, when there was a cry behind the scenes of "Mr. Denis!" Mr. Denis should have rushed on, but Mr. Denis did not rush on. The play stopped. Mr. Denis was not in the library, the improvised greenroom; Mr. Denis did not appear when his name was called in stentorian tones by Ralph, or in pathetic falsetto by Charles. In short, Mr. Denis was not forthcoming. A rush up-stairs on the part of most of the young men brought to light the awful fact that Mr. Denis had retired to his chamber, a prey to sudden and acute indisposition.

"Dear me!" said Charles to Lady Mary, with a dismal shake of his head, "how precarious is life! Here to-day, and in bed to-morrow. Support your aunt Mary, my dear Evelyn; she wishes to retire to rest. Indeed, we may as well all go to bed, for there will be no more acting to-night without poor Denis. I only trust he may be spared to us till to-morrow, and that he may be well enough to die by my hand to-morrow evening."

We all dispersed for the night in some anxiety. The play could not proceed without Mr. Denis, who took an important part; and Sir George ruefully informed me that all the neighboring houses had been filled for these theatricals, and that great numbers of people were expected. There was to be dancing afterwards, but the principal feature of the entertainment was the play. We all retired to rest, fervently hoping that the health of Mr. Denis might be restored by the following morning.

CHAPTER VI

But far from being better the following morning, Denis was much worse. Charles, who had sat up most of the night with him, and who came down to breakfast more cool and indifferent than ever, at once extinguished any hope that still remained that he would be able to take his part that night.

Great was the consternation of the whole party. A vague feeling of resentment against Denis prevailed among the womankind, who, having all preserved their own healths intact for the occasion (and each by her own account was a chronic invalid), felt it was extremely inconsiderate, not to say indelicate, of "a great man like him" to spoil everything by being laid up at the wrong moment.

But what was to be done? Denis was ill, and without Denis the play could not proceed. Must the whole thing be given up? There was a general chorus of lamentation.

"I see no alternative," said Charles, "unless some Curtius will leap into the gulf, and go through the piece reading the part, and that is always a failure at the best of times."

At that moment I had an idea; it broke upon me like a flash of lightning: *Valentine Carr*! I had seen him act the very part Denis was to have taken, in the theatricals on the steamer. How wonderfully fortunate that it should have occurred to me!

I told Charles that I had a friend who had acted that part only the week before.

"*You!*" cried Charles, losing all his customary apathy—"you don't say so! Great heavens, where is he? Out with him! Where is he at this moment? England, Ireland, Scotland, or Wales? Where is this treasure concealed?"

"Oh, Colonel Middleton! Oh, how delightful!" cried a number of gentle voices; and I was instantly surrounded, and all manner of questions put to me. Would he come? Was he tall? And oh! *had* he a beard? He had not a beard, had he? because it would not do for the part. Did he act well? When had he acted? Where had he acted?

Sir George interrupted the torrent of interrogation.

"Do you think he would come?" he asked.

"I am almost sure he would," I said; "he is a great friend of mine."

"It would be an exceedingly good-natured and friendly act," said Sir George. "Charles—no, I mean Ralph—bring a telegraph form, and if you will write a telegram at once, Middleton, I will send it to the station directly. We shall have an answer by twelve o'clock, and until then we will not give up all hope, though of course we must not count on your friend being able to come at such short notice."

The telegram was written and despatched, Carr having given me an address where letters would find him, though he said he did not put up there. I sincerely hoped he would not be out of the way on this occasion, and I was not a little pleased when, a few hours later, I received a telegram in reply saying that he could come, and should arrive by the afternoon train which had brought me the day before.

The spirits of the whole party revived. I (as is often the case) was in high favor with all. Even poor Denis, who had been very much depressed, was sufficiently relieved by the news—so Charles said—to smile over his beef-tea. Lady Mary, who appeared at luncheon-time, treated me with marked consideration. I had already laid them under an obligation, she said, graciously, by undertaking the care of the jewels, and now they were indebted to me a second time. Was Mr. Carr one of Lord Barrantyne's sons, or was he one of the Crampshire Carrs? She had known Lady Caroline Carr in her youth, but had not met her of late years. She seemed surprised when I told her that Carr was an American, and he sank, I could see, at once in her estimation; but she was kind enough to say that she was not a person who was prejudiced in any way by a man's nationality, and that she believed that very respectable people might be found among the Americans.

The day passed in the usual preparations for an entertainment. If I went into the hall I was sure to run against gardeners carrying in quantities of hot-house plants, with which the front of the stage was being hidden from the foot-lights to the floor; if I wandered into the library I interrupted Aurelia and Ralph rehearsing their parts alone, with their heads very close together; if I hastily withdrew into the morning-room, it was only to find Charles upon his knees luring Evelyn to immediate flight, in soul-stirring accents, before an admiring audience of not unenvious young ladyhood.

"Now, Evelyn, I ask you as a favor," said Charles, as I came in, moving towards her on his knees, "will you come a little closer when I am down? I don't mind wearing out my knees the least in a good cause; but I owe it to myself, as a wicked baron in hired tights, not to cross the stage in that position. Any impression I make will be quite lost if I do; and unless you keep closer, I shall never be able to reach your hand and clasp it to a heart at least two yards away. Now,"—rising, and crossing over to the other side—"I shall begin again. 'Ah! but my soul's adored—'"

"Is Middleton here?" asked a voice in the door-way. It was Sir George Danvers who had put his head into the room, and I went to him.

"I say, Middleton," he began, twirling his stick, and looking rather annoyed, "it is excessively provoking. I never thought of it before, but I find there is not a bed in the house. Every cranny has been filled. It never occurred to me that we had not a room for your friend, now that he is kind enough to come. And it looks so rude, when it is so exceedingly good-natured of him to come at all."

"Oh, dear! anywhere will do," I said.

"There is not even room for Ralph in the house," continued Sir George. "I have put him up at the lodge," pointing to a small house at the end of the drive, near the great entrance gates. "There is another nice little room leading out of his," he added, hesitating—"but really I don't like to suggest—"

"Oh, that will do perfectly!" I broke in. "Carr is not the sort of fellow to care a straw how he is put up. He will be quite content anywhere."

"Come and see it," he said, leading the way out-of-doors. "I would have turned out Charles in a moment, and given Carr his room; but Denis is really rather ill, and Charles sees to him, as he is next door."

I could not help saying how much I liked Charles.

"Strangers always do," he replied, coldly, as we walked towards the lodge. "I constantly hear him spoken of as a most agreeable young man."

"And he is so handsome."

"Yes," replied Sir George, in the same hard tone, "handsome and agreeable. I have no doubt he appears so to others; but I, who have had to pay the debts and hush up the scandals of my handsome and agreeable son, find Ralph, who has not a feature in his face, the better-looking of the two. I know Charles is head over ears in debt at this moment, but,"—with sudden acrimony—"he will not get another farthing from me. It is pouring water into a sieve."

"Ralph is marrying a sweetly pretty creature," I said, with warmth, desirous of changing the subject.

"Yes, she is very pretty," said Sir George, without enthusiasm; "but I wish she had belonged to one of our county families. It is nothing in the way of connection. She has no relations to speak of—one uncle living in Australia, and another, whom she goes to on Saturday, in Ireland. There seems to be no money either. It is Lady Mary's doing. She took a fancy to her abroad; and to say the truth, I did not wish to object, for at one time there seemed to be an attraction between Ralph and his cousin Evelyn Derrick, which his aunt and I were both glad to think had passed over. I do not approve of marriages between cousins."

We had reached the lodge by this time, and I was shown a tidy little room leading out of the one Ralph was occupying, in which I assured Sir George that Carr would be perfectly comfortable, much to the courteous old gentleman's relief, though I could see that he was evidently annoyed at not being able to put him up in the house.

In the afternoon, towards five o'clock, Carr arrived. I went into the hall to meet him, and to bring him into the drawing-room myself. Just as we came in, and while I was introducing him to Sir George, Ralph and Aurelia, who were sitting together as usual, started a lovers' squabble.

"Oh *my!*" said Ralph, suddenly.

"It is all your fault. You jogged my elbow," came Aurelia's quick rejoinder.

"My dearest love, I did *not,*" returned Ralph, on his knees, pocket-handkerchief in hand.

It appeared that between them they had managed to transfer Amelia's tea from her cup to the front of her dress.

"You did; you know you did," she said, evidently ready to cry with vexation. "I was just going to drink, and you had your arm round the back of my—"

"Hush, Aurelia, I beg," expostulated Charles. "Aunt Mary and I are becoming embarrassed. It is not necessary to enter into particulars as to the exact locality of Ralph's arm."

"Round the back of my chair," pouted Aurelia.

"It is all right, Aunt Mary," called Charles, cheerfully, to that lady. "Only the back of her *chair.* We took alarm unnecessarily. Just as it should be. I have done the same myself with—a different chair."

"He is *always* doing it," continued Aurelia, unmollified. "I have told him about it before. He made me drop a piece of bread and butter on the carpet only yesterday."

"I ate it afterwards," humbly suggested Ralph, still on his knees, "and there were hairs in it. There were, indeed, Aurelia."

"And now it is my tea-gown," continued Aurelia, giving way to the prettiest little outburst of temper imaginable. "I wish you would get up and go away, Ralph, and not come back. You are only making it worse by rubbing it in that silly way with your wet handkerchief."

"Here is another," said Charles, snatching up Lady Mary's delicate cambric one, which was lying on her work-table, while I was in the act of introducing Carr to her; and before that lady's politeness to Carr would allow her to turn from him to expostulate, Charles was on his knees beside Ralph, wiping the offending stain.

"'Out, d——d spot!' or rather series of spots. What, Aurelia! you don't wish it rubbed any more? Good! I will turn my attention to the *Aubusson* carpet. Ha! triumph! Here at least I am successful. Aunt Mary, you have no conception how useful your handkerchief is. The amount of tea or dirt, or both, which is leaving the carpet and taking refuge in your little square of cambric will surprise you when you see it. Ah!" rising from his knees as I brought up Carr, having by this time presented him to Sir George. "Very happy to see you, Mr. Carr. Most kind of you to come. Evelyn, are you pouring out some tea for Mr. Carr? Nature requires support before a last rehearsal. May I introduce you to my cousin Miss Derrick?"

After Carr had also been introduced to Aurelia, who, however, was still too much absorbed in her tea-gown to take much notice of him, he seemed glad to retreat to a chair by Evelyn, who gave him his tea, and talked pleasantly to him. He was very shy at first, but he soon got used to us, and many were the curious glances shot at him by the rest of the party as tea went on. There was to be a last rehearsal immediately afterwards, so that he might take part in it; and there was a general unacknowledged anxiety on the part of all the actors as to how he would bear that crucial test on which so much depended. I was becoming anxious myself, being in a manner responsible for him.

"You're not nervous, are you?" I said, taking him aside when tea was over. "Only act half as well as you did on the steamer and you will do capitally."

"Yes, I am nervous," he replied, with a short uneasy laugh. "It is enough to make a fellow nervous to be set down among a lot of people whom he has never seen before—to act a principal part, too. I had no idea it was going to be such a grand affair or I would not have come. I only did it to please you."

Of course I knew that, and I tried to reassure him, reminding him that the audience would not be critical, and how grateful every one was to him for coming.

"Tell me who some of the people are, will you?" he went on. "Who is that tall man with the fair mustache? He is looking at us now."

"That is Charles, the eldest son," I replied; "and the shorter one, with the pleasant face, near the window, is Ralph, his younger brother."

"That is a very good-looking girl he is talking to," he remarked. "I did not catch her name."

"Hush!" I said. "That is Miss Grant, whom he is engaged to. They have just had a little tiff, and are making it up. He *does* talk to her a good deal. I have noticed it myself. Such a sweet creature!"

"Is she going to act?"

"Yes," I replied. "They are going to begin at once. You need not dress. It is not a dress rehearsal."

"I think I will go and get my boots off, though," said Carr. "Can you show me where I am?"

"I am afraid you are not in the house at all," I said. "The fact is—did not Sir George tell you?" And then I explained.

For a moment his face fell, but it cleared instantly, though not before I had noticed it.

"You don't mind?" I said, astonished. "You quite understand—"

"Of course, of course!" he interrupted. "It is all right, I have a cold, that is all; and I have to sing next week. I shall do very well. Pray don't tell your friends I have a cold. I am sure Sir George is kindness itself, and it might make him uneasy to think I was not in his house."

The rehearsal now began, and in much trepidation I waited to see Carr come on. The moment he appeared all anxiety vanished; the other actors were reassured, and acted their best. A few passages had to be repeated, a few positions altered, but it was obvious that Carr could act, and act well; though, curiously enough, he looked less gentlemanlike and well-bred when acting with Charles than he had done when he was the best among a very mixed set on the steamer.

"You act beautifully, Mr. Carr!" said Aurelia, when it was over. "Doesn't he, Ralph?"

"Doesn't he?" replied Ralph, hot but good-humored. "I am sure, Carr, we are most grateful to you."

"So am I," said Charles. "Your death agonies, Carr, are a credit to human nature. No great vulgar writhings with legs all over the stage, like Denis; but a chaste, refined wriggle, and all was over. It is a pleasure to kill a man who dies in such a gentlemanlike manner. If only Evelyn will keep a little closer to me when I am on my wicked baronial knees, I shall be quite happy. You hear, Evelyn?"

"How you can joke at this moment," said Evelyn, who looked pale and nervous, "I cannot think. I don't believe I shall be able to remember a word when it comes to the point."

"Stage-fever coming on already," said Charles, in a different tone. "Ah! it is your first appearance, is it not? Go and rest now, and you will be all right when the time comes. I have a vision of a great success, and a call before the curtain, and bouquets, and other delights. Only go and rest now." And he went to light a candle for her. He seemed very thoughtful for Evelyn.

It was the signal for all of us to disperse, the ladies to their rooms, the men to the only retreat left to them, the smoking-room. As Aurelia went upstairs I saw her beckon Ralph and whisper to him:

"Am I really to wear them?"

"Wear what, my angel? The jewels! Why, good gracious, I had quite forgotten them. Of course I want you to wear them."

"So do I, dreadfully," she replied, with a killing glance over the balusters. "Only if I am, you must bring them down in good time, and put them on in the greenroom. I hope you have got them somewhere safe."

"Safe as a church," replied Ralph, forgetting that in these days the simile was not a good one. "Father has them in his strong-box. I will ask him to get them out—at least all that could be worn—and I will give them a rub up before you wear them."

"Ah!" said Charles, sadly, as we walked up-stairs, "if only I had known Sir John!"

CHAPTER VII

It was nearly eight o'clock when I came down. The play was to begin at eight. The hall, which was brilliantly lighted, was one moving mass of black coats, with here and there a red one, and evening-dresses many colored—the people in them, chatting, bowing, laughing, being ushered to their places. Lady Mary and Sir George Danvers side by side received their guests at the foot of the grand staircase, Lady Mary, resplendent in diamond tiara and riviere, smiling as if she could never frown; Sir George upright, courteous, a trifle stiff, as most English country gentlemen feel it incumbent on themselves to be on such occasions.

Presently the continual roll of the carriages outside ceased, the lamps were toned down, the orchestra struck up, and Sir George and Lady Mary took their seats, looking round with anxious satisfaction at the hall crowded with people. People lined the walls; chairs were being lifted over the heads of the sitting for some who were still standing; cushions were being arranged on the billiard-table at the back for a covey of white waistcoats who arrived late; the staircase was already crowded with servants; the whole place was crammed.

I wondered how they were getting on behind the scenes, and slipping out of the hall, I traversed the great gold and white drawing-room, prepared for dancing, and peeped into the morning-room, which, with the adjoining library, had been given up to the actors. They were all assembled in the morning-room, however, waiting for one of the elder ladies who had not come down. The prompter was getting fidgety, and walking about. The two scene-shifters, pale, weary-looking men, who had come down with the scenery, were sitting in the wings, perfectly apathetic amid the general excitement. Charles and several other actors were standing round a footman who was opening champagne bottles at a surprising rate. I saw Charles take a glass to Evelyn, who was shivering with a sharp attack of stage-fever in an arm-chair, looking over her part. She smiled gratefully, but as she did so her eyes wandered to the other side of the room, where Ralph, on his knees before Aurelia, was fastening a diamond star in her dress. Diamonds, rubies, and emeralds flashed in her hair, and on her white neck and arms. Ralph was fixing the last ornament onto her shoulder with wire off a champagne bottle, there being no clasp to hold it in its place. I saw Evelyn turn away again, and Charles, who was watching her, suddenly went off to the fire, and began to complain of the cold, and of the thinness of his silk stockings.

The elder lady—"the heavy mother," as Charles irreverently called her—now arrived; the orchestra, which was giving a final flourish, was begged in a hoarse whisper to keep going a few minutes longer; eyes were applied to the hole in the curtain, and then, every one being assembled, it was felt by all that the awful moment had come at last. A more miserable-looking set of people I never saw. I always imagined that the actors behind the scenes were as gay off the stage as on it; but I found to my astonishment that they were all suffering more or less from severe mental depression. Ralph and Aurelia were now sitting ruefully together on an ottoman beside the painting table, littered with its various rouges and creams and stage appliances. Even Charles, who had established Evelyn on a chair in the wings at the side she had to come on from, and was now drinking champagne with due regard to his paint—even Charles owned to being nervous.

"I wish to goodness Mrs. Wright would begin!" he said. "Ah, there she goes!"—as she ascended the stage steps. "There goes the bell. We are in for it now. She starts, and I come on next. Up goes the curtain. Where the devil has my book got to?"

In another moment he was in the wings, intent on his part; then I saw him throw down his book and go jauntily forward. A moment more, and there was a thunder of applause. All the actors looked at each other, and smiled a feeble smile.

"He will do," said General Marston, the Indian officer, who, now in the dress of an old-fashioned livery servant, proceeded to mount the steps. It dawned upon me that I was missing the play, and I hurried back to find Charles convulsing the audience with the utmost coolness, and evidently enjoying himself exceedingly. Then Evelyn came on—But who cares to read a description of a play? It is sufficient to say that Aurelia looked charming, and many were the whispered comments on her magnificent jewels; but on the stage Evelyn surpassed her, as much as Aurelia surpassed Evelyn off it.

Ralph and Carr did well, but Charles was the favorite with every one, from the Duchess of Crushington in the front seat to the scullery-maid on the staircase. He was so bold, so wicked, so insinuating, in his plumed cap and short cloak, so elegantly refined when he wiped his sword upon his second's handkerchief. He took every one's heart by storm. Ralph, who represented all the virtues, with rather thick ankles and a false mustache, was nowhere. When the curtain fell for the last time, amid great and continued applause, the "heavy mother," Ralph, Aurelia, all were well received as they passed before it; but Charles, who appeared last, was the hero of the evening.

"He is engaged to his cousin, Miss Derrick, isn't he?" said a lady near me, in a loud whisper to a friend.

"Hush! no. Charles can't marry. Head over ears in debt. They say *she* is attached to one of her cousins, but I forget which. I am not sure it was not the other one."

"Then it is the second son who is going to be married, is it? I know I heard something about one of them being engaged."

"Yes, the second son is engaged to that good-looking girl in diamonds, who acted Florence Mordaunt. A lot of money, I believe, but not much in the way of family. Grandfather sold mouse-traps in Birmingham, so people say."

"She looks like it!" replied the other, who had daughters out, and could not afford to let any praise of other girls pass. "No breeding or refinement; and she will be stout later, you will see."

The play being over, a general movement now set in towards the drawing-room, where the band was already installed, and making its presence known by an inspiriting valse tune. In a few moments twenty, thirty, forty couples were swaying to the music; Aurelia in her acting costume was dancing away with Ralph in his red stockings; Carr with the "heavy mother," and Charles in prosaic evening-dress was flying past with Evelyn, who, now that she had effaced her beautiful stage complexion, looked pale and grave as ever.

I suppose it was a capital ball. Every one seemed to enjoy it. I did not dance myself, but I liked watching the others; and after a time Charles, who had been dancing indefatigably with two school-room girls with pigtails, came and flung himself down on the other half of the ottoman on which I was sitting.

"Three times with each!" he said, in a voice of extreme exhaustion. "No favoritism. I have done for to-night now."

"What! Are you not going to dance any more?"

"No, not unless Evelyn will give me another turn later, which she probably won't. There she goes with Lord Breakwater again. How I do dislike that young man! And look at Carr—valsing with Aurelia! He seems to be leaping on her feet a good deal, and she looks as if she were telling him so, does not she? There! they have subsided into the bay-window. I thought she would not stand it long. He does not dance as well as he acts. Heigh-ho! Come in to supper with me, Middleton. The supper-room will be emptier now, and I am dying of hunger. You must be the same, for you had no regular dinner any more than we had. Come along. We will get a certain little table for two that I know of, in the bay-window where I took the fair pigtail just now, to the evident anxiety of the parental chignon who was at the large table. We will have a good feed in peace and quietness."

In a few minutes we were established in a quiet nook in the supper-room, which was now half empty, and were making short work of everything before us.

"How well Carr acted!" said Charles at last, leaning back, and leisurely sipping his champagne. "I can think of something besides food now. Did not you think he acted well?"

"Yes," I said, "but you cut him out."

"Did I!" said Charles, absently, beckoning to some lobster salad which was passing. "Have some? Do, Middleton. We can but die once. You won't? Well I will. Have you often seen Carr act before?"

"Never," I said. "I never met him till I came on board the *Bosphorus* at— —"

"Indeed! Oh! I fancied you were quite old friends."

"We made great friends on the steamer."

"Did you see much of him in London?" he asked, filling up his glass and mine.

"Not much, naturally," I said, laughing. "I was in London only two nights."

"Ah! I forgot. Very good of you, I am sure, to come down here so soon after your arrival. You would hardly have seen him at all since you landed, then?"

"Carr? Yes," I replied, thinking Charles's talk was becoming very vague; though when I rallied him about it next day he assured me it had been very much to the point indeed. "We dined and went to the play together, and had rather a nasty accident into the bargain on our way home."

"What kind of accident?"

I told him the particulars, which seemed to interest him very much.

"And you had all those jewels of poor Sir John's with you, no doubt," continued Charles. "You said you had them on you day and night. I wonder you were not relieved of them."

"That is just what Carr said," I went on; "for he lost something of his, poor fellow. However, I had left them with Jane in a—in a *safe place*."

I did not think it necessary to mention the tea-caddy.

"Oh! so Carr knew you had charge of them, did he?" said Charles. "Have some of these grapes, Middleton; the white ones are the best."

"Yes," I said, "he was the only person who had any idea of such a thing. I am very careful, I can tell you; and I did not mean to have half the ship's company know that I had valuables to such an amount upon me. When I told Jane about them—"

"Oh, then, Jane—I beg her pardon, Miss Middleton—was aware you had them with you?"

"Of course," I replied; "and she was quite astonished at them when I showed them to her."

"I hope," continued Charles, with his charming smile—all the more charming because it was so rare—"that Miss Middleton will add me to the number of her friends some day. I live in London, you know; but I wonder at ladies caring to live there. No poultry or garden, to which the feminine mind usually clings."

"Jane seems to like it," I said.

"Yes," replied Charles, meditatively. "I dare say she is very wise. A woman who lives alone is much safer in town than in an isolated house in the country, in case of fire, or thieves, or——"

"Well, I don't know that," I said. "I don't see that they are so very safe. Why, only the night before I came down here——" I stopped. I had looked up to catch a sudden glimpse of Carr's face, pale and uneasy, watching us in a mirror opposite. In a moment I saw his face turn smiling to another—Evelyn's, I think—and both were gone.

Charles's light steel eyes were fixed full upon me.

"'Only the night before you came down here,' you were saying," he remarked, leaning back and half shutting them as usual.

"Yes, only the night before I came down here our house was broken into;" and I gave him a short account of what had happened. "And only the night before *that*," I added, "a poor woman was murdered in Jane's old house. I remember it especially, because I went to the house by mistake, not knowing Jane had moved, and I saw her, poor thing, sitting by the fire. I don't see that living in town *is* so much safer for life and property, after all."

"Dear me! no. You are right, perfectly right," said Charles, dreamily. "Your sister's experience proves it. And that other poor creature—only the night before—and in Miss Middleton's former house, too. Well, Middleton," with a start, "I suppose we ought to be going back now. I have got all I want, if you have. I wonder what time it is? I'm dog tired."

We re-entered the ball-room to find the last valse being played, and a crowd of people taking leave of Lady Mary.

"Where's father?" asked Charles, as Ralph came up. "He ought to be here to say good-night."

"He's gone to bed," said Ralph. "Aunt Mary sent him. He was quite done up. He has been on his legs all day. I expect he will be laid up to-morrow."

In a quarter of an hour the ball-room was empty, and Lady Mary, who was dragging herself wearily towards the hall as the last carriage rolled away, felt that she might safely restore the balance of her mind by a sudden lapse from the gracious and benevolent to the acid and severe.

"To bed! to bed!" she kept repeating. "Where is Evelyn? I want her arm. General Marston, Colonel Middleton, will you have the goodness to go and glean up these young people? Mrs. Marston and Lady Delmour, you must both be tired to death. Let us go on, and they can follow."

General Marston and I found a whole flock of the said young people in the library, candle in hand, laughing and talking, thinking they were going that moment, but not doing it, and all, in fact, listening to Charles, who was expounding a theory of his own respecting ball dresses, which seemed to meet with the greatest feminine derision.

"First take your silk slip," he was saying as we came in. "There is nothing indiscreet in mentioning a slip; is there, Evelyn? I trust not; for I heard Lady Delmour telling Mrs. Wright that all well-brought-up young ladies had silk slips. Then—"

"He exposes his ignorance more entirely every moment," said Evelyn. "Let us all go to bed, and leave him to hold forth to men who know as little as himself."

"Oh, Ralph!" said Aurelia, pointing to the jewels on her neck and arms; "before we go I want you to take back these. I don't like keeping them myself; I am afraid of them." And she began to take them off and lay them on the table.

"Nonsense, my pet; keep them yourself, and lock them up in your dressing-case." And Ralph held them towards her.

"I haven't got a dressing-case," said Aurelia, pouting; "and my hat-box won't lock. I don't like having them. I wish you would keep them yourself."

"Bother!" said Ralph; "and father has gone to bed. He can't put them back into his safe, and he keeps the key himself. Where is the bag they go in?"

Aurelia said that she had seen him put it behind a certain jar on the chimney-piece in the morning-room, and Carr went for it, she following him with a candle, as all the lamps had been put out. They presently returned with it, and Ralph, who had been collecting all the jewels spread over the table, shovelled them in with little ceremony.

"Bother!" he said again, looking round and swinging the bag; "what on earth am I to do with them? Ah, well, here goes!" and he opened a side drawer in a massive writing-table and shoved the bag in.

"There!" he said, locking it, and putting the key in his pocket; "they will do very well there till to-morrow. Are you content now, Aurelia?"

"Oh yes," she said, "I am, if you are." And she bade us good-night and followed in the wake of the others, who were really under way at last.

As we all tramped wearily up-stairs to the smoking-room I saw Charles draw Ralph aside and whisper something to him.

"Nonsense!" I heard Ralph say. "Safe enough. Besides, who would suspect their being there? Just as safe as in the strong-box. Brahma lock. Won't be bothered any more about them."

Charles shrugged his shoulders and marched off to bed. Ralph and Carr likewise went off shortly afterwards to their rooms in the lodge. Carr looked tired to death. I went down with them, at Ralph's request, to lock the door behind them, as all the servants had gone to bed.

It was a fine night, still and cold, with a bright moon. It had evidently been snowing afresh, for there was not a trace of wheels upon the ground; but it had ceased now.

"Good-night!" called Ralph and Carr, as they went down the steps together. I watched the two figures for a moment in the moonlight, their footsteps making a double track in the untrodden snow. The cold was intense. I drew back shivering, and locked and bolted the door.

CHAPTER VIII

It is very seldom I cannot sleep, but I could not that night. There was something in the intense quiet and repose of the great house, after all the excitement of the last few hours, that oppressed me. Everything seemed, as I lay awake, so unnaturally silent. There was not a sound in the wide grate, where the last ashes of the fire were silently giving up the ghost, not a rumble of wind in the old chimney which had had so much to say the night before. I tossed and turned, and vainly sought for sleep, now on this side, now on that. At last I gave up trying, half in the hope that it might steal upon me unawares. I thought of the play and the ball, of poor Charles and his debts—of anything and everything—but it was no good. In the midst of a jumble of disconnected ideas I suddenly found myself listening again to the silence—listening as if it had been broken by a sound which I had not heard. My watch ticked loud and louder on the dressing-table, and presently I gave quite a start as the distant stable clock tolled out the hour: One, two, three, four. I had gone to bed before three. Had I been awake only an hour? It seemed incredible. Getting up on tiptoe, vaguely afraid myself of breaking the silence, I noiselessly pushed aside the heavy curtains and looked out.

The moon had set, but by the frosty starlight the outline of the great snow-laden trees and the wide sweep of white drive were still dimly visible. All was silent without as within. Not a branch moved or let fall its freight of snow. There was not a breath of wind stirring. I was on the point of getting back into bed, when I thought in the distance I heard a sound. I listened intently. No! I must have been mistaken. Ah! again, and nearer! I held my breath. I could distinctly hear a stealthy step coming up the stairs. My room was the nearest to the staircase end of the corridor, and any one coming up the stairs must pass my door. With a presence of mind which, I am glad to say, rarely deserts me, I blew out my candle, slipped to the door, and noiselessly opened it a chink.

Some one was coming down the corridor with the lightness of a cat, candle in hand, as a faint light showed me. Another moment, and I saw Charles, pale and haggard, still in evening-dress, coming towards me. He was without his shoes. He passed my door and went noiselessly into his own room, a little farther down the passage. There was the faintest suspicion of a sound, as of a key being gently turned in the lock, and then all was still again, stiller than ever.

What could Charles have been after? I wondered. He could not have been returning from seeing Denis, who was not only much better, but was in the room beyond his own. And why had he still got on his evening clothes at four o'clock in the morning? I determined to ask him about it next day, as I got back into bed again, and then, while wondering about it and trying to get warm, I fell fast asleep. I was only roused, after being twice called, to find that it was broad daylight, and to hear being carried down the boxes of many of the guests who were leaving by an early train.

I was late, but not so late as some. Breakfast was still going on. Evelyn and Ralph had been up to see their friends off, but General and Mrs. Marston and Carr, who was staying on, came in after I did. Lady Mary and Aurelia were having breakfast in their own rooms. I think nothing is more dreary than a long breakfast-table, laid for large numbers, with half a dozen picnicking at it among the débris left by earlier ravages. Evelyn, behind the great silver urn, looked pale and preoccupied, and had very little to say for herself when I journeyed up to her end of the table and sat down by her. She asked me twice if I took sugar, and was not bright and alert and ready in conversation, as I think girls should be. Carr, too, was eating his breakfast in silence beside Mrs. Marston.

It was not cheerful. And then Charles came in, listless and tired, and without an appetite. He sat down wearily on the other side of Evelyn, and watched her pour out his coffee without a word.

"The Carews and Edmonts and Lady Delmour and her daughter have just gone," said Evelyn, "and Mr. Denis."

"Yes," replied Charles, seeming to pull himself together; "Denis came to my room before he went. He looked a wreck, poor fellow; but not worse than some of us. These late hours, these friskings with energetic young creatures in the school-room, these midnight revels, are too much for me. I feel a perfect wreck this morning, too."

He certainly looked it.

"Have you had bad letters?" said Evelyn, in a low voice.

He laughed a little—a grim laugh—and shook his head. "But I had yesterday," he added presently, in a low tone. "I shall have to try a change of air again soon, I am afraid."

I was just going to ask Charles what he had been doing walking about in his socks the night before, when the door opened, and Ralph, whose absence

I had not noticed, came in. He looked much perturbed. It seemed his father had been taken suddenly and alarmingly ill while dressing. In a moment all was confusion. Evelyn precipitately left the room to go to him, while Charles rushed round to the stables to send a groom on horseback for the nearest doctor. Ralph followed him, and the remainder of the party gathered in a little knot round the fire, Mrs. Marston expressing the sentiment of each of us when she said that she thought visitors were very much in the way when there was illness in the house, and that she regretted that she and her husband had arranged to stay over Sunday, to-day being Friday.

"So have I," said Carr; "but I am sure I had better have refused. A stranger in a sick-house is a positive nuisance. I think I shall go to town by an afternoon train, if there is one."

"Upon my word I think we had better do the same," said Mrs. Marston. "What do you say, Arthur?" and she turned to her husband.

"I must go to-day, anyhow—on business," said General Marston.

"I hope no one is talking of leaving," said Charles, who had returned suddenly, rather out of breath.

As he spoke his eyes were fixed on Carr.

"Yes, that is exactly what we were doing," said Mrs. Marston. "Nothing is so tiresome as having visitors on one's hands when there is illness in the house. Mr. Carr was thinking of going up to London by the afternoon train; and I have a very good mind to go away with Arthur, instead of staying on, and letting him come back here for me to-morrow, as we had intended."

"Pray do not think of such a thing!" said Charles, really with unnecessary earnestness. "Mrs. Marston, pray do not alter your plans. Carr!" in a much sterner tone, "I must beg that you will not think of leaving us to-day. Your friend Colonel Middleton is staying on, and we cannot allow you to desert us so suddenly."

It was more like a command than an invitation; but Carr, usually so quick to take a slight, did not seem to notice it, and merely said that he should be happy to go or stay, whichever was most in accordance with the wishes of others, and took up the newspaper. He and Charles did not seem to get on well. I could see that Charles had not seemed to take to him from the very first; and Carr certainly did not appear at ease in the house. Perhaps Charles felt that he had rather failed in courtesy to him, for during the remainder of the morning he hardly let him out of his sight. He took him to see the stables, though Carr openly declared that he did not understand horses; he showed him his collection of Zulu weapons in the vestibule; he even started a game of billiards with him till the arrival of the doctor. I did not think Carr took his attentions in very good part, though he was too well-mannered to show it; but he looked relieved when Charles went up-stairs with the doctor, and pitched his cue into the rack at once, and came to the hall-fire where I was sitting, and where Aurelia presently joined us, fresh and smiling, in the prettiest of morning-gowns. Every one met in the hall. It was in the centre of the house, and every one coming up or down had to pass through it. Just now it was not so tempting an abode as usual, for the flowers and part of the stage had already been removed, and the bare boards, with their wooden supports, gave an air of discomfort to the whole place.

Aurelia opened wide eyes of horror at hearing Sir George was ill. She even got out a tiny laced pocket-handkerchief; but before she had had time to weep much into it, and spoil her pretty eyes, the doctor reappeared, accompanied by Charles and Ralph, and we all learned to our great relief that Sir George, though undoubtedly ill, was not dangerously so at present, though the greatest care would be necessary. Lady Mary had undertaken the nursing of her brother-in-law, and in her the doctor expressed the same confidence which parents are wont to feel in a stern school-master. In the mean time the patient was to be kept very quiet, and on no account to be disturbed.

When the doctor had left, Ralph and Aurelia, who had actually seen nothing of each other that morning, sauntered away together towards the library. Charles challenged Carr to finish his game of billiards, and Marston and I retired up-stairs to the smoking-room, where we could talk over our Indian experiences, and perhaps doze undisturbed. We might have been so occupied for half an hour or more when a flying step came up the stairs, the door was thrown open, and Ralph rushed into the room.

"General Marston! Colonel Middleton!" he gasped out, breathing hard, "will you, both of you, come to my father's room at once? He has sent for you."

"Good gracious! Is he worse?" I exclaimed.

"No. Hush! Don't ask anything, but just come," —and he turned and led the way to Sir George Danvers's room.

We followed in wondering silence, and, after passing along numerous passages, were ushered into a large oak-panelled room with a great carved bed in it, in the middle of which, bolt-upright, sat Sir George Danvers, pale as ivory, his light steel eyes (so like Charles's) seeming to be the only living thing about him.

As we came in he looked at each of us in turn.

"Where is Charles?" he said, speaking in a hoarse whisper.

"Dear me! Sir George," I said, sympathetically, "how you *have* lost your voice!"

He looked at me for a moment, and then turned to Ralph again.

"Where is Charles?" he asked a second time, in the same tone.

"Here!" said a quiet voice. And Charles came in, and shut the door.

CHAPTER IX

The two pairs of steel eyes met, and looked fixedly at each other.

A tap came to the door.

Sir George winced, and made a sign to Ralph, who rushed to it and bolted it.

"I am coming in, George," said Lady Mary's voice.

"Send her away," came a whisper from the bed.

This was easier said than done. But it *was* done after a sufficiently long parley; and Lady Mary retired under the impression that Ralph was sitting alone with his father, who thought he might get a little sleep.

"Now," whispered Sir George, motioning to Ralph.

"The fact is," said Ralph, "the jewels are gone! They have been stolen in the night."

He bolted out with this one sentence, and then was silent. Marston and I stared at him aghast.

"Is there no mistake?" said Marston at last.

"None," replied Ralph. "I put them in a drawer in the great inlaid writing-table in the library last night, before everybody. I went for them this morning, half an hour ago, at father's request. The lock was broken, and they were gone."

There was another long silence.

"I was a fool, of course, to put them there," resumed Ralph. "Charles told me so; but I thought they were as safe there as anywhere, if no one knew—and no one did except the house party."

"Were any of the servants about?" asked Marston.

"Not one. They had all gone to bed except one of the footmen, who was putting out the lamps in the supper-room, miles away."

Another silence.

"That is the dreadful part of it," burst out Ralph. "They must have been taken by some one staying in the house—some one who saw me put them there. The first thing I did was to send for the house-maids, and they assured me that they had found every shutter shut, and every door locked, this morning, as usual. Any one with time and wits *might* have got in through one of the library windows by taking out a pane and forcing the shutter. I suppose a practised hand might have done such a thing; but I went outside and there was not a footstep in the snow anywhere near the library windows, or, for that matter, anywhere near the house at all, except at the side and front doors, which are impracticable for any one to force an entrance by."

"When did it leave off snowing?" asked Marston.

"About three o'clock," replied Ralph. "It must have snowed heavily till then, for there was not a trace of all the carriage-wheels on the drive when we went out last night, but our footprints down to the lodge are clear in the snow now. There has been no snow since three o'clock this morning."

"It all points to the same thing," said Charles, quietly, speaking for the first time. "The jewels were taken by some one staying in the house."

"One of the servants—" began Marston.

"No!" said Charles, cutting him short, "not one of the servants."

"It is impossible it should have been one of them," said Ralph, after some thought. "First of all, none of them saw the jewels put into that drawer; and, secondly, how could they suspect me of hiding them in a place where I had never thought of putting them myself till that moment? Besides, that one drawer only was broken open—the centre drawer in the left-hand set of drawers. All the others were untouched, though they were all locked. No one who had not *seen* the jewels put in would have found them so easily. That is the frightful part of it."

For a few minutes no one spoke. At last Marston raised his head from his hands.

"There is no way out of it," he said, very gravely. "The robbery was committed by one of the visitors staying in the house!"

"Yes!" said Charles.

"Yes!" echoed a whisper from the bed.

Charles looked up slowly and deliberately, and the eyes of father and son met again.

"We do not often agree, father," he said, in a measured voice. "I mark this exception to the rule with pleasure."

"When I had made out as much as this," continued Ralph, "father told me to call both of you and Charles, to consider what ought to be done before we make any move."

"Have you an inventory of the jewels?" asked Marston at length.

"None," said Sir George, "unless Middleton had one from Sir John."

I thereupon recapitulated in full all the circumstances of the bequest, finally adding that Sir John had never so much as mentioned an inventory.

"So much the better for the thief," said Marston, his chin in his hands. "It is not a case for a detective," he added.

"I think not," said Charles.

A kind of hoarse ghostly laugh came from the bed. "Charles is always right," whispered the sick man. "Quite unnecessary, I am sure."

"Oh, I don't know," I said, feeling I had not yet been of as much assistance as I could have wished. "Now, I think detectives are of use—really useful, you know, in finding out things. There was a detective, I remember, trying to trace the people who murdered that poor lady at Jane's old house since my return."

"But who could it have been? who could it have been?" burst out Ralph, unheeding. "They were all friends. It is frightful to suspect one of them. One could as easily suspect one's self. Which of them all could have done a thing like that? Out of them all, which was it?"

"Carr!" replied Charles, quietly, looking full at his father.

If a bomb-shell had fallen among us at that moment it could not have produced a greater effect than that one word, uttered so deliberately. Sir George started in his bed, and clutched at the bedclothes with both hands. My brain positively reeled. Carr! my friend Carr! introduced into the family by myself, was being accused by Charles. I was speechless with indignation.

"I am sorry, Middleton," continued Charles; "I know he is your friend, but I can't help that. Carr took the jewels. I distrusted him from the moment he set foot in the house."

"Where is he at this instant?" said Marston, getting up. "Is no one with him?"

"There is no need to be anxious on his account," replied Charles. "I took him up to the smoking-room before I came here, and I turned the key in the door. The key is here." And he laid it on the table.

Marston sat down again.

"What are your grounds for suspecting Carr?" he asked. "Remember, this is a very serious thing, Charles, that you have done in locking him up, if you have not adequate reason for it."

"You had better leave Carr alone, Charles," said Ralph, significantly.

"Let him go on," said Sir George.

"I have no proof," continued Charles; "I did not see him take them, but I am as certain of it as if I had seen it with my own eyes. The jewels could only have been stolen by some one staying in the house. That is certain. Who, excepting Carr, was a stranger among us? Who, excepting Carr—"

"Stop, Charles," said Ralph again. "Don't you know that Carr slept with me down at the lodge?"

Charles turned on his brother and gripped his shoulder.

"Do you mean to say," he said, sharply, "that Carr did not sleep in the house last night?"

"Dear me, Charles, that was an oversight on your part," came Sir George's whisper.

"No," replied Ralph, "he did not. The house was full, and we had to put him in that second small room through mine in the lodge. If Carr had been dying to take them he had not the opportunity. He could not have left his room without passing through mine, and I never went to sleep at all. I had a sharp touch of neuralgia from the cold, which kept me awake all night."

"He got out through the window," said Charles.

"Nonsense!" said Ralph, getting visibly angry; "you are only making matters worse by trying to put it on him. Remember the size of the window. Besides, you know how the lodge stands, built against the garden wall. When I came out this morning there was not a single footstep in the snow, except those we had made as we went there the night before. I noticed our footmarks particularly, because I had been afraid there would be more snow. No one could by any possibility have left the house during the night. Even Jones himself had not been out, for there was a little eddy of snow before the back door, and I remember calling to him that he would want his broom."

"The snow clinches the matter, Charles," said Marston, gravely. "You have made a mistake."

"Quite unintentional, I'm sure," whispered Sir George.

There was something I did not like about that whisper. It seemed to imply more than met the ear.

Charles did not appear to hear him. He was looking fixedly before him, his hand had dropped from Ralph's shoulder, his face was quite gray.

"Then," he said, slowly, as if waking out of a dream, "it was *not* Carr."

"No," said Sir George; "I never thought it was."

"Good God!" ejaculated Charles, sinking into a low chair by the fire, and shading his face with his hand. "Not Carr, after all!"

But my indignation could not be restrained a moment longer. I had only been kept silent by repeated signs from Marston, and now I broke out.

"And so, sir, you suspect my friend," I said, "and insult him in your father's house by turning the key on him. You endeavor to throw suspicion on a man who never injured you in the slightest degree. You insult *me* in insulting my friend, sir. Suspicion is not always such an easy thing to shake off as it has been in this instance. I, on my side, might ask what *you* were doing walking about the passages in your socks at four o'clock this morning? In your socks, sir, still in your evening clothes—"

I had spoken it anger, not thinking much what I was saying, and I stopped short, alarmed at the effect of my own words.

"I knew it! I knew it!" gasped Sir George, in his hoarse, suffocated voice, and he fell back panting among his pillows.

Charles took his hand from his face, and looked hard at me with a strange kind of smile.

"At any rate we are quits, Middleton," he said. "You have done it now, and no mistake."

I did not quite see what I had done, but it soon became apparent.

"I knew it!" gasped out the sick man again; "I knew it from the first moment that he tried to throw suspicion on Carr."

"Sir George," said Marston, gravely, "Charles made a mistake just now. Do not you, on your side, make another. Come, Charles," turning to the latter, who was now sitting erect, with flashing eyes, "tell us about it. What were you doing when Middleton saw you?"

"I was coming up-stairs," said Charles, haughtily.

"From the library?" asked Sir George.

Charles bit his lip and remained silent.

I would not have spoken to him for a good deal at that moment. He looked positively dangerous.

"From the library, of course," he said at last, controlling himself, and speaking with something of his old careless manner, "laden with the spoils of my midnight depredations. Parental fondness will supply all minor details, no doubt; so, as the subject is a delicate one for me, I will withdraw, that it may be discussed more fully in my absence."

"Stop, Charles," said Marston; "the case is too serious for banter of this kind. My dear boy," he added, kindly, "I am glad to see you angry, but nevertheless, you must condescend to explain. The longer you allow suspicion to rest on yourself the longer it will be before it falls on the right person. Come, what were you doing in the passage at that time of night?"

Charles was touched, I could see. A very little kindness was too much for him.

"It is no good, Marston," he said, in quite a different voice—"I am not believed in this house."

He turned away and leaned against the mantle-piece, looking into the fire. Ralph cleared his throat once or twice, and then suddenly went up to him, and laid his hand affectionately on his shoulder.

"Fire away, old boy!" he said, in a constrained tone, and he choked again.

Charles turned round and faced his brother, with the saddest smile I ever saw.

"Well, Ralph!" he said, "I will tell you everything, and then you can believe me or not, as you like. I have never told you a lie, have I?"

"Not often," replied Ralph, unwillingly.

"You at least are truth itself," said Charles, reddening; "and if you are biassed in your opinion of me, perhaps it is more the fault of that exemplary Christian, Aunt Mary, than your own. According to her, I have told lies enough to float a company or carry an election, and I never like to disappoint her expectations of me in that respect; but you I have never to my knowledge deceived, and I am not going to begin now."

"You will be a clergyman yet," whispered the sick parent. "There is a good living in the family. Charles, I shall live to see the Reverend Charles Danvers in a surplice, preaching his first sermon on the ninth commandment."

"At any rate, he is practising the fifth under difficulties at this moment," said Marston, as Charles winced and turned his back on the parental sick-bed. "Come, my boy, we are losing time."

"Will somebody have the goodness to restrain Middleton if he gets excited?" said Charles. "I am afraid he won't like part of what I have got to say."

"Nonsense, sir!" I replied, with warmth. "I hope I can restrain myself as well as any man, even under such provocation as I have lately received. You may depend on me, sir, that—"

"We lose time," said Marston, seating himself by me, and cutting short what I was saying in an exceedingly brusque manner. "Come, Charles, you should not be interrupted."

But he was. I interrupted him the whole time, in spite of continual efforts on the part of Marston to make me keep silence. I am not the man calmly to let pass black insinuations against the character of a friend. No, I stood up for him. I am glad to think how I stood up for him, not only metaphorically, but in the most literal sense of the term; for I found myself continually getting up, and Marston as often pulling me down again into my chair.

"Am I to speak, or is Middleton?" said Charles at last, in despair. "I will do a solo, or I will keep silence; but really I am unequal to a duet."

"Sir George," said Marston, "will you have the goodness to desire Colonel Middleton to be silent, or to leave the room till Charles has finished his story?"

I was justly annoyed at Marston's manner of speaking of me, but as I had no intention to leave the room and miss what was going on, I merely bowed in answer to a civil request from Sir George, and took up an attitude of dignified silence. I felt that I had done my part in vindicating my friend; and after all, no one, evidently, was accustomed to believe what Charles said.

"As I was saying," he continued, "I suspected Carr from the first. I did not like the look of him, and I purposely pumped Middleton about him last night at supper."

I nearly burst out at the bare idea of Charles daring to say he had pumped me; but, as will be seen, he could twist anything that was said to such an extent that it was perfectly useless to contradict him any longer. I said not a single word, and he went on:

"All Middleton told me confirmed me in my suspicions. Sir John had been murdered the night before Middleton sailed for England, a whisper of the jewels having no doubt gone abroad. Carr came on board next day, and made friends with Middleton. Whether he had anything to do with the murder or not, God knows! but he found out—nay, Middleton openly told him—that he had jewels of great value in his possession, which he carried about on his person. Carr was the only person aware of that fact. What follows? Carr has Middleton's address in London. Middleton goes to the house, and finds that his sister has moved to the next street. That house to which he first went is broken into, and the poor woman in it is murdered, or dies of fright that same night. I mention this as coincidence number one. The following evening Middleton, having by chance left the jewels at home, dines, and goes to the theatre by appointment with Carr. Unique cab accident occurs, in which Middleton is knocked on the head and rendered unconscious. Coincidence number two. Miss Middleton's house is broken into that same night on Middleton's return to it. Coincidence number three. When I put all this together last night, remembering that Carr, by Middleton's own account, was the only person aware that he had jewels of great value in his keeping, I felt absolutely certain (as I feel still) that he had accepted the invitation, and come down from London solely for the purpose of stealing them. It was pure conjecture on my part, and I dared say nothing beyond begging Ralph not to leave the jewels in the library—which, however, he did. I went straight off to my room when the others went to smoke, but I did not go to bed. The more I thought it over the more certain I felt that Carr would not let slip such an opportunity, the more convinced that an attempt would be made that very night. I did not know that he was not sleeping in the house, but I knew Ralph was at the lodge, so I could not go and consult with him, as I should otherwise have done. I thought of going to Middleton, whose room was close to mine, but on second thoughts I gave up the idea. I am glad I did. At last I determined I would wait till the house was quiet, and that then I would go down alone, and watch in the library in the dark. I lay down on my bed in my clothes to wait, and then—I had been up most of the night before with Denis; I was dead beat with acting and dancing—by ill luck I fell asleep. When I woke up I found to my horror that it was close on four o'clock. I instantly slipped off my shoes, and crept out of my room and down the stairs. I could not get to the library from the hall, as the stage blocked the way, and I had to go all the way round by the drawing-room and morning-room. As I went I thought how easy it would be for Carr to force the lock of the drawer; and so, it flashed across me, could I. Oh, Ralph!" said Charles, "I went down solely to look after your property for you, but I *did* think of it. I hope I should not have done it, but I suddenly remembered how hard pressed I was for money, and I did think of the crescent, and how you would hardly miss it, and how—but what does it matter now? When I got to the library I found I was too late. The lock of the drawer had been forced, and it was empty. There was nothing for it but to go back to my room. I felt as certain that Carr had done it as that I am standing here; but I dared say nothing next morning, for fear of drawing an ever-ready parental suspicion on myself—which, however, Middleton did for me. All I could do was to keep Carr well in sight until the theft was found out, to prevent any possibility of his escaping, and then to accuse him. There!" said Charles, "that is the whole truth. Carr did not take the jewels; that is absolutely proved, and the sooner he is let out the better. Who took them Heaven only knows! I don't. But I know who meant to, and that was Carr."

"Charles," said Ralph, with glistening eyes, "if ever I get them back you shall have the crescent."

"A very neat little story altogether," said Sir George, "and the episode of temptation very effectively thrown in. It does you credit, my son, and is a great relief to your old father's mind."

"Thank you, Charles," said Marston, getting up. "Sir George, it is close on luncheon-time, and Carr must be let out at once. Now that Charles has so completely cleared himself I don't see that anything more can be done for the moment; and of one thing I am certain, namely, that you are making yourself much worse, and must keep absolutely quiet for the rest of the day. If I may advise, I would suggest that Carr should be allowed to leave, as he wishes to do, by the afternoon train, and should not be pressed to stay. There is nothing more to be got out of him; and, considering the circumstances, I should say the sooner he is out of the house the better. As he has been wrongly suspected, I think the robbery had better not be mentioned to any one, even the ladies in the house, until after he has left."

"Aurelia knows," said Ralph. "She was with me in the library. I left her crying bitterly about them."

"Let her cry, if she will only hold her tongue," said Sir George, making a last effort to speak, but evidently at the extreme point of exhaustion. "And you, Marston, you are right about Carr. See that he goes this afternoon. There is nothing more to be done at present. Charles, you will remain here, though I have no doubt you have an engagement in London. I cannot spare you just yet."

Charles bowed, and he and Marston went out. I remained a second behind with Ralph.

"I see it quite clearly," said Sir George. "I know Charles. He is sharp enough. He saw Carr meant mischief, and he was beforehand with him; and *he* took what Carr meant to take. It was not badly imagined, but he should have made certain Carr was sleeping in the house. It all turned on that. He never reckoned on the possibility of Carr's being cleared."

"Middleton is still here," said Ralph, significantly, who was pouring out something for his father.

"Is he? I thought he was gone!" said Sir George, so sharply, that I considered it advisable to retire at once.

Charles and Marston were talking together earnestly in the passage.

"He does not believe a word I say," said Charles, as I joined them; "and, what is more, I could see he had told Ralph he suspected me before we came in. Did not you see how Ralph tried to stop me when he thought I was committing myself by accusing Carr, who, it seems, was quite out of the question? I am glad you cut it short, Marston. He was making himself worse every moment."

"Come on with that key of yours, and let us go and let out Carr," replied Marston, patting Charles kindly on the back, "or he will be kicking all the paint off the door."

"Not he!" said Charles. "An honest man would have rung up the whole household and nearly battered the door down by this time, thinking it had been locked by mistake. Carr knows better."

We had reached the smoking-room by this time, just as the gong was beginning to sound for luncheon, and under cover of the noise Charles fitted the key into the key-hole and unlocked the door. He and Marston went slowly in, talking on some indifferent subject, and I followed.

CHAPTER X

The room seemed strangely quiet after the stormy interview in the sick-chamber which we had just left. The pale winter sunlight was stealing in aslant through the low windows. The fire had sunk to a deep red glow, and in an arm-chair drawn up in front of it, newspaper in hand, was Carr, evidently fast asleep.

"'Oh, my prophetic soul!'" whispered Charles, nudging Marston; and then he went forward and shouted "Luncheon!" in a voice that would have waked the dead.

Carr started up and rubbed his eyes.

"Why, I believe you have been here ever since I left you here, hours ago," said Charles, in a surprised tone, though really, under the circumstances, it did not require a great stretch of the imagination to suppose any such thing.

"Yes," said Carr, still rubbing his eyes. "Have you been gone long? I expect I fell asleep."

"I rather thought you were inclined for a nap when I left you," replied Charles, airily; "and now let us go to luncheon."

It was a very dismal meal. Lady Mary did not come down to it, and Aurelia sat with red eyes, tearful and silent. Ralph was evidently out of favor, for she hardly spoke to him, and snubbed him decidedly when he humbly tendered a peace-offering in the form of a potato. Evelyn, too, was silent, or made spasmodic attempts at conversation with Mrs. Marston, the only unconstrained person of the party. Evelyn and Aurelia had appeared together, and it was evident from Evelyn's expression that Aurelia had told her. What conversation there was turned upon Sir George's illness.

"We must go by the afternoon train, my dear," said Marston down the table to his wife. "In Sir George's present state *all* visitors are an incubus."

Carr looked up. "I think I ought to go, too," he said. "I wished to arrange to do so this morning, but Mr. Danvers," glancing at Charles, "would not hear of it. I am sure, when there is illness in a house, strangers are always in the way."

"I have seen my father since then," replied Charles, "and I fear his illness is much more serious than I had any idea of. That being the case, I feel it would be wrong to press any one, even Middleton, to stay and share the tedium of a sick-house."

After a few more civil speeches it was arranged that Carr should, after all, leave by the train which he had proposed in the morning. It was found that there was still time for him to do so, but that was all. He was evidently as anxious to be off as the Danverses were that he should go. The dog-cart was ordered, a servant despatched to the lodge in hot haste to pack his portmanteau, and in half an hour he was bidding us good-bye, evidently glad to say it. Poor fellow! He little guessed, as he shook hands with us, how shamefully he had been suspected, how villanously he had been traduced behind his back. Somehow or other I had not had a moment of conversation with him since the morning, or a single chance of telling him how I had stood up for him in his absence. Either Charles or Marston were always at hand, and when he took leave of me I could only shake his hand warmly, and tell him to come and see me again in town. I watched him spinning down the drive in the dog-cart, little thinking how soon I should see him again, and in what circumstances.

"We shall have more snow," said Ralph, coming in-doors. "I feel it in the air."

General and Mrs. Marston were the next to leave, starting an hour later, and going in the opposite direction. I saw Marston turn aside, when his wife was taking leave of the others, and go up to Charles. The young hand and the old one met, and were locked tight.

"Good-bye, my dear boy," said Marston.

"Don't go," said Charles, without looking up.

"I must!" said Marston. "I am due at Kemberley to-night, on business; but," in a lower tone, "I shall come back to-morrow, in case I can be of any use."

They were gone, and I was the only one remaining. It has occurred to me since that perhaps they expected me to go too, but I never thought of it at the time. I had been asked for a week, and to go before the end of it never so much as entered my head.

There was no chance of going out. The early winter afternoon was already closing in, and a few flakes of snow were drifting like feathers in the heavy air, promising more to come. Every one seemed to have dispersed, Ralph up-stairs to his father, Charles out-of-doors somewhere in spite of the weather. I remembered that I had not written to Jane since I left London, and went into the library to do so. As I came in I saw Evelyn sitting in a low chair by the fire, gazing abstractedly into it. She started when she saw me, and on my saying I wished to write some letters, showed me a writing-table near the fire, with pens, ink, and paper.

"You will find it very cold at the big table in the window," she said, looking at it with its broken drawer, a chink open, with a visible shudder.

I installed myself near the fire, talking cheerfully the while, for it struck me she was a little low in her spirits. She did not make much response, and I was settling down to my letters when she suddenly said:

"Colonel Middleton!"

"Yes, Miss Derrick."

"I am afraid I am interrupting your writing, but—"

I looked round. She was standing up, nervously playing with her rings. "But—I know I am not supposed to—but I know what happened last night; Aurelia told me."

"It is very sad, isn't it?" I said. "But cheer up. I dare say we may get them back yet." And I nodded confidentially at her. "In the mean time, you know, you must not talk of it to any one."

"Do you suspect any one in particular?" she asked, very earnestly, coming a step nearer.

I hardly knew what to say. Carr, I need hardly mention, I had never suspected for a moment; but Charles—Marston had evidently believed what Charles had said, but I am by nature more cautious and less credulous than Marston. Besides, I had not forgiven Charles yet for trying to incriminate Carr. Not knowing what to say, I shrugged my shoulders and smiled.

"You do suspect some one, then?"

"My dear young lady," I replied, "when jewels are stolen, one naturally suspects some one has taken them."

"So I should imagine. Whom do you naturally suspect?"

I could not tell her that I more than suspected Charles.

"I know nothing for certain," I said.

"But you have a suspicion?"

"I have a suspicion."

She went to the door to see if it were shut, and then came back and said, in a whisper:

"So have I."

"Perhaps we suspect the same person?" I said.

She did not answer, but fixed her dark eyes keenly on mine. I had never noticed before how dark they were.

I saw then that she knew, and that she suspected Charles, just as Sir George had done.

I nodded.

"Nothing is proved," I said.

"I dared not say even as much as this before," she continued, hurriedly. "It is only the wildest, vaguest suspicion. I have nothing to take hold of. It is so horrible to suspect any one; but—"

She stopped suddenly. Her quick ear had caught the sound of a distant step coming across the hall. In another moment Aurelia came in.

"Are you there, Evelyn?" she said. "I was looking for you, to ask where the time-table lives. I want to look out my journey for to-morrow. Ralph ought to do it, but he is up-stairs," with a little pout.

"You ought not to have quarrelled with him until he had made it out for you," said Evelyn, smiling. "It is a very cross journey, isn't it? Let me see. You are going to your uncle in Dublin, are not you? You had better go to London, and start from there. It will be the shortest way in the end."

The two girls laid their heads together over the Bradshaw, Evelyn's dark-soft hair making a charming contrast to Aurelia's yellow curls. At last the journey was made out and duly written down, and a post-card despatched to the uncle in Dublin.

"Have you seen Ralph anywhere?" asked Aurelia, when she had finished it. "I am afraid I was a little tiny wee bit cross to him this morning, and I am so sorry."

Evelyn always seemed to stiffen when Aurelia talked about Ralph, and, under the pretext of putting her post-card in the letter-bag for her, she presently left the room, and did not return.

Aurelia sat down on the hearth-rug, and held two plump little hands to the fire. It was quite impossible to go on writing to Jane while she was there, and I gave it up accordingly.

"I am glad Evelyn is gone," she said, confidentially. "Do you know why I am glad?"

I said I could not imagine.

"Because," continued Aurelia, nodding gravely at me, "I want to have a very, very, *very* serious conversation with you, Colonel Middleton."

I said I should be charmed, inwardly wondering what that little curly head would consider to be serious conversation.

"Really serious, you know," continued Aurelia, "not pretence. About that!" pointing with a pink finger at the inlaid writing-table. "You know I was with Ralph when he found it out, and I am afraid I was a little cross to him, only really it was so hard, and they were so lovely, and it *was* partly his fault, now, wasn't it, for leaving them there? He ought to have been more careful."

"Of course he ought," I said. I would not have contradicted her for worlds.

"And you know I am to be married next month; and Aunt Alice in Dublin, who is getting my things, says as it is to be a winter wedding I am to be married in a white *frisé* velvet, and I did think the diamonds would have looked so lovely with it. Wouldn't they?"

I agreed, of course.

"But I shall never be married in them now," she said, with a deep sigh. "And I was looking forward to the wedding so much, though I dare say I did tell a naughty little story when I said I was *not* to Ralph the other night. Of course Ralph is still left," she added, as an after-thought; "but it won't be so perfect, will it?"

I was morally certain Charles would have to give them up, so I said, reassuringly:

"Perhaps you may be married in them, after all."

"Oh!" she said, clasping her hands together, "do you really think so? Do you know anything? I have not seen Ralph since to ask him about it. Do you think we shall really get them back?"

"I should not wonder."

"Oh, Colonel Middleton, I see you know. You are a clever, wise man, and you have found out something. Who is it? Do tell me!"

"Will you promise not to tell any one?"

"Mayn't I tell Ralph? I tell him everything."

"Well, you may tell Ralph, because he knows already; but no one else, remember. The truth is, we are afraid it is Charles."

There was a long pause.

"I know Evelyn thinks so," said Aurelia, in a whisper, "though she tries not to show it, because—because—"

"Because what?"

"Well, of course, you can't have helped seeing, can you, that she and Charles—"

I had not seen it; indeed, I had fancied at times that Evelyn had a leaning towards Ralph; but I never care to seem slower than others in noticing these things, so I nodded.

"And then, you know, people can't be married that haven't any money; and Charles and Evelyn have none," said Aurelia. "Oh, I am glad Ralph is well off."

A light was breaking in on me. Perhaps it was not Charles after all. Perhaps—

"I am afraid Evelyn is very unhappy," continued Aurelia. "Her room is next to mine, and she walks up and down, and up and down, in the night. I hear her when I am in bed. Last night I heard her so late, so late that I had been to sleep and had waked up again. Do you know," and she crept close up to me with wide, awe-struck eyes, "I am going away to-morrow, and I don't like to say anything to any one but you; but I think Evelyn knows something."

"Miss Derrick!" I said, beginning to suspect that she possibly knew a good deal more than any of us, and then suddenly remembering that she had been on the point of telling me something and had been interrupted. I was getting quite confused. She certainly would not have wished to confide in me if my new suspicion were correct. Considering there was a mystery, it was curious how every one seemed to know something very particular about it.

"Yes," replied Aurelia, nodding once or twice. "I am sure she knows something. I went into her room before luncheon, and she was sitting with her head down on the dressing-table, and when she looked up I saw she had been crying. I don't know what to say about it to Ralph; but you know,"—with a shake of the curls—"though people may think me only a silly little thing, yet I do notice things, Colonel Middleton. Aunt Alice in Dublin often says how quickly I notice things. And I thought, as you were staying on, and seemed to be a friend, I would tell you this before I went away, as you would know best what to do about it."

Aurelia had more insight into character than I had given her credit for. She had hit upon the most likely person to follow out a clew, however slight, in a case that seemed becoming more and more complicated. I inwardly resolved that I would have it out with Miss Derrick that very evening. Lady Mary now came in, and servants followed shortly afterwards with lamps. The dreary twilight, with its dim whirlwinds of driving snow, was shut out, the curtains were drawn, and tea made its appearance. Evelyn presently returned, and Charles also, who civilly wished Lady Mary good-morning, not having seen her till then. She handed him his tea without a word in reply. It was evident that she, also, was aware of the robbery, and it is hardly necessary to add that she suspected Charles.

"How is my father?" he asked, taking no notice of the frigidity of her manner.

"He is asleep at this moment," she replied. "Ralph is remaining with him."

"He is better, then, I hope?"

"He is in a very critical state, and is likely to remain in it. His illness was quite serious enough, without having it increased by one of his own household."

"Ah, I was afraid that had been the case," returned Charles. "I knew you had been doctoring him when he was out of sorts yesterday. But you must not reproach yourself, Aunt Mary. We are none of us infallible. No doubt you acted for the best at the time, and I dare say what you gave him may not do him any permanent injury."

"If that is intended to be amusing," said Lady Mary, her teacup trembling in her hand, "I can only say that, in my opinion, wilfully misunderstanding a simple statement is a very cheap form of wit."

"I am so glad to hear you say so," said Charles, rising, "as it was at your expense." With which Parthian shot he withdrew.

I endeavored in vain to waylay Evelyn after tea, but she slipped away almost before it was over, and did not appear again till dinner-time. In the mean while my brain, fertile in expedients on most occasions, could devise no means by which I could speak to her alone, and without Charles's knowledge. I felt I must trust to chance.

CHAPTER XI

When I came down before dinner I found Ralph and Charles talking earnestly by the hall-fire, Ralph's hand on his brother's shoulder.

"You see we are no farther forward than we were," he was saying.

"We shall have Marston back to-morrow," said Charles, as the gong began to sound. "We cannot take any step till then, especially if we don't want to put our foot in it. I have been racking my brains all the afternoon without the vestige of a result. We must just hold our hands for the moment."

Dinner was announced, and we waited patiently for a few minutes, and impatiently for a good many more, until Evelyn hurried down, apologizing for being late, and with a message from Lady Mary that we were not to wait for her, as she was dining up-stairs in her own room—a practice to which she seemed rather addicted.

"And where is Aurelia?" asked Ralph.

"She is not coming down to dinner either," said Evelyn. "She has a bad headache again, and is lying down. She asked me to tell you that she wishes particularly to see you this evening, as she is going away to-morrow, and if she is well enough she will come down to the morning-room at nine; indeed, she said she would come down anyhow."

After Ralph's natural anxiety respecting his ladylove had been relieved, and he had been repeatedly assured that nothing much was amiss, we went in to dinner, and a more lugubrious repast I never remember being present at. The meals of the day might have been classified thus: breakfast *dismal*; luncheon, *dismaller* (or more dismal); dinner, *dismallest* (or most dismal). There really was no conversation. Even I, who without going very deep (which I consider is not in good taste) have something to say on almost every subject—even I felt myself nonplussed for the time being. Each of us in turn got out a few constrained words, and then relapsed into silence.

Evelyn ate nothing, and her hand trembled so much when she poured out a glass of water that she spilled some on the cloth. I saw Charles was watching her furtively, and I became more and more certain that Aurelia was right, and that Evelyn knew something about the mystery of the night before. I must and would speak to her that very evening.

"Bitterly cold," said Ralph, when at last we had reached the dessert stage. "It is snowing still, and the wind is getting up."

In truth, the wind was moaning round the house like an uneasy spirit.

"That sound in the wind always means snow," said Charles, evidently for the sake of saying something. "It is easterly, I should think. Yes," after a pause, when another silence seemed imminent, "there goes the eight o'clock train. It must be quite a quarter of an hour late, though, for it has struck eight some time. I can hear it distinctly. The station is three miles away, and you never hear the train unless the wind is in the east."

"Come, Charles, not three miles—two miles and a half," put in Ralph.

"Well, two and a half from here down to the station, but certainly three from the station up here," replied Charles; and so silence was laboriously avoided by diligent small-talk until we returned to the drawing-room, thankful that there at least we could take up a book, and be silent if we wished. We all did wish it, apparently. Evelyn was sitting by a lamp when we came in, with a book before her, her elbow on the table, shading her face with a slender delicate hand. She remained motionless, her eyes fixed upon the page, but I noticed after some time that she had never turned it over. Charles may have read his newspaper, but if he did it was with one eye upon Evelyn all the time. Between watching them both I did not, as may be imagined, make much progress myself. How was I to manage to speak to Evelyn alone, and without Charles's knowledge?

At last Ralph, who had gone into the morning-room, opened the drawing-room door and put his head in.

"Aurelia has not come down yet, and it is a quarter past nine. I wish you would run up, Evelyn, and see if she is coming."

"She is sure to come!" replied Evelyn, without raising her eyes. "She said she *must* see you."

Ralph disappeared again, and the books and papers were studied anew with unswerving devotion. At the end of another ten minutes, however, the impatient lover reappeared.

"It is half-past nine," he said, in an injured tone. "Do pray run up, Evelyn. I don't think she can be coming at all. I am afraid she is worse."

Evelyn laid down her book and left the room. Ralph sauntered back into the morning-room, where we heard him beguiling his solitude with a few chords on the piano.

Presently Evelyn returned. She was pale even to the lips, and her voice faltered as she said:

"She has not gone to bed, for there is a light in her room; but she would not answer when I knocked, and the door is locked."

"All of which circumstances are not sufficient to make you as white as a ghost," said Charles. "I think even if Aurelia has a headache, you would bear the occurrence with fortitude. My dear child, you do not act so well off the stage as on it. There is something on your mind. People don't upset water at dinner, and refuse all food except pellets of pinched bread, for nothing. What is it?"

Evelyn sank into a chair, and covered her face with her trembling hands.

"Yes, I thought so," said Charles, kneeling down by her, and gently withdrawing her hands. "Come, Evelyn, what is it?"

"I dare not say." And she turned away her face, and tried to disengage her hands, but Charles held them firmly.

"Is it about what happened last night?" he asked, in a tone that was kind, but that evidently intended to have an answer.

"Yes."

"And do you know that I am suspected?"

"You, Charles? Never!" she cried, starting up.

"Yes, I. Suspected by my own father. So, if you know anything, Evelyn—which I see you do—it is your duty to tell us, and to help us in every way you can."

He had let go her hands now, and had risen.

"I don't know anything for certain," she said, "but—but we soon shall. Aurelia knows, and she is going to tell Ralph."

"Miss Grant!" I exclaimed. "She knew nothing at tea-time. She was asking me about it."

"It is since then," continued Evelyn. "I went up to her room before dinner to ask her for a fan that I had lent her. She was packing some of her things, and the floor was strewn with packing-paper and parcels. She gave me my fan, and was going on putting her things together, talking all the time, when she asked me to hand her a glove-box on the dressing-table. As I did so my eye fell on a piece of paper lying together with others, and I instantly recognized it as the same that had been wrapped round the diamond crescent when Colonel Middleton first showed us the jewels. I should never have noticed it—for though it was rice paper, it looked just like the other pieces strewn about—if I had not seen two little angular tears, which I suddenly remembered making in it myself when General Marston asked me not to pull it to pieces, which I suppose I had been absently doing. I made some sort of exclamation of surprise, and Aurelia turned round sharply, and asked me what was the matter. As I did not answer, she left her packing and came to the table. She saw in a moment what I was looking at. I had turned as red as fire, and she was quite white. 'I did not mean you to see that,' she said, at last, quietly taking up the paper. 'I meant no one to know until I had shown it to Ralph. *Do you know where I found it?*' and she looked hard at me. I could only shake my head. I was too much ashamed of a suspicion I had had to be able to get out a word. 'I am very sorry,' continued Aurelia, 'but I am afraid it will be my duty to tell Ralph, whatever the consequences may be. I have been thinking it over, and I think he ought to know. I am going to show it him to-night after dinner,' and she put it in her pocket, and then began to cry. I did not know what to say or do, I was so frightened at the thought of what was coming; and, as the dressing-bell rang at that moment, I was just leaving the room when she called me back.

"'I can't come down to dinner,' she said. 'I hate Ralph to see me with red eyes. Tell him I shall come down afterwards, at nine o'clock, and that I want to see him particularly; only don't tell him what it is about, or mention it to any one else. I did not mean any one to know till he did.'

"She began to cry afresh, and I made her lie down and put a shawl over her, and then left her, as I had still to dress, and I knew that Aunt Mary was not coming down. I was late as it was."

"Is that all?" said Charles, who had been listening intently.

"All," replied Evelyn. "We shall soon know the worst now."

"Very soon," said Charles. "Ralph may come in here at any moment. Evelyn and Middleton, will you have the goodness to come with me?" And he led the way into the hall.

We could hear Ralph in the next room, humming over an old Irish melody, with an improvised accompaniment.

"Now show me her room," said Charles, "and please be quick about it."

Evelyn looked at him astonished, and then led the way up-stairs, along the picture-gallery to another wing of the house. She stopped at last before a door at the end of a passage, dimly lighted by a lamp at the farther end.

There was a light under the door, and a bright chink in the key-hole, but though we listened intently we could hear nothing stirring within.

"Knock again," said Charles to Evelyn. "Louder!" as her hand failed her.

There was no answer. As we listened the light within disappeared.

"Bring that lamp from the end of the passage," said Charles to Evelyn, and she brought it.

"Hold it there," he said; "and you, Middleton, stand aside."

He took a few steps backward, and then flung himself against the door with his whole force. It cracked and groaned, but resisted.

"The lock is old. It is bound to go," he said, panting a little.

"Really, Charles," I remonstrated—"a lady's private apartment! Miss Derrick, I wonder you allow this."

Charles retreated again, and then made a fresh and even fiercer onslaught on the door. There was a sound of splintering wood and of bursting screws, and in another moment the door flew open inward, and Charles was precipitated head-foremost into the room, his evening-pumps flourishing wildly in the air. In an instant he was on his feet again, gasping hard, and had seized the lamp out of Evelyn's hand. Before I had time to remonstrate on the liberty that he was taking, we were all three in the room.

It was empty!

In one corner stood a box, half packed, with various articles of clothing lying by it. On the dressing-table was a whole medley of little feminine knick-knacks, with a candlestick in the midst, the dead wick still smoking in the socket, and accounting for the disappearance of the light a few minutes before. The fire had gone out, but on a chair by it was laid a little black lace evening-gown, evidently put out to be worn; while over the fender a dainty pair of silk stockings had been hung, and two diminutive black satin shoes were waiting on the hearth-rug. The whole aspect of the room spoke of a sudden and precipitate flight.

"Bolted!" said Charles, when he had recovered his breath. "And so the mystery is out at last! I might have known there was a woman at the bottom of it. Unpremeditated, though," he continued, looking round. "She meant to have gone to-morrow; but your recognition of that paper frightened her, though she turned it off well to gain time. No fool that! She had only an hour, and she made the most of it, and got off, no doubt, while we were at dinner, by the 8.2 London train, which is the last to-night; and after the telegraph office was closed, too! She knew nothing could be done till to-morrow. She has more wit than I gave her credit for."

"I distrusted her before, though I had no reason for it, but I never thought she was gone," said Evelyn, trembling violently, and still looking round the room.

"I knew it," said Charles, "from the moment I saw the light through the key-hole. A key-hole with a key in it would not have shown half the amount of light through it; and a locked door without a key in it is safe to have been locked *from the outside*. Had she a maid with her?"

"No," replied Evelyn, "she used to come to me next door when she wanted help—but not often—because I think she knew I did not like her, though I tried not to show it."

"Well, we have seen the last of her, or I am much mistaken," said Charles. "And now," he added, compressing his lips, "I suppose I must go and tell Ralph."

"Oh, Ralph! Ralph!" gasped Evelyn, with a sudden sob; "and he was so fond of her!"

"And so you distrusted her before, Evelyn? And why did you not mention that fact a little sooner?"

"Without any reason for it? And when Ralph—Oh, I couldn't! I couldn't!" said the girl, crimsoning.

Charles gazed intently at her as she turned away, pressing her hands tightly together, and evidently struggling with some sudden emotion for which there really was no apparent reason. She was overwrought, I suppose; and indeed the exertion of breaking in the door had been rather too much for Charles too; for, now that the excitement was over, his hand shook so much that he had to put down the lamp, and even his voice trembled a little as he said:

"I don't think Ralph is very much to be pitied. He has had a narrow escape."

"Don't come down again, either of you," he continued a moment later, in his usual voice. "I had better go and get it over at once. He will be wondering what has become of us if I wait much longer. Evelyn, good-night. Good-night, Middleton. If it is too early for you to go to bed, you will find a fire in the smoking-room."

I bade Evelyn good-night, and followed Charles down the corridor. He replaced the lamp with a hand that was steady enough now, and went

slowly across the picture-gallery. The way to my room led me through it also. Involuntarily I stopped at the head of the great carved staircase which led into the hall, and watched him going down, step by step, with lagging tread. From the morning-room came the distant sound of a piano, and a man's voice singing to it; singing softly, as though no Nemesis were approaching; singing slowly, as if there were time enough and to spare. But Nemesis had reached the bottom of the staircase; Nemesis, with a heavy step, was going across the silent hall—was even now opening the door of the morning-room. The door was gently closed again, and then, in the middle of a bar, the music stopped.

CHAPTER XII

I passed an uneasy night. The wind moaned wearily round the house, at one moment seeming to die away altogether, at another returning with redoubled fury, roaring down the wide chimney, shaking the whole building. It dropped completely towards dawn, and after hours of fitful slumber I slept heavily.

In the gray of the early morning I was awakened by some one coming into my room, and started up to find Charles standing by my bedside, dressed, and with a candle in his hand. His face was worn and haggard from want of sleep.

"I have come to speak to you before I go, Middleton," he said, when I was thoroughly awake. "Ralph and I are off by the early train. Will you tell my father that we may not be able to return till to-morrow, if then; and may I count upon you to keep all you saw and heard secret till after our return?"

"Where are you going?"

"To London. We start in twenty minutes. I don't think it is the least use, but Ralph insists on going, and I cannot let him go alone."

"My dear Charles," I said (all my anger had vanished at the sight of his worn face), "I will accompany you."

"Not for worlds!" he replied, hastily. "It would be no good. Indeed, I should not wish it."

But I knew better.

"An old head is often of use," I replied, rapidly getting into my clothes. "You may count on me, Charles. I shall be ready in ten minutes."

Charles made some pretence at annoyance, but I was not to be dissuaded. I knew very well how invaluable the judgment of an elder man of experience could be on critical occasions; and besides, I always make a point of seeing everything I can, on all occasions. In ten minutes I was down in the dining-room, where, beside a spluttering fire, the brothers, both heavily booted and ulstered, were drinking coffee by candle-light. A hastily laid breakfast was on the table, but it had not been touched. The gray morning light was

turning the flame of the candles to a rusty yellow, and outside, upon the wide stone sills, the snow lay high against the panes.

Ralph was sitting with bent head by the fire, stick and cap in hand, his heavy boot beating the floor impatiently. He looked up as I came in, but did not speak. The ruddy color in his cheeks was faded, his face was drawn and set. He looked ten years older.

"We ought to be off," he said at last, in a low voice.

"No hurry," replied Charles; "finish your coffee."

I hastily drank some also, and told Charles that I was coming with them.

"No!" said Charles.

"Yes!" I replied. "You are going to London, and so am I. I have decided to curtail my visit by a few days, under the circumstances. I shall travel up with you. My luggage can follow."

As soon as Charles grasped the idea that I was not going to return to Stoke Moreton his opposition melted away; he even seemed to hail my departure with a certain sense of relief.

"As you like," he said. "You can leave at this unearthly hour if you wish, and travel with us as far as Paddington."

I nodded, and went after my great-coat. Of course I had not the slightest intention of leaving them at Paddington; but I felt that the time had not arrived to say so.

"Here comes the dog-cart," said Charles, as I returned.

Ralph was already on his feet. But the dog-cart, with its great bay horse, could not be brought up to the door. The snow had drifted heavily before the steps, and right up into the archway, and the cart had to go round to the back again before we could get in and start. Charles took the reins, and his brother got up beside him. The groom and I squeezed ourselves into the back seat. I could see that I was only allowed to come on sufferance, and that at the last moment they would have been willing to dispense with my presence. However, I felt that I should never have forgiven myself if I had let them go alone. Charles was not thirty, and Ralph several years younger. An experienced man of fifty to consult in case of need might be of the greatest assistance in an emergency.

"Quicker!" said Ralph; "we shall miss the train."

"No quicker, if we mean to catch it," said Charles. "I allowed ten minutes extra for the snow. We shall do it if we go quietly, but not if I let him go. An upset would clinch the matter."

We drove noiselessly through the great gates with their stone lions on either side, rampant in wreaths of snow, and up the village street, where life was hardly stirring yet. The sun was rising large and red, a ball of dull fire in the heavy sky. It seemed to be rising on a dead world. Before us (only to be seen on my part by craning round) stretched the long white road. At intervals, here and there among the shrouded fields, lay cottages half hidden by a white network of trees. Groups of yellow sheep stood clustered together under hedge-rows, motionless in the low mist, and making no sound. A lonely colt, with tail erect, ran beside us on the other side of the hedge as far as his field would allow him, his heavy hoofs falling noiseless in the snow. The cold was intense.

"There will be a drift at the bottom of Farrow hill," said Ralph; "we shall be late for the train."

And in truth, as we came cautiously down the hill, on turning a corner we beheld a smooth sheet of snow lapping over the top of the hedge on one side, like iced sugar on a cake, and sloping downward to the ditch on the other side of the road.

"Hold on!" cried Charles, as I stood up to look; and in another moment we were pushing our way through the snow, keeping as near the ditch as possible—too near, as it turned out. But it was not to be. A few yards in front of us lay the road—snowy, but practicable; but we could not reach it. We swayed backward and forward; we tilted up and down; Charles whistled, and made divers consolatory and encouraging sounds to the bay horse; but the bay horse began to plunge—he made a side movement—one wheel crunched down through the ice in the ditch, and all was over—at least, all in the cart were. We fell soft—I most providentially alighting on the groom, who was young, and inclined to be plump, and thus breaking a fall which to a heavy man of my age might have been serious. Charles and Ralph were up in a moment.

"I thought I could not do it; but it was worth a trial," said Charles, shaking himself. "George, look after the horse and cart, and take them straight back. Now, Ralph, we must run for it if we mean to catch the train. Middleton, you had better go back in the cart." And off they set, plunging through the snow without further ceremony. I watched the two dark figures disappearing, aghast with astonishment. They were positively leaving me behind! In a moment my mind was made up; and, leaving the gasping young groom to look after the horse and cart, I set off to run too. It was only a chance, of course; but in this weather the train might be late. It was all the way downhill. I thought I could do it, and I did. My feet were balled with snow; I was hotter than I had been for years; I was completely out of breath; but when I puffed into the little road-side station, five minutes after the train was due, I could see that it was not yet in, and that Ralph and Charles were waiting on the platform.

"My word, Middleton!" said Charles, coming to meet me. "I thought I had seen the last of you when I left you reclining on George in the drift. I do believe you have got yourself into this state of fever-heat purely to be of use to us two; and I treated you very cavalierly, I am sure. Let by-gones be by-gones, and let us shake hands while you are in this melting mood."

I could not speak, but we shook hands cordially; and I hurried off to get my ticket.

"You can only book to Tarborough!" he called after me, "where we change, and catch the London express."

The station-master gave me my ticket, and then approached Charles, and touched his cap.

"Might any of you gentlemen be going to London, sir?" he inquired.

"All three of us."

"I don't think you will get on, sir. The news came down this morning that the evening express from Tarborough last night was thrown off the rails by a drift, and got knocked about, and I don't expect the line is clear yet. There will be no trains running till later in the day, I am afraid."

"The night express?" said Ralph, suddenly.

"Do you mean the 9 train, which you can catch by the 8.2 from here?"

"Yes, sir."

"She was in it!" said Ralph, in a hoarse voice, as the man walked away.

"How late the train is!" said Charles; "quarter of an hour already. I say, Jervis," calling after him, "any particulars about the accident? Serious?"

"Oh dear no, sir, not to my knowledge. Never heard of anything but that the train had been upset, and had stopped the traffic."

"Not many people travelling in such weather, at any rate. I dare say there was not a creature who went from here by the last train last night?"

"Only two, sir. One of the young gentlemen from the rectory, and a young lady, who was very near late, poor thing, and all wet with snow. Ah, there she is, at last!" as the train came in sight; and he went through the ceremony of ringing the bell, although we were the only travellers on the platform.

It was only an hour's run to Tarborough, where we were to join the main line.

"What are we to do now?" said Charles, as the chimneys of Tarborough hove in sight, and the train slackened. "Ten to one we shall not be able to get on to London!"

"Nor she either," said Ralph. "I shall see her! I shall see her here!"

There was an air of excitement about the whole station as we drew up before the platform. Groups of railway officials were clustered together, talking eagerly; the bar-maids were all looking out of the refreshment-room door; policemen were stationed here and there; and outside the iron gates of the station a little crowd of people were waiting in the trodden yellow snow, peering through the bars.

We got out, and Charles went up to a respectable-looking man in black, evidently an official of some consequence, and asked what was the matter. The man informed him that a special had been sent down the line with workmen to clear the rails, and that its return, with the passengers in the ill-fated express, was expected at any moment.

"You don't mean to say the wretched passengers have been there all night?" exclaimed Charles. From the man's account it appeared that the travellers had taken refuge in a farm near the scene of the accident, and, the snow-storm continuing very heavily, it had not been thought expedient to send a train down the line to bring them away till after daybreak. "It has been gone an hour," he said, looking at the clock; "and it is hardly nine yet. Considering how late we received notice of the accident—for the news had to travel by night, and on foot for a considerable distance—I don't think there has been much delay."

"Will all the passengers come back by this train?" asked Ralph.

"Yes sir."

"We will wait," said Ralph; and he went and paced up and down the most deserted part of the platform. The man followed him with his eyes.

"Anxious about friends, sir?" he asked Charles.

"Yes," I heard Charles say, as I went off to warm myself by the waiting-room fire, keeping a sharp lookout for the arrival of the train. When I came out some time later, wondering if it were ever going to arrive at all, I found Charles and the man in black walking up and down together, evidently in earnest conversation. When I joined them they ceased talking (I never can imagine why people generally do when I come up), and the latter said that he would make inquiry at the booking-office, and left us.

"Who is that man?" I asked.

"How should I know?" said Charles, absently. "He says he has been a London detective till just lately, but he is an inspector of police now. Well?" as the man returned.

"Booking-clerk can't remember, sir; but the clerk at the telegraph office remembers a young lady leaving a telegram last night, to be sent on first thing this morning."

"Has it been sent yet?"

"Yes, sir; some time."

"Where was it sent to?"

"That is against rules, sir. The clerk has no right to give information. Anyhow, it is as good as certain, from what you say, that the party was in the train, and at all events you will not be kept in doubt much longer;" and he pointed to the long-expected puff of white smoke in the direction in which all eyes had been so anxiously turned. The train came slowly round a broad curve and crawled into the station. Ralph had come up, and his eyes were fixed intently upon it. The hand he laid on Charles's arm shook a little as he whispered, in a hoarse voice, "I must speak to her alone before anything is said."

"You shall," replied Charles; and he moved forward a little, and waited for the passengers to alight. I felt that any chance of escape which lay in eluding those keen light eyes would be small indeed.

Then ensued a scene of confusion, a Babel of tongues, as the passengers poured out upon the platform. "What was the meaning of it all?" hotly demanded an infuriated little man before he was well out of the carriage. "Why had a train been allowed to start if it was to be overturned by a snow-drift? What had the company been about not to make itself aware of the state of the line? What did the railway officials mean by—" etc. But he was not going to put up with such scandalous treatment. He should cause an inquiry to be made; he should write to the *Times*, he should—in short, he behaved like a true Englishman in adverse circumstances, and poured forth abuse like water. Others followed—some angry, some silent, all cold and miserable. A stout woman in black, who had been sent for to a dying child, was weeping aloud; a dazed man with bound-up head and a terrified wife were pounced upon immediately by expectant friends, and borne off with voluble sympathy. One or two people slightly hurt were helped out after the others. The train was emptied at last. Aurelia was not there. Charles went down the length of the train looking into each carriage, and then came back, answering Ralph's glance with a shake of the head. The man in black, who seemed to have been watching him, came up.

"Have *all* come back by this train?" Charles asked.

"All, sir, except,"—and he hesitated—"except a few. The doctor who went has not returned; and the guard says there were some of the passengers, badly hurt, that he would not allow to be moved from the farm when the train came for them. The engine-driver and one or two others were—"

Charles made a sign to him to be silent.

"How far is it?" he asked.

"Twenty miles, sir."

"Are the roads practicable?"

"No, sir. At least they would be very uncertain once you got into the lanes."

"We can walk along the line," said Ralph. "That must be clear. Let us start at once."

"Could not the station-master send us down on an engine?" asked Charles. "We would pay well for it."

The police-inspector shook his head, but Charles went off to inquire, nevertheless, and he followed him. I thought him a very pushing, inquisitive kind of person. I have always had a great dislike to the idle curiosity which is continually prying into the concerns of others. Ralph and I walked up and down, up and down, the now deserted platform. I spoke to him once or twice, but he hardly answered; and after a time I gave it up, and we paced in silence.

At last Charles returned. His request for an engine had been refused, but a further relay of workmen was being sent down the line in a couple of hours' time, and he had obtained leave for himself and us to go with them. After two long interminable hours of that everlasting pacing we found ourselves in an open truck, full of workmen, steaming slowly out of the station. At the last moment the man in black jumped in, and accompanied us.

The pace may have been great, but to us it seemed exasperatingly slow, and in the open truck the cold was piercing. The workmen, who laughed and talked among themselves, appeared to take no notice of it; but I saw that Charles was shivering, and presently he made his brother light his pipe, and began to smoke hard himself.

Ralph's pipe, however, went out unheeded in his fingers. He sat quite still with his back against the side of the truck, his eyes fixed upon the gray horizon. Once he turned suddenly to his brother, and said, as if unable to keep silence on what was in his mind, "What was her object?"

Charles shook his head.

"They were hers already!" he went on. "She would have had them all. If she had had debts, I would have paid them. What could her object have been?" And seemingly, without expecting a reply, he relapsed into silence.

We had left the suburbs now, and were passing through a lonely country. Here and there a village of straggling cottages met the eye, clustering round their little church. In places the hedge-rows alone marked the lie of the hidden lanes; in others men were digging out the roads through drifts of snow, and carts and horses were struggling painfully along. In one place a little walking funeral was laboring across the fields from a lonely cottage, in the direction of the church, high on the hill, the bell of which was tolling through the quiet air. The sound reached us as we passed, and seemed to accompany us on our way. I heard the men talking among themselves that there had been no snow-storm like to this for thirty years; and as they spoke some of them began shading their eyes, and trying to look in the direction in which we were going.

We had now reached a low waste of unenclosed land, with sedge and gorse pricking up everywhere through the snow, and with long lines of pollards marking the bed of a frozen stream. Near the line was a deserted brick-kiln, surrounded by long uneven mounds and ridges of ice, with three poplars mounting guard over it. Flights of rooks hung over the barren ground, and wheeled in the air with discordant clamor as we passed—the only living moving things in the utter desolation of the scene. As I looked there was an exclamation from one of the workmen, and the engine began to slacken. We were there at last.

CHAPTER XIII

The engine and trucks stopped, the men shouldered their tools and tumbled out, and we followed them. A few hundred paces in front of us was a railway bridge, over which a road passed, and under which the rail went at a sharp curve. The snow had drifted heavily against the bridge, with its high earth embankment, making manifest at a glance the cause of the disaster.

The bridge was crowded with human figures, and on the line below men were working in the drift, amid piles of débris and splintered wood. The wrecked train had all been slightly draped in snow; the engine alone, barely cold, lying black and grim, like some mighty giant, formidable in death. A sheet of glass ice near it showed how the boiler had burst. Some of the hindermost carriages were still standing, or had fallen comparatively uninjured; but others seemed to have leaped upon their fellows, and ploughed right through them into the drift. It was well that it began to snow as we reached the spot. There were traces of dismal smears on the white ground which it would be seemly to hide.

Our friend in black went forward and asked a few questions of the man in charge, and presently returned.

"The remainder of the passengers are at the farm," he said, pointing to a house at a little distance; and without further delay we began to scramble up the steep embankment, and clamber over the stone-wall of the bridge into the road. My mind was full of other things, but I remember still the number of people assembled on the bridge, and how a man was standing up in his donkey-cart to view the scene. It was Saturday, and there were quantities of village school-boys sitting astride on the low wall, or perched on adjacent hurdles, evidently enjoying the spectacle, jostling, bawling, eating oranges, and throwing the peel at the engine. Some older people touched their hats sympathetically, and one went and opened a gate for us into a field, through which many feet seemed to have come and gone; but for the greater number the event was evidently regarded as an interesting variation in the dull routine of every-day life; and to the school-boys it was an undoubted treat.

Ralph and Charles walked on in front, following the track across the field. It was not particularly heavy walking after what we had had earlier in the day, but Ralph stumbled perpetually, and presently Charles drew his arm through his own, and the two went on together, the police-inspector following with me.

In a few minutes we reached the farm, and entered the farm-yard, which was the nearest way to the house. A little knot of calves, intrenched on a mound of straw in the centre of the yard, lowered their heads and looked askance at us as we came in, and a party of ducks retreated hastily from our path with a chorus of exclamations, while a thin collie dog burst out of a barrel at the back door, and made a series of gymnastics at the end of a chain, barking hoarsely, as if he had not spared himself of late.

An elderly woman with red arms met us at the door, and, on a whisper from the police-inspector, first shook her head, and then, in answer to a further whisper, nodded at another door, and, a voice calling her from within, hastily disappeared.

The inspector opened the door she had indicated and went in, I with him. Charles, who had grown very grave, hung back with Ralph, who seemed too much dazed to notice anything in heaven above or the earth beneath. The door opened into an out-house, roughly paved with round stones, where barrels, staves, and divers lumber had been put away. There was straw in the farther end of it, out of which a yellow cat raised two gleaming eyes, and then flew up a ladder against the wall, and disappeared among the rafters. In the middle of the floor, lying a little apart, were three figures with sheets over them. Instinctively we felt that we were in the presence of death. I looked back at Charles and Ralph, who were still standing outside in the falling snow. Charles was bareheaded, but Ralph was looking absently in front of him, seeming conscious of nothing. The inspector made me a sign. He had raised one of the sheets, and now withdrew it altogether. My heart seemed to stand still. *It was Aurelia!* Aurelia changed in the last great change of all, but still Aurelia. The fixed artificial color in the cheek consorted ill with the bloodless pallor of the rest of the face, which was set in a look of surprise and terror. She was altered beyond what should have been. She looked several years older. But it was still Aurelia. Those little gloved hands, tightly clinched, were the same which she had held to the library fire as we talked the day before; even the dress was the same. Alas! she had been in too great a hurry to change it before she left, or her thin shoes. Poor little Aurelia! And then—I don't know how it was, but in another moment Ralph was kneeling by her, bending over her, taking the stiffened hands in his trembling clasp, imploring the deaf ears to hear him, calling wildly to the pale lips to speak to him, which had done with human speech. I could not bear it, and I turned away and looked out through the open door at the snow falling. The inspector came and stood beside me. In the silence which followed we could hear Charles speaking gently from time to time; and when at last we both turned towards them again, Ralph had flung himself down on an old bench at the farther end of the out-house, with his back turned towards us, his arms resting on a barrel, and his head bowed down upon them. He neither spoke nor moved.

Charles left him, and came towards us, and he and the inspector spoke apart for a moment, and then the latter dropped on his knees beside the dead woman, and, after looking carefully at a dark stain on one of the wrists, turned back the sleeve. Crushed deep into the round white arm gleamed something bright. It was an emerald bracelet which we both knew. Charles cast a hasty glance at Ralph, but he had not moved, and he drew me beside him, so as to interpose our two figures between him and the inspector. The latter quietly turned down the sleeve and recomposed the arm.

"I knew she would have them on her, if she had them at all," he said, in a low voice. "We need look no farther at present. Not one will be missing. They are all there."

He gazed long and earnestly at the dead face, and then to my horror he suddenly unfastened the little hat. I made an involuntary movement as if to stop him, but Charles laid an iron grip upon me, and motioned to me to be still. The stealthy hand quietly pushed back the fair curls upon the forehead, and in another moment they fell still farther back, showing a few short locks of dark hair beneath them, which so completely altered the dead face that I could hardly recognize it as belonging to the same person. The inspector raised his head, and looked significantly at Charles. Then he quietly drew forward the yellow hair over the forehead again, replaced the hat, and rose to his feet. Charles and I glanced apprehensively at Ralph, but he had not stirred. As we looked, a hurried step came across the yard, a hand raised the latch of the door, and some one entered abruptly. It was Carr. For one moment he stood in the door-way, for one moment his eyes rested horror-struck on the dead woman, then darted at us, from us to the inspector, who was coolly watching him, and—he was gone! gone as suddenly as he had come; gone swiftly out again into the falling snow, followed by the wild barking of the dog.

Charles, who had had his back to the door, turned in time to see him, and he made a rush for the door, but the inspector flung himself in his way, and held him forcibly.

"Let me go! Let me get at him!" panted Charles, struggling furiously.

"I shall do no such thing, sir. It can do no good, and might do harm. He is armed, and you are not; and he would not be over-scrupulous if he were pushed. Besides, what can you accuse him of? Intent to rob? For he did not do it. If you have lost anything, remember, you have found it again. If you caught him a hundred times, you have no hold on him. I know him of old."

"You?"

"Yes; I have known him by sight long enough. He is not a new hand by any means—nor she either, as to that, poor thing."

"But what on earth brought him here?"

"He was waiting for news of her in London, most likely, and he knew she would have the jewels on her, and came down when he got wind of the accident."

"Knew she would have the jewels! Then do you mean to say there was collusion between the two?"

The inspector glanced furtively at Ralph, but he had never stirred, or raised his head since he had laid it down on his clinched hands.

"They are both well known to the police," he said at last, "and I think it probable there was collusion between them, considering they were *man and wife*."

CONCLUSION

I am told that I ought to write something in the way of a conclusion to this account of the Danvers jewels, as if the end of the last chapter were not conclusion enough. Charles, who has just read it, says especially that his character requires what he calls "an elegant finish," and suggests that a slight indication of a young and lovely heiress in connection with himself would give pleasure to the thoughtful reader. But I do not mean at the last moment to depart from the exact truth, and dabble in fiction just to make a suitable conclusion. If I must write something more, I must beg that it will be kept in mind that if further details concerning the robbery are now added against my own judgment, they will rest on Charles's authority—not mine—as anything I afterwards heard was only through Charles, whose information I never consider reliable in the least degree.

It was not till three months later that I saw him again, on a wet April afternoon. I was still living in London with Jane when he came to see me, having just returned from a long tour abroad with Ralph.

Sir George, he said, was quite well again, but the coolness between himself and his father had dropped almost to freezing-point since it had come to light that he had been innocent after all. His father could not forgive his son for putting him in the wrong.

"I seldom disappoint him in matters of this kind," he said. "Indeed, I may say I have, as a rule, surpassed his expectations, and I must be careful never to fall short of them in this way again. But ah! Miss Middleton, I am sure you will agree with me how difficult it is to preserve an even course without relaxing a little at times."

"My dear Mr. Charles," said Jane, beaming at him over her knitting, but not quite taking him in the manner he intended, "you are young yet, but don't be downhearted. I am sure by your face that as you grow older these deviations, which you so properly regret, will grow fewer and fewer, until, as life goes on, they will gradually cease altogether."

"I consider it not improbable myself," said Charles, with a faint smile, and he changed the conversation. I really cannot put down here all that he proceeded to say in the most cold-blooded manner concerning Carr and Aurelia, or as he *would* call them, Mr. and Mrs. Brown, *alias* Sinclair, *alias*

Tibbits. I for one don't believe a word of it; and I don't see how he could have found it all out, as he said he had, through the police, and people of that kind. I don't consider it is at all respectable consorting with the police in that way; but then Charles never was respectable, as I told Jane after he left, arousing excited feelings on her part which made me regret having mentioned it.

According to him, Carr, who had never been seen or heard of since the day after the accident, was a professional thief, who had probably gone to — — in India with the express design of obtaining possession of Sir John's jewels, which had, till near the time of his death, been safely stowed away in a bank in Calcutta. He and his wife usually worked together; but on this occasion she had, by means of her engaging manners and youthful appearance, struck up an acquaintance abroad with Lady Mary Cunningham, who, it will be remembered, had jewels of considerable value, with a view to those jewels. Ralph she had used as her tool, and engaged herself to him in the expectation that on her return to England she might, by means of her intimacy with the family, have an opportunity of taking them—Lady Mary having left them, while abroad, with her banker in London. The opportunity came while she was at Stoke Moreton; but in the mean while Sir John's priceless legacy had arrived, having eluded her husband's vigilance. (That certainly was true. The jewels were safe enough as long as I had anything to do with them.) Her husband, who followed them, saw that he was suspected, and threw the game into her hands, devoting himself entirely to putting his own innocence beyond a doubt; in which, with Ralph's assistance, he succeeded.

"I see now," continued Charles, "why she spilled her tea when Carr arrived. She was taken by surprise on seeing him enter the room, having had, probably, no idea that he was the friend whom you had telegraphed for. I suspect, too, that same evening, after the ball, when she and Carr went together to find the bag, it was to have a last word to enable them to play into each other's hands, being aware, if I remember rightly, that father had gone to bed in company with the key of the safe, and that, consequently, the jewels might be left within easier reach than usual. No doubt she weighed the matter in her own mind, and decided to give up all thought of Lady Mary's jewels, and to secure those which were ten times their value. She could not have taken both without drawing suspicion upon herself. Like a wise woman she left the smaller, and went in for the larger prize; a less clever one would have tried for both, and have failed. She failed, it is true, by an oversight. She could never have noticed that the piece of paper wrapped round the crescent was peculiar in any way, or she would not have left it on the table among the others. She turned it off well when Evelyn recognized it, and made the most of her time. She was within an ace of success, but fate was against her. And Carr lost no time, either, for that matter; for I have since found out that the telegram she sent was to Birmingham, where he was no doubt hiding, bidding him meet her in London earlier than had been arranged. Of course he set off for the scene of the accident directly he heard of it, having received no further communication from her. We arrived only ten minutes before him. For my part, I admired *her* more than I ever did before, when the truth about her came out. I considered her to be a pink-and-white nonentity, without an idea beyond a neat adjustment of pearl-powder, and then found that she possessed brains enough to outwit two minds of no mean calibre, namely, yours, Middleton, and my own. Evelyn was the only person who had the slightest suspicion of her, and that hardly amounted to more than an instinct, for she owned that she had no reason to show for it."

"I wonder Lady Mary was so completely taken in by her to start with," I said.

"I don't," replied Charles. "I have even heard of elderly men being taken in by young ones. Besides, suspicious people are always liable to distrust their own nearest relatives, especially their prepossessing nephews, and then lay themselves open to be taken in by entire strangers. She wanted to get Ralph married, and she took a fancy to this girl, who was laying herself out to be taken a fancy to. In short, she trusted to her own judgment, and it failed her, as usual. I wrote very kindly to her from abroad, telling her how sincerely I sympathized with her in her distress at finding how entirely her judgment had been at fault, how lamentably she had been deceived from first to last, and how much trouble she had been the innocent means of bringing on the family. I have had no reply. Dear Aunt Mary! That reminds me that she is in London now; and I think a call from me, and a personal expression of sympathy, might give her pleasure." And he rose to take his leave.

I had let Charles go without contradicting a word he had said, because, unfortunately, I was not in a position to do so. As I have said before, I am not given to suspecting a friend, even though appearances may be against him; and I still believed in Carr's innocence, though I must own that I was sorry that he never answered any of the numerous letters I wrote to him, or ever came to see me in London, as I had particularly asked him to do. Of course I did not believe that he was married to Aurelia, for it was only on the word of a stranger and a police-inspector, while I knew from his own lips that he was engaged to a countrywoman of his own. However, be that how it may, my own rooted conviction at the time, which has remained unshaken ever since, is that in some way he became aware that he was unjustly suspected, and being, like all Americans, of a sensitive nature, he retired to his native land. Anyhow, I have never seen or heard anything of him since. I am aware that Jane holds a different opinion, but then Charles had prejudiced her against him—so much so that it has ended by becoming a subject on which we do not converse together.

I saw Charles again a few months later on a sultry night in July. I was leaving town the next day to be present at Ralph's wedding, and Jane and I were talking it over towards ten o'clock, the first cool time in the day, when he walked in. He looked pale and jaded as he sat down wearily by us at the open window and stroked the cat, which was taking the air on the sill. He said that he felt the heat, and he certainly look very much knocked up. I do not feel heat myself, I am glad to say.

"I am going abroad to-morrow," he said, after a few remarks on other subjects. "It is not merely a question of pleasure, though I shall be glad to be out of London; but I have of late become an object of such increasing interest to those who possess my autograph that I have decided on taking change of air for a time."

"Do you mean to say you are not going down to Stoke Moreton for Ralph's wedding?" I exclaimed. "I thought we should have travelled together, as we once did six months ago."

"I can't go," said Charles, almost sharply. "I have told Ralph so."

"I am sure he will be very much disappointed, and Evelyn too; and the wedding being from her uncle's house, as she has no home of her own, will make your absence all the more marked."

"It *must* be marked, then; but the young people will survive it, and Aunt Mary will be thankful. She has not spoken to me since I made that little call upon her in the spring. When I pass her carriage in the Row she looks the other way."

"I am glad Ralph has consoled himself," I said. "A good and charming woman like Evelyn, and a nice steady fellow like Ralph, are bound to be happy together."

"Yes," said Charles, "I suppose they are. She deserves to be happy. She always liked Ralph, and he *is* a good fellow. The model young men make all the running nowadays. In novels the good woman always marries the scapegrace, but it does not seem to be the case in real life."

"Anyhow, not in this instance," I remarked, cheerfully.

"No, not in this instance, as you so justly observe," he replied, with a passing gleam of amusement in his restless, tired eyes. "And now," producing a small packet, "as I am not going myself, I want to give my wedding-present to the bride into your charge. Perhaps you will take it down to-morrow, and give it into her own hands, with my best wishes."

"Might we see it first?" said Jane, with all a woman's curiosity, evidently scenting a jewel-case from afar.

Charles unwrapped a small morocco case, and, touching a spring, showed the diamond crescent, beautifully reset and polished, blazing on its red satin couch.

"Ralph said I should have it, and he sent it me some time since," he said, turning it in his hand; "but it seems a pity to fritter it away in paying bills; and," in a lower tone, "I should like to give it to Evelyn. I hear she has refused to wear any of Sir John's jewels on her wedding-day, but perhaps, if you were to ask her—she and I are old friends—she might make an exception in favor of the crescent."

And she did.

SIR CHARLES DANVERS

CHAPTER I

"Dear heart, Miss Ruth, my dear, now don't ye be a-going yet, and me that hasn't set eyes on ye this month and more—and as hardly hears a body speak from morning till night."

"Come, come, Mrs. Eccles, I am always finding people sitting here. I expect to see the latch go every minute."

"Well, and if they do; and some folks are always a-dropping in, and a-setting theirselves down, and a clack-clacking till a body can't get a bit of peace! And the things they say! Eh? Miss Ruth, the things I have heard folks say, a setting as it might be there, in poor Eccles his old chair by the chimley, as the Lord took him in."

To the uninitiated, Mrs. Eccles's allusion might have seemed to refer to photography. But Ruth knew better; a visitation from the Lord being synonymous in Slumberleigh Parish with a fall from a ladder, a stroke of paralysis, or the midnight cart-wheel that disabled Brown when returning late from the Blue Dragon "not quite hisself."

"Lor'!" resumed Mrs. Eccles, with an extensive sigh, "there's a deal of talk in the village now," glancing inquisitively at the visitor, "about him as succeeds to old Mr. Dare; but I never listen to their tales."

They made a pleasant contrast to each other, the neat old woman, with her shrewd spectacled eyes and active, hard-worked fingers, and the young girl, tranquil, graceful, sitting in the shadow, with her slender ungloved hands in her lap.

They were not sitting in the front parlor, because Ruth was an old acquaintance; but Mrs. Eccles *had* a front parlor—a front parlor with the bottled-up smell in it peculiar to front parlors; a parlor with a real mahogany table, on which photograph albums and a few select volumes were symmetrically arranged round an inkstand, nestling in a very choice wool-work mat; a parlor with wax-flowers under glass shades on the mantle-piece, and an avalanche of paper roses and mixed paper herbs in the fireplace.

Ruth knew that sacred apartment well. She knew the name of each of the books; she had expressed a proper admiration for the wax-flowers; she had heard, though she might have forgotten, for she was but young, the price of the "real Brussels" carpet, and so she might safely be permitted to sit in the kitchen, and watch Mrs. Eccles darning her son's socks.

I am almost afraid Ruth liked the kitchen best, with its tiled floor and patch of afternoon sun; with its tall clock in the corner, its line of straining geraniums in the low window-shelf, and its high mantle-piece crowned by two china dogs with red lozenges on them, holding baskets in their mouths.

"Yes, a deal of talk there is, but nobody rightly seems to know anything for certain," continued Mrs. Eccles, spreading out her hand in the heel of a fresh sock, and pouncing on a modest hole. "Ye see, we never gave a thought to *him*, with that great hearty Mr. George, his eldest brother, to succeed when the old gentleman went. And such a fine figure of a man in his clothes as poor Mr. George used to be, and such a favorite with his old uncle. And then to be took like that, horseback riding at polar, only six weeks after the old gentleman. But I can't hear as anybody's set eyes on his half-brother as comes in for the property now. He never came to Vandon in his uncle's lifetime. They say old Mr. Dare couldn't bide the French madam as his brother took when his first wife died—a foreigner, with black curls; it wasn't likely. He was always partial to Mr. George, and he took him up when his father died; but he never would have anything to say to this younger one, bein' nothin' in the world, so folks say, but half a French, and black, like his mother. I wonder now—" began Mrs. Eccles, tentatively, with her usual love of information.

"I wonder, now," interposed Ruth, quietly, "how the rheumatism is getting on? I saw you were in church on Sunday evening."

"Yes, my dear," began Mrs. Eccles, readily diverted to a subject of such interest as herself. "Yes, I always come to the evening service now, though I won't deny as the rheumatics are very pinching at times. But, dear Lord! I never come up to the stalls near the chancel, so you ain't likely to see me. To see them Harrises always a-goin' up to the very top, it does go agen me. I don't say as it's everybody as ought to take the lowest place. The Lord knows I'm not proud, but I won't go into them chairs down by the font myself; but to see them Harrises, that to my certain knowledge hasn't a bite of butcher's meat in their heads but onst a week, a-settin' theirselves up—"

"Now, Mrs. Eccles, you know perfectly well all the seats are free in the evening."

"And so they may be, Miss Ruth, my dear—and don't ye be a-getting up yet—and good Christians, I'm sure, the quality are to abide it. And it did my heart good to hear the Honorable John preaching as he did in his new surplice (as Widder Pegg always puts too much blue in the surplices to my thinking), all about rich and poor, and one with another. A beautiful sermon it was; but I wouldn't come up like they Harrises. There's things as is suitable, and there's things as is not. No, I keep to my own place; and I had to turn out old Bessie Pugh this very last Sunday night, as I found a-cocked up there, tho' I was not a matter of five minutes late. Bessie Pugh always was one to take upon herself, and, as I often says to her, when I hear her a-goin' on about free grace and the like, 'Bessie,' I says, 'if I was a widder on the parish, and not so much as a pig to fat up for Christmas, and coming to church reg'lar on Loaf Sunday, which it's not that I ain't sorry for ye, but I wouldn't take upon myself, if I was you, to talk of things as I'd better leave to them as is beholden to nobody and pays their rent reg'lar. I've no patience—But eh, dear Miss Ruth! look at that gentleman going down the road, and the dog too. Why, ye haven't so much as got up! He's gone. He was a foreigner, and no mistake. Why, good Lord! there he is coming back again. He's seen me through the winder. Mercy on us! he's opening the gate; he's coming to the door!"

As she spoke, a shadow passed before the window, and some one knocked.

Mrs. Eccles hastily thrust her darning-needle into the front of her bodice, the general *rendezvous* of the pins and needles of the establishment, and proceeded to open the door and plant herself in front of it.

Ruth caught a glimpse of an erect light gray figure in the sunshine, surmounted by a brown face, and the lightest of light gray hats. Close behind stood a black poodle of a dignified and self-engrossed deportment, wearing its body half shaved, but breaking out in ruffles round its paws, and a tuft at the end of a stiffly undemonstrative tail.

"The key of the church is kep' at Jones's, by the pump," said Mrs. Eccles, in the brusque manner peculiar to the freeborn Briton when brought in contact with a foreigner.

"Thank you, madam," was the reply, in the most courteous of tones, and the gray hat was off in a moment, showing a very dark, cropped head, "but I do not look for the church. I only ask for the way to the house of the pastor, Mr. Alwynn."

Mrs. Eccles gave full and comprehensive directions in a very high key, accompanied by much gesticulation, and then the gray hat was replaced, and the gray figure, followed by the black poodle, marched down the little garden path again, and disappeared from view.

Mrs. Eccles drew a long breath, and turned to her visitor again.

"Well, my dear, and did ye ever see the like of that? And his head, Miss Ruth! Did ye take note of his head? Not so much as a shadder of a parting. All the same all the way over; and asking the way to the rectory. Why, you ain't never going yet? Well, good-bye, my dear, and God bless ye! And now," soliloquized Mrs. Eccles, as Ruth finally escaped, "I may as well run across to Jones's, and see if *they* know anything about the gentleman, and if he's put up at the inn."

It was a glorious July afternoon, but it was hot. The roads were white, and the tall hedge-rows gray with dust. A wagon-load of late hay, with a swarm of children just out from school careering round it, was coming up the road in a dim cloud of dust. Ruth, who had been undecided which way to take, beat a hasty retreat towards the church-yard, deciding that, if she must hesitate, to do so among cool tombstones in the shade. She glanced up at the church clock, as she selected her tombstone under one of the many yew-trees in the old church-yard. Half-past four, and already an inner voice was suggesting *tea!* To miss five o'clock tea on a thirsty afternoon like this was not to be thought of for a moment. She had no intention of going back to tea at Atherstone, where she was staying with her cousins, Mr. and Mrs. Danvers. Two alternatives remained. Should she go to Slumberleigh Hall, close by, and see the Thursbys, who she knew had all returned from London yesterday, or should she go across the fields to Slumberleigh Rectory, and have tea with Uncle John and Aunt Fanny?

She knew that Sir Charles Danvers, Ralph Danvers's elder brother, was expected at Atherstone that afternoon. His aunt, Lady Mary Cunningham, was also staying there, partly with a view of meeting him. Ralph Danvers had not seen his brother, nor Lady Mary her nephew, for some time, and, judging by the interest they seemed to feel in his visit, Ruth had determined not to interrupt a family meeting, in which she imagined she might be *de trop.*

"My fine tact," she thought, "will enable them to have a quiet talk among themselves till nearly dinner-time. But I must not neglect myself any longer. The Hall is the nearer, and the drive is shady; but, to put against that, Mabel will insist on showing me her new gowns, and Mrs. Thursby will make her usual remarks about Aunt Fanny. No; in spite of that burning expanse of glebe, I will go to tea at the rectory. I have not seen Uncle John for a week, and—who knows?—perhaps Aunt Fanny may be out."

So the gloves were put on, the crisp white dress shaken out, the parasol put up, and Ruth took the narrow church path across the fields up to Slumberleigh Rectory.

For many years since the death of her parents, Ruth Deyncourt had lived with her grandmother, a wealthy, witty, and wise old lady, whose house had been considered one of the pleasantest in London by those to whom pleasant houses are open.

Lady Deyncourt, a beauty in her youth, a beauty in middle life, a beauty in her old age, had seen and known all the marked men of the last two generations, and had reminiscences to tell which increased in point and flavor, like old wine, the longer they were kept. She had frequented as a girl the Misses Berrys' drawing-room, and people were wont to say that hers was the nearest approach to a *salon* which remained after the Misses Berry disappeared. She had married a grave politician, a rising man, whom she had pushed into a knighthood, and at one time into the ministry. If he had died before he could make her the wife of a premier, the disappointment had not been without its alleviations. She had never possessed much talent for domestic life, and, the yoke once removed, she had not felt the least inclination to take it upon herself again. As a widow, her way through life was one long triumphal procession. She had daughters—dull, tall, serious girls, with whom she had nothing in common, whom she educated well, brought out, laced in, and then married, one after another, relinquishing the last with the utmost cheerfulness, and refusing the condolences of friends on her lonely position with her usual frankness.

But her son, her only son, she had loved. He was like her, and understood her, and was at ease with her, as her daughters had never been. The trouble of her life was the death of her son. She got over it, as she got over everything; but when several years afterwards his widow, with whom, it is hardly necessary to say, she was not on speaking terms, suddenly died (being a faint-hearted, feeble creature), Lady Deyncourt immediately took possession of her grandchildren—a boy and two girls—and proceeded as far as in her lay to ruin the boy for life.

"A woman," she was apt to remark in after years, "is not intended by nature to manage any man except her husband. I am a warning to the mothers, aunts, and grandmothers, particularly the grandmothers, of the future. A husband is a sufficient field for the employment of a woman's whole energies. I went beyond my sphere, and I am punished."

And when Raymond Deyncourt finally disappeared in America for the last time, having been fished up therefrom on several occasions, each time in worse case than the last, she excommunicated him, and cheerfully altered her will, dividing the sixty thousand pounds she had it in her power to leave, between her two granddaughters, and letting the fact become known, with the result that Anna was married by the end of her second season; and if at the end of five seasons Ruth was still unmarried, she had, as Lady Deyncourt took care to inform people, no one to thank for it but herself.

But in reality, now that Anna was provided for, Lady Deyncourt was in no hurry to part with Ruth. She liked her as much as it was possible for her to like any one—indeed, I think she even loved her in a way. She had taken but small notice of her while she was in the school-room, for she cared little about girls as a rule; but as she grew up tall, erect, with the pale, stately beauty of a lily, Lady Deyncourt's heart went out to her. None of her own daughters had been so distinguished-looking, so ornamental. Ruth's clothes always looked well on her, and she had a knack of entertaining people, and much taste in the arrangement of flowers. Though she had inherited the Deyncourt earnestness of character, together with their dark serious eyes, and a certain annoying rigidity as to right and wrong, these defects were counterbalanced by flashes of brightness and humor which reminded Lady Deyncourt of herself in her own brilliant youth, and inclined her to be lenient, when in her daughters' cases she would have been sarcastic. The old woman and the young one had been great friends, and not the less so, perhaps, because of a tacit understanding which existed between them that certain subjects should be avoided, upon which, each instinctively felt, they were not likely to agree. And if the shrewd old woman of the world ever suspected the existence of a strength of will and depth of character in Ruth such as had, in her own early life, been a source of annoyance and perplexity to herself in her dealings with her husband, she was skilful enough to ignore any traces of it that showed themselves in her granddaughter, and thus avoided those collisions of will, the result of which she felt might have been doubtful.

And so Ruth had lived a life full of varied interests, and among interesting people, and had been waked up suddenly in a gray and frosted dawn to find that chapter of her life closed. Lady Deyncourt, who never thought of travelling without her maid and footman, suddenly went on a long journey alone one wild January morning, starting, without any previous preparation, for a land in which she had never professed much interest heretofore. It seemed a pity that she should have to die when she had so thoroughly acquired the art of living, with little trouble to herself, and much pleasure to others; but so it was.

And then, in Ruth's confused remembrance of what followed, all the world seemed to have turned to black and gray. There was no color anywhere, where all had been color before. Miles of black cloth and crape seemed to extend before her; black horses came and stamped black hoof-marks in the snow before the door. Endless arrangements had to be made, endless letters to be written. Something was carried heavily down-stairs, all in black, scoring the wall at the turn on the stairs in a way which would have annoyed Lady Deyncourt exceedingly if she had been there to see it, but she had left several days before it happened. The last pale shadow of the kind, gay little grandmother was gone from the great front bedroom up-stairs. Mr. Alwynn, one of Ruth's uncles, came up from the country and went to the funeral, and took Ruth away afterwards. Her own sister Anna was abroad with her husband, her brother Raymond had not been heard of for years. As she drove away from the house, and looked up at the windows with wide tearless eyes, she suddenly realized that this departure was final, that there would be no coming back, no home left for her in the familiar rooms where she and another had lived so long together.

Mr. Alwynn was by her side in the carriage, patting her cold hands and telling her not to cry, which she felt no inclination to do; and then, seeing the blank pallor in her face, he suddenly found himself fumbling for his own pocket-handkerchief.

CHAPTER II

On this particular July afternoon Mr. Alwynn, or, as his parishioners called him, "The Honorable John," was sitting in his arm-chair in the little drawing-room of Slumberleigh Rectory. Mrs. Honorable John was pouring out tea; and here, once and for all, let it be known that meals, particularly five o'clock tea, will occupy a large place in this chronicle, not because of any importance especially attaching to them, but because in the country, at least in Slumberleigh, the day is not divided by hours but by the meals that take place therein, and to write of Slumberleigh and its inhabitants with disregard to their divisions of time is "impossible, and cannot be done."

So I repeat, boldly, Mr. and Mrs. Alwynn were at tea. They were alone together, for they had no children, and Ruth Deyncourt, who had been living with them since her grandmother's death in the winter, was now staying with her cousin, Mrs. Ralph Danvers, at Atherstone, a couple of miles away.

If it had occasionally crossed Mr. Alwynn's mind during the last few months that he would have liked to have a daughter like Ruth, he had kept the sentiment to himself, as he did most sentiments in the company of his wife, who, while she complained of his habit of silence, made up for it nobly herself at all times and in all places. It had often been the subject of vague wonder among his friends, and even at times to Mr. Alwynn himself, how he had come to marry "Fanny, my love." Mr. Alwynn dearly loved peace and quiet, but these dwelt not under the same roof with Mrs. Alwynn. Nay, I even believe, if the truth were known, he liked order and tidiness, judging by the exact arrangement of his own study, and the rueful glances he sometimes cast at the litter of wools and letters on the newspaper-table, and the gay garden hats and goloshes, hidden, but not concealed, under the drawing-room sofa. Conversation about the dearness of butchers' meat and the enormities of servants palled upon him, I think, after a time, but he had taken his wife's style of conversation for better for worse when he took her gayly dressed self under those ominous conditions, and he never showed impatience. He loved his wife, but I think it grieved him when smart-colored glass vases were strewn among the cherished bits of old china and enamel which his soul loved. He did not like chromo-lithographs, or the framed photographs which Mrs. Alwynn called her "momentums of travel," among his rare old prints, either. He bore them, but after their arrival in company with large and inappropriate nails, and especially after the cut-glass candlesticks appeared on the drawing-room chimney-piece, he ceased to make his little occasional purchases of old china and old silver. The curiosity shops knew him no more, or if he still at times brought home some treasure in his hat-box, on his return from Convocation, it was unpacked and examined in private, and a little place was made for it among the old Chelsea figures on the bookcase in his study, which had stood, ever since he had inherited them from his father, on the drawing-room mantle-piece, but had been silently removed when a pair of comic china elephants playing on violins had appeared in their midst.

Mr. Alwynn sighed a little when he looked at them this afternoon, and shook his head; for had he not brought back in his empty soup-tin an old earthen-ware cow of Dutch extraction, which he had long coveted on the shelf of a parishioner? He had bought it very dear, for when in all his life had he ever bought anything cheap? And now, as he was tenderly wiping a suspicion of beef-tea off it, he wondered, as he looked round his study, where he could put it. Not among the old Oriental china, where bits of Wedgwood had already elbowed in for want of room elsewhere. Among his Lowestoft cups and saucers? Never! He would rather not have it than see it there. He had a vision of a certain bracket, discarded from the hall, and put aside by his careful hands in the lowest drawer of the cupboard by the window, in which he kept little stores of nails and string and brown paper, among which "Fanny, my love" performed fearful ravages when minded to tie up a parcel.

Mr. Alwynn nailed up the bracket under an old etching and placed the cow thereon, and, after contemplating it over his spectacles, went into the drawing-room to tea with his wife.

Mrs. Alwynn was a stout, florid, good-humored-looking woman, with a battered fringe, considerably younger than her husband in appearance, and with a tendency to bright colors in dress.

"Barnes is very poorly, my dear," said Mr. Alwynn, patiently fishing out one of the lumps of sugar which his wife had put in his tea. He took one lump, but she took two herself, and consequently always gave him two. "I should say a little strong soup would—"

At this juncture the front door-bell rang, and a moment afterwards "Mr. Dare" was announced.

The erect, light gray figure which had awakened the curiosity of Mrs. Eccles came in close behind the servant. Mrs. Alwynn received a deep bow in return for her look of astonishment; and then, with an eager exclamation, the visitor had seized both Mr. Alwynn's hands, regardless of the neatly folded slice of bread and butter in one of them, and was shaking them cordially.

Mr. Alwynn looked for a moment as astonished as his wife, and the blank, deprecating glance he cast at his visitor showed that he was at a loss.

The latter let go his hands and spread his own out with a sudden gesture.

"Ah, you do not know me," he said, speaking rapidly; "it is twenty years ago, and you have forgotten. You do not remember Alfred Dare, the little boy whom you saw last in sailing costume, the little boy for whom you cut the whistles, the son of your old friend, Henry Dare?"

"Good gracious!" ejaculated Mr. Alwynn, with a sudden flash of memory. "Henry's other son. I remember now. It *is* Alfred, and I remember the whistles too. You have your mother's eyes. And, of course, you have come to Vandon now that your poor brother—We have all been wondering when you would turn up. My dear boy, I remember you perfectly now; but it is a long time ago, and you have changed very much."

"Between eight years and twenty-eight there is a great step," replied Dare, with a brilliant smile. "How could I expect that you should remember all at once? But *you* are not changed. I knew you the first moment. It is the same kind, good face which I remember well."

Mr. Alwynn blushed a faint blush, which any word of praise could always call up; and then, reminded of the presence of Mrs. Alwynn by a short cough, which that lady always had in readiness wherewith to recall him to a sense of duty, he turned to her and introduced Dare.

Dare made another beautiful bow; and while he accepted a cup of tea from Mrs. Alwynn, Mr. Alwynn had time to look attentively at him with his mild gray eyes. He was a slight, active-looking young man of middle height, decidedly un-English in appearance and manner, with dark roving eyes, mustaches very much twirled up, and a lean brown face, that was exceedingly handsome in a style to which Mr. Alwynn was not accustomed.

And this was Henry Dare's second son, the son by his French wife, who had been brought up abroad, of whom no one had ever heard or cared to hear, who had now succeeded, by his half-brother's sudden death, to Vandon, a property adjoining Slumberleigh.

The eager foreign face was becoming familiar to Mr. Alwynn. Dare was like his mother; but he sat exactly as Mr. Alwynn had seen his father sit many a time in that very chair. The attitude was the same. Ah, but that flourish of the brown hands! How unlike anything Henry would have done! And those sudden movements! He was roused by Dare turning quickly to him again.

"I am telling Mrs. Alwynn of my journey here," he began; "of how I miss my train; of how I miss my carriage, sent to meet me from the inn; of how I walk on foot up the long hills; and when I get there they think I am no longer coming. I arrived only last night at Vandon. To-day I walk over to see my old friend at Slumberleigh."

Dare leaned forward, laying the tips of his fingers lightly against his breast.

"You seem to have had a good deal of walking," said Mr. Alwynn, rather taken aback, but anxious to be cordial; "but, at any rate, you will not walk back. You must stay the night, now you are here; mustn't he, Fanny?"

Dare was delighted—beaming. Then his face became overcast. His eyebrows went up. He shook his head. Mr. and Mrs. Alwynn were most kind, but—he became more and more dejected—a bag, a simple valise—

It could be sent for.

Ah! Mr. Alwynn was too good. He revived again. He showed his even white teeth. He was about to resume his tea, when suddenly a tall white figure came lightly in through the open French window, and a clear voice began:

"Oh, Uncle John, there is such a heathen of a black poodle making excavations in the flower-beds! Do—"

Ruth stopped suddenly as her eyes fell upon the stranger. Dare rose instinctively.

"This is Mr. Dare, Ruth," said Mr. Alwynn. "He has just arrived at Vandon."

Ruth bowed. Dare surpassed himself, and was silent. All his smiles and flow of small-talk had suddenly deserted him. He began patting his dog, which had followed Ruth in-doors, and a moment of constraint fell upon the little party.

"She is shy," said Dare to himself. "She is adorably shy."

Ruth's quiet, self-possessed voice dispelled that pleasing illusion.

"I have had a very exhausting afternoon with Mrs. Eccles, Aunt Fanny, and I have come to you for a cup of tea before I go back to Atherstone."

"Why did you walk so far this hot afternoon, my dear? and how are Mrs. Danvers and Lady Mary? and is any one else staying there? and, my dear, *are* the dolls finished?"

"They are," said Ruth. "They are all outrageously fashionable. Even Molly is satisfied. There is to be a school-feast here to-morrow," she added, turning to Dare, who appeared bewildered at the turn the conversation was taking. "All our energies for the last fortnight have been brought to bear on dolls. We have been dressing dolls morning, noon, and night."

"When is it to be, this school-feast?" said Dare, eagerly. "I will buy one—three dolls!"

After a lengthy explanation from Mrs. Alwynn as to the nature of a school-feast as distinct from a bazaar, Ruth rose to go, and Mr. Alwynn offered to accompany her part of the way.

"And so that is the new Mr. Dare about whom we have all been speculating," she said, as they strolled across the fields together. "He is not like his half-brother."

"No; he seems to be entirely a Frenchman. You see, he was educated abroad, and that makes a great difference. He was a very nice little boy twenty years ago. I hope he will turn out well, and do his duty by the place."

The neighboring property of Vandon, with its tumble-down cottages, its neglected people, and hard agent, were often in Mr. Alwynn's thoughts.

"Oh, Uncle John, he will, he must! You must help him and advise," said Ruth, eagerly. "He ought to stay and live on the place, and look into things for himself."

"I am afraid he will be poor," said Mr. Alwynn, meditatively.

"Anyhow, he will be richer than he was before," urged Ruth, "and it is his duty to do something for his own people."

When Ruth had said it was a duty, she imagined, like many another young soul before her, that nothing remained to be said, having yet to learn how much beside often remained to be done.

"We shall see," said Mr. Alwynn, who had seen something of his fellow-creatures; and they walked on together in silence.

The person whose duty Ruth had been discussing so freely looked after the two retreating figures till they disappeared, and then turned to Mrs. Alwynn.

"You and Mr. Alwynn also go to the school-feast to-morrow?"

Mrs. Alwynn, a little nettled, explained that of course she went, that it was her *own* school-feast, that Mrs. Thursby, at the Hall, had nothing to do with it. (Dare did not know who Mrs. Thursby was, but he listened with great attention.) She, Mrs. Alwynn, gave it herself. Her own cook, who had been with her five years, made the cakes, and her own donkey-cart conveyed the same to the field where the repast was held.

"Miss Deyncourt, will she be there?" asked Dare.

Mrs. Alwynn explained that all the neighborhood, including the Thursbys, would be there; that she made a point of asking the Thursbys.

"I also will come," said Dare, gravely.

CHAPTER III

Atherstone was a rambling, old-fashioned, black-and-white house, half covered with ivy, standing in a rambling, old-fashioned garden—a charming garden, with clipped yews, and grass paths, and straggling flowers and herbs growing up in unexpected places. In front of the house, facing the drawing-room windows, was a bowling-green, across which, at this time of the afternoon, the house had laid a cool green shadow.

Two ladies were sitting under its shelter, each with her work.

It was hot still, but the shadows were deepening and lengthening. Away in the sun hay was being made and carried, with crackings of whips and distant voices. Beyond the hay-fields lay the silver band of the river, and beyond again the spire of Slumberleigh Church, and a glimpse among the trees of Slumberleigh Hall.

"Ralph has started in the dog-cart to meet Charles. They ought to be here in half an hour, if the train is punctual," said Mrs. Ralph.

She was a graceful woman, with a placid, gentle face. She might be thirty, but she looked younger. With her pleasant home and her pleasant husband, and her child to be mildly anxious about, she might well look young. She looked particularly so now as she sat in her fresh cotton draperies, winding wool with cool, white hands.

The handiwork of some women has a hard, masculine look. If they sew, it is with thick cotton in some coarse material; if they knit, it is with cricket-balls of wool, which they manipulate into wiry stockings and comforters. Evelyn's wools, on the contrary, were always soft, fleecy, liable to weak-minded tangles, and so turning, after long periods of time, into little feminine futilities for which it was difficult to divine any possible use.

Lady Mary Cunningham, her husband's aunt, made no immediate reply to her small remark. Evelyn Danvers was not a little afraid of that lady, and, in truth, Lady Mary, with her thin face and commanding manner, was a very imposing person. Though past seventy, she sat erect in her chair, her stick by her side, some elaborate embroidery in her delicate old ringed hands. Her pale, colorless eyes were as keen as ever. Her white hair was covered by a wonderful lace cap, which no one had ever succeeded in imitating, that fell in soft lappets and graceful folds round the severe, dignified face. Molly, Evelyn's little daughter, stood in great awe of Lady Mary, who had such a splendid stick with a silver crook of her very own, and who made remarks in French in Molly's presence which that young lady could not understand, and felt that it was not intended she should. She even regarded with a certain veneration the cap itself, which she had once met in equivocal circumstances, journeying with a plait of white hair towards Lady Mary's rooms.

It was the first time since their marriage, of which she had not approved, that Lady Mary had paid a visit to Ralph and Evelyn at Atherstone. Lady Mary had tried to marry Ralph, in days gone by, to a woman who—but it was an old story and better forgotten. Ralph had married his first cousin when he had married Evelyn, and Lady Mary had strenuously objected to the match, and had even gone so far as to threaten to alter certain clauses in her will, which she had made in favor of Ralph, her younger nephew, at a time when she was at daggers drawn with her eldest nephew, Charles, now Sir Charles Danvers. But that was an old story, too, and better forgotten.

When Charles succeeded his father some three years ago, and when, after eight years, Molly had still remained an only child, and one of the wrong kind, of no intrinsic value to the family, Lady Mary decided that by-gones should be by-gones, and became formally reconciled to Charles, with whom she had already found it exceedingly inconvenient, and consequently unchristian, not to be on speaking terms. As long as he was the scapegrace son of Sir George Danvers her Christian principles remained in abeyance; but when he suddenly succeeded to the baronetcy and Stoke Moreton, the air of which suited her so well, and, moreover, to that convenient *pied à terre*, the house in Belgrave Square, she allowed feelings, which she said she had hitherto repressed with difficulty, their full scope, expressed a Christian hope that, now that he had come to this estate, Charles would put away Bohemian things, and instantly set to work to find a suitable wife for him.

At first Lady Mary felt that the task which she had imposed upon herself would (D.V.) be light indeed. Charles received her overtures with the same courteous demeanor which had been the chief sting of their former warfare. He paid his creditors, no one knew how, for his father had left nothing to him unentailed; and once out of money difficulties, he seemed in no hurry to plunge into them again. If he had not as yet thoroughly taken up the life of an English country gentleman, for want of that necessary adjunct which Lady Mary was so anxious to supply, at least he lived in England and in good society. In short, Lady Mary was fond of telling her friends Charles had entirely reformed, hinting, at the same time, that she had been the humble instrument, in the hands of an all-wise Providence, which had turned him back into the way in which the English aristocracy should walk, and from which he had deviated so long. But one thing remained—to marry him. Every one said Charles *must* marry. Lady Mary did not say it, but with her whole soul she meant it. What she intended to do, she, as a rule, performed—occasionally at the expense of those who were little able to afford it, but still the thing was (always, of course, by the co-operation of Providence) done. Ralph certainly had proved an exception to the rule. He had married Evelyn against Lady Mary's will, and consequently without the blessing of Providence. After that, of course, she had never expected there would be a son, and with each year her anxiety to see Charles safely married had increased. He had seemed so amenable that at first she could hardly believe that the steed which she had led to waters of such divers merit would refuse to drink from any of them. If rank had no charm for him, which apparently it had not, she would try beauty. When beauty failed, even beauty with money in its hand, Lady Mary hesitated, and then fell back on goodness. But either the goodness was not good enough, or, as Lady Mary feared, it was not sufficiently High Church to be really genuine: even goodness failed. For three years she had strained every nerve, and at the end of them she was no nearer the object in view than when she began.

An inconvenient death of a sister, with whom she had long since quarrelled about church matters (and who had now gone where her folly in differing from Lady Mary would be fully, if painfully, brought home to her), had prevented Lady Mary continuing her designs this year in London. But if thwarted in one direction, she knew how to throw her energies into another. The first words she uttered indicated what that direction was.

Evelyn's little remark about the dog-cart, which had gone to meet Charles, had so long remained without any response that she was about to coin another of the same stamp, when Lady Mary suddenly said, with a decision that was intended to carry conviction to the heart of her companion:

"It is an exceedingly suitable thing."

Evelyn evidently understood what it was that was so suitable, but she made no reply.

"A few years ago," continued Lady Mary, "I should have looked higher. I should have thought Charles might have done better, but—"

"He never could do better than—than—" said Evelyn, with a little mild flutter. "There is no one in the world more—"

"Yes, yes, my dear—of course we all know that," returned the elder lady. "She is much too good for him, and all the rest of it. A few years ago, I was saying, I might not have regarded it quite in the light I do now. Charles, with his distinguished appearance and his position, might have married anybody. But time passes, and I am becoming seriously anxious about him; I am, indeed. He is eight-and-thirty. In two years he will be forty; and at forty you never know what a man may not do. It is a critical age, even when they are married. Until he is forty, a man may be led under Providence into forming a connection with a woman of suitable age and family. After that age he will never look at any girl out of her teens, and either perpetrates a folly or does not marry at all. If the Danvers family is not to become extinct, or to be dragged down by a *mésalliance*, measures must be taken at once."

Evelyn winced at the allusion to the extinction of the Danvers family, of which Charles and Ralph were the only representatives. She felt keenly having failed to give Ralph a son, and the sudden smart of the old hurt added a touch of sharpness to her usually gentle voice as she said, "I cannot see what *has* been left undone."

"No, my dear," said Lady Mary, more suavely, "you have fallen in with my views most sensibly. I only hope Ralph—"

"Ralph knows nothing about it."

"Quite right. It is very much better he should not. Men never can be made to look at things in their proper light. They have no power of seeing an inch in front of them. Even Charles, who is less dense than most men, has never been allowed to form an idea of the plans which from time to time I have made for him. Nothing sets a man more against a marriage than the idea that it has been put in his way. They like to think it is all their own doing, and that the whole universe will be taken by surprise when the engagement is given out. Charles is no exception to the rule. Our duty is to provide a wife for him, and then allow him to think his own extraordinary cleverness found her for himself. How old is this cousin of yours, Miss Deyncourt?"

"About three-and-twenty."

"Exceedingly suitable. Young, and yet not too young. She is not beautiful, but she is decidedly handsome, and very high-bred-looking, which is better than beauty. I know all about her family; good blood on both sides; no worsted thread. I forget if there is any money."

This was a pious fraud on Lady Mary's part, as she was, of course, aware of the exact sum.

"Lady Deyncourt left her thirty thousand pounds," said Evelyn, unwillingly. She hated herself for the part she was taking in her aunt's plans, although she had been so unable to support her feeble opposition by any show of reason that it had long since melted away before the consuming fire of Lady Mary's determined authority.

"Twelve hundred a year," said that lady. "I fear Lady Deyncourt was far, very far, from the truth, but she seems to have made an equitable will. I am glad Miss Deyncourt is not entirely without means; and she has probably something of her own as well. The more I see of that girl the more convinced I am that she is the very wife for Charles. There is no objection to the match in any way, unless it lies in that disreputable brother, who seems to have entirely disappeared. Now, Evelyn, mark my words. You invited her here at my wish, after I saw her with that dreadful Alwynn woman at the flower-show. You will never regret it. I am seventy-five years of age, and I have seen something of men and women. Those two will suit."

"Here comes the dog-cart," said Evelyn, with evident relief.

"Where is Miss Deyncourt?"

"She went off to Slumberleigh some time ago. She said she was going to the rectory, I believe."

"It is just as well. Ah! here is Charles."

A tall, distinguished-looking man in a light overcoat came slowly round the corner of the house as she spoke, and joined them on the lawn. Evelyn went to meet him with, evident affection, which met with as evident a return, and he then exchanged a more formal greeting with his aunt.

"Come and sit down here," said Evelyn, pulling forward a garden-chair. "How hot and tired you look!"

"I am tired to death, Evelyn. I went to London in May a comparatively young man. Aunt Mary said I ought to go, and so, of course, I went. I have come back not only sadder and wiser—that I would try to bear—but visibly aged."

He took off his hat as he spoke, and wearily pushed back the hair from his forehead. Lady Mary looked at him over her spectacles with grave scrutiny. She had not seen her nephew for many months, and she was not pleased with what she saw. His face looked thin and worn, and she even feared she could detect a gray hair or two in the light hair and mustache. His tired, sarcastic eyes met hers.

"I was afraid you would think I had *gone off*," he said, half shutting his eyes in the manner habitual to him. "I fear I took your exhortations too much to heart, and overworked myself in the good cause."

"A season is always an exhausting thing," said Lady Mary; "and I dare say London is very hot now."

"Hot! It's more than hot. It is a solemn warning to evil-doers; a foretaste of a future state."

"I suppose everybody has left town by this time?" continued Lady Mary, who often found it necessary even now to ignore parts of her nephew's conversation.

"By everybody I know you mean *one* family. Yes, they are gone. Left London to-day. Consequently, I also conveyed my remains out of town, feeling that I had done my duty."

"Where is Ralph?" asked Evelyn, rising, dimly conscious that Charles and his aunt were conversing in an unknown tongue, and feeling herself *de trop*.

"I left him in the shrubbery. A stoat crossed the road before the horse's nose as we drove up, and Ralph, who seems to have been specially invented by Providence for the destruction of small vermin, was in attendance on it in a moment. I had seen something of the kind before, so I came on."

Evelyn laid down her work, and went across the lawn, and round the corner of the house, in the direction of the shrubbery, from which the voice of her lord and master "rose in snatches," as he plunged in and out among the laurels.

"And how is Lord Hope-Acton?" continued Lady Mary, with an air of elaborate unconcern. "I used to know him in old days as one of the best waltzers in London. I remember him very slim and elegant-looking; but I suppose he is quite elderly now, and has lost his figure? or so some one was saying."

"Not lost, but gone before, I should say, to judge by appearances," said Charles, meditatively, gazing up into the blue of the summer sky.

The mixed impiety and indelicacy of her nephew's remark caused a sudden twitch to the High Church embroidery in Lady Mary's hand; but she went on a moment later in her usual tone:

"And Lady Hope-Acton. Is she in stronger health?"

"I believe she was fairly well; not robust, you know, but, like other fond mothers with daughters out, 'faint yet pursuing.'"

Lady Mary bit her lip; but long experience had taught her that it was wiser to refrain from reproof, even when it was so urgently needed.

"And their daughter, Lady Grace. How beautiful she is! Was she looking as lovely as usual?"

"More so," replied Charles, with conviction. "Her nose is even straighter, her eyelashes even longer than they were last summer. I do not hesitate to say that her complexion is—all that her fancy paints it."

"You are so fond of joking, Charles, that I don't know when you are serious. And you saw a good deal of her?"

"Of course I did. I leaned on the railings in the Row, and watched her riding with Lord Hope-Acton, whose personal appearance you feel such an interest in. At the meeting of the four-in-hands, was not she on the box-seat beside me? At Henley, were we not in the same boat? At Hurlingham, did we not watch polo together, and together drink our tea? At Lord's, did not I tear her new muslin garment in helping her up one of those poultry-ladders on the Torringtons' drag? Have I not taken her in to dinner five several times? Have I not danced with her at balls innumerable? Have I not, in fact, seen as much of her as—of several others?"

"Oh, Charles!" said Lady Mary, "I wish you would talk seriously for one moment, and not in that light way. Have you spoken?"

"In a light way, I should say I had spoken a good deal; but *seriously*, no. I have never ventured to be serious."

"But you will be. After all this, you *will* ask her?"

"Aunt Mary," replied Charles, with gentle reproach, "a certain delicacy should be observed in probing the exact state of a man's young affections. At five-and-thirty (I know I am five-and-thirty, because you have told people so for the last three years) there exists a certain reticence in the youthful heart which declines to lay bare its inmost feelings even for an aunt to— we won't say peck at, but speculate upon. I have told you all I know. I have done what I was bidden to do, up to a certain point. I am now here to recruit, and restore my wasted energies, and possibly to heal (observe, I say possibly) my wounded affections in the intimacy of my family circle. That reminds me that that little ungrateful imp Molly has not yet made the slightest demonstration of joy at my arrival. Where is she?" and without waiting for an answer, which he was well aware would not be forthcoming, Charles rose and strolled towards the house with his hands behind his back.

"Molly!" he called, "Molly!" standing bareheaded in the sunshine, under a certain latticed window, the iron bars of which suggested a nursery within.

There was a sudden answering cackle of delight, and a little brown head was thrust out amid the ivy.

"Come down this very moment, you little hard-hearted person, and embrace your old uncle."

"I'm comin', Uncle Charles, I'm comin';" and the brown head disappeared, and a few seconds later a white frock and two slim black legs rushed round the corner, and Molly precipitated herself against the waistcoat of "Uncle Charles."

"What do you mean by not coming down and paying your respects sooner?" he said, when the first enthusiasm of his reception was over, looking down at Molly with a great kindness in the keen light eyes which had looked so apathetic and sarcastic a moment before.

As he spoke, Ralph Danvers, a square, ruddy man in gray knickerbockers, came triumphantly round from the shrubbery, holding by its tail a minute corpse with out-stretched arms and legs.

"Got him!" he said, smiling, and wiping his brow with honest pride. "See, Charles? See, Molly? Got him!"

"Don't bring it here, Ralph, please. We are going to have tea," came Evelyn's gentle voice from the lawn; and Ralph and the terrier Vic retired to hang the body of the slain upon a fir-tree on the back premises, the recognized long home of stoats and weasels at Atherstone.

Molly, in the presence of Lady Mary and the stick with the silver crook, was always more or less depressed and shy. She felt the pale cold eye of that lady was upon her, as indeed it generally was, if she moved or spoke. She did not therefore join in the conversation as freely as was her wont in the family circle, but sat on the grass by her uncle, watching him with adoring eyes, trying to work the signet ring off his big little finger, which in the memory of man—of Molly, I mean—had never been known to work off, while she gave him the benefit of small pieces of local and personal news in a half whisper from time to time as they occurred to her.

"Cousin Ruth is staying here, Uncle Charles."

"Indeed," said Charles, absently.

His eyes had wandered to Evelyn taking Ralph his cup of tea, and giving him a look with it which he returned—the quiet, grave look of mutual confidence which sometimes passes between married people, and which for the moment makes the single state seem very single indeed.

Molly saw that he had not heard, and that she must try some more exciting topic in order to rivet his attention.

"There was a mouse at prayers yesterday, Uncle Charles."

"There *wasn't*?"

Uncle Charles was attending again now.

Molly gave an exact account of the great event, and of how "Nanny" had gathered her skirts round her, and how James had laughed, only father did not see him, and how—There was a great deal more, and the story ended tragically for the mouse, whose final demise under a shovel, when prayers were over, Molly described in graphic detail.

"And how are the guinea-pigs?" asked Charles, putting down his cup.

"Come and see them," whispered Molly, insinuating her small hand delightedly into his big one; and they went off together, each happy in the society of the other. Charles was introduced to the guinea-pigs, which had multiplied exceedingly since he had presented them, the one named after him being even then engaged in rearing a large family.

Then, after Molly had copiously watered her garden, and Charles's unsuspecting boots at the same time, objects of interest still remained to be seen and admired; confidences had to be exchanged; inner pockets in Charles's waistcoat to be explored; and it was not till the dressing-bell and the shrill voice of "Nanny" from an upper window recalled them, that the friends returned towards the house.

As they turned to go in-doors Charles saw a tall white figure skimming across the stretches of low sunshine and long shadow in the field beyond the garden, and making swiftly for the garden gate.

"Oh, Molly! Molly!" he said, in a tone of sudden consternation, squeezing the little brown hand in his. "*Who* is that?"

Molly looked at him astonished. A moment ago Uncle Charles had been talking merrily, and now he looked quite sad.

"It's only Ruth," she said, reassuringly.

"Who is Ruth?"

"Cousin Ruth," replied Molly. "I told you she was here."

"She's not *staying* here?"

"Yes, she is. She is rather nice, only she says the guinea-pigs smell nasty, which isn't true. She *will* be late," —with evident concern—"if she is going to be laced up; and I know she is, because I saw it on her bed. She doesn't see us yet. Let us go and meet her."

"Run along, then," said Charles, in a lone of deep dejection, loosing Molly's hand. "I think I'll go in-doors."

CHAPTER IV

"I've done Uncle Charles a button-hole, and put it in his water-bottle," said Molly, in an important *affairé* whisper, as she came into Ruth's room a few minutes before dinner, where Ruth and her maid were struggling with a black-lace dress. "Mrs. Jones, you must be very quick. Why do you have pins in your mouth, Mrs. Jones? James has got his coat on, and he is going to ring the bell in one minute. I told him you had only just got your hair done; but he said he could not help that. Uncle Charles,"—peeping through the door—"is going down now, and he's got on a beautiful white waistcoat. He's brought that nice Mr. Brown with him that unpacks his things and plays on the concertina. Ah! there's the bell;" and Molly hurried down to give a description of the exact stage at which Ruth's toilet had arrived, which Ruth cut short by appearing hard upon her heels.

"It is a shame to come in-doors now, isn't it?" said Charles, as he was introduced and took her in to dinner in the wake of Lady Mary and Ralph. "Just the first cool time of the day."

"Is it?" said Ruth, still rather pink with her late exertions. "When I heard the dressing-bell ring across the fields, and the last gate would not open, and I found the railings through which I precipitated myself had been newly painted, I own I thought it had never been so hot all day."

"How trying it is to be forgotten!" said Charles, after a pause. "We have met before, Miss Deyncourt; but I see you don't remember me. I gave you time to recollect me by throwing out that little remark about the weather, but it was no good."

Ruth glanced at him and looked puzzled.

"I am afraid I don't," she said at last. "I have seen you playing polo once or twice, and driving your four-in-hand; but I thought I only knew you by sight. When did we meet before?"

"You have no recollection of a certain ball after some theatricals at Stoke Moreton, which you and your sister came to as little girls in pigtails?"

"Of course I remember that. And were you there?"

"Was I there? Oh, the ingratitude of woman! Did not I dance three times with each of you, and suggest chicken at supper instead of lobster salad?

Does not the lobster salad awaken memories? Surely you have not forgotten that?"

Ruth began to smile.

"I remember now. So you were the kind man, name unknown, who took such care of Anna and me? How good-natured you were!"

"Thanks! You evidently do remember now, if you say that. I recognized you at once, when I saw you again, by your likeness to your brother Raymond. You were very like him then, but much more so now. How is he?"

Ruth's dark gray eyes shot a sudden surprised glance at him. People had seldom of late inquired after Raymond.

"I believe he is quite well," she replied, in a constrained tone. "I have not heard from him for some time."

"It is some years since I met him," said Charles, noting but ignoring her change of tone. "I used to see a good deal of him before he went to—was it America? I heard from him about three years ago. He was prospecting, I think, at that time."

Ruth remembered that Charles had succeeded his father about three years ago. She remembered also Raymond's capacities for borrowing. A sudden instinct told her what the drift of that letter had been. The blood rushed into her face.

"Oh, he didn't—did he?"

The other three people were talking together; Lady Mary, opposite, was joining with a bland smile of inward satisfaction in the discussion between Ralph and Evelyn as to the rival merits of "Cochin Chinas" and "Plymouth Rocks."

"If he did," said Charles, quietly, "it was only what we had often done for each other before. There was a time, Miss Deyncourt, when your brother and I both rowed in the same boat; and both, I fancy, split on the same rock. It was not so long since—"

There was a sudden silence. The chicken question was exhausted. It dropped dead. Charles left his sentence unfinished, and, turning to his brother, the conversation became general.

In the evening, when the others had said good-night, Charles and Ralph went out into the cool half-darkness to smoke, and paced up and down on the lawn in the soft summer night. The two brothers had not met for some time, and in an undemonstrative way they had a genuine affection for each other, which showed itself on this occasion in walking about together without exchanging a word.

At last Charles broke the silence. "I thought, when I settled to come down here, you said you would be alone!" There was a shade of annoyance in his tone.

"Well, now, that is just what I said at the time," said Ralph, sleepily, with a yawn that would have accommodated a Jonah, "only I was told I did not understand. They always say I don't understand if they're set on anything. I thought you wanted a little peace and quietness. I said so; but Aunt Mary settled we must have some one. I say, Charles," with a chuckle of deep masculine cunning, "you just look out. There's some mystery up about Ruth. I believe Aunt Mary got Evelyn to ask her here with an eye to business."

"I would not do Aunt Mary the injustice to doubt *that* for a moment," replied Charles, rather bitterly; and they relapsed into silence and smoke.

Presently Ralph, who had been out all day, yawned himself into the house, and left Charles to pace up and down by himself.

If Lady Mary, who was at that moment composing herself to slumber in the best spare bedroom, had heard the gist of Ralph's remarks to his brother, I think she would have risen up and confronted him then and there on the stairs. As it was, she meditated on her couch with much satisfaction, until the sleep of the just came upon her, little recking that the clumsy hand of brutal man had even then torn the veil from her carefully concealed and deeply laid feminine plans.

Charles, meanwhile, remained on the lawn till late into the night. After two months of London smuts and London smoke and London nights, the calm scented darkness had a peculiar charm for him. The few lights in the windows were going out one by one, and thousands and thousands were coming out in the quiet sky. Through the still air came the sound of a corn-crake perpetually winding up its watch at regular intervals in a field hard by. A little desultory breeze hovered near, and just roused the sleepy trees to whisper a good-night. And Charles paced and paced, and thought of many things.

Only last night! His mind went back to the picture-gallery where he and Lady Grace had sat, amid a grove of palms and flowers. Through the open archway at a little distance came a flood of light, and a surging echo of plaintive, appealing music. It was late, or rather early, for morning was looking in with cold, dispassionate eyes through the long windows. The gallery was comparatively empty for a London gathering, for the balconies and hall were crowded, and the rooms were thinning. To all intents and purposes they were alone. How nearly—how nearly he had asked for what he knew would not have been refused! How nearly he had decided to do at once what might still be put off till to-morrow! And he *must* marry; he often told himself so. She was there beside him on the yellow brocade ottoman. She was much too good for him; but she liked him. Should he do it—now? he asked himself, as he watched the slender gloved hand swaying the feather fan with monotonous languor.

But when he took her back to the ball-room, back to an expectant, tired mother, he had not done it. He should be at their house in Scotland later. He thought he would wait till then. He breathed a long sigh of relief, in the quiet darkness now, at the thought that he had not done it. He had a haunting presentiment that neither in the purple heather, any more than in a London ball-room, would he be able to pass beyond that "certain point" to which, in divers companionship, with or without assistance, he had so often attained.

For Charles was genuinely anxious to marry. He regarded with the greatest interest every eligible and ineligible young woman whom he came across. If Lady Mary had been aware of the very serious light in which he had considered Miss Louisa Smith, youngest daughter of a certain curate Smith, who in his youth had been originally extracted from a refreshment-room at Liverpool to become an ornament of the Church, that lady would have swooned with horror. But neither Miss Louisa Smith, with her bun and sandwich ancestry, nor the eighth Lord Breakwater's young and lovely sister, though both willing to undertake the situation, were either of them finally offered it. Charles remained free as air, and a dreadful stigma gradually attached to him as a heartless flirt and a perverter of young girls' minds from men of more solid worth. A man who pleases easily and is hard to please soon gets a bad name among—mothers. I don't think Lady Hope-Acton thought very kindly of him, as she sped up to Scotland in the night mail.

Perhaps he was not so much to blame as she thought. Long ago, ten long years ago, in the reckless days of which Lady Mary had then made so much, and now made so little, poor Charles had been deeply in love with a good woman, a gentle, quiet girl, who after a time had married his brother Ralph. No one had suspected his attachment—Ralph and Evelyn least of all—but several years elapsed before he found time to visit them at Atherstone; and I think his fondness for Molly had its origin in his feeling for her mother. Even now it sometimes gave him a momentary pang to meet the adoration in Molly's eyes which, with their dark lashes, she had copied so exactly from Evelyn's.

And now that he could come with ease on what had been forbidden ground, he had seen of late clearly, with the insight that comes of dispassionate consideration, that Evelyn, the only woman whom he had ever earnestly loved, whom he would have turned heaven and earth to have been able to marry, had not been in the least suited to him, and that to have married her would have entailed a far more bitter disappointment than the loss of her had been.

Evelyn made Ralph an admirable wife. She was so placid, so gentle, and—with the exception of muddy boots in the drawing-room—so unexacting. It was sweet to see her read to Molly; but did she never take up a book or a paper? What she said was always gracefully put forth; but oh! in old days, used she in that same gentle voice to utter such platitudes, such little stereotyped remarks? Used she, in the palmy days that were no more (when she was not Ralph's wife), so mildly but so firmly to adhere to a pre-conceived opinion? Had she formerly such fixed opinions on every subject in general, and on new-laid eggs and the propriety of chicken-hutches on the lawn in particular? Disillusion may be for our good, like other disagreeable things, but it is seldom pleasant at the time, and is apt to leave in all except the most conceited natures (whose life-long mistakes are committed for our learning) a strange self-distrustful caution behind, which is mortally afraid of making a second mistake of the same kind.

Charles suddenly checked his pacing.

And yet surely, surely, he said to himself, there were in the world somewhere good women of another stamp, who might be found for diligent seeking.

He turned impatiently to go in-doors.

"Oh, Molly! Molly!" he said, half aloud, gazing at the darkened windows behind which the body of Molly was sleeping, while her little soul was frisking away in fairy-land, "why did you complicate matters by being a little girl?" With which reflection he brought his meditations to a close for the night.

CHAPTER V

Molly awoke early on the following morning, and early informed the rest of the household that the weather was satisfactory. She flew into Ruth's room with the hot water, to wake her and set her mind at rest on a subject of such engrossing interest; she imparted it repeatedly to Charles through his key-hole, until a low incoherent muttering convinced her that he also was rejoicing in the good news. She took all the dolls out of the baskets in which Ruth's careful hands had packed them the evening before, in the recognized manner in which dolls travel without detriment to their toilets, namely, head downward, with their orange-top-boots turned upward to the sky. In short, Molly busied herself in the usual ways in which an only child finds employment.

It really was a glorious day. Except in Molly's eyes it was almost too good a day for a school-feast; too good a day, Ruth thought, as she looked out, to be spent entirely in playing at endless games of "Sally Water" and "Oranges and Lemons," and in pouring out sweet tea in a tent. She remembered a certain sketch at Arleigh, an old deserted house in the neighborhood, which she had long wished to make. What a day for a sketch! But she shut her eyes to the temptation of the evil one, and went out into the garden, where Molly's little brown hands were devastating the beds for the approaching festival, and Molly's shrill voice was piping through the fresh morning air.

There had been rain in the night, and to-day the earth had all her diamonds on, just sent down reset from heaven. The trees came out resplendent, unable to keep their leaves still for very vanity, and dropping gems out of their settings at every rustle. No one had been forgotten. Every tiniest shrub and plant had its little tiara to show; rare jewels, cut by a Master Hand, which at man's rude touch, or, for that matter, Molly's either, slid away to tears.

"You don't mean to say, Molly," said Charles, later in the day, when all the dolls had been passed in review before him, and he had criticised each, "that you are going to leave me all day by myself? What shall I do between luncheon and tea-time, when I have fed the guinea-pigs and watered the 'blue-belia,' as you call it—Where has that imp disappeared to now? I think," with a glance at Ruth, who was replacing the cotton wool on the doll's faces,

"I really think, though I own I fancied I had a previous engagement, that I shall be obliged to come to the school-feast too."

"Don't," said Ruth, looking up suddenly from her work with gray serious eyes. "Be advised. No man who respects himself makes himself common by attending village school-feasts and attempting to pour out tea, which he is never allowed to do in private life."

"I could hand buns," suggested Charles. "You take a gloomy view of your fellow-creatures, Miss Deyncourt. I see you underrate my powers with plates of buns."

"Far from it. I only wished to keep you from quitting your proper sphere."

"What, may I ask, is my proper sphere?"

"Not to come to school-feasts at all; or, if you feel that is beyond you, only to arrive when you are too late to be of any use; to stand about with a hunting-crop in your hand—for, of course, you will come on horseback—and then, after refreshing all of us workers by a few well-chosen remarks, to go away again at an easy canter."

"I think I could do that, if it would give pleasure; and I am most grateful to you for pointing out my proper course to me. I have observed it is the prerogative of woman in general not only to be absolutely convinced as to her own line of action, but also to be able to point out that of man to his obtuser perceptions."

"I believe you are perfectly right," said Ruth, becoming serious. "If men, especially prime-ministers, were to apply to almost any woman I know (except, of course, myself) for advice as to the administration of the realm or their own family affairs, I have not the slightest doubt that not one of them would be sent empty away, but would be furnished instantly with a complete guide-book as to his future movements on this side the grave."

"Oh, some people don't stop there," said Charles. "Aunt Mary, in my young days, used to think nothing of the grave if I had displeased her. She still revels in a future court of justice, and an eternal cat-o'-nine tails beyond the tomb. Well, Molly, so here you are, back again! What's the last news?"

The news was the extraordinary arrival of five new kittens, which, according to Molly, the old stable cat had just discovered in a loft, and took the keenest personal interest in. Charles was dragged away, only half acquiescent, to help in a decision that must instantly be come to, as to which of the two spotted or the three plain ones should be kept.

It was a day of delight to Molly. She had the responsibility and honor of driving Ruth and the dolls in her own donkey-cart to the scene of action, where the school children, and some of the idlest or most good-natured of Mrs. Alwynn's friends, were even then assembling, and where Mrs. Alwynn herself was already dashing from point to point, buzzing like a large "bumble" bee.

As the donkey-cart crawled up a gray figure darted out of the tent, and flew to meet them from afar. Dare, who had been on the lookout for them for some time, offered to lift out Molly, helped out Ruth, held the baskets, wished to unharness the donkey, let the wheel go over his patent leather shoe, and in short made himself excessively agreeable, if not in Ruth's, at least in Molly's eyes, who straightway entered into conversation with him, and invited him to call upon herself and the guinea-pigs at Atherstone at an early date.

Then ensued the usual scene at festivities of this description. Tea was poured out like water (very like warm water), buns, cakes, and bread and butter were eaten, were crumbled, were put in pockets, were stamped underfoot. Large open tarts, covered with thin sticks of pastry, called by the boys "the tarts with the grubs on 'em," disappeared apace, being constantly replaced by others made in the same image, from which the protecting but adhesive newspaper had to be judiciously peeled. When the last limit of the last child had been reached, the real work of the day began—the games. Under a blazing sun, for the space of two hours, "Sally Water" or "Nuts in May" must be played, with an occasional change to "Oranges and Lemons."

Ruth, who had before been staying with the Alwynns at the time of their school-feast, hardened her heart, and began that immoral but popular game of "Sally Water."

"Sally, Sally Water, come sprinkle your pan;
Rise up a husband, a handsome young man.
Rise, Sally, rise, and don't look sad,
You shall have a husband, good or bad."

The last line showing how closely the state of feeling of village society, as regards the wedded state, resembles the view taken of it in the highest circles.

Other games were already in full swing. Mrs. Alwynn, flushed and shrill, was organizing an infant troop. A good-natured curate was laying up for himself treasure elsewhere, by a present expenditure of half-pence secreted in a tub of bran. Dare, not to be behind-hand, took to swinging little girls with desperate and heated good-nature. His bright smile and genial brown face soon gained the confidence of the children; and then he swung them as they had never been swung before. It was positively the first time that some of the girls had ever seen their heels above their heads. And his powers of endurance were so great. First his coat and then his waistcoat were cast aside as he warmed to his work, until at last he dragged the sleeve of his shirt out of the socket, and had to retire into private life behind a tree, in company with Mrs. Eccles and a needle and thread. But he reappeared again, and was soon swept into a game of cricket that was being got up among the elder boys; bowled the school-master; batted brilliantly and with considerable flourish for a few moments, only to knock his own wickets down with what seemed singular want of care; and then fielded with cat-like activity and an entire oblivion of the game, receiving a swift ball on his own person, only to choke, coil himself up, and recover his equanimity and the ball in a moment.

All things come to an end, and at last the Slumberleigh church clock struck four, and Ruth could sink giddily onto a bench, and push back the few remaining hair-pins that were left to her, and feebly endeavor, with a pin eagerly extracted by Dare from the back of his neck, to join the gaping ruin of torn gathers in her dress, so daintily fresh two hours ago, so dilapidated now.

"There they come!" said Mrs. Alwynn, indignantly, who was fanning herself with her pocket-handkerchief, which stout women ought to be forbidden by law to do. "There are Mrs. Thursby and Mabel. Just like them, arriving when the games are all over! And, dear me! who is that with them? Why, it is Sir Charles Danvers. I had no idea he was staying with them. Brown particularly told me they had not brought back any friend with them yesterday. Dear me! How odd! And Brown—"

"Sir Charles Danvers is staying at Atherstone," said Ruth.

"At Atherstone, is he? Well, my dear, this is the first I have heard of it, if he is. I don't see what there is to make a secret of in *that*. Most natural he should be staying there, I should have thought. And, if that's one of Mabel's new gowns, all I can say is that yours is quite as nice, Ruth, though I know it is from last year, and those full fronts as fashionable as ever."

As Mr. and Mrs. Alwynn went forward to meet the Thursbys, Charles strolled up to Ruth, and planted himself deliberately in front of her.

"You observe that I am here?" he said.

"I do."

"At the proper time?"

"At the proper time."

"And in my sphere? I have tampered with no buns, you will remark, and teapots have been far from me."

"I am exceedingly rejoiced my little word in season has been of such use."

"It has, Miss Deyncourt. The remark you made this morning I considered honest, though poor, and I laid it to heart accordingly. But," with a change of tone, "you look tired to death. You have been out in the sun too long. I am going off now. I only came because I met the Thursbys, and they dragged me here. Come home with me through the woods. You have no idea how agreeable I am in the open air. It will be shady all the way, and not half so fatiguing as being shaken in Molly's donkey-cart."

"In the donkey-cart I must return, however, if I die on the way," said Ruth, with a tired smile. "I can't leave Molly. Besides, all is not over yet. The races and prizes take time; and when at last they are dismissed, a slice of—"

"No, Miss Deyncourt, *no*! Not more food!"

"A slice of cake will be applied *externally* to each of the children, which rite brings the festivities to a close. There! I see the dolls are being carried out. I must go;" and a moment later Ruth and Molly and Dare, who had been hovering near, were busily unpacking and shaking out the dolls; and Charles, after a little desultory conversation with Mabel Thursby, strolled away, with his hands behind his back and his nose in the air in the manner habitual to him.

And so the day wore itself out at last; and after a hymn had been shrieked the children were dismissed, and Ruth and Molly at length drove away.

"Hasn't it been delicious?" said Molly. "And my doll was chosen first. Lucy Bigg, with the rash on her face, got it. I wish little Sarah had had it. I do love Sarah so very much; but Sarah had yours, Ruth, with the real pocket and the handkerchief in it. That will be a surprise for her when she gets home. And that new gentleman was so kind about the teapots, wasn't he? He always filled mine first. He's coming to see me very soon, and to bring a curious black dog that he has of his very own, called—"

"Stop, Molly," said Ruth, as the donkey's head was being sawed round towards the blazing high-road; "let us go home through the woods. I know it is longer, but I can't stand any more sun and dust to-day."

"You do look tired," said Molly, "and your lips are quite white. My lips turned white once, before I had the measles, and I felt very curious inside, and then spots came all over. You don't feel like spots, do you, Cousin Ruth?

We will go back by the woods, and I'll open the gates, and you shall hold the reins. I dare say Balaam will like it better too."

Molly had called her donkey Balaam, partly owing to a misapprehension of Scripture narrative, and partly owing to the assurance of Charles, when in sudden misgiving she had consulted him on the point, that Balaam *had* been an ass.

Balaam's reluctant underjaw was accordingly turned in the direction of the woods, and, little thinking the drive might prove an eventful one, Ruth and Molly set off at that easy amble which a well-fed pampered donkey will occasionally indulge in.

CHAPTER VI

After the glare and the noise, the shrill blasts of penny trumpets, and the sustained beating of penny drums, the silence of the Slumberleigh woods was delightful to Ruth; the comparative silence, that is to say, for where Molly was, absolute silence need never be feared.

Long before the first gate had been reached Balaam had, of course, returned to the mode of procedure which suited him and his race best, and it was only when the road inclined to be downhill that he could be urged into anything like a trot.

"Never mind," said Molly, consolingly to Ruth, as he finally settled into a slow lounge, gracefully waving his ears and tail at the army of flies which accompanied him, "when we get to the place where the firs are, and the road goes between the rocks, it's downhill all the way, and we'll gallop down."

But it was a long way to the firs, and Ruth was in no hurry. It was an ideal afternoon, verging towards evening; an afternoon of golden lights and broken shadows, of vivid greens in shady places. It must have been on such a day as this, Ruth thought, that the Almighty walked in the garden of Eden when the sun was low, while as yet the tree of knowledge was but in blossom, while as yet autumn and its apples were far off, long before fig-leaves and millinery were thought of.

On either side the bracken and the lady-fern grew thick and high, almost overlapping the broad moss-grown path, across which the young rabbits popped away in their new brown coats, showing their little white linings in their lazy haste. A dog-rose had hung out a whole constellation of pale stars for Molly to catch at as they passed. A family of honeysuckles clung, faint and sweet, just beyond the reach of the little hand that stretched after them in turn.

They had reached the top of an ascent that would have been level to anything but the mean spirit of a donkey, when Molly gave a start.

"Cousin Ruth, there's something creeping among the trees—don't you hear it? Oh-h-h!"

There really was a movement in the bracken, which grew too thick and high to allow of anything being easily seen at a little distance.

"If it's a lion," said Molly, in a faint whisper, "and I feel in my heart it is, he must have Balaam."

Balaam at this moment pricked his large ears, and Molly and Ruth both heard the snapping of a twig, and saw a figure slip behind a tree. Molly's spirits rose, and Ruth's went down in proportion. The woods were lonely, and they were nearing the most lonely part.

"It's only a man," said Ruth, rather sharply. "I expect it is one of the keepers." (Oh, Ruth!) "Come, Molly, we shall never get home at this rate. Whip up Balaam, and let us trot down the hill."

Much relieved about Balaam's immediate future, Molly incited him to a really noble trot, and did not allow him to relapse even on the flat which followed. Through the rattling and the jolting, however, Ruth could still hear a stealthy rustle in the fern and under-wood. The man was following them.

"He's coming after us," whispered Molly, with round frightened eyes, "and Balaam will stop in a minute, I know. Oh, Cousin Ruth, what shall we do?"

Ruth hesitated. They were nearing the steep pitch, where the firs overhung the road, which was cut out between huge bowlders of rock and sandstone. The ground rose rough and precipitous on their right, and fell away to their left. Just over the brow of the hill, out of sight, was, as she well knew, the second gate. The noise in the brushwood had ceased. Turning suddenly, her quick eye just caught sight of a figure disappearing behind the slope of the falling ground to the left. He was a lame man, and he was running. In a moment she saw that he was making a short cut, with the intention of waylaying them at the gate. He would get there long before they would; and even then Balaam was beginning the ascent, which really was an ascent this time, at his slowest walk.

Molly's teeth were chattering in her little head.

"Now, Molly," said Ruth, sharply, "listen to me, and don't be a baby. He'll wait for us at the gate, so he can't see us here. Get out this moment, and we will both run up the hill to the keeper's cottage at the top of the bank. We shall get there first, because he is lame."

They had passed the bracken now, and were among the moss and sandstone beneath the firs. Ruth hastily dragged Molly out of the cart without stopping Balaam, who proceeded, twirling his ears, leisurely without them.

"Oh, my poor Balaam!" sobbed Molly, with a backward glance at that unconscious favorite marching towards its doom.

"There is no time to think of poor Balaam now," replied Ruth. "Run on in front of me, and don't step on anything crackly."

"Never in this world," thought Ruth, "will I come alone here with Molly again. Never again will I—"

But it was stiff climbing, and the remainder of the resolution was lost.

They are high to the right above the white gate now. The keeper's cottage is in sight, built against a ledge of rock, up to which wide rough steps have been cut in the sandstone. Ruth looks down at the gate below. He is waiting—the dreadful man is waiting there, as she expected; and Balaam, toying with a fern, is at that moment coming round the corner. She sees that he takes in the situation instantly. There is but one way in which they can have fled, and he knows it. In a moment he comes halting and pounding up the slope. He sees their white dresses among the firs. Run, Molly! run, Ruth! Spare no expense. If your new black sash catches in the briers, let it catch; heed it not, for he is making wonderful play with that lame leg up the hill. It is an even race. Now for the stone steps! How many more there are than there ever were before! Quick through the wicket, and up through the little kitchen-garden. Molly is at the door first, beating upon it, and calling wildly on the name of Brown.

And then Ruth's heart turns sick within her. The door is locked. Through the window, which usually blossoms with geraniums, she can see the black fireplace and the bare walls. No Brown within answers to Molly's cries. Brown has been turned away for drinking. Mrs. Brown, who hung a slender "wash" on the hedge only last week, has departed with her lord. Brown's cottage is tenantless. The pursuer must have known it when he breasted the hill. A mixed sound, as of swearing and stumbling, comes from the direction of the stone steps. The pursuer is evidently intoxicated, probably lunatic!

"Quick, Molly!" gasps Ruth, "round by the back, and then cut down towards the young plantation, and make for the road again. Don't stop for me."

The little yard, the pigsty, the water-butt, fly past. Past fly the empty kennels. Past does *not* fly the other gate. Locked; padlocked! It is like a bad dream. Molly, with a windmill-like exhibition of black legs, gives Ruth a lead over. Now for it, Ruth! The bars are close together and the gate is high. It is not a time to stick at trifles. What does it matter if you can get over best by assuming a masculine equestrian attitude for a moment on the top bar? There! And now, down the hill again, away to your left. Take to your heels, and be thankful they are not high ones. Never mind if your hair is coming down. You have a thousand good qualities, Ruth, high principles and a tender conscience, but you are not a swift runner, and you have not played "Sally Water" all day for nothing. Molly is far in front now. A heavy trampling is not far behind; nay, it is closer than you thought. And your eyes are becoming misty, Ruth, and armies of drums are beating every other sound out of your ears—that shouting behind you, for instance. The intoxicated, murderous lunatic is close behind. One minute! Two minutes! How many more seconds can you keep it up? Through the young plantation, down the hill, into the sandy road again, the sandy, uphill road. How much longer can you keep it up?

Charles strolled quietly homeward, enjoying the beauties of nature, and reflecting on the quantity of rabbit-shooting that Mr. Thursby must enjoy. He may also have mused on Lady Grace, for anything that can be known to the contrary, and have possibly made a mental note that if it had been she whom he had asked to walk home with him, instead of Ruth, he would not have been alone at that moment. Be that how it may, he leisurely pursued his path until a fallen tree beside the bank looked so inviting that (Evelyn and Ralph having gone out to friends at a distance) Charles, who was in no hurry to return to Lady Mary, seated himself thereon, with a cigarette to bear him company.

To him, with rent garments and dust upon her head, and indeed all over her, suddenly appeared Molly; Molly, white with panic, breathless, unable to articulate, pointing in the direction from which she had come. In a moment Charles was tearing down the road at full speed. A tall, swaying figure almost ran against him at the first turn, and Ruth only avoided him to collapse suddenly in the dry ditch, her face in the bank, and a yard of sash biting the dust along the road behind her.

Her pursuer stopped short. Charles made a step towards him and stopped short also. The two men stood and looked at each other without speaking.

When Ruth found herself in a position to make observations she discovered that she was sitting by the road-side, with her head resting against—was it a tweed arm or the bank? She moved a little, and found that first impressions are apt to prove misleading. It was the bank. She opened her eyes to see a brown, red-lined hat on the ground beside her, half full of water, through which she could dimly discern the golden submerged name of the maker. She seemed to have been contemplating it with vague interest for about an hour, when she became aware that some one was dabbing her forehead with a wet silk handkerchief.

"Better?" asked Charles's voice.

"Oh!" gasped Ruth, suddenly trying to sit up, but finding the attempt resulted only in the partial movement of a finger somewhere in the distance. "Have I really—surely, surely, I was not so abject as to *faint*?"

"Truth," said Charles, with a reassured look in his quick, anxious eyes, "obliges me to say you did."

"I thought better of myself than that."

"Pride goes before a fall or a faint."

"Oh, dear!" turning paler than ever. "Where is Molly?"

"She is all right," said Charles, hastily, applying the pocket-handkerchief again. "Don't alarm yourself, and pray don't try to get up. You can see just as much of the view sitting down. Molly has gone for the donkey-cart."

"And that dreadful man?"

"That dreadful man has also departed. By-the-way, did you see his face? Would you know him again if the policeman succeeds in finding him?"

"No; I never looked round. I only saw, when he began to run to cut us off at the gate, that he was lame."

"H'm!" said Charles, reflectively. Then more briskly, with a new access of dabbing, "How is the faintness going on?"

"Capitally," replied Ruth, with a faint, amused smile; "but if it does not seem ungrateful, I should be very thankful if I might be spared the rest of the water in the hat, or if it might be poured over me at once, if you don't wish it to be wasted."

"Have I done too much? I imagined my services were invaluable. Let me help you to find your own handkerchief, if you would like a dry one for a change. Ah, what a good shot into that labyrinth of drapery! You have found it for yourself. You are certainly better."

"But my self-respect," replied Ruth, drying her face, "is gone forever!"

"I lost mine years ago," said Charles, carefully dusting Ruth's hat, "but I got over it. I had no idea those bows were supported by a wire inside. One lives and learns."

"I never did such a thing before," continued Ruth, ruefully. "I have always felt a sort of contempt for girls who scream or faint just when they ought not."

"For my part, I am glad to perceive you have some little feminine weakness. Your growing solicitude also as to the state of your back hair is pleasing in the extreme."

"I am too confused and shaken to retaliate just now. You are quite right to make hay while the sun shines; but, when I am myself again, beware!"

"And your gown," continued Charles. "What yawning gulfs, what chasms appear! and what a quantity of extraneous matter you have brought away with you—reminiscences of travel—burrs, very perfect specimens of burrs, thistledown, chips of fir, several complete spiders' webs; and your sash, which seems to have a particularly adhesive fringe, is a museum in itself. Ah, here comes that coward of little cowards, Molly, with Balaam and the donkey-cart!"

Molly, who had left Ruth for dead, greeted her cousin with a transport of affection, and then proceeded to recount the fearful risks that Balaam had encountered by being deserted, and the stoic calm with which he had waited for them at the gate.

"He's not a common donkey," she said, with pride. "Get in, Ruth. Are you coming in, Uncle Charles? There's just room for you to squeeze in between Ruth and me—isn't there, Ruth? Oh, you're not going to walk beside, are you?"

But Charles was determined not to let them out of his sight again, and he walked beside them the remainder of the way to Atherstone. He remained silent and preoccupied during the evening which followed, pored over a newspaper, and went off to his room early, leaving Ralph dozing in the smoking-room.

It was a fine moonlight night, still and clear. He stood at the open window looking out for a few minutes, and then began fumbling in a dilapidated old travelling-bag such as only rich men use.

"Not much," he said to himself, spreading out a few sovereigns and some silver on the table, "but it will do."

He put the money in his pocket, took off his gold hunting watch, and then went back to the smoking-room.

"I am going out again, Ralph, as I did last night. If I come in late, you need not take me for a burglar."

Ralph murmured something unintelligible, and Charles ran downstairs, and let himself out of the drawing-room French window, that long French window to the ground, which Evelyn had taken a fancy to in a neighbor's drawing-room, and which she could never be made to see was not in keeping with the character of her old black-and-white house. He put the shutter back after he had passed through, and carefully drawing the window to behind him, without actually closing it, he took a turn or two upon the bowling-green, and then walked off in the direction of the Slumberleigh woods.

After the lapse of an hour or more he returned as quietly as he had gone, let himself in, made all secure, and stole up to his room.

CHAPTER VII

Vandon was considered by many people to be the most beautiful house in ----shire.

In these days of great brand-new imitation of intensely old houses, where the amount of ground covered measures the purse of the builder, it is pleasant to come upon a place like Vandon, a quiet old manor-house, neither large nor small, built of ancient bricks, blent to a dim purple and a dim red by that subtle craftsman Time.

Whoever in the years that were no more had chosen the place whereon to build had chosen well. Vandon stood on the slope of a gentle hill, looking across a sweep of green valley to the rising woods beyond, which in days gone by had been a Roman camp, and where the curious might still trace the wide ledges cut among the regular lines of the trees.

Some careful hand had planned the hanging gardens in front of the house, which fell away to the stream below. Flights of wide stone steps led down from terrace to terrace, each built up by its south wall covered with a wealth of jasmine and ivy and climbing roses. But all was wild and deserted now. Weeds had started up between the stone slabs of the steps, and the roses blossomed out sweet and profuse, for it was the time of roses, amid convolvulus and campion. The quaint old dove-cot near the house had almost disappeared behind the trees that had crowded up round it, and held aloft its weathercock in silent protest at their encroachment. The stables close at hand, with their worn-out clock and silent bell, were tenantless. The coach-houses were full of useless old chariots and carriages. Into one splendid court coach the pigeons had found their way through an open window, and had made nests, somewhat to the detriment of the green-and-white satin fittings.

Great cedars, bent beneath the weight of years, grew round the house. The patriarch among them had let fall one of his gnarled supplicating arms in the winter, and there it still lay where it had fallen.

Anything more out of keeping with the dignified old place than its owner could hardly be imagined, as he stood in his eternal light gray suit (with a badge of affliction lightly borne on his left arm), looking at his heritage, with his cropped head a little on one side.

The sun was shining, but, like a smile on a serious face, Vandon caught the light on all its shuttered windows, and remained grave, looking out across its terraces to the forest.

"If it were but a villa on the Mediterranean, or a house in London," he said to himself; "but I have no chance." And he shrugged his shoulders, and wandered back into the house again. But, if the outside oppressed him, the interior was not calculated to raise his spirits.

Dare had an elegant taste, which he had never hitherto been able to gratify, for blue satin furniture and gilding; for large mirrors and painted ceilings of lovers and cupids, and similar small deer. The old square hall at Vandon, with its great stained glass windows, representing the various quarterings of the Dare arms, about which he knew nothing and cared less, oppressed him. So did the black polished oak floor, and the walls with their white bass-reliefs of twisting wreaths and scrolls, with busts at intervals of Cicero and Dante, and other severe and melancholy personages. The rapiers upon the high white chimney-piece were more to his taste. He had taken them down the first day after his arrival, and had stamped and cut and thrust in the most approved style, in the presence of Faust, the black poodle.

Dare was not the kind of man to be touched by it; but to many minds there would have been something pathetic in seeing a house, which had evidently been an object of the tender love and care of a by-gone generation, going to rack and ruin from neglect. Careful hands had embroidered, in the fine exquisite work of former days, marvellous coverlets and hangings, which still adorned the long suites of empty bedrooms. Some one had taken an elaborate pleasure in fitting up those rooms, had put *pot-pourri* in tall Oriental jars in the passages, had covered the old inlaid Dutch chairs with dim needle-work.

The Dare who had lived at court, whose chariot was now the refuge of pigeons, whose court suits, with the tissue paper still in the sleeves, yet remained in one of the old oak chests, and whose jewelled swords still hung in the hall, had filled one of the rooms with engravings of the royal family and ministers of his day. The Dare who had been an admiral had left his miniature surrounded by prints of the naval engagements he had taken part in, and on the oak staircase a tattered flag still hung, a trophy of unremembered victory.

But they were past and forgotten. The hands which had arranged their memorials with such pride and love had long since gone down to idleness, and forgetfulness also. Who cared for the family legends now? They, too, had gone down into silence. There was no one to tell Dare that the old blue enamel bowl in the hall, in which he gave Faust refreshment, had been brought back from the loot of the Winter Palace of Pekin; or that the drawer in the Reisener table in the drawing-room was full of treasured medals and miniatures, and that the key thereof was rusting in a silver patch-box on the writing-table.

The iron-clamped boxes in the lumber-room kept the history to themselves of all the silver plate that had lived in them once upon a time, although the few odd pieces remaining hinted at the splendor of what had been. In one corner of the dining-room the mahogany tomb still stood of a great gold racing cup, under the portrait of the horse that had won it; but the cup had followed the silver dinner service, had followed the diamonds, had followed in the wake of a handsome fortune, leaving the after generations impoverished. If their money is taken from them, some families are left poor indeed, and to this class the Dares belonged. It is curious to notice the occasional real equality underlying the apparent inequality of different conditions of life. The unconscious poverty, and even bankruptcy, of some rich people in every kind of wealth except money affords an interesting study; and it seems doubly hard when those who have nothing to live upon, and be loved and respected for, except their money, have even that taken from them. As Dare wandered through the deserted rooms the want of money of his predecessors, and consequently of himself, was borne in upon him. It fell like a shadow across his light pleasure-loving soul. He had expected so much from this unlooked-for inheritance, and all he had found was a melancholy house with a past.

He went aimlessly through the hall into the library. It was there that his uncle had lived; there that he had been found when death came to look for him; among the books which he had been unable to carry away with him at his departure; rare old tomes and first editions, long shelves of dead authors, who, it is to be hoped, continue to write in other worlds for those who read their lives away in this. Old Mr. Dare's interests and affections had all been bound in morocco and vellum. A volume lay open on the table, where the old man had put it down beside the leather arm-chair where he had sat, with his back to the light, summer and winter, winter and summer, for so many years.

No one had moved it since. A wavering pencil-mark had scored the page here and there. Dare shut it up, and replaced it among its brethren. How *triste* and silent the house seemed! He wondered what the old uncle had been like, and sauntered into the staircase hall, much in need of varnish, where the Dares that had gone before him lived. But these were too ancient to have his predecessor among them. He went into the long oak-panelled dining-room, where above the high carved dado were more Dares. Perhaps that man with the book was his namesake, the departed Alfred Dare. He wondered vaguely how he should look when he also took his place among his relations. Nature had favored him with a better mustache than most men, but he had a premonitory feeling that the very mustache itself, though undeniable in real life, would look out of keeping among these bluff, frank, light-haired people, of whom it seemed he—he who had never been near them before—was the living representative.

A sudden access of pleasurable dignity came over him as he sat on the dining-table, the great mahogany dining-table, which still showed vestiges of a by-gone polish, and was heavily dented by long years of hammered applause. These ancestors of his! He would not disgrace them. A few minutes ago he had been wondering whether Vandon might not be let. Now, with one of the rapid transitions habitual to him, he resolved that he would live at Vandon, that in all things he would be as they had been. He would become that vague, indefinable, to him mythical personage—a "country squire." Fortunately, he had a neat leg for a stocking. It was lost, so to speak, in his present mode of dress; but he felt that it would appear to advantage in the perpetual knickerbockers which he supposed it would be his lot to wear. It would also become his duty and his pleasure to marry. For those who tread in safety the slippery heights of married life he felt a true esteem. It would be a strain, no doubt, a great effort; but at this moment he was capable of anything. The finger of duty was plain. And with that adorable Miss Ruth, with or without a fortune—Alas! he trusted she had a fortune, for, as he came to think thereon, he remembered that he was desperately poor. As far as he could make out from his agent, a grim, silent man, who had taken an evident dislike to him from the first, there was no money anywhere. The rents would come in at Michaelmas; but the interest of heavy mortgages had to be paid, the estate had to be kept up. There was succession duty; there were debts—long outstanding debts—which came pouring in now, which Waters spread before him with an iron smile, and which poor Dare contemplated with his head on one side, and solemn, arched eyebrows. When Dare was not smiling he was always preternaturally solemn. There was no happy medium in his face, or consequently in his mind, which was generally gay, but, if not, was involved in a tragic gloom.

"These bills, my friend," he would say at last, tapping them in deep dejection, and raising his eyebrows into his hair, "how do we pay them?"

But Waters did not know. How should he, Waters, know? Waters only knew that the farmers would want a reduction in these bad times—Mr. Dare might be sure of *that*. And what with arrears, and one thing and another, he need not expect more than two-thirds of his rents when they did arrive. Mr. Dare might lay his account for *that*.

The only money which Dare received to carry on with, on his accession to the great honor and dignity of proprietor of Vandon, was brought to him by the old dairywoman of the house, a faithful creature, who produced out of an old stocking the actual coins which she had received for the butter and cheese she had sold, of which she showed Dare an account, chalked up in some dead language on the dairy door.

She was a little doubled-up woman, who had served the family all her life. Dare's ready smile and handsome face had won her heart before he had been many days at Vandon, in spite of "his foreign ways," and he found himself constantly meeting her unexpectedly round corners, where she had been lying in wait for him, each time with a secret revelation to whisper respecting what she called the "goin's on."

"You'll not tell on me, sir, but it's only right you should know as Mrs. Smith" (the house-keeper, of whom Dare stood in mortal terror) "has them fine damask table-cloths out for the house-keeper's room; I see 'em myself; and everything going to rag and ruin in the linen closet!" Or, "Joseph has took in another flitch this very day, sir, as Mrs. Smith sent for, and the old flitch all cut to waste. Do'e go and look at the flitches, sir, and the hams. They're in the room over the stables. And it's always butter, butter, butter, in the kitchen! Not a bit o' dripping used! There's not a pot of dripping in the larder, or so much as a skin of lard. Where does it all go to? You ask Mrs. Smith; and how she sleeps in her bed at night I don't know!"

Dare listened, nodded, made his escape, and did nothing. In the village it was as bad. Time, which had dealt so kindly with Vandon itself, had taken the straggling village in hand too. Nothing could be more picturesque than the crazy black-and-white houses, with lichen on their broken-in thatch, and the plaster peeling off from between the irregular beams of black wood; nothing more picturesque—and nothing more miserable.

When Time puts in his burnt umbers and brown madders with a lavish hand, and introduces his beautiful irregularities of outline, and his artistic disrepair, he does not look to the drainage, and takes no thought for holes in the roof.

Dare could not go out without eager women sallying out of cottages as he passed, begging him just to come in and walk up-stairs. They would say no more—but would the new squire walk up-stairs? And Dare would stumble up and see enough to promise. Alas! how much he promised in those early days. And in the gloaming, heavy dull-eyed men met him in the lanes coming back from their work, and followed him to "beg pardon, sir," and lay before the new squire things that would never reach him through Waters—bitter things, small injustices, too trivial to seem worthy of mention, which serve to widen the gulf between class and class. They looked to Dare to help them, to make the crooked straight, to begin a new régime. They looked to the new king to administer his little realm; the new king, who, alas! cared for none of these things. And Dare promised that he would do what he could, and looked anxious and interested, and held out his brown hand, and raised hopes. But he had no money—no money.

He spoke to Waters at first; but he soon found that it was no good. The houses were bad? Of course they were bad. Cottage property did not pay; and would Mr. Dare kindly tell him where the money for repairing them was to come from? Perhaps Mr. Dare might like to put a little of his private fortune into the cottages and the drains and the new pumps? Dare winced. His fortune had not gone the time-honored way of the fortunes of spirited young men of narrow means with souls above a sordid economy, but still it had gone all the same, and in a manner he did not care to think of.

It was after one of these depressing interviews with Waters that Ralph and Evelyn found the new owner of Vandon, when they rode over together to call, a day or two after the school-feast. Poor Dare was sitting on the low ivy-covered wall of the topmost terrace, a prey to the deepest dejection. If he had lived in Spartan days, when it was possible to conceal gnawing foxes under wearing apparel, he would have made no use of the advantages of Grecian dress for such a purpose. Captivated by Evelyn's gentleness and sympathetic manner (strangers always thought Evelyn sympathetic), and impressed by Ralph's kindly, honest face, he soon found himself telling them something of his difficulties, of the maze in which he found himself, of the snubs which Waters had administered.

Ralph slapped himself with his whip, whistled, and gave other masculine signs of interest and sympathy. Evelyn looked from one to the other, amiably distressed in her well-fitting habit. After a long conversation, in which Evelyn disclosed that Ralph was possessed of the most extraordinary knowledge and experience in such matters, the two good-natured young people, seeing he was depressed and lonely, begged him to come and stay with them at Atherstone the very next day, when he might discuss his affairs with Ralph, if so disposed, and take counsel with him. Dare accepted with the most genuine pleasure, and his speaking countenance was in a moment radiant with smiles. Was not the little Molly of the school-feast their child? and was not Miss Deyncourt likewise staying with them?

When his visitors departed, Dare took a turn at the rapiers; then opened the piano with the internal derangement, and sang to his own accompaniment a series of little confidential French songs, which would have made the hair of his ancestors stand on end, if painted hair could do such a thing. And the "new squire," as he was already called, shrugged his shoulders, and lowered his voice, and spread out his expressive rapid hands, and introduced to Vandon, one after another, some of those choice little ditties, French and English, which had made him such a favorite companion in Paris, so popular in a certain society in America.

CHAPTER VIII

"Sir Charles!"

"Miss Deyncourt!"

"I fear," with a glance at the yellow-back in his hand, "I am interrupting a studious hour, but—"

"Not in the least, I assure you," said Charles, shutting his novel. "What is regarded as study by the feminine intellect is to the masculine merely relaxation. I was 'unbending over a book,' that was all."

The process of "unbending" was being performed in the summer-house, whither he had retired after Evelyn and Ralph had started on their afternoon's ride to Vandon, in which he had refused to join.

"I thought I should find you here," continued Ruth, frankly. "I have been wishing to speak to you for several days, but you are as a rule so surrounded and encompassed on every side by Molly that I have not had an opportunity."

It had occurred to Charles once or twice during the last few days that Molly was occasionally rather in the way. Now he was sure of it. As Ruth appeared to hesitate, he pulled forward a rustic contorted chair for her.

"No, thanks," she said. "I shall not long interrupt the unbending process. I only came to ask—"

"To ask!" repeated Charles, who had got up as she was standing, and came and stood near her.

"You remember the first evening you were here?"

"I do."

"And what we spoke of at dinner?"

"Perfectly."

"I came to ask you how much you lent Raymond?" Ruth's clear, earnest eyes were fixed full upon him.

At this moment Charles perceived Lady Mary at a little distance, propelling herself gently over the grass in the direction of the summer-house. In another second she had perceived Charles and Ruth, and had turned precipitately, and hobbled away round the corner with surprising agility.

"Confound her!" inwardly ejaculated Charles.

"I wish to know how much you lent him," said Ruth again, as he did not answer, happily unconscious of what had been going on behind her back.

"Only what I was well able to afford."

"And has he paid it back since?"

"I am sure he understood I should not expect him to pay it back at once."

"But he has had it three years."

Charles did not answer.

"I feel sure he is not able to pay it. Will you kindly tell me how much it was?"

"No, Miss Deyncourt; I think not."

"Why not?"

"Because—excuse me, but I perceive that if I do you will instantly wish to pay it."

"I do wish to pay it."

"I thought so."

There was a short silence.

"I still wish it," said Ruth at last.

Charles was silent. Her pertinacity annoyed and yet piqued him. Being unmarried, he was not accustomed to opposition from a woman. He had no intention of allowing her to pay her brother's debt, and he wished she would drop the subject gracefully, now that he had made that fact evident.

"Perhaps you don't know," continued Ruth, "that I am very well off." (As if he did not know it! As if Lady Mary had not casually mentioned Ruth's fortune several times in his hearing!) "Lady Deyncourt left me twelve hundred a year, and I have a little of my own besides. You may not be aware that I have fourteen hundred and sixty-two pounds per annum."

"I am very glad to hear it."

"That is a large sum, you will observe."

"It is riches," assented Charles, "if your expenditure happens to be less."

"It does happen to be considerably less in my case."

"You are to be congratulated. And yet I have always understood that society exacts great sacrifices from women in the sums they feel obliged to devote to dress."

"Dress is an interesting subject, and I should be delighted to hear your views on it another time; but we are talking of something else just at this moment."

"I beg your pardon," said Charles, quickly, who did not quite like being brought back to the case in point. "I—the truth was, I wished to turn your mind from what we were speaking of. I don't want you to count sovereigns into my hand. I really should dislike it very much."

"You intend me to think from that remark that it was a small sum," said Ruth, with unexpected shrewdness. "I now feel sure it was a large one. It ought to be paid, and there is no one to do it but me. I know that what is firmness in a man is obstinacy in a woman, so do not on your side be too firm, or, who knows? you may arouse some of that obstinacy in me to which I should like to think myself superior."

"If," said Charles, with sudden eagerness, as if an idea had just struck him, "if I let you pay me this debt, will you on your side allow me to make a condition?"

"I should like to know the condition first."

"Of course. If I agree,"—Charles's light gray eyes had become keen and intent—"if I agree to receive payment of what I lent Deyncourt three years ago, will you promise not to pay any other debt of his, or ever to lend him money without the knowledge and approval of your relations?"

Ruth considered for a few minutes.

"I have so few relations," she said at length, with rather a sad smile, "and they are all prejudiced against poor Raymond. I think I am the only friend he has left in the world. I am afraid I could not promise that."

"Well," said Charles, eagerly, "I won't insist on relations. I know enough of those thorns in the flesh myself. I will say instead, 'natural advisers.' Come, Miss Deyncourt, you can't accuse me of firmness now!"

"My natural advisers," repeated Ruth, slowly. "I feel as if I ought to have natural advisers somewhere; but who are they? Where are they? I could not ask my sister or her husband for advice. I mean, I could not take it if I did. I should think I knew better myself. Uncle John? Evelyn? Lord Polesworth? Sir Charles, I am afraid the truth is I have never asked for advice in my life. I have always tried to do what seemed best, without troubling to know what other people thought about it. But as I am anxious to yield gracefully, will you substitute the word 'friends' for 'natural advisers'? I hope and think I have friends whom I could trust."

"Friends, then, let it be," said Charles. "Now," holding out his hand, "do you promise never, et cetera, et cetera, without first consulting your *friends*?"

Ruth put her hand into his.

"I do."

"That is right. How amiable we are both becoming! I suppose I must now inform you that two hundred pounds is the exact sum I lent your brother."

Ruth went back to the house, and in a few minutes returned with a check in her hand. She held it towards Charles, who took it, and put it in his pocket-book.

"Thank you," she said, with gratitude in her eyes and voice.

"We have had a pitched battle," said Charles, relapsing into his old indifferent manner. "Neither of us has been actually defeated, for we never called out our reserves, which I felt would have been hardly fair on you; but we do not come forth with flying colors. I fear, from your air of elation, you actually believe you have been victorious."

"I agree with you that there has been no defeat," replied Ruth; "but I won't keep you any longer from your studies. I am just going out driving with Lady Mary to have tea with the Thursbys."

"Miss Deyncourt, don't allow a natural and most pardonable vanity to delude you to such an extent. Don't go out driving the victim of a false impression. If you will consider one moment—"

"Not another moment," replied Ruth; "our bugles have sung truce, and I am not going to put on my war-paint again for any consideration. There comes the carriage," as a distant rumbling was heard. "I must not keep Lady Mary waiting;" and she was gone.

Charles heard the carriage roll away again, and when half an hour later he sauntered back towards the house, he was surprised to see Lady Mary sitting in the drawing-room window.

"What! Not gone, after all!" he exclaimed, in a voice in which surprise was more predominant than pleasure.

"No, Charles," returned Lady Mary in her measured tones, looking slowly up at him over her gold-rimmed spectacles. "I felt a slight return of my old enemy, and Miss Deyncourt kindly undertook to make my excuses to Mrs. Thursby."

No one knew what the old enemy was, or in what manner his mysterious assaults on Lady Mary were conducted; but it was an understood thing that she had private dealings with him, in which he could make himself very disagreeable.

"Has Molly gone with her?"

"No; Molly is making jam in the kitchen, I believe. Miss Deyncourt most good-naturedly offered to take her with her; but,"—with a shake of the head—"the poor child's totally unrestrained appetites and lamentable self-will made her prefer to remain where she was."

"I am afraid," said Charles, meditatively, as if the idea were entirely a novel one, "Molly is getting a little spoiled among us. It is natural in you, of course; but there is no excuse for me. There never is. There are, I confess, moments when I don't regard the child's immortal welfare sufficiently to make her present existence less enjoyable. What a round of gayety Molly's life is! She flits from flower to flower, so to speak; from me to cook and the jam-pots; from the jam-pots to some fresh delight in the loft, or in your society. Life is one long feast to Molly. Whatever that old impostor the Future may have in store for her, at any rate she is having a good time now."

There was a shade of regretful sadness in Charles's voice that ruffled his aunt.

"The child is being ruined," she said, with resigned bitterness.

"Not a bit of it. I was spoiled as a child, and look at me!"

"You *are* spoiled. I don't spoil you; but other people do. Society does. And the result is that you are so hard to please that I don't believe you will ever marry. You look for a perfection in others which is not to be found in yourself."

"I don't fancy I should appear to advantage side by side with perfection," said Charles, in his most careless manner; and he rose, and wandered away into the garden.

He was irritated with Lady Mary, with her pleased looks during the last few days, with her annoying celerity that afternoon in the garden. It was all the more annoying because he was conscious that Ruth amused and interested him in no slight degree. She had the rare quality of being genuine. She stood for what she was, without effort or self-consciousness. Whether playful or serious, she was always real. Beneath a reserved and rather quiet manner there lurked a piquant unconventionality. The mixture of earnestness and humor, which were so closely interwoven in her nature that he could never tell which would come uppermost, had a strange attraction for him. He had grown accustomed to watch for and try to provoke the sudden gleam of fun in the serious eyes, which always preceded a retort given with an air of the sweetest feminine meekness, which would make Ralph rub himself all over with glee, and tell Charles, chuckling, he "would not get much change out of Ruth."

If only she had not been asked to Atherstone on purpose to meet him. If only Lady Mary had not arranged it; if only Evelyn did not know it; if only Ralph had not guessed it; if only he himself had not seen it from the first instant! Ruth and Molly were the only two unconscious persons in the house.

"I wonder," said Charles to himself, "why people can't allow me to manage my own affairs? Oh, what a world it is for unmarried men with money! Why did I not marry fifteen years ago, when every woman with a straight nose was an angel of light; when I felt a noble disregard for such minor details as character, mind, sympathy, if the hair and the eyes were the right shade? Why did I not marry when I was out of favor with my father, when I was head over ears in debt, and when at least I could feel sure no one would marry me for my money? Molly," as that young lady came running towards him with lingering traces of jam upon her flushed countenance, "you have arrived just in time. Uncle Charles was getting so dull without you. What have you been after all this time?"

"Cook and me have made thirty-one pots and a little one," said Molly, inserting a very sticky hand into Charles's. "And your Mr. Brown helped. Cook told him to go along at first, which wasn't kind, was it? but he stayed all the same; and I skimmed with a big spoon, and she poured it in the pots. Only they aren't covered up with paper yet, if you want to see them. And oh! Uncle Charles, what *do* you think? Father and mother have come back from their ride, and that nice funny man who was at the school-feast is coming here to-morrow, and I shall show him my guinea-pigs. He said he wanted to see them very much."

"Oh, he did, did he? When was that?"

"At the school-feast. Oh!" with enthusiasm, "he was so nice, Uncle Charles, so attentive, and getting things when you want them; and the wheel went over his foot when he was shaking hands, and he did not mind a bit; and he filled our teapots for us—Ruth's big one, you know, that holds such a lot."

"Oh! He filled the big teapot, did he?"

"Yes, and mine too; and then he helped us to unpack the dolls. He was so kind to me and Cousin Ruth."

"Kind to Miss Deyncourt, was he?"

"Yes; and when we went away he ran and opened the gate for us. Oh, there comes Cousin Ruth back again in the carriage. I'll run and tell her he's coming. She *will* be glad."

"Aunt Mary is right," said Charles, watching his niece disappear. "Molly has formed a habit of expressing herself with unnecessary freedom. Decidedly she is a little spoiled."

CHAPTER IX

Dare arrived at Atherstone the following afternoon. Evelyn and Ralph, who had enlarged on the state of morbid depression of the lonely inhabitant of Vandon, were rather taken aback by the jaunty appearance of the sufferer when he appeared, overflowing with evident satisfaction and small-talk, his face wreathed with smiles.

"He bears up wonderfully," said Charles aside to Ruth, later in the evening, as Dare warbled a very discreet selection of his best songs after dinner. "No one knows better than myself that many a breaking heart beats beneath a smiling waistcoat, but unless we had been told beforehand we should never have guessed it in his case."

Dare, who was looking at Ruth, and saw Charles go and sit down by her, brought his song to an abrupt conclusion, and made his way to her also.

"You also sing, Miss Deyncourt?" he asked. "I am sure, from your face, you sing."

"I do."

"Thank Heaven!" said Charles, fervently. "I did you an injustice. I thought you were going to say 'a little.' Every singing young lady I ever met, when asked that question, invariably replied 'a little.'"

"I leave my friends to say that for me," said Ruth.

"Perhaps you yourself sing a *little*?" asked Dare, wishing Charles would leave Ruth's ball of wool alone.

"No," said Charles; "I have no tricks." And he rose and went off to the newspaper-table. Dare's songs were all very well, but really his voice was nothing so very wonderful, and he was not much of an acquisition in other ways.

Then Dare took his opportunity. He dropped into Charles's vacant chair; he wound wool; he wished to learn to knit; his inquiring mind craved for information respecting shooting-stockings. He talked of music; of songs—Italian, French, and English; of American nigger melodies. Would Miss Deyncourt sing? Might he accompany her? Ah! she preferred the simple old English ballads. He *loved* the simple English ballad.

And Ruth, nothing loath, sang in her fresh, clear voice one song after another, Dare accompanying her with rapid sympathy and ease.

Charles put down his paper and moved slightly, so that he had a better view of the piano. Evelyn laid down her work and looked affectionately at Ruth.

"Exquisite," said Lady Mary from time to time, who had said the same of Lady Grace's wavering little soprano.

"You also sing duets? You sing duets?" eagerly inquired Dare, the music-stool creaking with his suppressed excitement; and, without waiting for an answer, he began playing the opening chords of "Greeting."

The two voices rose and fell together, now soft, now triumphant, harmonizing as if they sung together for years. Dare's second was low, pathetic, and it blended at once with Ruth's clear young contralto. Charles wondered that the others should applaud when the duet was finished. Ruth's voice went best alone in his opinion.

"And the 'Cold Blast'?" asked Dare, immediately afterwards. "The 'Cold Blast' was here a moment ago,"—turning the leaves over rapidly. "You are not tired, Miss Deyncourt?"

"Tired!" replied Ruth, her eyes sparkling. "It never tires me to sing. It rests me."

"Ah! so it is with me. That is just how I feel," said Dare. "To sing, or to listen to the voice of—of—"

"Of what? Confound him!" wondered Charles.

"Of *another*," said Dare. "Ah, here he is!" and he pounced on another song, and lightly touched the opening chords.

"'Oh! wert thou in the cold blast,'"

sang Ruth, fresh and sweet.

"'I'd shelter thee,'"

Dare assured her with manly fervor. He went on to say what he would do if he were monarch of the realm, affirming that the brightest jewel of his crown would be his queen.

"Anyhow, he can't pronounce Scotch," Charles thought.

"Would be his queen," Dare repeated, with subdued emotion and an upward glance at Ruth, which she was too much absorbed in the song to see, but which did not escape Charles. Dare's dark sentimental eyes spoke volumes of—not sermons—at that moment.

"Oh, Uncle Charles!" whispered Molly, who had been allowed to sit up about two hours beyond her nominal bedtime, at which hour she rarely felt disposed to retire—"oh, Uncle Charles! 'The brightest jewel in his crown!' Don't you wish you and me could sing together like that?"

Charles moved impatiently, and took up his paper again.

The evening passed all too quickly for Dare, who loved music and the sound of his own voice, and he had almost forgotten, until Charles left him and Ralph alone together in the smoking-room, that he had come to discuss his affairs with the latter.

"Dear me," said Evelyn, who had followed her cousin to her room after they had dispersed for the night, and was looking out of Ruth's window, "that must be Charles walking up and down on the lawn. Well, now, how thoughtful he is to leave Mr. Dare and Ralph together. You know, Ruth, poor Mr. Dare's affairs are in a very bad way, and he has come to talk things over with my Ralph."

"I hope Ralph will make him put his cottages in order," said Ruth, with sudden interest, shaking back her hair from her shoulders. "Do you think he will?"

"Whatever Ralph advises will be sure to be right," replied Evelyn, with the soft conviction of his infallibility which caused her to be considered by most of Ralph's masculine friends an ideal wife. It is women without reasoning powers of any kind whom the nobler sex should be careful to marry if they wish to be regarded through life in this delightful way by their wives. Men not particularly heroic in themselves, who yet are anxious to pose as heroes in their domestic circle, should remember that the smallest modicum of common-sense on the part of the worshipper will inevitably mar a happiness, the very existence of which depends entirely on a blind unreasoning devotion. In middle life the absence of reason begins perhaps to be felt; but why in youth take thought for such a far-off morrow!

"I hope he will," said Ruth, half to herself. "What an opportunity that man has if he only sees it. There is so much to be done, and it is all in his hands."

"Yes, it's not entailed; but I don't think there is so very much," said Evelyn. "But then, so long as people are nice, I never care whether they are rich or poor. That is the first question I ask when people come into the neighborhood. Are they really nice? Dear me, Ruth, what beautiful hair you have; and mine coming off so! And, talking of hair, did you ever see anything like Mr. Dare's? Somebody must really speak to him about it. If he would keep his hands still, and not talk so quick, and let his hair grow a little, I really think he would not look so like a foreigner."

"I don't suppose he minds looking like one."

"My *dear!*"

"His mother was a Frenchwoman, wasn't she? I am sure I have heard so fifty times since his uncle died."

"And if she was," said Evelyn, reprovingly, "is not that an extra reason for his giving up anything that will remind people of it? And we ought to try and forget it, Ruth, and behave just the same to him as if she had been an Englishwoman. I wonder if he is a Roman Catholic?"

"Ask him."

"I hope he is not," continued Evelyn, taking up her candle to go. "We never had one to stay in the house before. I don't mean," catching a glimpse of Ruth's face, "that Catholics are—well—I don't mean *that*. But still, you know, one would not like to make great *friends* with a Catholic, would one, Ruth? And he is so nice and so amusing that I do hope, as he is going to be a neighbor, he is a Protestant." And after a few more remarks of about the same calibre from Evelyn, the two cousins kissed and parted for the night.

"Will he do it?" said Ruth to herself, when she was alone. "Has he character enough, and perseverance enough, and money enough? Oh, I wish Uncle John would talk to him!"

Ruth was not aware that one word from herself would have more weight with a man like Dare than any number from an angel of heaven, if that angel were of the masculine gender. If at the other side of the house Dare could have known how earnestly Ruth was thinking about him, he would not have been surprised (for he was not without experience), but he would have felt immensely flattered.

Vandon lay in a distant part of Mr. Alwynn's parish, and a perpetual curate had charge of the district. Mr. Alwynn consequently seldom went there, but on the few occasions on which Ruth had accompanied him in his periodical visits she had seen enough. Who cares for a recital of what she saw? Misery and want are so common. We can see them for ourselves any day. In Ruth's heart a great indignation had kindled against old Mr. Dare, of Vandon, who was inaccessible as a ghost in his own house, haunting the same rooms, but never to be found when Mr. Alwynn called upon him to "put things before him in their true light." And when Mr. Dare descended to the Vandon vault, all Mr. Alwynn's interest, and consequently a good deal of Ruth's, had centred in the new heir, who was so difficult to find, and who ultimately turned up from the other end of nowhere just when people were beginning to despair of his ever turning up at all.

And now that he had come, would he make the crooked straight? Would the new broom sweep clean? Ruth recalled the new broom's brown handsome face, with the eager eyes and raised eyebrows, and involuntarily shook her head. It is difficult to be an impartial judge of any one with a feeling for music and a pathetic tenor voice; but the face she had called to mind did not inspire her with confidence. It was kindly, amiable, pleasant; but was it strong? In other words, was it not a trifle weak?

She found herself comparing it with another, a thin, reserved face, with keen light eyes and a firm mouth; a mouth with a cigar in it at that moment on the lawn. The comparison, however, did not help her meditations much, being decidedly prejudicial to the "new broom;" and the faint chime of the clock on the dressing-table breaking in on them at the same moment, she dismissed them for the night, and proceeded to busy herself putting to bed her various little articles of jewellery before betaking herself there also.

Any doubts entertained by Evelyn about Dare's religious views were completely set at rest the following morning, which happened to be a Sunday. He appeared at breakfast in a black frock-coat, the splendor of which quite threw Ralph's ancient Sunday garment into the shade. He wore also a chastened, decorous aspect, which seemed unfamiliar to his mobile face, and rather ill suited to it. After breakfast, he inquired when service would be, and expressed a wish to attend it. He brought down a high hat and an enormous prayer-book, and figured with them in the garden.

"Who is going to Greenacre, and who is going to Slumberleigh?" called out Ralph, from the smoking-room window. "Because, if any of you are going to foot it to Slumberleigh, you had better be starting. Which are you going to, Charles?"

"I am going where Molly goes. Which is it to be, Molly?"

"Slumberleigh," said Molly, with decision, "because it's the shortest sermon, and I want to see the little foal in Brown's field."

"Slumberleigh be it," said Charles. "Now, Miss Deyncourt," as Ruth appeared, "which church are you going to support—Greenacre, which is close in more senses than one, where they never open the windows, and the clergyman preaches for an hour; or Slumberleigh, shady, airy, cool, lying past a meadow with a foal in it? If I may offer that as any inducement, Molly and I intend to patronize Slumberleigh."

Ruth said she would do the same.

"Now, Dare, *you* will be able to decide whether Greenacre, with a little fat tower, or Slumberleigh, with a beautiful tall steeple, suits your religious views best."

"I will also go to Slumberleigh," said Dare, without a moment's hesitation.

"I thought so. I suppose,"—to Ralph and Evelyn—"you are going to Greenacre with Aunt Mary? Tell her I have gone to church, will you? It will cheer her up. Sunday is a very depressing day with her, I know. She thinks of all she has done in the week, preparatory to doing a little more on Monday. Good-bye. Now then, Molly, have you got your prayer-book? Miss Deyncourt, I don't see yours anywhere. Oh, there it is! No, don't let Dare carry it for you. Give it to me. He will have enough to do, poor fellow, to travel with his own. Come, Molly! Is Vic chained up? Yes, I can hear him howling. The craving for church privileges of that dumb animal, Miss Deyncourt, is an example to us Christians. Molly, have you got your penny? Miss Deyncourt, can I accommodate you with a threepenny bit? Now, *are* we all ready to start?"

"When this outburst of eloquence has subsided," said Ruth, "the audience will be happy to move on."

And so they started across the fields, where the grass was already springing faint and green after the haymaking. There was a fresh wandering air, which fluttered the ribbons in Molly's hat, as she danced on ahead, frisking in her short white skirt beside her uncle, her hand in his. Charles was the essence of wit to Molly, with his grave face that so seldom smiled, and the twinkle in the kind eyes, that always went before those wonderful, delightful jokes which he alone could make. Sometimes, as she laughed, she looked back at Ruth and Dare, half a field behind, in pity at what they were missing.

"Shall we wait and tell them that story, Uncle Charles?"

"No, Molly. I dare say he is telling her another which is just as good."

"I don't think he knows any like yours."

"Some people like the old, old story best."

"Do I know the old, old one, Uncle Charles?"

"No, Molly."

"Can you tell it?"

"No. I have never been able to tell that particular story."

"And do you really think he is telling it to her now?" with a backward glance.

"Not at this moment. It's no good running back. He's only thinking about it now. He will tell it her in about a month or six weeks' time."

"I hope I shall be there when he tells it."

"I hope you may; but I don't think it is likely. And now, Molly, set your hat straight, and leave off jumping. I never jump when I go to church with Aunt Mary. Quietly now, for there's the church, and Mr. Alwynn's looking out of the window."

Dare, meanwhile, walking with Ruth, caught sight of the church and lych-gate with heart-felt regret. The stretches of sunny meadowland, the faint glamour of church bells, the pale refined face beside him, had each individually and all three together appealed to his imagination, always vivid when he himself was concerned. He suddenly felt as if a great gulf had fixed itself, without any will of his own, between his old easy-going life and the new existence that was opening out before him.

He had crossed from the old to the new without any perception of such a gulf, and now, as he looked back, it seemed to yawn between him and all that hitherto he had been. He did not care to look back, so he looked forward. He felt as if he were the central figure (when was he *not* a central figure?) in a new drama. He was fond of acting, on and off the stage, and now he seemed to be playing a new part, in which he was not yet thoroughly at ease, but which he rather suspected would become him exceedingly well. It amused him to see himself going to church—*to church*—to hear himself conversing on flowers and music with a young English girl. The idea that he was rapidly falling in love was specially delightful. He called himself a *vieux scélérat*, and watched the progress of feelings which he felt did him credit with extreme satisfaction. He and Ruth arrived at the church porch all too soon for Dare; and though he had the pleasure of sitting on one side of her during the service, he would have preferred that Charles, of whom he felt a vague distrust, had not happened to be on the other.

CHAPTER X

"My dear," said Mrs. Alwynn to her husband that morning, as they started for church across the glebe, "if any of the Atherstone party are in church, as they ought to be, for I hear from Mrs. Smith that they are not at all regular at Greenacre—only went once last Sunday, and then late—I shall just tell Ruth that she is to come back to me to-morrow. A few days won't make any difference to her, and it will fit in so nicely her coming back the day you go to the palace. After all I've done for Ruth—new curtains to her room, and the piano tuned and everything—I don't think she would like to stay there with friends, and me all by myself, without a creature to speak to. Ruth may be only a niece by marriage, but she will see in a moment—"

And in fact she did. When Mrs. Alwynn took her aside after church, and explained the case in the all-pervading whisper for which she had apparently taken out a patent, Ruth could not grasp any reason why she should return to Slumberleigh three days before the time, but she saw at once that return she must if Mrs. Alwynn chose to demand it; and so she yielded with a good grace, and sent Mrs. Alwynn back smiling to the lych-gate, where Mr. Alwynn and Mabel Thursby were talking with Dare and Molly, while Charles interviewed the village policeman at a little distance.

"No news of the tramp," said Charles, meeting Ruth at the gate; and they started homeward in different order to that in which they had come, in spite of a great effort at the last moment on the part of Dare, who thought the old way was better. "The policeman has seen nothing of him. He has gone off to pastures new, I expect."

"I hope he has."

"Mrs. Alwynn does not want you to leave Atherstone to-morrow, does she?"

"I am sorry to say she does."

"But you won't go?"

"I must not only go, but I must do it as if I liked it."

"I hope Evelyn won't allow it."

"While I am living with Mrs. Alwynn, I am bound to do what she likes in small things."

"H'm!"

"I should have thought, Sir Charles, that this particularly feminine and submissive sentiment would have met with your approval."

"It does; it does," said Charles, hastily. "Only, after the stubborn rigidity of your—shall I say your—week-day character, especially as regards money, this softened Sabbath mood took me by surprise for a moment."

"You should see me at Slumberleigh," said Ruth, with a smile half sad, half humorous. "You should see me tying up Uncle John's flowers, or holding Aunt Fanny's wools. Nothing more entirely feminine and young lady-like can be imagined."

"It must be a great change, after living with a woman like Lady Deyncourt—to whose house I often went years ago, when her son was living—to come to a place like Slumberleigh."

"It *is* a great change. I am ashamed to say how much I felt it at first. I don't know how to express it; but everything down here seems so small and local, and hard and fast."

"I know," said Charles, gently; and they walked on in silence. "And yet," he said at last, "it seems to me, and I should have thought you would have felt the same, that life is very small, very narrow and circumscribed everywhere; though perhaps more obviously so in Cranfords and Slumberleighs. I have seen a good deal during the last fifteen years. I have mixed with many sorts and conditions of men, but in no class or grade of society have I yet found independent men and women. The groove is as narrow in one class as in another, though in some it is better concealed. I sometimes feel as if I were walking in a ball-room full of people all dancing the lancers. There are different sets, of course—fashionable, political, artistic—but the people in them are all crossing over, all advancing and retiring, with the same apparent aimlessness, or setting to partners."

"There is occasionally an aim in that."

Charles smiled grimly.

"They follow the music in that as in everything else. You go away for ten years, and still find them, on your return, going through the same figures to new tunes. I wonder if there are any people anywhere in the world who stand on their own feet, and think and act for themselves; who don't set their watches by other people's; who don't live and marry and die by rote, expecting to go straight up to heaven by rote afterwards?"

"I believe there are such people," said Ruth, earnestly; "I have had glimpses of them, but the real ones look like the shadows, and the shadows like the real ones, and—we miss them in the crowd."

"Or one thinks one finds them, and they turn out only clever imitations after all. In these days there is a mania for shamming originality of some kind. I am always imagining people I meet are real, and not shadows, until one day I unintentionally put my hand through them, and find out my mistake. I am getting tired of being taken in."

"And some day you will get tired of being cynical."

"I am very much obliged to you for your hopeful view of my future. You evidently imagine that I have gone in for the fashionable creed of the young man of the present day. I am not young enough to take pleasure in high collars and cheap cynicism, Miss Deyncourt. Cynical people are never disappointed in others, as I so often am, because they expect the worst. In theory I respect and admire my fellow-creatures, but they continually exasperate me because they won't allow me to do so in real life. I have still—I blush to own it—a lingering respect for women, though they have taken pains to show me, time after time, what a fool I am for such a weakness."

Charles looked intently at Ruth. Women are so terribly apt in handling any subject to make it personal. Would she fire up, or would she, like so many women, join in abuse of her own sex? She did neither. She was looking straight in front of her, absently watching the figures of Dare and Molly in the next field. Then she turned her grave, thoughtful glance towards him.

"I think respect is never weakness," she said. "It is a sign of strength, even when it is misplaced. There is not much to admire in cunning people who are never taken in. The best people I have known, the people whom it did me good to be with, have been those who respected others and themselves. Do not be in too great a hurry to get rid of any little fragment that still remains. You may want it when it is gone."

Charles's apathetic face had become strangely earnest. There was a keen, searching look in his tired, restless eyes. He was about to make some answer, when he suddenly became aware of Dare and Molly sitting perched on a gate close at hand waiting for them. Never had he perceived Molly's little brown face with less pleasure than at that moment. She scrambled down with a noble disregard of appearances, and tried to take his hand. But it was coolly withdrawn. Charles fell behind on some pretence of fastening the gate, and Molly had to content herself with Ruth's and Dare's society for the remainder of the walk.

Ruth had almost forgotten, until Molly suggested at luncheon a picnic for the following day, that she was returning to Slumberleigh on Monday morning; and when she made the fact known, Ralph had to be "hushed" several times by Evelyn for muttering opinions behind the sirloin respecting

Mrs. Alwynn, which Evelyn seemed to have heard before, and to consider unsuited to the ears of that lady's niece.

"But if you go away, Cousin Ruth, we can't have the picnic. Can we, Uncle Charles?"

"Impossible, Molly. Rather bread and butter at home than a mixed biscuit in the open air without Miss Deyncourt."

"Is Mrs. Alwynn suffering?" asked Lady Mary, politely, down the table.

Ruth explained that she was not in ill-health, but that she did wish to be left alone; and Ralph was "hushed" again.

Lady Mary was annoyed, or, more properly speaking, she was "moved in the spirit," which in a Churchwoman seems to be the same thing as annoyance in the unregenerate or unorthodox mind. She regretted Ruth's departure more than any one, except perhaps Ruth herself. She had watched the girl very narrowly, and she had seen nothing to make her alter the opinion she had formed of her; indeed, she was inclined to advance beyond it. Even she could not suspect that Ruth had "played her cards well;" although she would have aided and abetted her in any way in her power, if Ruth had shown the slightest consciousness of holding cards at all, or being desirous of playing them. Her frank yet reserved manner, her distinguished appearance, her sense of humor (which Lady Mary did not understand, but which she perceived others did), and the quiet *savoir faire* of her treatment of Dare's advances, all enhanced her greatly in the eyes of her would-be aunt. She bade her good-bye with genuine regret; the only person who bore her departure without a shade of compunction being Dare, who stood by the carriage till the last moment, assuring Ruth that he hoped to come over to the rectory very shortly; while Charles and Molly held the gate open meanwhile, at the end of the short drive.

"I know that Frenchman means business," said Lady Mary wrathfully to herself, as she watched the scene from the garden. Her mind, from the very severity of its tension, was liable to occasional lapses of this painful kind from the spiritual and ecclesiastical to the mundane and transitory. "I saw it directly he came into the house; and with *his* opportunities, and living within a stone's-throw, I should not wonder if he were to succeed. Any man would fetch a fancy price at Slumberleigh; and the most fastidious woman in the world ceases to be critical if she is reduced to the proper state of dulness. He is handsome, too, in his foreign way. But she does not like him now. She is inclined to like Charles, though she does not know it. There is an attraction between the two. I knew there would be. And he likes her. Oh, what fools men are! He will go away; and Dare, on the contrary, will ride over to Slumberleigh every day, and by the time he is engaged to her Charles will see her again, and find out that he is in love with her himself. Oh, the folly, the density, of unmarried men! and, indeed," (with a sudden recollection of the deceased Mr. Cunningham), "of the whole race of them! But of all men I have ever known, I really think the most provoking is Charles."

"Musing?" inquired her nephew, sauntering up to her.

"I was thinking that we had just lost the pleasantest person of our little party," said Lady Mary, viciously seizing up her work.

"I am still here," suggested Charles, by way of consolation. "I don't start for Norway in Wyndham's yacht for three days to come."

"Do you mean to say you are going to Norway?"

"I forget whether it was to be Norway; but I know I'm booked to go yachting somewhere. It's Wyndham's new toy. He paid through the parental nose for it, and he made me promise in London to go with him on his first cruise. I believe a very charming Miss Wyndham is to be of the party."

"And how long, pray, are you going to yacht with Miss Wyndham?"

"It is with her brother I propose to go. I thought I had explained that before. I shall probably cruise about, let me see, for three weeks or so, till the grouse-shooting begins. Then I am due in Scotland, at the Hope-Actons', and several other places."

Lady Mary laid down her work, and rose to her feet, her thin hand closing tightly over the silver crook of her stick.

"Charles," she said, in a voice trembling with anger, looking him full in the face, "you are a fool!" and she passed him without another word, and hobbled away rapidly into the house.

"Am I?" said Charles, half aloud to himself, when the last fold of her garment had been twitched out of sight through the window.

"*Am I?* Molly," with great gravity, as Molly appeared, "yes, you may sit on my knee; but don't wriggle. Molly, what is a fool?"

"I think it's Raca, only worse," said Molly. "Uncle Charles, Mr. Dare is going away too. His dog-cart had just come into the yard."

"Has it? I hope he won't keep it waiting."

"You are not going away, are you?"

"Not for three days more."

"Tuesday, Wednesday, Thursday. Why, they will be gone in a moment."

But to Charles they seemed three very long days indeed. He was annoyed with himself for having made so many engagements before he left London. At the time there did not seem anything better to be done, and he supposed he must go somewhere; but now he thought he would have liked to stay on at Atherstone, though he would not have said so to Lady Mary for worlds. He was tired of rushing up and down. He was not so fond of yachting, after all; and he remembered that he had been many times to Norway.

"I would get out of it if I could," he said to Lady Mary on the last morning; "and of this blue serge suit, too (you should see Miss Wyndham in blue serge!); but it is not a question of pleasure, but of principle. I don't like to throw over Wyndham at the last moment, after what you said when I failed the Hope-Actons last year. Twins could not feel more exactly together than you and I do where a principle is involved. I see you are about to advise me to keep my engagement. Do not trouble to do so; I am going to Portsmouth by the mid-day train. Brown is at this moment packing my telescope and life-belt."

CHAPTER XI

It was the end of August. The little lawn at Slumberleigh Rectory was parched and brown. The glebe beyond was brown; so was the field beyond that. The thirsty road was ash-white between its gray hedge-rows. It was hotter in the open air than in the house, but Ruth had brought her books out into the garden all the same, and had made a conscientious effort to read under the chestnut-tree.

For under the same roof with Mrs. Alwynn she had soon learned that application or study of any kind was an impossibility. Mrs. Alwynn had several maxims as to the conduct of herself, and consequently of every one else, and one of those to which she most frequently gave utterance was that "young people should always be cheery and sociable, and should not be left too much to themselves."

When in the winter Mr. Alwynn had brought home Ruth, quite overwhelmed for the time by the shock of the first real trouble she had known, Mrs. Alwynn was kindness itself in the way of sweet-breads and warm rooms; but the only thing Ruth craved for, to be left alone, she would not allow for a moment. No! Mrs. Alwynn was cheerful, brisk, and pious at intervals. If she found her niece was sitting in her own room, she bustled up-stairs, poked the fire, gave her a kiss, and finally brought her down to the drawing-room, where she told her she would be as quiet as in her own room. She need not be afraid her uncle would come in; and she must not allow herself to get moped. What would she, Mrs. Alwynn, have done, she would like to know, if, when she was in trouble—and she knew what trouble meant, if any one did—she had allowed herself to get moped. Ruth must try and bear up. And at Lady Deyncourt's age it was quite to be expected. And Ruth must remember she still had a sister, and that there was a happy home above. And now, if she would get that green wool out of the red plush iron (which really was a work-box—such a droll idea, wasn't it?), Ruth should hold the wool, and they would have a cosey little chat till luncheon time.

And so Mrs. Alwynn did her duty by her niece; and Ruth, in the dark days that followed her grandmother's death, took all the little kindnesses in the spirit in which they were meant, and did her duty by her aunt.

But after a time Mrs. Alwynn became more exacting. Ruth was visibly recovering from what Mrs. Alwynn called "her bereavement." She could smile again without an effort; she took long walks with Mr. Alwynn, and later in the spring paid a visit to her uncle, Lord Polesworth. It was after this visit that Mrs. Alwynn became more exacting. She had borne with half attention and a lack of interest in crewel-work while Ruth was still "fretting," as she termed it. But when a person lays aside crape, and goes into half-mourning, the time had come when she may—nay, when she ought to be "chatty." This time had come with Ruth, but she was not "chatty." Like Mrs. Dombey, she did not make an effort, and, as the months passed on, Mrs. Alwynn began to shake her head, and to fear that "there was some officer or something on her mind." Mrs. Alwynn always called soldiers officers, and doctors physicians.

Ruth, on her side, was vaguely aware that she did not give satisfaction. The small-talk, the perpetual demand on her attention, the constant interruptions, seemed to benumb what faculties she had. Her mind became like a machine out of work—rusty, creaking, difficult to set going. If she had half an hour of leisure she could not fix her attention to anything. She, who in her grandmother's time had been so keen and alert, seemed to have drifted, in Mrs. Alwynn's society, into a torpid state, from which she made vain attempts to emerge, only to sink the deeper.

When she stood once more, fresh from a fortnight of pleasant intercourse with pleasant people, in the little ornate drawing-room at Slumberleigh, on her return from Atherstone, the remembrance of the dulled, confused state in which she had been living with her aunt returned forcibly to her mind. The various articles of furniture, the red silk handkerchiefs dabbed behind pendent plates, the musical elephants on the mantle-piece, the imitation Eastern antimacassars, the shocking fate, in the way of nailed and glued pictorial ornamentation, that had overtaken the back of the cottage piano— indeed, all the various objects of luxury and *vertu* with which Mrs. Alwynn had surrounded herself, seemed to recall to Ruth, as the apparatus of the sick-room recalls the illness to the patient, the stupor into which she had fallen in their company. With her eyes fixed upon the new brass pig (that was at heart a pen-wiper) which Mrs. Alwynn had pointed out as a gift of Mabel Thursby, who always brought her back some little "tasty thing from London"—with her eyes on the brass pig, Ruth resolved that, come what would, she would not allow herself to sink into such a state of mental paralysis again.

To read a book of any description was out of the question in the society of Mrs. Alwynn. But Ruth, with the connivance of Mr. Alwynn, devised a means of eluding her aunt. At certain hours of the day she was lost regularly, and not to be found. It was summer, and the world, or at least the neighborhood of Slumberleigh Rectory, which was the same thing, was all before her where to choose. In after-years she used to say that some books had always remained associated with certain places in her mind. With Emerson she learned to associate the scent of hay, the desultory remarks of hens, and the sudden choruses of ducks. Carlyle's "Sartor Resartus," which she read for the first time this year, always recalled to her afterwards the leathern odor of the box-room, with an occasional *soupçon* of damp flapping linen in the orchard, which spot was not visible from the rectory windows.

Gradually Mrs. Alwynn became aware of the fact that Ruth was never to be seen with a book in her hand, and she expressed fears that the latter was not keeping up her reading.

"And if you don't like to read to yourself, my dear, you can read to me while I work. German, now. I like the sound of German very well. It brings back the time when your Uncle John and I went up the Rhine on our honey-moon. And then, for English reading there's a very nice book Uncle John has somewhere on natural history, called 'Animals of a Quiet Life,' by a Mr. Hare, too—so comical, I always think. It's good for you to be reading something. It is what your poor dear granny would have wished if she had been alive. Only it must not be poetry, Ruth, not poetry."

Mrs. Alwynn did not approve of poetry. She was wont to say that for her part she liked only what was perfectly *true*, by which it is believed she meant prose.

She had no books of her own. In times of illness she borrowed from Mrs. Thursby (who had all Miss Young's works, and selections from the publications of the S.P.C.K.). On Sundays, when she could not work, she read, half aloud, of course, with sighs at intervals, a little manual called "Gold Dust," or a smaller one still called "Pearls of Great Price," which she had once recommended to Charles, whom she knew slightly, and about whom she affected to know a great deal, which nothing (except pressing) would induce her to repeat; which rendered the application of the "Pearls," to be followed by the "Dust," most essential to his future welfare.

On this particular morning in August, Ruth had slipped out as far as the chestnut-tree, the lower part of which was hidden from the rectory windows by a blessed yew hedge. It was too hot to walk, it was too hot to draw, it was even too hot to read. It did not seem, however, to be too hot to *ride*, for presently she heard a horse's hoofs clattering across the stones of the stable-yard, and she knew, from the familiarity of the sound at that hour of the day, that Dare had probably ridden over, and, more probably still, would stay to luncheon.

The foreign gentleman, as all the village people called him, had by this time become quite an institution in the neighborhood of Vandon. Every one liked him, and he liked every one. Like the sun, he shone upon the just and unjust. He went to every tennis-party to which he was invited. He was pleased if people were at home when he called. He became in many houses a privileged person, and he never abused his privileges. Women especially liked him. He had what Mrs. Eccles defined as "such a way with him;" his way being to make every woman he met think that she was particularly interesting in his eyes—for the time being. Men did not, of course, care for him so much. When he stayed anywhere, it was vaguely felt by the sterner sex of the party that he stole a march upon them. While they were smoking, after their kind, in clusters on the lawn, it would suddenly be observed that he was sitting in the drawing-room, giving a lesson in netting, or trying over a new song encircled by young ladyhood. It was felt that he took an unfair advantage. What business had he to come down to tea in that absurd amber plush smoking-suit, just because the elder ladies had begged to see it? It was all the more annoying, because he looked so handsome in it. Like most men who are admired by women, he was not much liked by men.

But the house to which he came the oftenest was Slumberleigh Rectory. He was faithful to his early admiration of Ruth; and the only obstacle to his making her (in his opinion) happy among women, namely, her possible want of fortune, had long since been removed by the confidential remarks of Mrs. Alwynn. To his foreign habits and ideas fourteen or fifteen hundred a year represented a very large sum. In his eyes Ruth was an heiress, and in all good earnest he set himself to win her. Mr. Alwynn had now become the proper person to consult regarding his property; and at first, to Ruth's undisguised satisfaction, he consulted him nearly every other day, his horse at last taking the turn for Slumberleigh as a matter of course. Many a time, in these August days, might Mrs. Eccles and all the other inhabitants of Slumberleigh have seen Dare ride up the little street, taking as much active exercise as his horse, only skyward; the saddle being to him merely a point of rebound.

But if the object of his frequent visits was misunderstood by Ruth at first, Dare did not allow it to remain so long. And not only Ruth herself, but

Mr. and Mrs. Alwynn, and the rectory servants, and half the parish were soon made aware of the state of his affections. What was the good of being in love, of having in view a social aim of such a praiseworthy nature, if no one were aware of the same? Dare was not the man to hide even a night-light under a bushel; how much less a burning and a shining hymeneal torch such as this. His sentiments were strictly honorable. If he raised expectations, he was also quite prepared to fulfil them. Miss Deyncourt was quite right to treat him with her adorable, placid assumption of indifference until his attentions were more avowed. In the mean while she was an angel, a lily, a pearl, a star, and several other things, animal, vegetable, and mineral, which his vivid imagination chose to picture her. But whatever Dare's faults may have been—and Ruth was not blind to them—he was at least head over ears in love with her, fortune or none; and as his attachment deepened, it burned up like fire all the little follies with which it had begun.

A clergyman has been said to have made love to the helpmeet of his choice out of the Epistle to the Galatians. Dare made his out of material hardly more promising—plans for cottages, and estimates of repairs. He had quickly seen how to interest Ruth, though the reason for such an eccentric interest puzzled him. However, he turned it to his advantage. Ruth encouraged, suggested, sympathized in all the little he was already doing, and the much that he proposed to do.

Of late, however, a certain not ungrounded suspicion had gradually forced itself upon her which had led her to withdraw as much as she could from her former intercourse with Dare; but her change of manner had not quite the effect she had intended.

"She thinks I am not serious," Dare had said to himself; "she thinks that I play with her feelings. She does not know me. To-morrow I ride over; I set her mind at rest. To-morrow I propose; I make an offer; I claim that adored hand; I—become engaged."

Accordingly, not long after the clatter of horse's hoofs in the stable-yard, Dare himself appeared in the garden, and perceiving Ruth, for whom he was evidently looking, informed her that he had ridden over to ask Mr. Alwynn to support him at a dinner his tenants were giving in his honor—a custom of the Vandon tenantry from time immemorial on the accession of a new landlord. He spoke absently; and Ruth, looking at him more closely as he stood before her, wondered at his altered manner. He had a rose in his button-hole. He always had a rose in his button-hole; but somehow this was more of a rose than usual. His mustaches were twirled up with unusual grace.

"You will find Mr. Alwynn in the study," said Ruth, hurriedly.

His only answer was to cast aside his whip and gloves, as possible impediments later on, and to settle himself, with an elegant arrangement of the choicest gaiters, on the grass at her feet.

It is probably very disagreeable to repeat in any form, however discreetly worded, the old phrase—

"The reason why I cannot tell,
But I don't like you, Doctor Fell."

But it must be especially disagreeable, if a refusal is at first not taken seriously, to be obliged to repeat it, still more plainly, a second time. It was Ruth's fate to be obliged to do this, and to do it hurriedly, or she foresaw complications might arise.

At last Dare understood, and the sudden utter blankness of his expression smote Ruth to the heart. He had loved her in his way after all. It is a bitter thing to be refused. She felt that she had been almost brutal in her direct explicitness, called forth at the moment by an instinct that he would proceed to extreme measures unless peremptorily checked.

"I am so sorry," she said, involuntarily.

Poor Dare, who had recovered a certain amount of self-possession, now that he was on his feet again, took up his gloves and riding-whip in silence. All his jaunty self-assurance had left him. He seemed quite stunned. His face under his brown skin was very pale.

"I am so sorry," said Ruth again, feeling horribly guilty.

"It is I who am sorry," he said, humbly. "I have made a great mistake, for which I ask pardon;" and, after looking at her for a moment, in blank incertitude as to whether she could really be the same person whom he had come to seek in such happy confidence half an hour before, he raised his hat, his new light gray hat, and was gone.

Ruth watched him go, and when he had disappeared, she sat down again mechanically in the chair from which she had risen a few moments before, and pressed her hands tightly together. She ought not to have allowed such a thing to happen, she said to herself. Somehow it had never presented itself to her in its serious aspect before. It is difficult to take a vain man seriously. Poor Mr. Dare! She had not known he was capable of caring so much about anything. He had never appeared to such advantage in her eyes as he had done when he had left her the moment before, grave and silent. She felt she had misjudged him. He was not so frivolous, after all. And now that her influence was at an end, who would keep him up to the mark about the various duties which she knew now he had begun to fulfil only to please her? Oh, who would help and encourage him in that most difficult of positions, a land-owner without means sufficient for doing the best by land and tenantry? She instinctively felt that he could not be relied upon for continuous exertion by himself.

"I wish I could have liked him," said Ruth to herself. "I wish, I wish, I could!"

CHAPTER XII

During the whole of the following week Dare appeared no more at Slumberleigh. Mrs. Alwynn, whose time was much occupied as a rule in commenting on the smallest doings of her neighbors, and in wondering why they left undone certain actions which she herself would have performed in their place, Mrs. Alwynn would infallibly have remarked upon his absence many times during every hour of the day, had not her attention been distracted for the time being by a one-horse fly which she had seen go up the road on the afternoon of the day of Dare's last visit, the destination of which had filled her soul with anxious conjecture.

She did not ascertain till the following day that it had been ordered for Mrs. Smith, of Greenacre; though, as she told Ruth, she might have known that, as Mr. Smith was going for a holiday with Mrs. Smith, and their pony lame in its feet; that they would have to have a fly, and with that hill up to Greenacre she was surprised one horse was enough.

When the question of the fly had been thus satisfactorily settled, and Mrs. Alwynn had ceased wondering whether the Smiths had gone to Tenby or to Rhyl (she always imagined people went to one or other of these two places), her whole attention reverted to a screen which she was making, the elegance and novelty of which supplied her with a congenial subject of conversation for many days.

"There is something so new in a screen, an entire screen of Christmas cards," Mrs. Alwynn would remark. "Now, Mrs. Thursby's new screen is all pictures out of the *Graphic*, and those colored Christmas numbers. She has put all her cards in a book. There is something rather *passy* about those albums, I think. Now I fancy this screen will look quite out of the common, Ruth; and when it is done, I shall get some of those Japanese cranes and stand them on the top. Their claws are made to twist round, you know, and I shall put some monkeys—you know those droll chenille monkeys, Ruth—creeping up the sides to meet the cranes. I don't honestly think, my dear"—with complacency—"that many people will have anything like it."

Ruth did not hesitate to say that she felt certain very few would.

Mrs. Alwynn was delighted at the interest she took in her new work. Ruth was coming out at last, she told her husband; and she passed many happy hours entirely absorbed in the arrangement of the cards upon the panels. Ruth, thankful that her attention had been providentially distracted from the matter that filled her own thoughts, in a way that surprised and annoyed her, sorted, and snipped, and pasted, and decided weighty questions as to whether a goitred robin on a twig should be placed next to a smiling plum-pudding, dancing a polka with a turkey, or whether a congealed cross, with "Christian greeting" in icicles on it, should separate the two.

To her uncle Ruth told what had happened; and as he slowly wended his way to Vandon on the day fixed for the tenant's dinner, Mr. Alwynn mused thereon, and I believe, if the truth were known, he was sorry that Dare had been refused. He was a little before his time, and he stopped on the bridge, and looked at the river, as it came churning and sweeping below, fretted out of its usual calm by the mill above. I think that as he leaned over the low stone parapet he made many quiet little reflections besides the involuntary one of himself in the water below. He would have liked (he was conscious that it was selfish, but yet he *would* have liked) to have Ruth near him always. He would have liked to see this strange son of his old friend in good hands, that would lead him—as it is popularly supposed a woman's hand sometimes can—in the way of all others in which Mr. Alwynn was anxious that he should walk; a way in which he sometimes feared that Dare had not made any great progress as yet. Mr. Alwynn felt at times, when conversing with him, that Dare's life could not have been one in which the nobler feelings of his nature had been much brought into play, so crude and unformed were his ideas of principle and responsibility, so slack and easy-going his views of life.

But if Mr. Alwynn felt an occasional twinge of anxiety and misgiving about his young friend, it speedily turned to self-upbraiding for indulging in a cynical, unworthy spirit, which was ever ready to seek out the evil and overlook the good; and he gradually convinced himself that only favorable circumstances were required for the blossoming forth of those noble attributes, of which the faintest indications on Dare's part were speedily magnified by the powerful lens of Mr. Alwynn's charity to an extent which would have filled Dare with satisfaction, and would have overwhelmed a more humble nature with shame.

And Ruth would not have him! Mr. Alwynn remembered a certain passage in his own youth, a long time ago, when somebody (a very foolish somebody, I think) would not have him either; and it was with that remembrance still in his mind that he met Dare, who had come as far as the lodge gates to meet him, and whose forlorn appearance touched Mr. Alwynn's heart the moment he saw him.

There was not time for much conversation. To his astonishment Mr. Alwynn found Dare actually nervous about the coming ordeal; and on the way to the Green Dragon, where the dinner was to be given, he reassured him as best he could, and suggested the kind of answer he should make when his health was drunk.

When, a couple of hours later, all was satisfactorily over, when the last health had been drunk, the last song sung, and Dare was driving Mr. Alwynn home in the shabby old Vandon dog-cart, both men were at first too much overcome by the fumes of tobacco, in which they had been hidden, to say a word to each other. At last, however, Mr. Alwynn drew a long breath, and said, faintly:

"I trust I may never be so hot again. Drive slowly under these trees, Dare. It is cooling to look at them after sitting behind that steaming volcano of a turkey. How is your head getting on? I saw you went in for punch."

"Was that punch?" said Dare. "Then I take no more punch in the future."

"You spoke capitally, and brought in the right sentiment, that there is no place like home, in first-rate style. You see, you need not have been nervous."

"Ah! but it was you who spoke really well," said Dare, with something of his old eager manner. "You know these people. You know their heart. You understand them. Now, for me, I said what you tell me, and they were pleased, but I can never be with them like you. I understand the words they speak, but themselves I do not understand."

"It will come."

"No," with a rare accession of humility. "I have cared for none of these things till—till I came to hear them spoken of at Slumberleigh by you and—and now at first it is smooth, because I say I will do what I can, but soon they will find out I cannot do much, and then—" He shrugged his shoulders.

They drove on in silence.

"But these things are nothing—nothing," burst out Dare at last, in a tremulous voice, "to the one thing I think of all night, all day—how I love Miss Deyncourt, and how," with a simplicity which touched Mr. Alwynn, "she does not love me at all."

There is something pathetic in seeing any cheerful, light-hearted animal reduced to silence and depression. To watch a barking, worrying, jovial puppy suddenly desist from parachute expeditions on unsteady legs, and from shaking imaginary rats, and creep, tail close at home, overcome by affliction, into obscurity, is a sad sight. Mr. Alwynn felt much the same kind of pity for Dare as he glanced at him, resignedly blighted, handsomely forlorn, who but a short time ago had taken life as gayly and easily as a boy home for the holidays.

"Sometimes," said Mr. Alwynn, addressing himself to the mill, and the bridge, and the world in general, "young people change their minds. I have known such things happen."

"I shall never change mine."

"Perhaps not; but others might."

"Ah!" and Dare turned sharply towards Mr. Alwynn, scanning his face with sudden eagerness. "You think—you think, possibly—"

"I don't think anything at all," interposed Mr. Alwynn, rather taken aback at the evident impression his vague words had made, and anxious to qualify them. "I was only speaking generally; but—ahem! there is one point, as we are on the subject, that—"

"Yes, yes?"

"Whether you consider any decision as final or not"—Mr. Alwynn addressed the clouds in the sky—"I think, if you do not wish it to be known that anything has taken place, you had better come and see me occasionally at Slumberleigh. I have missed your visits for the past week. The fact is, Mrs. Alwynn has a way of interesting herself in all her friends. She has a kind heart, and—you—understand—any little difference in their behavior might be observed by her, and might possibly—might possibly"—Mr. Alwynn was at a loss for a word—"be, in short, commented on to others. Suppose now you were to come back with me to tea to-day?"

And Dare went, nothing loath, and arrived at a critical moment in the manufacture of the screen, when all the thickest Christmas cards threatened to resist the influence of paste, and to curl up, to the great anxiety of Mrs. Alwynn.

One of the principle reasons of Dare's popularity was the way in which he threw his whole heart into whatever he was doing, for the time; never for a long time, certainly, for he rarely bored himself or others by adherence to one set of ideas after its novelty had worn off.

And now, as if nothing else existed in the world, and with a grave manner suggesting repressed suffering and manly resignation, he concentrated his whole mind on Mrs. Alwynn's recalcitrant cards, and made Ruth grateful to him by his tact in devoting himself to her aunt and the screen.

"Well, I never!" said Mrs. Alwynn, after he was gone. "I never did see any one like Mr. Dare. I declare he has made the church stick, Ruth, and 'Blessings on my friend,' which turned up at the corners twice when you put it on, and the big middle one of the kittens skating, too! Dear me! I am pleased. I hope Mrs. Thursby won't call till it's finished. But he did not look well, Ruth, did he? Rather pale now, I thought."

"He has had a tiring day," said Ruth.

CHAPTER XIII

At Slumberleigh you have time to notice the change of the seasons. There is no hurry at Slumberleigh. Spring, summer, autumn, and winter, each in their turn, take quite a year to come and go. Three months ago it was August; now September had arrived. It was actually the time of damsons. Those damsons which Ruth had seen dangling for at least three years in the cottage orchards were ripe at last. It seemed ages ago since April, when the village was a foaming mass of damson blossom, and the "plum winter" had set in just when spring really seemed to have arrived for good. It was a well-known thing in Slumberleigh, though Ruth till last April had not been aware of it, that God Almighty always sent cold weather when the Slumberleigh damsons were in bloom, to harden the fruit. And now the lame, the halt, and the aged of Slumberleigh, all with one consent, mounted on tottering ladders to pick their damsons, or that mysterious fruit, closely akin to the same, called "black Lamas ploums."

There were plum accidents, of course, in plenty. The Lord took Mrs. Eccles's own uncle from his half-filled basket to another world, for which, as a "tea and coffee totaller," he was no doubt well prepared. The too receptive organisms of unsuspecting infancy suffered in their turn. In short, it was a busy season for Mr. and Mrs. Alwynn.

Ruth had plenty of opportunities now for making her long-projected sketch of the ruined house of Arleigh, for the old woman who lived in the lodge close by, and had charge of the place, had "ricked" her back in a damson-tree, and Ruth often went to see her. She had been Ruth's nurse in her childhood, and having originally come from Slumberleigh, returned there when the Deyncourt children grew up, and lived happily ever after, with the very blind and entirely deaf old husband of her choice, in the gray stone lodge at Arleigh.

It was on her return from one of these almost daily visits that Mrs. Eccles pounced on Ruth as she passed her gate, and under pretence of inquiring after Mrs. Cotton, informed her that she herself was suffering in no slight degree. Ruth, who suddenly remembered that she had been remiss in "dropping in" on Mrs. Eccles of late, dropped in then and there to make up for past delinquencies.

"Is it rheumatism again?" she asked, as Mrs. Eccles seemed inclined to run off at once into a report of the goings on of Widow Jones's Sally.

"Not that, my dear, so much as a sinking," said Mrs. Eccles, passing her hand slowly over what seemed more like a rising than a depression in her ample figure. "But there! I've not been myself since the Lord took old Samiwell Price, and that's the truth."

Samuel Price was the relation who had entered into rest off a ladder, and Ruth looked duly serious.

"I have no doubt it upset you very much," she said.

"Well, miss," returned Mrs. Eccles, with dignity, "it's not as if I'd had my 'ealth before. I've had something wrong in the cistern" (Ruth wondered whether she meant system) "these many years. From a gell I suffered in my inside. But lor'! I was born to trouble, baptized in a bucket, and taken with collects at a week old. And how did you say Mrs. Cotton of the lodge might be, miss, as I hear is but poorly too?"

Ruth replied that she was better.

"She's no size to keep her in 'ealth," said Mrs. Eccles, "and so bent as she does grow, to be sure. Eh, dear, but it's a good thing to be tall. I always think little folks they're like them little watches, they've no room for their insides. And I wonder now"—Mrs. Eccles was coming to the point that had made her entrap Ruth on her way past—"I wonder now—"

Ruth did not help her. She knew too well the universal desire for knowledge of good and evil peculiar to her sex to doubt for a moment that Mrs. Eccles had begged her to "step in" only to obtain some piece of information, about which her curiosity had been aroused.

"I wonder, now, if Cotton at the lodge has heard anything of the poachers again this year, round Arleigh way?"

"Not that I know of," said Ruth, surprised at the simplicity of the question.

"Dear sakes! and to think of 'em at Vandon last night, and Mr. Dare and the keepers out all night after 'em."

Ruth was interested in spite of herself.

"And the doctor sent for in the middle of the night," continued Mrs. Eccles, covertly eying Ruth. "Poor young gentleman! For all his forrin ways, there's a many in Vandon as sets store by him."

"I don't think you need be uneasy about Mr. Dare," said Ruth, coldly, conscious that Mrs. Eccles was dying to see her change color. "If anything had happened to him Mr. Alwynn would have heard of it. And now," rising, "I must be going; and if I were you, Mrs. Eccles, I should not listen to all the gossip of the village."

"Me listen!" said Mrs. Eccles, much offended. "Me, as is too poorly so much as to put my foot out of the door! But, dear heart!" with her usual quickness of vision, "if there isn't Mr. Alwynn and Dr. Brown riding up the street now in Dr. Brown's gig! Well, I never! and Mr. Alwynn a-getting out, and a-talking as grave as can be to Dr. Brown. Poor Mr. Dare! Poor dear young gentleman!"

Ruth was conscious that she beat rather a hurried retreat from Mrs. Eccles's cottage, and that her voice was not quite so steady as usual when she asked the doctor if it were true that Mr. Dare had been hurt.

"All the village will have it that he is killed; but he is all right, I assure you, Miss Deyncourt," said the kind old doctor, so soothingly and reassuringly that Ruth grew pink with annoyance at the tone. "Not a scratch. He was out with his keepers last night, and they had a brush with poachers; and Martin, the head keeper was shot in the leg. Bled a good deal, so they sent for me; but no danger. I picked up your uncle here on his way to see him, and so I gave him a lift there and back. That is all, I assure you."

And Dr. Brown and Mrs. Eccles, straining over her geraniums, both came to the same conclusion, namely, that, as Mrs. Eccles elegantly expressed it, "Miss Ruth wanted Mr. Dare."

"And he'll have her, too, I'm thinking, one of these days," Mrs. Eccles would remark to the circle of her acquaintance.

Indeed, the match was discussed on numerous ladders, with almost as much interest as the unfailing theme of the damsons themselves.

And Dare rode over to the rectory as often as he used to do before a certain day in August, when he had found Ruth under the chestnut-tree—the very day before Mrs. Alwynn started on her screen, now the completed glory of the drawing-room.

And was Ruth beginning to like him?

As it had not occurred to her to ask herself that question, I suppose she was *not*.

Dare had grown very quiet and silent of late, and showed a growing tendency to dark hats. His refusal had been so unexpected that the blow, when it came, fell with all the more crushing force. His self-love and self-esteem had been wounded; but so had something else. Under the velvet corduroy waistcoat, which he wore in imitation of Ralph, he had a heart. Whether it was one of the very best of its kind or warranted to wear well is not for us to judge; but, at any rate, it was large enough to take in a very real affection, and to feel a very sharp pang. Dare's manner to Ruth was now as diffident as it had formerly been assured. To some minds there is nothing more touching than a sudden access of humility on the part of a vain man.

Whether Ruth's mind was one of this class or not we do not pretend to know.

CHAPTER XIV

It was Sunday morning at Atherstone. In the dining-room, breakfasting alone, for he had come down late, was Sir Charles Danvers. His sudden arrival on the previous Saturday was easily accounted for. When he had casually walked into the drawing-room late in the evening, he had immediately and thoroughly explained the reasons of his unexpected arrival. It seemed odd that he should have come to Atherstone, in the midland counties, "on his way" between two shooting visits in the north, but so it was. It might have been thought that one of his friends would have been willing to keep him two days longer, or receive him two days earlier; but no doubt every one knows his own affairs best, and Charles might certainly, "at his age," as he was so fond of saying, be expected to know his.

Anyhow, there he was, leaning against the open window, coffee-cup in hand, lazily watching the dwindling figures of Ralph and Evelyn, with Molly between them, disappearing in the direction of Greenacre church, hard by.

The morning mist still lingered on the land, and veiled the distance with a tender blue. And up across the silver fields, and across the standing armies of the yellowing corn, the sound of church bells came from Slumberleigh, beyond the river; bringing back to Charles, as to us all, old memories, old hopes, old visions of early youth, long cherished, long forgotten.

The single bell of Greenacre was giving forth a slow, persistent, cracked invitation to true believers, as an appropriate prelude to Mr. Smith's eloquence; but Charles did not hear its testimony.

He was listening to the Slumberleigh bells. Was that the first chime or the second?

Suddenly a thought crossed his mind. Should he go to church?

He smiled at the idea. It was a little late to think of that. Besides he had let the others start, and he disliked that refuge of mildew and dust, Greenacre.

There was Slumberleigh!

There went the bells again!

Slumberleigh! Absurd! Why, he should positively have to run to get there before the First Lesson; and that mist meant heat, or he was much mistaken.

Charles contemplated the mist for a few seconds.

Tang, teng, ting, tong, tung!

He certainly always made a point of going to church at his own home. A good example is, after all, just as important in one place as another.

Tang, tong, teng, tung, *ting*! went the bells.

"Why not run?" suggested an inner voice. "Put down your cup. There! Now! Your hat's in the hall, with your gloves beside it. Never mind about your prayer-book. Dear me! Don't waste time looking for your own stick. Take any. Quick! out through the garden-gate! No one can see you. The servants have all gone to church except the cook, and the kitchen looks out on the yew hedge."

"Over the first stile," said Charles to himself. "I am out of sight of the house now. Let us be thankful for small mercies. I shall do it yet. Oh, what a fool I am! I'm worse than Raca, as Molly said. I shall be rushing precipitately down a steep place into the sea next. Confound this gate! Why can't people leave them open? At any rate, it will remain open now. I am not going to have my devotions curtailed by a gate. I fancied it would be hot, but never anything half as hot as this. I hope I sha'n't meet Brown taking a morning stroll. I value Brown; but I should have to dismiss him if he saw me now. I could never meet his eye again. What on earth shall I say to Ralph and Evelyn when I get back? What a merciful Providence it is that Aunt Mary is at this moment intoning a response in the highest church in Scarborough!"

Ting, ting, ting!

"Mr. Alwynn is getting on his surplice, is he? Well, and if he is, I can make a final rush through the corn, can't I? There's not a creature in sight. The bell's down! What of that? There is the voluntary. Easy over the last fields. There are houses in sight, and there may be wicked Sabbath-breakers looking out of windows. Brown's foal has grown since July. Here we are! I am not the only Christian hurrying among the tombs. I shall get in with 'the wicked man' after all."

Some people do not look round in church; others do. Mrs. Alwynn always did, partly because she wished to see what was going on behind her, and partly because, in turning back again, she could take a stealthy survey of Mrs. Thursby's bonnet, in which she always felt a burning interest, which she would not for worlds have allowed that lady to suspect.

If the turning round had been all, it would have mattered little; but Mrs. Alwynn suffered so intensely from keeping silence that she was obliged to relieve herself at intervals by short whispered comments to Ruth.

On this particular morning it seemed as if the comments would never end.

"I am so glad we asked Mr. Dare into our pew, Ruth. The Thursbys are full. That's Mrs. Thursby's sister in the red bonnet."

Ruth made no reply. She was following the responses in the psalms with a marked attention, purposely marked to check conversation, and sufficient to have daunted anybody but her aunt.

Mrs. Alwynn took a spasmodic interest in the psalm, but it did not last.

"Only two basses in the choir, and the new *Te Deum*, Ruth. How vexed Mr. Alwynn will be!"

No response from Ruth. Mrs. Alwynn took another turn at her prayer-book, and then at the congregation.

"'I am become as it were a monster unto—' Ruth! *Ruth!*"

Ruth at last turned her head a quarter of an inch.

"Sir Charles Danvers is sitting in the free seats by the font!"

Ruth nailed her eyes to her book, and would vouchsafe no further sign of attention during the rest of the service; and Dare, on the other side, anxious to copy Ruth in everything, being equally obdurate, Mrs. Alwynn had no resource left but to follow the service half aloud to herself, at the times when the congregation were *not* supposed to join in, putting great emphasis on certain words which she felt applicable to herself, in a manner that effectually prevented any one near her from attending to the service at all.

It was with a sudden pang that Dare, following Ruth out into the sunshine after service, perceived for the first time Charles, standing, tall and distinguished-looking, beside the rather insignificant heir of all the Thursbys, who regarded him with the mixed admiration and gnawing envy of a very young man for a man no longer young.

And then—Charles never quite knew how it happened, but with the full intention of walking back to the rectory with the Alwynns, and staying to luncheon, he actually found himself in Ruth's very presence, accepting a cordial invitation to luncheon at Slumberleigh Hall. For the first time during the last ten years he had done a thing he had no intention of doing. A temporary long-lost feeling of shyness had seized upon him as he saw

Ruth coming out, tall and pale and graceful, from the shadow of the church porch into the blaze of the mid-day sunshine. He had not calculated either for that sudden disconcerting leap of the heart as her eyes met his. He had an idiotic feeling that she must be aware that he had run most of the way to church, and that he had contemplated the burnished circles of her back hair for two hours, without a glance at the fashionably scraped-up head-dress of Mabel Thursby, with its hogged mane of little wire curls in the nape of the neck. He felt he still looked hot and dusty, though he had imagined he was quite cool the moment before. To his own astonishment, he actually found his self-possession leaving him; and though its desertion proved only momentary, *in* that moment he found himself walking away with the Thursbys in the direction of the Hall. He was provoked, angry with himself, with the Thursbys, and, most of all, with Mr. Alwynn, who had come up a second later, and asked him to luncheon, as a matter of course, also Dare, who accepted with evident gratitude. Charles felt that he had not gone steeple-chasing over the country only to talk to Mrs. Thursby, and to see Ruth stroll away over the fields with Dare towards the rectory.

However, he made himself extremely agreeable, which was with him more a matter of habit than those who occasionally profited by it would have cared to know. He asked young Thursby his opinion on E.C. cartridges; he condoled with Mrs. Thursby on the loss of her last butler, and recounted some alarming anecdotes of his own French cook. He admired a pallid water-color drawing of Venice, in an enormous frame on an enormous easel, which he rightly supposed to be the manual labor of Mabel Thursby.

When he rose to take his leave, young Thursby, intensely flattered by having been asked for that opinion on cartridges by so renowned a shot as Charles, offered to walk part of the way back with him.

"I am afraid I am not going home yet," said Charles, lightly. "Duty points in the opposite direction, I have to call at the rectory. I want Mr. Alwynn's opinion on a point of clerical etiquette, which is setting my young spiritual shepherd at Stoke Moreton against his principal sheep, namely, myself."

And Charles took his departure, leaving golden opinions behind him, and a determination to invite him once more to shoot, in spite of his many courteous refusals of the last few years.

Mrs. Alwynn always took a nap after luncheon in her smart Sunday gown, among the mustard-colored cushions of her high-art sofa. Mr. Alwynn, also, was apt at the same time to sink into a subdued, almost apologetic doze, in the old arm-chair which alone had resisted the march of discomfort, and so-called "taste," which had invaded the rest of the little drawing-room of Slumberleigh Rectory. Ruth was sitting with her dark head leaned against the open window-frame. Dare had not stayed after luncheon, being at times nervously afraid of giving her too much of his society; and she was at liberty to read over again, if she chose, the solitary letter which the Sunday post had brought her. But she did not do so; she was thinking.

And so her sister Anna was actually returning to England at last! She and her husband had taken a house in Rome, and had arranged that Ruth should join them in London in November, and go abroad with them after Christmas for the remainder of the winter. She had pleasant recollections of previous winters in Rome, or, on the Riviera with her grandmother, and she was surprised that she did not feel more interested in the prospect. She supposed she would like it when the time came, but she seemed to care very little about it at the present moment. It had become very natural to live at Slumberleigh, and although there were drawbacks—here she glanced involuntarily at her aunt, who was making her slumbers vocal by a running commentary on them through her nose—still she would be sorry to go. Mr. Alwynn gave the ghost of a miniature snore, and, opening his eyes, found Ruth bent affectionately upon him. Her mind went back to another point in Anna's letter. After dilating on the extreme admiration and regard entertained for herself by her husband, his readiness with shawls, etc., she went on to ask whether Ruth had heard any news of Raymond.

Ruth sighed. Would there ever be any news of Raymond? The old nurse at Arleigh always asked the same question. "Any news of Master Raymond?" It was with a tired ache of the heart that Ruth heard that question, and always gave the same answer. Once she had heard from him since Lady Deyncourt's death, after she had written to tell him, as gently as she could, that she and Anna had inherited all their grandmother had to leave. A couple of months later she had received a hurried note in reply, inveighing against Lady Deyncourt's injustice, saying (as usual) that he was hard up for money, and that, when he knew where it might safely be sent, he should expect her and her sister to make up to him for his disappointment. And since then, since April—not a word. June, July, August, September. Four months and no sign. When he was in want of money his letters heretofore had made but little delay. Had he fallen ill and died out there, or met his death suddenly, perhaps in some wild adventure under an assumed name? Her lips tightened, and her white brows contracted over her absent eyes. It was an old anxiety, but none the less wearing because it was old. Ruth put it wearily from her, and took up the first book which came to her hand, to distract her attention.

It was a manual out of which Mrs. Alwynn had been reading extracts to her in the morning, while Ruth had been engaged in preparing herself to teach in the Sunday-school. She wondered vaguely how pleasure could be derived, even by the most religious persons, from seeing favorite texts twined in and out among forget-me-nots, or falling aslant in old English letters off bunches of violets; but she was old enough and wise enough to know that one man's religion is another man's occasion of stumbling. Books are made to fit all minds, and small minds lose themselves in large-minded books. The thousands in which these little manuals are sold, and the confidence with which their readers recommend them to others, indicates the calibre of the average mind, and shows that they meet a want possibly "not known before," but which they alone, with their little gilt edges, can adequately fill. Ruth was gazing in absent wonder at the volume which supplied all her aunt's spiritual needs when she heard the wire of the front door-bell squeak faintly. It was a stiff-necked and obdurate bell, which for several years Mr. Alwynn had determined to see about.

A few moments later James, the new and inexperienced footman, opened the door about half a foot, put in his head, murmured something inaudible, and withdrew it again.

A tall figure appeared in the door-way, and advanced to meet her, then stopped midway. Ruth rose hastily, and stood where she had risen, her eyes glancing first at Mr. and then at Mrs. Alwynn.

The alien presence of a visitor had not disturbed them. Mrs. Alwynn, her head well forward and a succession of chins undulating in perfect repose upon her chest, was sleeping as a stout person only can—all over. Mr. Alwynn, opposite, his thin hands clasped listlessly over his knee, was as unconscious of the two pairs of eyes fixed upon him as Nelson himself, laid out in Madame Tussaud's.

Charles's eyes, twinkling with suppressed amusement, met Ruth's. He shook his head energetically, as she made a slight movement as if to wake them, and stepping forward, pointed with his hat towards the open window, which reached to the ground. Ruth understood, but she hesitated. At this moment Mrs. Alwynn began a variation on the simple theme in which she had been indulging, and in so much higher a key that all hesitation vanished. She stepped hastily out through the window, and Charles followed. They stood together for a moment in the blazing sunshine, both too much amused to speak.

"You are bareheaded," he said, suddenly; "is there any"—looking round—"any shade we could take refuge under?"

Ruth led the way round the yew hedge to the horse-chestnut; that horse-chestnut under which Dare had once lost his self-esteem.

"I am afraid," said Charles, "I arrived at an inopportune moment. As I was lunching with the Thursbys, I came up in the hope of finding Mr. Alwynn, whom I wanted to consult about a small matter in my own parish."

Charles was quite pleased with this sentence when he had airily given it out. It had a true ring about it he fancied, which he remembered with gratitude was more than the door-bell had. Peace be with that door-bell, and with the engaging youth who answered it.

"I wish you had let me wake Mr. Alwynn," said Ruth. "He will sleep on now till the bells begin."

"On no account. I should have been shocked if you had disturbed him. I assure you I can easily wait until he naturally wakes up; that is," with a glance at the book in her hand, "if I am not disturbing you—if you are not engaged in improving yourself at this moment."

"No. I have improved myself for the day, thanks. I can safely afford to relax a little now."

"So can I. I resemble Lady Mary in that. On Sunday mornings she reflects on her own shortcomings; on Sunday afternoons she finds an innocent relaxation in pointing out mine."

"Where is Lady Mary now?"

"I should say she was in her Bath-chair on the Scarborough sands at this moment."

"I like her," said Ruth, with decision.

"Tastes differ. Some people feel drawn towards wet blankets, and others have a leaning towards pokers. Do you know why you like her?"

"I never thought about it, but I suppose it was because she seemed to like *me*."

"Exactly. You admired her good taste. A very natural vanity, most pardonable in the young, was gratified at seeing marks of favor so well bestowed."

"I dare say you are right. At any rate, you seem so familiar with the workings of vanity in the human breast that it would be a pity to contradict you."

"By-the-way," said Charles, speaking in the way people do who have nothing to say, and are trying to hit on any subject of conversation, "have you heard any more of your tramp? There was no news of him when I left. I asked the Slumberleigh policeman about him again on my way to the station."

"I have heard no more of him, though I keep his memory green. I have not forgotten the fright he gave me. I had always imagined I was rather a self-possessed person till that day."

"I am a coward myself when I am frightened," said Charles, consolingly, "though at other times as bold as a lion."

They were both sitting under the flickering shadow of the already yellowing horse-chestnut-tree, the first of all the trees to set the gorgeous autumn fashions. But as yet it was paling only at the edges of its slender fans. The air was sweet and soft, with a voiceless whisper of melancholy in it, as if the summer knew, for all her smiles, her hour had wellnigh come.

The rectory cows—the mottled one, and the red one, and the big white one that was always milked first—came slowly past on their way to the pond, blinking their white eyelashes leisurely at Charles and Ruth.

"It is almost as hot as that Sunday in July when we walked over from Atherstone. Do you remember?" said Charles, suddenly.

"Yes."

She knew he was thinking of their last conversation, and she felt a momentary surprise that he had remembered it.

"We never finished that conversation," he said, after a pause.

"No; but then conversations never are finished, are they? They always seem to break off just when they are coming to the beginning. A bell rings, or there is an interruption, or one is told it is bedtime."

"Or fools rush in with their word where you and I should fear to tread, and spoil everything."

"Yes."

"And have you been holding the wool and tying up the flowers, as you so graphically described, ever since you left Atherstone in July?"

"I hope I have; I have tried."

"I am sure of that," he said, with sudden earnestness, then added more slowly, "I have not wound any wool; I have only enjoyed myself."

"Perhaps," said Ruth, turning her clear, frank gaze upon him, "that may have been the harder work of the two; it sometimes is."

His light, restless eyes, with the searching look in them which she had seen before, met hers, and then wandered away again to the level meadows and the woods and the faint sky.

The Danvers Jewels And Sir Charles Danvers | 183

"I think it was," he said at last; and both were silent. He reflected that his conversations with Ruth had a way of beginning in fun, becoming more serious, and ending in silence.

The bells rang out suddenly.

Charles thought they were full early.

"Mr. Alwynn will wake up now," said Ruth; "I will tell him you are here."

But before she had time to do more than rise from her chair, Mr. Alwynn came slowly round the yew hedge, and stopped suddenly in front of the chestnut-tree, amazed at what he saw beneath it. His mild eyes gazed blankly at Charles through his spectacles, gathering a pained expression as they peered over the top of them, which did not lessen when they fell on Ruth.

Charles explained in a few words the purport of his visit, which had already explained itself quite sufficiently to Mr. Alwynn; and mentioning that he had waited in the hope of presently finding Mr. Alwynn "disengaged" (at this Mr. Alwynn blushed a little), asked leave to walk as far as the church with him to consult him on a small matter, etc. It was a neat sentence, but it did not sound quite so well the third time. It had lost by the heathenish and vain repetitions to which it had been subjected.

"Certainly, certainly," said Mr. Alwynn, mollified, but still discomposed. "You should have waked me, Ruth;" turning reproachfully to his niece, whose conduct had never, in his eyes, fallen short of perfection till this moment. "Little nap after luncheon. Hardly asleep. You should have waked me."

"There was Aunt Fanny," said Ruth, feeling as if she had committed some grave sin.

"Ah-h!" said Mr. Alwynn, as if her reason were a weighty one, his memory possibly recalling the orchestral flourish which as a rule heralded his wife's return to consciousness. "True, true, my dear. I must be going," as the chime ceased. "Are you coming to church this afternoon?"

Ruth replied that she was not, and Mr. Alwynn and Charles departed together, Charles ruefully remembering that he had still to ask advice on a subject the triviality of which would hardly allow of two opinions.

Ruth watched them walk away together, and then went back noiselessly into the drawing-room.

Mrs. Alwynn was sitting bolt upright, her feet upon the floor, her gown upon the sofa. Her astonished eyes were fixed upon the dwindling figures of Mr. Alwynn and Charles.

"Goodness, Ruth!" she exclaimed, "who is that white waistcoat walking with your uncle?"

Ruth explained.

"Dear me! And as likely as not he came to see the new screen. I know Mrs. Thursby tells everybody about it. And his own house so full of beautiful things too. Was ever anything so annoying! We should have had so much in common, for I hear his taste is quite—well, really quite out of the way. How contrary things are, Ruth! You awake and me asleep, when it might just as well have been the other way; but it is Sunday, my dear, so we must not complain. And now, as we have missed church, I will lie down again, and you shall read me that nice sermon, which I always like to hear when I can't go to church; the one in the green book about Nabob's vineyard."

CHAPTER XV

Great philosophers and profound metaphysicians should by rights have lived at Slumberleigh. Those whose lines have fallen to them "ten miles from a lemon," have time to think, if so inclined.

Only elementary natures complain of their surroundings; and though at first Ruth had been impatient and depressed, after a time she found that, better than to live in an atmosphere of thought, was to be thrown entirely on her own resources, and to do her thinking for herself.

Some minds, of course, sink into inanition if an outward supply of nutriment is withheld. Others get up and begin to forage for themselves. Happy are these—when the transition period is over—when, after a time, the first and worst mistakes have been made and suffered for, and the only teaching that profits anything at all, the bitter teaching of experience, has been laid to heart.

Such a nature was Ruth's, upright, self-reliant, without the impetuosity and impulsiveness that so often accompanies an independent nature, but accustomed to look at everything through her own eyes, and to think, but not till now to act for herself.

She had been brought up by her grandmother to believe that before all things *noblesse oblige*; to despise a dishonorable action, to have her feelings entirely under control, to be intimate with few, to be courteous to all. But to help others, to give up anything for them, to love an unfashionable or middle-class neighbor, or to feel a personal interest in religion, except as a subject of conversation, had never found a place in Lady Deyncourt's code, or consequently in Ruth's, though, as was natural with a generous nature, the girl did many little kindnesses to those about her, and was personally unselfish, as those who live with self-centred people are bound to be if there is to be any semblance of peace in the house.

But now, new thoughts were stirring within her, were leavening her whole mind. All through these monotonous months she had watched the quiet routine of patient effort that went to make up the sum of Mr. Alwynn's life. He was a shy man. He seldom spoke of religion out of the pulpit; but all through these long months he preached it without words to Ruth, as she had never heard it preached before, by

"The best portion of a good man's life—
His little, nameless, unremembered acts
Of kindness and of love."

It was the first time that she had come into close contact with a life spent for others, and its beauty appealed to her with a new force, and gradually but surely changed the current of her thoughts, until, as "we needs must love the highest when we see it," she unconsciously fell in love with self-sacrifice.

The opinions of most young persons, however loudly and injudiciously proclaimed, rarely do the possessors much harm, because they are not, as a rule, acted upon; but with some few people a change of views means a change of life. Ruth was on the edge of a greater change than she knew.

At first she had often regretted the chapter of her life that had been closed by Lady Deyncourt's death. Now, she felt she could not go back to it, and find it all-sufficient as of old. It would need an added element, without which she began to see that any sort or condition of life is but a stony, dusty concern after all—an element which made even Mr. Alwynn's colorless existence a contented and happy one.

Ruth had been telling him one day, as they were walking together, of her sister's plans for the winter, and that she was sorry to think her time at Slumberleigh was drawing to a close.

"I am afraid," he said, "in spite of all you say, my dear, it has been very dull for you here. No little gayeties or enjoyments such as it is right young people should have. I wish we had had a picnic, or a garden-party, or something. Mabel Thursby cannot be happy without these things, and it is natural at your age that you should wish for them. Your aunt and I lead very quiet lives. It suits us, but it is different for young people."

"Does it suit you?" asked Ruth, with sudden earnestness. "Do you really like it, or do you sometimes get tired of it?"

Mr. Alwynn looked a little alarmed and disconcerted. He never cared to talk about himself.

"I used to get tired," he said at last, with reluctance, "when I was younger. There were times when I foolishly expected more from life than— than, in fact, I quite got, my dear; and the result was, I fear I had a very discontented spirit—an unthankful, discontented spirit," he repeated, with sad retrospection.

Something in his tone touched Ruth to the quick.

"And now?"

"I am content now."

"Uncle John, tell me. How did you grow to feel content?"

He saw there were tears in her eyes.

"It took a long time," he said. "Anything that is worth knowing, Ruth, takes a long time to learn. I think I found in the end, my dear, that the only way was to put my whole heart into what I was doing," (Mr. Alwynn's voice was simple and earnest, as if he were imparting to Ruth a great discovery). "I had tried before, from time to time, of course, but never quite as hard as I might have done. That was where I failed. When I put myself on one side, and really settled down to do what I could for others, life became much simpler and happier."

He turned his grave, patient eyes to Ruth's again. Was something troubling her?

"I have often thought since then," he went on, speaking more to himself than to her, "that we should consider well what we are keeping back our strength for, if we find ourselves refusing to put the whole of it into our work. When at last one does start, one feels it is such a pity one did not do it earlier in life. When I look at all the young faces growing up around me, I often hope, Ruth, they won't waste as much time as I did."

How simple it seemed while she listened to him; how easy, how natural, this life for others!

She could not answer. One sentence of Mr. Alwynn's was knocking at the door of her heart for admission; was drowning with its loud beating the sound of all the rest:

"We should consider well what we are keeping back our strength for, if we refuse to put the whole of it into our work."

She and Mr. Alwynn walked on in silence; and after a time, always afraid of speaking much on the subject that was first in his own mind, he began to talk again on trivial matters, to tell her how he had met Dare that morning, and had promised on her behalf that she would sing at a little local concert which the Vandon school-master was getting up that week to defray the annual expense of the Vandon cricket club, and in which Dare was taking a vivid interest.

"You won't mind singing, will you, Ruth?" asked Mr. Alwynn, wishing she would show a little more interest in Dare and his concert.

"Oh no, of course not," rather hurriedly. "I should be glad to help in any way."

"And I thought, my dear, as it would be getting late, we had better accept his offer of staying the night at Vandon."

Ruth assented, but so absently that Mr. Alwynn dropped the subject with a sigh, and walked on, revolving weighty matters in his mind. They had left the woods now, and were crossing the field where, two months ago, the school-feast had been held. Mr. Alwynn made some slight allusion to it, and then coughed. Ruth's attention, which had been distracted, came back in a moment. She knew her uncle had something which he did not like, something which yet he felt it his duty to say, when he gave that particular cough.

"That was when you were staying with the Danvers, wasn't it, Ruth?" in a would-be casual, disengaged tone.

"Yes; I came over from Atherstone with Molly Danvers."

"I remember," said Mr. Alwynn, looking extremely uncomfortable; "and—if I am not mistaken—ahem! Sir Charles Danvers was staying there at the same time?"

"Certainly he was."

"Yes, and I dare say, Ruth—I am not finding fault, far from it—I dare say he made himself very agreeable for the time being?"

"I don't think he made himself so. I should have said he was naturally so, without any effort, just as some people are naturally the reverse."

"Indeed! Well, I have always heard he was most agreeable; but I am afraid—I think perhaps it is just as well you should know—forewarned is forearmed, you know—that, in fact, he says a great deal more than he means sometimes."

"Does he? I dare say he does."

"He has a habit of appearing to take a great interest in people, which I am afraid means very little. I dare say he is not fully aware of it, or I am sure he would struggle against it, and we must not judge him; but still, his manner does a great deal of harm. It is peculiarly open to misconstruction. For instance," continued Mr. Alwynn, making a rush as his courage began to fail him, "it struck me, Ruth, the other day—Sunday, was it? Yes, I think it *was* Sunday—that really he had not much to ask me about his week-day services. I—ahem! I thought he need not have called."

"I dare say not."

"But now, that is just the kind of thing he *does*—calls, and, er—under chestnut-trees, and that sort of thing—and how *are* young people to know unless their elders tell them that it is only his way, and that he has done just the same ever so often before?"

"And will again," said Ruth, trying to keep down a smile. "Is it true (Mabel is full of it) that he is engaged, or on the point of being so, to one of Lord Hope-Acton's daughters?"

"People are always saying he is engaged, to first one person and then another," said Mr. Alwynn, breathing more freely now that his duty was discharged. "It often grieves me that your aunt mentions his engagement so confidently to friends, because it gives people the impression that we know, and we really don't. He is a great deal talked about, because he is such a conspicuous man in the county, on account of his wealth and his place, and the odd things he says and does. There is something about him that is different from other people. I am sure I don't know why it is, but I like him very much myself. I have known him do such kind things. Dear me! What a pleasant week I had at Stoke Moreton last year. It is beautiful, Ruth; and the collection of old papers and manuscripts unique! Your aunt was in Devonshire with friends at the time. I wish he would ask me again this autumn, to see those charters of Edward IV.'s reign that have been found in the secret drawer of an old cabinet. I hear they are quite small, and have green seals. I wish I had thought of asking him about them on Sunday. If they are really small—but it was only Archdeacon Eldon who told me about them, and he never sees anything any particular size—if they should happen to be really small—" And Mr. Alwynn turned eagerly to the all-engrossing subject of the Stoke Moreton charters, which furnished him with conversation till they reached home.

"We should consider well what we are keeping back our strength for, if we refuse to put the whole of it into our work."

All through the afternoon and the quiet, monotonous evening these words followed Ruth. She read them between the lines of the book she took up. She stitched them into her sewing. They went up-stairs with her at night, they followed her into her room, and would not be denied. When she had sent away her maid, she sat down by the window, and, with the full harvest-moon for company, faced them and asked them what they meant. But they only repeated themselves over and over again. What had they to do with her? Her mind tried to grapple with them in vain. As often as she came to close quarters with them they eluded her and disappeared, only to return with the old formula.

Her thoughts drifted away at last to what Mr. Alwynn had said of Charles, and all the disagreeable things which Mabel had come up on Monday morning, with a bunch of late roses, on purpose to tell her respecting him. She had taken Mabel's information at its true worth, which I fear was but small; but she felt annoyed that both Mabel and Mr. Alwynn should have thought it necessary to warn her. As if, she said to herself, she had not known! Really, she had not been born and bred in Slumberleigh, nor had she lived there all her life. She had met men of that kind before. She always liked them. Charles especially amused her, and she could see that she amused him; and, now she came to think of it, she supposed he had paid her a good deal of attention at Atherstone, and perhaps he had not come over to Slumberleigh especially to see Mr. Alwynn. It was as natural to men like Charles to be always interested in some one, as it would be unnatural in others ever to be so, except as the result of long forethought, and with a wedding-ring and a set of bridesmaids well in view. But to attach any importance to the fact that Charles liked to talk to her would have been absurd. With another man it might have meant much; but she had heard of Charles and his misdoings long before she had met him, and knew what to expect. Lord Breakwater's sister had confided to her many things respecting him, and had wept bitter tears on her shoulder, when he suddenly went off to shoot grizzlies in the Rocky Mountains.

"He has not sufficient vanity to know that he is exceedingly popular," said Ruth to herself. "I should think there are few men, handicapped as he is, who have been liked more entirely for themselves, and less for their belongings; but all the time he probably imagines people admire his name, or his place, or his income, and not himself, and consequently he does not care much what he says or does. I am certain he does not mean to do any harm. His manner never deceived me for a moment. I can't see why it should others; but, from all accounts, he seems to be frequently misunderstood. That is just the right word for him. He is misunderstood. At any rate, I never misunderstood him. That Sunday call might have made me suspicious of any ordinary mortal; but I knew no common rule could apply to such an exception as he is. I only wonder, when he really does find himself in earnest, how he is to convey his meaning to the future Lady Danvers. What words would be strong enough; what ink would be black enough to carry conviction to her mind?"

She smiled at the thought, and, as she smiled, another face rose suddenly before her—Dare's pale and serious, as it had been of late, with the wistful, anxious eyes. *He*, at least, had meant a great deal, she thought with remorse. *He* had been in earnest, sufficiently in earnest to make himself very unhappy, and on her account.

Ruth had known for some time that Dare loved her; but to-night that simple, unobtrusive fact suddenly took larger proportions, came boldly out of the shadow and looked her in the face.

He loved her. Well, what then?

She turned giddy, and leaned her head against the open shutter.

In the silence the words that had haunted her all the afternoon came back; not loud as heretofore, but in a whisper, speaking to her heart, which had begun to beat fast and loud.

"We should consider well what we are keeping back our strength for, if we refuse to put the whole of it into our work."

What work was there for her to do?

The giddiness and the whirl in her mind died down suddenly like a great gust on the surface of a lake, and left it still and clear and cold.

The misery of the world and the inability to meet it had so often confused and weighed her down that she had come back humbly of late to the only possibility with which it was in her power to deal, come back to the well-worn groove of earnest determination to do as much as in her lay, close at hand, when she could find a field to labor in. And now she suddenly saw, or thought she saw, that she had found it. She had been very anxious as to whether Dare would do his duty, but till this moment it had never struck her that it might be *her* duty to help him.

She liked him; and he was poor—too poor to do much for the people who were dependent on him, the poor, struggling people of Vandon. Their sullen, miserable faces rose up before her, and their crazy houses. Fever had broken out again in the cottages by the river. He needed help and encouragement, for he had a difficult time before him. And she had these to give, and money too. Could she do better with them? She knew Mr. Alwynn wished it. And as to herself? Was she never going to put self on one side? She had never liked any one very much—at least, not in that way—but she liked him.

The words came like a loud voice in the silence. She liked him. Well, what then?

She shut her eyes, but she only shut out the moon's pale photographs of the fields and woods. She could not shut out these stern besieging thoughts.

What was she holding back for? For some possible ideal romantic future; for the prince of a fairy story? No? Well, then, for what?

The moon went behind a cloud, and took all her photographs with her. The night had turned very cold.

"To-morrow," said Ruth to herself, rising slowly; "I am too tired to think now. To-morrow!"

And as she spoke the faint chime of the clock upon her table warned her that already it was to-morrow.

And soon, in a moment, as it seemed to her, before she had had time to think, it was again to-morrow, a wet, dim to-morrow, and she was at Vandon, running up the wide stone steps in the starlight, under Dare's protecting umbrella, and allowing him to take her wraps from her before the hall fire.

The concert had gone off well. Ruth was pleased, Mr. Alwynn was pleased. Dare was in a state of repressed excitement, now flying into the drawing-room to see if there were a good fire, as it was a chilly evening; now rushing thence to the dining-room to satisfy himself that all the immense and elaborate preparations which he had enjoined on the cook had been made. Then, Ruth must be shown to her room. Who was to do it? He flew to find the house-keeper, and after repeated injunctions to the house-maid, whom he met in the passage, not to forget the hot water, took Mr. Alwynn off to his apartment.

The concert had begun, as concerts always seem to do, at the exact time at which it is usual to dine, so that it was late before the principal performers and Mr. Alwynn reached Vandon. It was later still before supper came, but when it came it was splendid. Dare looked with anxious satisfaction, over a soup tureen, at the various spiced and glazed forms of indigestion, sufficient for a dozen people, which covered the table. It grieved him that Ruth, confronted by a spreading ham, and Mr. Alwynn, half hidden by a bowlder of turkey, should have such moderate appetites. But at least she was there, under his roof, at his table. It was not surprising that he could eat nothing himself.

After supper, Mr. Alwynn, who combined the wisdom of the worldly serpent with the harmlessness of the clerical dove, fell—not too suddenly—asleep by the fire in the drawing-room, and Ruth and Dare went into the hall, where the piano was. Dare opened it and struck a few minor chords. Ruth sat down in a great carved arm-chair beside the fire.

The hall was only lighted by a few tall lamps high on pedestals against the walls, which threw great profiles of the various busts upon the dim bass-reliefs of twining scroll-work; and Dare, with his eyes fixed on Ruth, began to play.

There is in some music a strange appeal beyond the reach of words. Those mysterious sharps and flats, and major and minor chords, are an alphabet that in some occult combinations forms another higher language than that of speech, a language which, as we listen, thrills us to the heart.

It was an old piano, with an impediment in its speech, out of the yellow notes of which Ruth could have made nothing; but in Dare's hands it spoke for him as he never could have spoken for himself.

His eyes never left her. He feared to look away, lest he should find the presence of that quiet, graceful figure by his fireside had been a dream, and that he was alone again with the dim lamps, alone with Dante and Cicero and Seneca.

The firelight dwelt ruddily upon her grave clear-cut face and level brows, and upon the folds of her white gown. It touched the slender hands clasped lightly together on her knee, and drew sudden sparks and gleams out of the diamond pin at her throat.

His hands trembled on the keys, and as he looked his heart beat high and higher, loud and louder, till it drowned the rhythm of the music. And as he looked her calm eyes met his.

In another moment he was on his knees beside her, her hands caught in his trembling clasp, and his head pressed down upon them.

"I know," he gasped, "it is no good. You have told me so once. You will tell me so again. I am not good enough. I am not worthy. But I love you; I love you!"

In moments of real feeling the old words hold their own against all modern new-comers. Dare repeated them over and over again in a paroxysm of overwhelming emotion which shook him from head to foot.

Something in his boyish attitude and in his entire loss of self-control touched Ruth strangely. She knew he was five or six years her senior, but at the moment she felt as if she were much older than he, and a sudden vague wish passed through her mind that he had been nearer her in age; not quite so young.

"Well?" she said, gently; and he felt her cool, passive hands tremble a little in his. Something in the tone of her voice made him raise his head, and meet her eyes looking down at him, earnestly, and with a great kindness in them.

A sudden eager light leaped into his face.

"Will you?" he whispered, breathlessly, his hands tightening their hold of hers. "Will you?"

There was a moment's pause, in which the whole world seemed to stand quite still and wait for her answer.

"Yes," she said at last, "I will."

"I am glad I did it," she said to herself, half an hour later, as she leaned her tired head against the carved oak chimney-piece in her bedroom, and absently traced with her finger the Latin inscription over the fireplace. "I like him very much. I am glad I did it."

CHAPTER XVI

For many years nothing had given Mr. Alwynn such heart-felt pleasure as the news Ruth had to tell him, as he drove her back next morning to Slumberleigh, behind Mrs. Alwynn's long-tailed ponies.

It was a still September morning, with a faint pearl sky and half-veiled silver sun. Pale gleams of sunshine wandered across the busy harvest fields, and burnished the steel of the river.

Decisions of any kind rarely look their best after a sleepless night; but as Ruth saw the expression of happiness and relief that came into her uncle's face, when she told him what had happened, she felt again that she was glad—very glad.

"Oh, my dear! my dear!"—Mr. Alwynn was driving the ponies first against the bank, and then into the opposite ditch—"how glad I am; how thankful! I had almost hoped, certainly; I wished so much to think it possible; but then, one can never tell. Poor Dare! poor fellow! I used to be so sorry for him. And how much you will be able to do at Vandon among the people. It will be a different place. And it is such a relief to think that the poor old house will be looked after. It went to my heart to see the way it had been neglected. I ventured this morning, as I was down early, to move some of that dear old Worcester farther back into the cabinet. They really were so near the edge, I could not bear to see them; and I found a Sèvres saucer, my dear, in the library that belonged to one of those beautiful cups in the drawing-room. I hope it was not very wrong, but I had to put it among its relations. It was sitting with a Delf mug on it, poor thing. Dear me! I little thought then—Really, I have never been so glad about anything before."

After a little more conversation, and after Mr. Alwynn had been persuaded to give the reins to his niece, who was far more composed than himself, his mind reverted to his wife.

"I think, my dear, until your engagement is more settled, till I have had a talk with Dare on the subject (which will be necessary before you write to your uncle Francis), it would be as well not to refer to it before—in fact, not to mention it to Mrs. Alwynn. Your dear aunt's warm heart and conversational bent make it almost impossible for her to refrain from speaking of anything that interests her; and indeed, even if she does not say anything in so many words, I have observed that opinions are sometimes formed by others as to the subject on which she is silent, by her manner when any chance allusion is made to it."

Ruth heartily agreed. She had been dreading the searching catechism through which Mrs. Alwynn would certainly put her—the minute inquiries as to her dress, the hour, the place; whether it had been "standing up or sitting down;" all her questions of course interwoven with personal reminiscences of "how John had done it," and her own emotion at the time.

It was with no small degree of relief at the postponement of that evil hour that Ruth entered the house. As she did so a faint sound reached her ear. It was that of a musical-box.

"Dear! dear!" said Mr. Alwynn, as he followed her. "It is a fine day. Your aunt must be ill."

For the moment Ruth did not understand the connection of ideas in his mind, until she suddenly remembered the musical-box, which, Mrs. Alwynn had often told her, was "so nice and cheery on a wet day, or in time of illness."

She hurriedly entered the drawing-room, followed by Mr. Alwynn, where the first object that met her view was Mrs. Alwynn extended on the sofa, arrayed in what she called her tea-gown, a loose robe of blue cretonne, with a large vine-leaf pattern twining over it, which broke out into grapes at intervals. Ruth knew that garment well. It came on only when Mrs. Alwynn was suffering. She had worn it last during a period of entire mental prostration, which had succeeded all too soon an exciting discovery of mushrooms in the glebe. Mr. Alwynn's heart and Ruth's sank as they caught sight of it again.

With a dignity befitting the occasion, Mrs. Alwynn recounted in detail the various ways in which she had employed herself after their departure the previous evening, up to the exact moment when she slipped going up-stairs, and sprained her ankle, in a blue and green manner that had quite alarmed the doctor when he had seen it, and compared with which Mrs. Thursby's gathered finger in the spring was a mere bagatelle.

"Mrs. Thursby stayed in bed when her finger was bad," said Mrs. Alwynn to Ruth, when Mr. Alwynn had condoled, and had made his escape to his study. "She always gives way so; but I never was like that. I was up all the same, my dear."

"I hope it does not hurt very much," said Ruth, anxious to be sympathetic, but succeeding only in being commonplace.

"It's not only the pain," said Mrs. Alwynn, in the gentle resigned voice which she always used when indisposed—the voice of one at peace with all the world, and ready to depart from a scene consequently so devoid of interest; "but to a person of my habits, Ruth—never a day without going into the larder, and always seeing after the servants as I do—first one duty and then another—and the chickens and all. It seems a strange thing that I should be laid aside."

Mrs. Alwynn paused, as if she had not for the nonce fathomed the ulterior reasons for this special move on the part of Providence, which had crippled her, while it left Ruth and Mrs. Thursby with the use of their limbs.

"However," she continued, "I am not one to repine. Always cheery and busy, Ruth: that is my motto. And now, my dear, if you will wind up the musical-box, and then read me a little bit out of 'Texts with Tender Twinings'" (the new floral manual which had lately superseded the "Pearls"), "after that we will start on one of my scrap-books, and you shall tell me all about your visit to Vandon."

It was not the time Ruth would have chosen for a *tête-à-tête* with her aunt. She was longing to be alone, to think quietly over what had happened, and it was difficult to concentrate her attention on pink and yellow calico, and cut out colored royal families, and foreign birds, with a good grace. Happily Mrs. Alwynn, though always requiring attention, was quite content with the half of what she required; and, with the "Buffalo Girls" and the "Danube River" tinkling on the table, conversation was somewhat superfluous.

In the afternoon Dare came, but he was waylaid in the hall by Mr. Alwynn, and taken into the study before he could commit himself in Mrs. Alwynn's presence. Mrs. Thursby and Mabel also called to condole, and a little later Mrs. Smith of Greenacre, who had heard the news of the accident from the doctor. Altogether it was a delightful afternoon for Mrs. Alwynn, who assumed for the time an air of superiority over Mrs. Thursby to which that lady's well-known chronic ill-health seldom allowed her to lay claim.

Mrs. Alwynn and Mrs. Thursby had remained friends since they had both arrived together as brides at Slumberleigh, in spite of a difference of opinion, which had at one time strained friendly relations to a painful degree, as to the propriety of wearing the hair over the top of the ear. The hair question settled, a temporary difficulty, extending over a few years, had sprung up in its place, respecting what Mrs. Thursby called "family." Mrs. Alwynn's family was not her strong point, nor was its position strengthened by her assertion (unsupported by Mrs. Markham), that she was directly descended from Queen Elizabeth. Consequently, it was trying to Mrs.

Thursby—who, as every one knows, was one of the brainless Copleys of Copley—that Mrs. Alwynn, who in the lottery of marriage had drawn an honorable, should take precedence of herself. To obviate this difficulty, Mrs. Thursby, with the ingenuity of her sex, had at one time introduced Mr. and Mrs. Alwynn as "our rector," and "our rector's wife," thus denying them their name altogether, for fear lest its connection with Lord Polesworth should be remembered, and the fact that Mr. Alwynn was his brother, and consequently an honorable, should transpire.

This peculiarity of etiquette entirely escaped Mr. Alwynn, but aroused feelings in the breast of his wife which might have brought about one of those deeply rooted feuds which so often exist between the squire's and clergyman's families, if it had not been for the timely and serious illness in which Mrs. Thursby lost her health, and the principal part of the other subject of disagreement—her hair.

Then Queen Elizabeth and the honorable were alike forgotten. With her own hands Mrs. Alwynn made a certain jelly, which Mrs. Thursby praised in the highest manner, saying she only wished that it had been the habit in *her* family to learn to do anything so useful. Mrs. Thursby's new gowns were no longer kept a secret from Mrs. Alwynn, to be suddenly sprung upon her at a garden-party, when, possibly in an old garment herself, she was least able to bear the shock. By-gones were by-gones, and, greatly to the relief of the two husbands, their respective wives made up their differences.

"And a very pleasant afternoon it has been," said Mrs. Alwynn, when the Thursbys and Dare, who had been loath to go, had taken their departure. "Mrs. Thursby and Mabel, and Mrs. Smith and Mr. Dare. Four to tea. Quite a little party, wasn't it, Ruth? And so informal and nice; and the buns came in as naturally as possible, which no one heard me whisper to James for. I think those little citron buns are nicer than a great cake like Mrs. Thursby's; and hers are always so black and overbaked. That is why the cook sifts such a lot of sugar over them. I do think one should be real, and not try to cover up things. And Mr. Dare so pleasant. Quite sorry to go he seemed. I often wonder whether it will be you or Mabel in the end. He ought to be making up his mind. I expect I shall have a little joke with him about it before long. And such an interest he took in the scrap-book. I asked him to come again to-morrow."

"I don't expect he will be able to do so," said Mr. Alwynn. "I rather think he will have to go to town on business."

Later in the evening, Mr. Alwynn told Ruth that in the course of his interview he had found that Dare had the very vaguest ideas as to the necessity of settlements; had evidently never given the subject a thought, and did not even know what he actually possessed.

Mr. Alwynn was secretly afraid of what Ruth's trustee, his brother, Lord Polesworth (now absent shooting in the Rocky Mountains), would say if, during his absence, their niece was allowed to engage herself without suitable provision; and he begged Ruth not "to do anything rash" in the way of speaking of her engagement, until Dare could, with the help of his lawyer, see his way to making some arrangement.

"I know he has no money," said Ruth, quietly; "that is one of the reasons why I am going to marry him."

Mr. Alwynn, to whom this seemed the most natural reason in the world, was not sure whether it would strike his brother with equal force. He had a suspicion that when Lord Polesworth's attention should be turned from white goats and brown bears to the fact that his niece, who had means of her own, had been allowed to engage herself to a poor man, and that Mr. Alwynn had greatly encouraged the match, unpleasant questions might be asked.

"Francis will be back in November," said Mr. Alwynn. "I think, Ruth, we had better wait till his return before we do anything definite."

"Anything *more* definite, you mean," said Ruth. "I have been very definite already, I think. I shall be glad to wait till he comes back, if you wish it, Uncle John. I shall try to do what you both advise. But at the same time I am of age; and if my word is worth anything, you know I have given that already."

Dare felt no call to go to London by the early train on the following morning, so he found himself at liberty to spend an hour at Slumberleigh Rectory on his way to the station, and by the advice of Mr. Alwynn went into the garden, where the sound of the musical-box reached the ear, but in faint echoes, and where Ruth presently joined him.

In his heart Dare was secretly afraid of Ruth; though, as he often told himself, it was more than probable she was equally afraid of him. If that was so, she controlled her feelings wonderfully, for as she came to meet him, nothing could have been more frankly kind, more friendly, or more composed than her manner towards him. He took her out-stretched hand and kissed it. It was not quite the way in which he had pictured to himself that they would meet; but if his imagination had taken a somewhat bolder flight in her absence, he felt now, as she stood before him, that it had taken that flight in vain. He kept her hand, and looked intently at her. She did not change color, nor did that disappointing friendliness leave her steady eyes.

"She does not love me," he said to himself. "It is strange, but she does not. But the day will come."

"You are going to London, are you not?" asked Ruth, withdrawing her hand at last; and after hearing a detailed account of his difficulties and anxieties about money matters, and after taking an immense weight off his mind by telling him that they would have no influence in causing her to alter her decision, she sent him beaming and rejoicing on his way, quite a different person to the victim of anxiety and depression who had arrived at Slumberleigh an hour before.

Mrs. Alwynn was much annoyed at Dare's entire want of heart in leaving the house without coming to see her, and during the remainder of the morning she did not cease to comment on the differences that exist between what people really are and what they seem to be, until, in her satisfaction at recounting the accident to Evelyn Danvers, a new and sympathetic listener, she fortunately forgot the slight put upon her ankle earlier in the day. The complete enjoyment of her sufferings was, however, destined to sustain a severe shock the following morning.

She and Ruth were reading their letters, Mrs. Alwynn, of course, giving Ruth the benefit of the various statements respecting the weather which her correspondents had confided to her, when Mr. Alwynn came in from the study, an open letter in his hand. He was quite pink with pleasure.

"He has asked me to go and see them," he said, "and they *are* small, and have green seals, all excepting one,"—referring to the letter—"which has a big red seal in a tin box, attached by a tape. Ruth, I am perfectly *convinced* beforehand that those charters are grants of land of the fourteenth or fifteenth century. Sir Charles mentions that they are in black letter, and only a few lines on each, but he says he won't describe them in full, as I must come and see them for myself. Dear me! how I shall enjoy arranging them for him, which he asked me to do. I had really become so anxious about them that a few days ago I determined to set my mind at rest, and I wrote to him to ask for particulars, and that is his answer."

Mr. Alwynn put Charles's letter into her hand, and she glanced over it.

"Why, Uncle John, he asks Aunt Fanny as well; and—'if Miss Deyncourt is still with you, pleasure,' etc.—and *me*, too!"

"When is it for?" asked Mrs. Alwynn, suddenly sitting bolt-upright.

"Let me see. 'Black letter size about'—where is it? Here. 'Tuesday, the 25th, for three nights. Leaving home following week for some time. Excuse short notice,' etc. It is next week, Aunt Fanny."

"I shall not be able to go," gasped Mrs. Alwynn, sinking back on her sofa, while something very like tears came into her eyes; "and I've never been there, Ruth. The Thursbys went once, in old Sir George's time, and Mrs. Thursby always says it is the show-place in the county, and that it is such a pity I have not seen it. And last autumn, when John went, I was in Devonshire, and never even heard of his going till I got home, or I'd have come back. Oh, Ruth! Oh, dear!"

Mrs. Alwynn let her letters fall into her lap, and drew forth the colored pocket-handkerchief which she wore, in imitation of Mabel Thursby, stuck into the bodice of her gown, and at the ominous appearance of which Mr. Alwynn suddenly recollected a duty in the study and retreated.

With an unerring instinct Ruth flew to the musical-box and set it going, and then knelt down by the prostrate figure of her aunt, and administered what sympathy and consolation she could, to the "cheery" accompaniment of the "Buffalo Girls."

"Never mind, dear Aunt Fanny. Perhaps he will ask you again when you are better. There will be other opportunities."

"I always was unlucky," said Mrs. Alwynn, faintly. "I had a swelled face up the Rhine on our honey-moon. Things always happen like that with me. At any rate," —after a pause—"there is *one* thing. We ought to try and look at the bright side. It is not as if we had not been asked. We have not been overlooked."

"No," said Ruth, promptly; and in her own mind she registered a vow that in her future home she would never give the pain that being overlooked by the larger house can cause to the smaller house.

"And I will stay with you, Aunt Fanny," she went on, cheerfully. "Uncle John can go by himself, and we will do just what we like while he is away, won't we?"

But at this Mrs. Alwynn demurred. She was determined that if she played the rôle of a martyr she would do it well. She insisted that Ruth should accompany Mr. Alwynn. She secretly looked forward to telling Mabel that Ruth was going. She did not mind being left alone, she said. She desired, with a sigh of self-sacrifice, that Mr. Alwynn should accept for himself and his niece. She had not been brought up to consider herself, thank God! She had her faults she knew. No one was more fully aware of them than herself; but she was not going to prevent others enjoying themselves because she herself was laid aside.

"And now, my dear," she said, with a sudden return to mundane interests that succeeded rather unexpectedly to the celestial spirit of her previous remarks, "you must be thinking about your gowns. If I had been going, I should have had my ruby satin done up—so beautiful by candle-light. What have you to wear? That white lace tea-gown with the silver-gray train is very nice; but you ought not to be in half mourning now. I like to see young people in colors. And then there is that gold-and-white brocade, Ruth, that you wore at the drawing-room last year. It is a beautiful dress, but rather too quiet. Could not you brighten it up with a few cherry-colored bows about it, or a sash? I always think a sash is so becoming. If you were to bring it down, I dare say I could suggest something. And you must be well dressed, for though he only says 'friends,' you never can tell whom you may not meet at a place like that."

CHAPTER XVII

The last week of September found Charles back at Stoke Moreton to receive the "friends" of whom Mrs. Alwynn spoke. People whose partridges he had helped to kill were now to be gathered from the east and from the west to help to kill his. From the north also guests were coming, were leaving their mountains to—But the remainder of the line is invidious. The Hope-Actons had written to offer a visit at Stoke Moreton on the strength of an old promise to Charles, a promise so old that he had forgotten it, until reminded, that next time they were passing they would take his house on their way. They had offered their visit exactly at the same time for which he had just invited the Alwynns and Ruth. Charles felt that they were not quite the people whom he would have arranged to meet each other, but, as Fate had so decreed it, he acquiesced calmly enough.

But when Lady Mary also wrote tenderly from Scarborough, to ask if she could be of any use helping to entertain his guests, he felt it imperative to draw the line, and wrote a grateful effusion to his aunt, saying that he could not think of asking her to leave a place where he felt sure she was deriving spiritual and temporal benefit, in order to assist at so unprofitable a festivity as a shooting-party. He mentioned casually that Lady Grace Lawrence, Miss Deyncourt, and Miss Wyndham were to be of the party, which details he imagined might have an interest for her amid her graver reflections.

The subject of Ruth's coming certainly had a prominent place in his own graver reflections. For the last fortnight, as he went from house to house, he had been wondering how he could meet her again, and, when Mr. Alwynn's letter concerning the charters was forwarded to him, a sudden inspiration made him then and there send the invitation which had arrived at Slumberleigh Rectory a few days before. He groaned in spirit as he wrote it, at the thought of Mrs. Alwynn disporting herself, dressed in the brightest colors, among his other guests; and it was with a feeling of thankfulness that he found Ruth and Mr. Alwynn were coming without her.

He had felt very little interest so far in the party, which, with the exception of the Hope-Actons, had been long arranged, but now he found himself looking forward to it with actual impatience, and he returned home a day before the time, instead of an hour or two before his guests were expected, as was his wont.

The Wyndhams and Hope-Actons, with Lady Grace in tow, were the first to appear upon the scene. Mr. Alwynn and Ruth arrived a few hours later, amid a dropping fire of young men and gun-cases, who kept on turning up at intervals during the afternoon, and, according to the mysterious nocturnal habits of their kind, till late into the night.

If ever a man appears to advantage it is on his native hearth, and as Charles stood on his in the long hall, where it was the habit of the house to assemble before dinner, Ruth found that her attempts at conversation were rather thrown away upon Lady Grace, with whom she had been renewing an old acquaintance, and whose interest, for the time being, entirely centred in the carved coats of arms and heraldic designs with which the towering white stone chimney-piece was covered.

Lady Grace was one of those pretty, delicate creatures who remind one of a very elaborate rose-bud. There was an appearance of ultra-refinement about her, a look of that refinement which is in itself a weakness, a poverty of blood, so to speak, the opposite and more pleasing but equally unhealthy extreme of coarseness. She looked very pretty as, having left Ruth, she stood by Charles, passing her little pink hand over the lowest carvings, dim and worn with the heat of many generations of fires, and listened with rapt attention to his answers to her questions.

"And the Hall is so beautiful," she said, looking round with childlike curiosity at the walls covered with weapons, and with a long array of armor, and at the massive pillars of carved white stone which rose up out of the polished floor to meet the raftered ceiling. "It is so—so uncommon."

Whatever Charles's other failings may have been, he was an admirable host. The weather was fine. What can be finer than September when she is in a good-humor? The two first days of Ruth's visit were unalloyed enjoyment. It seemed like a sudden return to the old life with Lady Deyncourt, when the round of country visits regularly succeeded the season in London. Of Mr. Alwynn she saw little or nothing. He was buried in the newly discovered charters. Of Charles she saw a good deal, more than at the time she was quite aware of, for he seemed to see a great deal of everybody, from Lady Grace to the shy man of the party, who at Stoke Moreton first conceived the idea that he was an acquisition to society. But, whether Charles made the opportunities or not which came so ready to his hand, still he found time, amid the pressure of his shooting arrangements and his duties as host, to talk to Ruth.

One day there was cub-hunting in the gray of the early morning, to which she and Miss Wyndham went with Charles and others of the party who could bear to get up betimes. Losing sight of the others after a time,

Ruth and Charles rode back alone together, when the sun was high, walking their tired horses along the black-berried lanes, and down the long green rides cut in the yellowing bracken of the park.

"And so you are going to winter in Rome?" said Charles, who had the previous day, contrary to his wont, accepted an invitation to Slumberleigh Hall for the middle of October. "I sometimes go to Rome for a few weeks when the shooting is over. And are you glad or sorry at the prospect of leaving your Cranford?"

"Very sorry."

"Why?"

"I have seen an entirely new phase of life at Slumberleigh."

"I think I can guess what you mean," said Charles, gravely. "One does not often meet any one like Mr. Alwynn."

"No. I was thinking of him. Until I came to Slumberleigh the lines had not fallen to me in very clerical places, so my experience is limited; but he seems to me to be the only clergyman I have known who does not force on one a form of religion that has been dead and buried for years."

"The clergy have much to answer for on that head," said Charles with bitterness. "I sometimes like and respect them as individuals, but I do not love them as a class. One ought to make allowance for the fact that they are tied and bound by the chain of their Thirty-nine Articles; that at three-and-twenty they shut the doors deliberately on any new and possibly unorthodox idea; and it is consequently unreasonable to expect from them any genuine freedom or originality of thought. I can forgive them their assumption of superiority, their inability to meet honest scepticism with anything like fairness, their continual bickering among themselves; but I cannot forgive them the harm they are doing to religion, the discredit they are bringing upon it by their bigoted views and obsolete ideas. They busy themselves doing good—that is the worst of it; they mean well, but they do not see that, in the mean while, their Church is being left unto them desolate; though perhaps, after all, the Church having come to be what it is, that is the best thing that can happen."

"There are men among the clergy who will not come under that sweeping accusation," said Ruth. "Look at some of the London churches. Are they desolate? Goodness and earnestness will be a power to the end of time, however narrow the accompanying creed may be."

"That is true, but we have heads as well as hearts. Goodness and earnestness appeal to the heart alone. The intellect is left out in the cold.

However good and earnest, and eloquent one of these great preachers may be, the reason we go to hear him is not only because of that, but because he appears to be thinking in a straight line, because he seems to recognize the long-resisted claim of the intellect, and we hope he will have a word to say to us. He promises well, but listen to him a little longer, follow his thought, and you will begin to see that he will only look for truth within a certain area, that his steps are describing an arc, that he is tethered. Give him time enough, and you will see him tread out the complete circle in which he and his brethren are equally bound to walk."

"You forget," said Ruth, "that you are regarding the Church from the stand-point of the cultivated and intellectual class, for whom the Church has ceased to represent religion; but there are lots of people neither cultivated nor intellectual—women even of our own class are not so as a rule—to whom the Church, with its ritual and dogma, is a real help and comfort. If, as you say, it does not suit the more highly educated, I think you have no right to demand that it *should* suit what is, after all, a very small minority. It would be most unfair if it did."

Charles did not answer. He had been looking at her, and thinking how few women could have disagreed with him as quietly and resolutely as this young girl riding at his side, carefully avoiding chance rabbit-holes as she spoke.

"There is, and there always will be, a certain number of people, not only among the clergy," she went on, "who, as somebody says, 'put the church clock back,' and are unable to see that they cannot alter the time of day for all that; only they can and do prevent many well-intentioned people from trusting to it any longer. But there are others here and there whom a dogmatic form of religion has been quite unable to spoil, whose more simple turn of mind draws out of the very system that appears to you so lifeless and effete, a real faith, a personal possession, which no one can take from them."

Her eyes sparkled as she spoke, and Charles saw that she was thinking of Mr. Alwynn.

"He has got it," he said, slowly, "this something which we all want, and for the greater part never find. He has got it. To see and recognize it early is a great thing," he continued, earnestly. "To disbelieve in it in early life, and cavil at all the caricatures and imitations, and only come to find out its reality comparatively later on, is a great misfortune—a great misfortune."

She felt that he was speaking of himself, and they rode on in silence, each grave with a sense of mutual understanding and companionship.

They forded the stream, and trotted up the little village street, the cottagers gazing admiringly after them till they disappeared within the great arched gate-way. And Charles looked at his old house as they paced up the wide drive, and wondered whether it were indeed possible that the lonely years he had spent in it had come to an end at last—at last.

Ruth had noticed that he had lost no opportunity of talking to her, and when she heard him conversing with Lady Grace, or plunging into fashionable slang with Miss Wyndham, found herself admiring the facility with which he adapted himself to different people.

The following afternoon, as she was writing in the library, she was amused to see that he found it incumbent on him to write too, even going so far as to produce a letter from Molly, whose correspondence he said he invariably answered by return.

"You seem very fond of giving Molly pleasure," said Ruth.

"I am glad to see, Miss Deyncourt, that you are beginning to estimate me at my true worth."

"You have it in your power just now to give a great pleasure," said Ruth, earnestly, laying down the pen which she had taken up.

"How?"

"It seems so absurd when it is put into words, but—by asking Mrs. Alwynn some time to stay here. She has always longed to see Stoke Moreton, because—well, because Mrs. Thursby has; and real, positive, actual tears were shed that she could not come when you asked us."

"Is it possible?" said Charles. "It is the first time that any letter of mine has caused emotion of that description."

"Ah! you don't know how important the smallest things appear if one lives in a little corner of the world where nothing ever happens. If Mrs. Alwynn had been able to come, her visit would have been an event which she would have remembered for years. I assure you, I myself, from having lived at Slumberleigh eight months, became quite excited at the prospect of so much dissipation."

And Ruth leaned back in her chair with a little laugh.

Charles looked narrowly at her and his face fell.

"I am glad you told me," he said, after a moment's pause. "People generally mention these things about ten years afterwards; when there is probably no possibility of doing anything. Thank you."

Ruth was disconcerted by the sudden gravity of his tone, and almost regretted the impulse that had made her speak. She forgot it, however, in the *tableaux vivants* which they were preparing for the evening, in which she and Charles illustrated the syllable *nun* to enthusiastic applause. Ruth represented the nun, engaged in conversation, over the lowest imaginable convent wall, with Charles, in all the glory of his cocked hat and deputy-lieutenant's uniform, who, while he held the nun's hand in one of his, pointed persuasively with the other towards an elaborately caparisoned war-horse, trembling beneath the joint weight of a yeomanry saddle and a side-saddle attached behind it, which considerably overlapped the charger's impromptu fur boa tail.

After the *tableaux* there was dancing in acting costume, at which the two men, who acted the war-horse between them were the only persons to protest, Lady Grace being beautiful as an improvised Anne Boleyn, and the shy man resplendent in a fancy dress of Charles's.

When the third morning came, Ruth gave a genuine sigh at the thought that it was the last day. Lady Grace, who was also leaving the following morning, may be presumed to have echoed it with far more sorrow. The Wyndhams were going that day, and disappeared down the drive, waving handkerchiefs, and carriage-rugs, and hats on sticks, out of the carriage-windows, as is the custom of really amusing people when taking leave.

In the afternoon, Lady Grace and Charles went off for a ride alone together, to see some ruin in which Lady Grace had manifested a sudden interest, the third horse, which had been brought round for another of the men, being sent back to the stables, his destined rider having decided, at the eleventh hour, to join the rest of the party in a little desultory rabbit shooting in the park, which he proceeded to do with much chuckling over his extraordinary penetration and tact.

The elder ladies went out driving, looking, as seen from an upper window, like four poached eggs on a dish; and the coast being clear, Ruth, who had no love of driving, escaped with her paint-box to the garden, where she was making a sketch of Stoke Moreton.

Some houses, like people, have dignity. Stoke Moreton, with ivy creeping up its mellow sandstone, and peeping into its long lines of mullioned windows, stood solemn and stately amid its level gardens; the low sun, bringing out every line of carved stone frieze and quaint architrave, firing all the western windows, and touching the tall heads of the hollyhocks and sunflowers, that stood in ordered regiments within their high walls of clipped box. And Ruth dabbed and looked, and dabbed again, until she suddenly found that if she put another stroke she would spoil all, and also that her hands were stiff with cold. After a few admiring glances at her work, she set off on a desultory journey round the gardens to get warm, and finally, seeing an oak door in the garden-wall open, wandered through it into the church-yard. The church door was open, too, and Ruth, after reading some of the epitaphs on the tombstones, went in.

It was a common little church enough, with a large mortuary chapel, where all the Danvers family reposed; ancient Danvers lying in armor, with their mailed hands joined, beside their wives; more modern Danvers kneeling in bass-relief in colored plaster and execrable taste in recesses. The last generations were there also; some of them anticipating the resurrection and feathered wings, but for the most part still asleep. Charles's mother was there, lying in white marble among her husband's people, with the child upon her arm which she had taken away with her.

And in the middle of the chapel was the last Sir Charles Danvers, whom his brother, Sir George, the father of the present owner, had succeeded. The evening sun shone full on the kneeling soldier figure, leaning on its sword, and on the grave, clear-cut face, which had a look of Charles. The long, beautifully modelled hands, clasped over the battered steel sword-hilt, were like Charles's too. Ruth read the inscription on the low marble pedestal, relating how he had fallen in the taking of the Redan, and then looked again. And gradually a great feeling of pity rose in her heart for the family which had lived here for so many generations, and which seemed now so likely to die out. Providence does not seem to care much for old families, or to value long descent. Rather it seems to favor the new race—the Browns, and the Joneses, and the Robinsons, who yesterday were not, and who to-day elbow the old county families from the place which has known them from time immemorial.

"I suppose Molly will some day marry a Smith," said Ruth to herself, "and then it will be all over. I don't think I will come and see her here when she is married."

With which reflection she returned to the house, and, after disturbing Mr. Alwynn, who was deep in a catalogue of the Danvers manuscripts, in which it was his firm conviction that he should find some mention of the charters, she went into the library, and wondered which of the several thousands of books would interest her till the others came in.

The library was a large room, the walls of which were lined with books from the floor to the ceiling. In order to place the higher shelves within reach, a light balcony of polished oak ran round the four walls, about equidistant from the floor and the ceiling. Ruth went up the tiny corkscrew staircase in the wall, which led to the balcony, and settling herself comfortably in the low, wide window-seat, took out one volume after another of those that came within her reach. These shelves by the window where she was sitting had somehow a different look to the rest. Old books and new, white vellum and card-board, were herded together without any apparent order, and with no respect of bindings. Here a splendid morocco "Novum Organum" was pushed in beside a cheap and much worn edition of Marcus Aurelius; there Emerson and Plato and Shakespeare jostled each other on the same shelf, while, just below, "Don Quixote" was pressed into the uncongenial society of Carlyle on one side and Confucius on the other. As she pulled out one book after another, she noticed that the greater part of them had Charles's name in them. Ruth's curiosity was at once aroused. No doubt this was the little corner in his great house in which he chose to read, and these were his favorite books which he had arranged so close to his hand. If we can judge our fellow-creatures at all, which is doubtful, it is by the books they read, and by those which, having read, they read again. She looked at the various volumes in the window-seat beside her with new interest, and opened the first one she took up. It was a collection of translations from the Persian poets, gentlemen of the name of Jemshíd, Sádi, and Hafiz, of whom she had never heard. As she turned over the pages, she heard the ringing of horses' hoofs, and, looking out from her point of observation, saw Charles and Lady Grace cantering up the short wide approach, and clattering out of sight again behind the great stone archway. She turned back to her book, and was reading an ode here and there, wondering to see how the same thoughts that work within us to-day had lived with man so many hundred years ago, when her eye was caught by some writing on the margin of a page as she turned it over. A single sentence on the page was strongly underlined:

"*True self-knowledge is knowledge of God.*"

Jemshíd was a wise man, Ruth thought, if he had found out that; and then she read, in Charles's clear handwriting in the margin:

"*With this compare 'Look within. Within is the fountain of good, and it will ever bubble up if thou wilt ever dig.'—Marcus Aurelius.*"

At this moment Charles came into the library, and looked up to where she was sitting, half hidden from below by the thickness of the wall.

"What, studying?" he called, gayly. "I saw you sitting in the window as I rode up. I might have known that if you were lost sight of for half an hour you would be found improving yourself in some exasperating way." And he ran up the little stairs and came round the balcony towards her. "My own special books, I see—Eve, as usual, surreptitiously craving for a knowledge of good and evil. What have you got hold of?"

The remainder of the window-seat was full of books; so, to obtain a better view of what she was reading, he knelt down by her, and looked at the open book on her knee.

Ruth did not attempt to close it. She felt guilty, she hardly knew of what. After a moment's pause she said:

"I plead guilty. I was curious. I saw these were your own particular shelves; but I never can resist looking at the books people read."

"Will you be pleased to remember in future that, in contemplating my character, Miss Deyncourt—a subject not unworthy of your attention—you are on private property. You are requested to keep on the gravel paths, and to look at the grounds I am disposed to show you. If, as is very possible, admiration seizes you, you are at liberty to express it. But there must be no going round to the back premises, no prying into corners, no trespassing where I have written up, 'No road.'"

Ruth smiled, and there was a gleam in her eyes which Charles well knew heralded a retort, when suddenly through the half-open door a silken rustle came, and Lady Hope-Acton slowly entered the room, as if about to pass through it on her way to the hall.

Now, kneeling is by no means an attitude to be despised. In church, or in the moment of presentation to majesty, it is appropriate, even essential; but it is dependent, like most things, upon circumstances and environment. No attitude, for instance, could be more suitable and natural to any one wishing to read the page on which a sitting fellow-creature was engaged. Charles had found it so. But, as Lady Hope-Acton sailed into the room, he felt that, however conducive to study, it was not the attitude in which he would at that moment have chosen to be found. Ruth felt the same. It had seemed so natural a moment before, it was so hideously suggestive now.

Perhaps Lady Hope-Acton would pass on through the other door, so widely, so invitingly open. Neither stirred, in the hope that she might do so. But in the centre of the room she stopped and sighed—the slow, crackling sigh of a stout woman in a too well-fitting silk gown.

Charles suddenly felt as if his muddy boots and cords were trying to catch her eye, as if every book on the shelves were calling to her to look up.

For a second Ruth and Charles gazed down upon the top of Lady Hope-Acton's head, the bald place on which showed dimly through her semi-transparent cap. She moved slightly, as if to go; but no, another step was drawing near. In another moment Lady Grace came in through the opposite door in her riding-habit.

Ruth felt that it was now or never for a warning cough; but, as she glanced at Charles kneeling beside her, she could not give it. Surely they would pass out in another second. The thought of the two pairs of eyes which would be raised, and the expression in them was intolerable.

"Grace," said Lady Hope-Acton, with dreadful distinctness, advancing to meet her daughter, "has he spoken?"

"No," said Lady Grace, with a little sob; "and," —with a sudden burst of tears—"oh, mamma, I don't think he ever will."

Oh, to have coughed, to have sneezed, to have choked a moment earlier! Anything would have been better than this.

"Run up-stairs this moment, then, and change your habit and bathe your eyes," said Lady Hope-Acton, sharply. "You need not come down till dinner-time. I will say you are tired."

And then, to the overwhelming relief of those two miserable spectators, the mother and daughter left the door.

But to the momentary sensation of relief in Ruth's mind a rush of pity succeeded for the childlike grief and tears; and with and behind it, like one hurrying wave overtopping and bearing down its predecessor, came a burning indignation against the cause of that picturesque emotion.

It is indeed a lamentable peculiarity of our fallen nature that the moment of relief from the smart of anxiety is seldom marked by so complete a mental calmness and moderation as could be wished.

Ruth rose slowly, with the book still in her hand, and Charles got off his knees as best he could, and stood with one hand on the railing of the balcony, as if to steady himself. His usually pale face was crimson.

Ruth closed the book in silence, and with a dreadful precision put it back in its accustomed place. Then she turned and faced him, with the western light full upon her stern face, and another light of contempt and indignation burning in her direct eyes.

"Poor little girl," she said, in a low distinct voice. "What a triumph to have succeeded in making her unhappy. She is very young, and she did not understand the rules of the game. Poor, foolish little girl!"

If he had been red before, he was pale enough now. He drew himself up, and met her direct gaze without flinching. He did not speak, and she left him standing in the window, and went slowly along the balcony and down the little staircase into the room below.

As she was about to leave the room he moved forward suddenly, and said, "Miss Deyncourt!"

Involuntarily she stopped short, in obedience to the stern authority of the tone.

"You are unjust."

She did not answer and left the room.

CHAPTER XVIII

"Uncle John," said Ruth next morning, taking Mr. Alwynn aside after breakfast, "we are leaving by the early train, are we not?"

"No, my love, it is quite impossible. I have several papers to identify and rearrange."

"We have stayed a day longer than we intended as it is. Most of the others go early. Do let us go too."

"It is most natural, I am sure, my dear, that you should wish to get home," said Mr. Alwynn, looking with sympathetic concern at his niece; "and why your aunt has not forwarded your letters I can't imagine. But still, if we return by the mid-day train, Ruth, you will have plenty of time to answer any letters that—ahem!—seem to require immediate attention, before the post goes; and I don't see my way to being ready earlier."

Ruth had not even been thinking of Dare and his letters; but she saw that by the early train she was not destined to depart, and watched the other guests take leave with an envious sigh. She was anxious to be gone. The last evening, after the episode in the library, had been interminably long. Already the morning, though breakfast was hardly over, seemed to have dragged itself out to days in length. A sense of constraint between two people who understand and amuse each other is very galling. Ruth had felt it so. All the previous evening Charles had hardly spoken to her, and had talked mainly to Lady Hope-Acton, who was somewhat depressed, and another elder lady. A good-night and a flat candlestick can be presented in a very distant manner, and as Ruth received hers from Charles that evening, and met the grave, steady glance that was directed at her, she perceived that he had not forgiven her for what she had said.

She felt angry again at the idea that he should venture to treat her with a coldness which seemed to imply that she had been in the wrong. The worst of it was that she felt she was to blame; that she had no right whatever to criticise Charles and his actions. What concern were they of hers? How much more suitable, how much more eloquent a dignified silence would have been. She could not imagine now, as she thought it over, why she had been so unreasonably annoyed at the moment as to say what she had done. Yet the reason was not far to seek, if she had only known where to lay her hand on it. She was uneasy, impatient; she longed to get out of the house. And it was still early; only eleven. Eleven till twelve. Twelve till one. One till half-past. Two whole hours and a half to be got through before the Stoke Moreton omnibus would bear her away. She looked round for a refuge during that weary age, and found it nearer than many poor souls do in time of need, namely, at her elbow, in the shape, the welcome shape of the shy man—almost the only remnant of the large party whose dispersion she had just been watching. Whenever Ruth thought of that shy man afterwards, which was not often, it was with a sincere hope that he had forgotten the forwardness of her behavior on that particular morning. She wished to see the picture-gallery. She would of all things like a walk afterwards. No, she had not been as far as the beech-avenue; but she would like to go. Should they look at the pictures first—now—no time like the present? How pleased he was! How proud! He felt that his shyness had gone forever; that Miss Deyncourt would, no doubt, like to hear a few anecdotes of his college life; that a quiet man, who does not make himself cheap to start with, often wins in the end; that Miss Deyncourt had unusual appreciation, not only for pictures, but for reserved and intricate characters that yet (here he ventured on a little joke, and laughed at it himself) had their lighter side. And in the long picture-gallery Ruth and he studied the old masters, as they had seldom been studied before, with an intense and ignorant interest on the one hand, and an entire absence of mind on the other.

Charles, who had done a good deal of pacing up and down his room the night before, and had arrived at certain conclusions, passed through the gallery once, but did not stop. He looked grave and preoccupied, and hardly answered a question of Mr. Conway's about one of the pictures.

Half-past eleven at last. A tall inlaid clock in the gallery mentioned the hour by one sedate stroke; the church clock told the village the time of day a second later. They had nearly finished the pictures. Never mind. She could take half an hour to put on her hat, and surely any beech-avenue, even on a dull day like this might serve to while away the remaining hour before luncheon.

They had come to the last picture of the Danvers collection, and Ruth was dwelling fondly on a very well-developed cow by Cuyp, as if she could hardly tear herself away from it, when she heard a step coming up the staircase from the hall, and presently Charles pushed open the carved folding-doors which shut off the gallery from the rest of the house, and looked in. She was conscious that he was standing in the door-way, but new beauties in the cow, which had hitherto escaped her, engaged her whole attention at the moment, and no one can attend to two things at once.

Charles did not come any farther; but, standing in the door-way, he called to the shy man who went to him, and the two talked together for a few moments. Ruth gazed upon the cow until it became so fixed upon the retina of her eye that, when she tried to admire an old Florentine cabinet near it, she still saw its portrait; and when, in desperation, she turned away to look out of the window across the sky and sloping park, the shadow of the cow hung like a portent.

A moment later Mr. Conway came hurrying back to her much perturbed, to say he had quite forgotten till this moment, had not in the least understood, in fact, etc. Danvers' gray cob, that he had thoughts of buying, was waiting at the door for him to try—in fact, had been waiting some time. No idea, upon his soul—

Ruth cut his apology short before he had done more than flounder well into it.

"You must go and try it at once," she said with decision; and then she added, as Charles drew near: "I have changed my mind about going out. It looks as if it might turn to rain. I shall get through some arrears of letter-writing instead."

Mr. Conway stammered, and repeated himself, and finally rushed out of the gallery. Ruth expected that Charles would accompany him, but he remained standing near the window, apparently engaged like herself in admiring the view.

"It struck me," he said, slowly, with his eyes half shut, "that Conway proved rather a broken reed just now."

"He did," said Ruth. She suddenly felt that she could understand what it was in Charles that exasperated Lady Mary so much.

He came a step nearer, and his manner altered.

"I sent him away," he said, looking gravely at her, "because I wished to speak to you."

Ruth did not answer or turn her head, though she felt he was watching her. Her eyes absently followed two young fallow-deer in the park, cantering away in a series of hops on their long stiff legs.

"I cannot speak to you here," said Charles, after a pause.

Ruth turned round.

"Silence is golden sometimes. I think quite enough has been said already."

"Not by me. You expressed yourself with considerable frankness. I wish to follow your example."

"You said I was unjust at the time. Surely that was sufficient."

"So insufficient that I am going to repeat it. I tell you again that you are unjust in not being willing to hear what I have to say. I have seen a good deal of harm done by misunderstandings, Miss Deyncourt. Pride is generally at the bottom of them. We are both suffering from a slight attack of that malady now; but I value your good opinion too much to hesitate, if, by any little sacrifice of my own pride, I can still retain it. If, after your remarks yesterday, I can make the effort (and it *is* an effort) to ask you to hear something I wish to say, you, on your side, ought not to refuse to listen. It is not a question of liking; you *ought* not to refuse."

He spoke in an authoritative tone, which gave weight to his words, and in spite of herself she saw the truth of what he said. She was one of those rare women who, being convinced against their will, are *not* of the same opinion still. It was ignominious to have to give way; but, after a moment's struggle with herself, she surmounted her dislike to being overruled, together with a certain unreasoning tenacity of opinion natural to her sex, and said, quietly:

"What do you wish me to do?"

Charles saw the momentary struggle, and honored her for a quality which women seldom give men occasion to honor them for.

"Do you dislike walking?"

"No."

"Then, if you will come out-of-doors, where there is less likelihood of interruption than in the house, I will wait for you here."

She went silently down the picture-gallery, half astonished to find herself doing his bidding. She put on her walking things mechanically, and came back in a few minutes to find him standing where she had left him. In silence they went down-stairs, and through the piazza with its flowering orange-trees, out into the gardens, where, on the stone balustrade, the peacocks were attitudinizing and conversing in the high key in which they always proclaim a change of weather and their innate vulgarity to the world. Charles led the way towards a little rushing brook which divided the gardens from the park.

"I think you must have had a very low opinion of me beforehand to say what you did yesterday," he remarked, suddenly.

"I was angry," said Ruth. "However true what I said may have been, I had no right to say it to—a comparative stranger. That is why I repeat that it would be better not to make matters worse by mentioning the subject again. It is sure to annoy us both. Let it rest."

"Not yet," said Charles, dryly. "As a comparative stranger, I want to know,"—stopping and facing her—"exactly what you mean by saying that she, Lady Grace, did not understand the rules of the game."

"I cannot put it in other words," said Ruth, her courage rising as she felt that a battle was imminent.

"Perhaps I can for you. Perhaps you meant to say that you believed I was in the habit of amusing myself at other people's expense; that—I see your difficulty in finding the right words—that it was my evil sport and pastime to—shall we say—raise expectations which it was not my intention to fulfil?"

"It is disagreeably put," said Ruth, reddening a little; "but possibly I did mean something of that kind."

"And how have you arrived at such an uncharitable opinion of a comparative stranger?" asked Charles, quietly enough, but his light eyes flashing.

She did not answer.

"You are not a child, to echo the opinion of others," he went on. "You look as if you judged for yourself. What have I done since I met you first, three months ago, to justify you in holding me in contempt?"

"I did not say I held you in contempt."

"You must, though, if you think me capable of such meanness."

Silence again.

"You have pushed me into saying more than I meant," said Ruth at last; "at least you have said I mean a great deal more than I really do. To be honest, I think you have thoughtlessly given a good deal of pain. I dare say you did it unconsciously."

"Thank you. You are very charitable, but I cannot shield myself under the supposition that at eight-and-thirty I am a creature of impulse, unconscious of the meaning of my own actions."

"If that is the case," thought Ruth, "your behavior to me has been inexcusable, especially the last few days; though, fortunately for myself, I was not deceived by it."

"If you persist in keeping silence," said Charles, after waiting for her to speak, "any possibility of conversation is at an end."

"I did not come out here for conversation," replied Ruth. "I came, not by my own wish, to hear something you said you particularly desired to say. Do you not think the simplest thing, under the circumstances, would be—to say it?"

He gave a short laugh, and looked at her in sheer desperation. Did she know what she was pushing him into?

"I had forgotten," he said. "It was in my mind all the time; but now you have made it easy for me indeed by coming to my assistance in this way. I will make a fresh start."

He compressed his lips, and seemed to pull himself together. Then he said, in a very level voice:

"Kindly give me your whole attention, Miss Deyncourt, so that I shall not be obliged to repeat anything. The deer are charming, I know; but you have seen deer before, and will no doubt again. I am sorry that I am obliged to speak to you about myself, but a little autobiography is unavoidable. Perhaps you know that about three years ago I succeeded my father. From being penniless, and head over ears in debt, I became suddenly a rich man—not by my father's will, who entailed every acre of the estates here and elsewhere on Ralph, and left everything he could to him. I had thought of telling you what my best friends have never known, why I am not still crippled by debt. I had thought of telling you why, at five-and-thirty, I was still unmarried, for my debts were not the reason; but I will not trouble you with that now. It is enough to say that I found myself in a position which, had I been a little younger, with rather a different past, I should have enjoyed more than I did. I was well received in English society when, after a lapse of several years and a change of fortune, I returned to it. If I had thought I was well received for myself, I should have been a fool. But I came back disillusioned. I saw the machinery. When you reflect on the vast and intricate machinery employed by mothers with grown-up daughters, you may imagine what I saw. In all honesty and sincerity I wished to marry; but in the ease with which I saw I could do so lay my chief difficulty. I did not want a new toy, but a companion. I suppose I still clung to one last illusion, that I might meet a woman whom I could love, and who would love me, and not my name or income. I could not find her, but I still believed in her. I went everywhere in the hope of meeting her, and, if others have ever been disappointed in me, they have never known how disappointed I have been in them. For three years I looked for her everywhere, but I could not find her, and at last I gave her up. And then I met Lady Grace Lawrence, and liked her. I had reason to believe she could be disinterested. She came of good people—all Lawrences are good; she was simple and unspoiled, and she seemed to like me. When I look back I believe that I had decided to ask her to marry me, and that it was only by the merest chance that I left London without speaking to her. What prevented me I hardly know, unless it was a reluctance at the last moment to cast the die. I came down to Atherstone, harassed and anxious, tired of everything and everybody, and there," said Charles, with sudden passion, turning and looking full at Ruth, "there I met *you.*"

The blood rushed to her face, and she hastily interposed, "I don't see any necessity to bring my name in."

"Perhaps not," he returned, recovering himself instantly; "unfortunately, I do."

"You expect too much of my vanity," said Ruth, her voice trembling a little; "but in this instance I don't think you can turn it to account. I beg you will leave me out of the question."

"I am sorry I cannot oblige you," he said, grimly; "but you can't be left out. I only regret that you dislike being mentioned, because that is a mere nothing to what is coming."

She trusted that he did not perceive that the reason she made no reply was because she suddenly felt herself unable to articulate. Her heart was beating wildly, as that gentle, well conducted organ had never beaten before. What was coming? Could this stern, determined man be the same apathetic, sarcastic being whom she had hitherto known?

"From that time," he continued, "I became surer and surer of what at first I hardly dared to hope, what it seemed presumption in me to hope, namely, that at last I had found what I had looked for in vain so long. I had to keep my engagement with the Hope-Actons in Scotland; but I regretted it. I stayed as short a time as I could. I did not ask them to come here. They offered themselves. I think, if I have been to blame, it has not been in so heartless a manner as you supposed; and it appears to me Lady Hope-Acton should not have come. This is my explanation. You can add the rest for yourself. Have I said enough to soften your harsh judgment of yesterday?"

Ruth could not speak. The trees were behaving in the most curious manner, were whirling round, were swaying up and down. The beeches close in front were dancing quadrilles; now ranged in two long rows, now setting to partners, now hurrying back to their places as she drew near.

"Sit down," said Charles's voice, gently; "you look tired."

The trunk of a fallen tree suddenly appeared rising up to meet her out of a slight mist, and she sat down on it more precipitately than she could have wished. In a few seconds the trees returned to their places, and the mist, which appeared to be very local, cleared away.

Charles was sitting on the trunk beside her, looking at her intently. The anger had gone out of his face, and had given place to a look of deep anxiety and suspense.

"I have not finished yet," he said, and his voice had changed as much as his face. "There is still something more."

"No, no!" said Ruth. "At least, if there is, don't say it."

"I think I would rather say it. You wish to save me pain, I see; but I am quite prepared for what you are going to say. I did not intend to speak to you on the subject for a long time to come, but yesterday's event.has forced my hand. There must be no more misunderstandings between us. You intend to refuse me, I can see. All the same, I wish to tell you that I love you, and to ask you to be my wife."

"I am afraid I cannot," said Ruth, almost inaudibly.

"No," said Charles, looking straight before him, "I have asked you too soon. You are quite right. I did not expect anything different; I only wished you to know. But, perhaps, some day—"

"Don't!" said Ruth, clasping her hands tightly together. "You don't know what you are saying. Nothing can make any difference, because—I am engaged."

She dared not look at his face, but she saw his hand clinch.

For an age neither spoke.

Then he turned his head slowly and looked at her. His face was gray even to the lips. With a strange swift pang at the heart, she saw how her few words had changed it.

"To whom?" he said at last, hardly above a whisper.

"To Mr. Dare."

"Not that man who has come to live at Vandon?"

"Yes."

Another long silence.

"When was it?"

"Ten days ago."

"Ten days ago," repeated Charles, mechanically, and his face worked. "Ten days ago!"

"It is not given out yet," said Ruth, hesitating, "because Mr. Alwynn does not wish it during Lord Polesworth's absence. I never thought of any mistake being caused by not mentioning it. I would not have come here if I had had the least idea that—"

"You cannot mean to say that you had never seen that I—what I—felt for you?"

"Indeed I never thought of such a thing until two minutes before you said it. I am very sorry I did not, but I imagined—"

"Let me hear what you imagined."

"I noticed you talked to me a good deal; but I thought you did exactly the same to Lady Grace, and others."

"You could not imagine that I talked to others—to any other woman in the world—as I did to you."

"I supposed," said Ruth, simply, "that you talked gayly to Lady Grace because it suited her; and more gravely to me, because I am naturally grave. I thought at the time you were rather clever in adapting yourself to different people so easily; and I was glad that I understood your manner better than some of the others."

"Better!" said Charles, bitterly. "Better, when you thought that of me! No, you need not say anything. I was in fault, not you. I don't know what right I had to imagine you understood me—you seemed to understand me—to fancy that we had anything in common, that in time—" He broke into a low wretched laugh. "And all the while you were engaged to another man! Good God, what a farce! what a miserable mistake from first to last!"

Ruth said nothing. It was indeed a miserable mistake.

He rose wearily to his feet.

"I was forgetting," he said; "it is time to go home." And they went back together in silence, which was more bearable than speech just then.

The peacocks were still pirouetting and minuetting on the stone balustrade as they came back to the garden. The gong began to sound as they entered the piazza.

To Ruth it was a dreadful meal. She tried to listen to Mr. Conway's account of the gray cob, or to the placid conversation of Mr. Alwynn about the beloved manuscripts. Fortunately the morning papers were full of a recent forgery in America, and a murder in London, which furnished topics when these were exhausted, and Charles used them to the utmost.

At last the carriage came. Mr. Alwynn and Mr. Conway simultaneously broke into incoherent ejaculations respecting the pleasure of their visit; Ruth's hand met Charles's for an embarrassed second; and a moment later they were whirling down the straight wide approach, between the columns of fantastically clipped hollies, leaving Charles standing in the door-way. He was still standing there when the carriage rolled under the arched gate-way with its rampant stone lions. Ruth glanced back once, as they turned into the road, at the stately old house, with its pointed gables and forests of chimneys cutting the gray sky-line. She saw the owner turn slowly and go up the steps, and looked hastily away again.

"Poor Danvers!" said Mr. Alwynn, cheerfully, also looking, and putting Ruth's thoughts into words. "He must be desperately lonely in that house all by himself; but I suppose he is not often there."

And Mr. Alwynn, whose mind had been entirely relieved since Ruth's engagement from the dark suspicion he had once harbored respecting Charles, proceeded to dilate upon the merits of the charters, and of the owner of the charters, until he began to think Ruth had a headache, and finding it to be the case, talked no more till they reached, at the end of their little journey, the door of Slumberleigh Rectory.

"Is it very bad?" he asked, kindly, as he helped her out of the carriage.

Ruth assented, fortunately with some faint vestige of truth, for her hat hurt her forehead.

"Then run up straight to your own room, and I will tell your aunt that you will come and have a chat with her later on, perhaps after tea, when the post will be gone." Mr. Alwynn spoke in the whisper of stratagem.

Ruth was only too thankful to be allowed to slip on tiptoe to her own room, but she had not been there many minutes when a tap came to the door.

"There, my dear," said Mr. Alwynn, putting his head in, and holding some letters towards her. "Your aunt ought to have forwarded them. I brought them up at once. And there is nearly an hour to post-time, and she won't expect you to come down till then. I think the headache will be better now, eh?"

He nodded kindly to her, and closed the door again. Ruth sat down mechanically, and began to sort the packet he had put into her hands. The first three letters were in the same handwriting, Dare's large vague handwriting, that ran from one end of the envelope to the other, and partly hid itself under the stamp.

She looked at them, but did not open them. A feeling of intense lassitude and fatigue had succeeded to the unconscious excitement of the morning. She could not read them now. They must wait with the others. Presently she could feel an interest in them; not now.

She leaned her head upon her hand, and a rush of pity swept away every other feeling as she recalled that last look at Stoke Moreton, and how Charles had turned so slowly and wearily to go in-doors. There was an ache at her heart as she thought of him, a sense of regret and loss. And he had loved her all the time!

"If I had only known!" she said to herself, pressing her hands against her forehead. "But how could I tell—how could I tell?"

She raised her head with a sudden movement, and began with nervous fingers to open Dare's letters, and read them carefully.

CHAPTER XIX

In the long evening that followed Ruth's departure from Stoke Moreton, Charles was alone for once in his own home. He was leaving again early on the morrow, but for the time he was alone, and heavy at heart. He sat for hours without stirring, looking into the fire. He had no power or will to control his thoughts. They wandered hither and thither, and up and down, never for a moment easing the dull miserable pain that lay beneath them all.

Fool! fool that he had been!

To have found her after all these years, and to have lost her without a stroke! To have let another take her, and such a man as Dare! To have such a fool's manner that he was thought to be in earnest when he was least so; that now, when his whole future hung in the balance, retribution had overtaken him, and with bitter irony had mocked at his earnestness and made it of none effect. She had thought it was his natural manner to all! His cursed folly had lost her to him. If she had known, surely it would have been, it must have been different. At heart Charles was a very humble man, though it was not to be expected many would think so; but nevertheless he had a deep, ever-deepening consciousness (common to the experience of the humblest once in a lifetime) that between him and Ruth that mysterious link of mutual understanding and sympathy existed which cannot be accounted for, which eludes analysis, which yet makes, when the sex happens to be identical, the indissoluble friendship of a David and a Jonathan, a Karlos and a Posa; and, where there is a difference of sex, brings about that rarest wonder of the world, a happy marriage.

Like cleaves to like. He knew she would have loved him. She was his by right. The same law of attraction which had lifted them at once out of the dreary flats of ordinary acquaintanceship would have drawn them ever closer and closer together till they were knit in one. He knew, with a certainty that nothing could shake, that he could have made her love him, even as he loved her; unconsciously at first, slowly perhaps—for the current of strong natures, like that of deep rivers, is sometimes slow. Still the end would have been the same.

And he had lost her by his own act, by his own heedless folly; her want of vanity having lent a hand the while to put her beyond his reach forever.

It was a bitter hour.

And as he sat late into the night beside the fire, that died down to dust and ashes before his absent eyes, ghosts of other heavy hours, ghosts of the past, which he had long since buried out of his sight, came back and would not be denied.

To live much in the past, is a want of faith in the Power that gives the present. Comparatively few men walk through their lives looking backward. Women more frequently do so from a false estimate of life fostered by romantic feeling in youth, which leads them, if the life of the affections is ended, resolutely to refuse to regard existence in any other maturer aspect, and to persist in wandering aimlessly forward, with eyes turned ever on the dim flowery paths of former days.

"Let the dead past bury its dead."

But there comes a time, when the grass has grown over those graves, when we may do well to go and look at them once more; to stand once again in that solitary burial-ground, "where," as an earnest man has said, "are buried broken vows, worn-out hopes, joys blind and deaf, faiths betrayed or gone astray—lost, lost love; silent spaces where only one mourner ever comes."

And to the last retrospective of us our dead past yet speaks at times, and speaks as one having authority.

Such a time had come for Charles now. From the open grave of his love for Ruth he turned to look at others by which he had stood long ago, in grief as sharp, but which yet in all its bitterness had never struck as deep as this.

Memory pointed back to a time twenty years ago, when he had hurried home through a long summer night to arrive at Stoke Moreton too late; to find only the solemn shadow of the mother whom he had loved, and whom he had grieved; too late to ask for forgiveness; too late for anything but a wild passion of grief and remorse, and frantic self-accusation.

The scene shifted to ten years later. It was a sultry July evening of the day on which the woman whom he had loved for years had married his brother. He was standing on the deck of the steamer which was taking him from England, looking back at the gray town dwindling against the tawny curtain of the sunset. In his brain was a wild clamor of wedding-bells, and across the water, marking the pulse of the sea, came to his outward ears the slow tolling of a bell on a sunken rock near the harbor mouth.

It seemed to be tolling for the death of all that remained of good in him. In losing Evelyn, whom he had loved with all the idealism and reverence of a reckless man for a good woman, he believed, in the bitterness of his spirit, that he had lost all; that he had been cut adrift from the last mooring to a better future, that nothing could hold him back now. And for a time it had been so, and he had drowned his trouble in a sea in which he wellnigh drowned himself as well.

Once more memory pointed—pointed across five dark years to an evening when he had sat as he was sitting now, alone by the wide stone hearth in the hall at Stoke Moreton, after his father's death, and after the reading of the will. He was the possessor of the old home, which he had always passionately loved, from which he had been virtually banished so long. His father, who had never liked him, but who of late years had hated him as men only hate their eldest sons, had left all in his power to his second son, had entailed every acre of the Stoke Moreton and other family properties upon him and his children. Charles could touch nothing, and over him hung a millstone of debt, from which there was now no escape. He sat with his head in his hands—the man whom his friends were envying on his accession to supposed wealth and position—ruined.

A few days later he was summoned to London by a friend whom he had known for many years. He remembered well that last meeting with the stern old man whom he had found sitting in his arm-chair with death in his face. He had once or twice remonstrated with Charles in earlier days, and as he came into his presence now for the last time, and met his severe glance, he supposed, with the callousness that comes from suffering which has reached its lowest depths, that he was about to rebuke him again.

"And so," said General Marston, sternly, "you have come into your kingdom; into what you deserve."

"Yes," said Charles. "If it is any pleasure to you to know that what you prophesied on several occasions has come true, you can enjoy it. I am ruined!"

"You fool!" said the sick man slowly. "To have come to five-and-thirty, and to have used up everything which makes life worth having. I am not speaking only of money. There is a bankruptcy in your face that money will never pay. And you had talent and a good heart and the making of a man in you once. I saw that when your father turned you adrift. I saw that when you were at your worst after your brother's marriage. Yes, you need not start. I knew your secret and kept it as well as you did yourself. I tried to stop you; but you went your own way."

Charles was silent. It was true, and he knew it.

"And so you thought, I suppose, that if your father had made a just will you could have retrieved yourself?"

"I know I could," said Charles, firmly; "but he left the — —shire property to Ralph, and every shilling of his capital; and Ralph had my mother's fortune already. I have Stoke Moreton and the place in Surrey, which he could not take from me, but everything is entailed, down to the trees in the park. I have nominally a large income; but I am in the hands of the Jews. I can't settle with them as I expected, and they will squeeze me to the uttermost. However, as you say, I have the consolation of knowing I brought it on myself."

"And if your father acted justly, as you would call it, which I knew he never would, you would have run through everything in five years' time."

"No, I should not. I know I have been a fool; but there are two kinds of fools—the kind that sticks to folly all its life, and the kind that has its fling, and has done with it. I belong to the second kind. My father had no right to take my last chance from me. If he had left it me, I should have used it."

"You look tired of your fling," said the elder man. "Very tired. And you think money would set you right, do you?" He looked critically at the worn, desperate face opposite him. "I made my will the other day," he went on, his eyes still fixed on Charles. "I had not much to leave, and I have no near relations, so I divided it among various charitable institutions. I see no reason to alter my will. If one leaves money, however small the sum may be, one likes to think it has been left to some purpose, with some prospect of doing good. A few days ago I had a surprise. I fancy it was to be my last surprise in this world. I inherited from a distant relation, who died intestate, a large fortune. After being a poor man all my days, wealth comes to me when I am on the point of going where money won't follow. Curious, isn't it? I am going to leave this second sum in the same spirit as the first, but in rather a different manner. I like to know what I am doing, so I sent for you. I am of opinion that the best thing I can do with it, is to set you on your legs again. What do you owe?"

Charles turned very red, and then very white.

"What do you owe?" repeated the sick man, testily. "I am getting tired. How much is it?" He got out a check-book, and began filling it in. "Have you no tongue?" he said, angrily, looking up. "Tell me the exact figure. Well? Keep nothing back."

"I won't be given the whole," said Charles, with an oath. "Give me enough to settle the Jews, and I will do the rest out of my income. I won't get off scot free."

"Well, then, have your own way, as usual, and name the sum you want. There, take it," he said, feebly, when Charles had mentioned with shame a certain hideous figure, "and go. I shall never know what you do with it, so you can play ducks and drakes with it if you like. But you won't like. You have burned your fingers too severely to play with fire again. You have turned over so many new leaves that now you have come to the last in the book. I have given you another chance, Charles; but one man can't do much to help another. The only person who can really help you is yourself. Give yourself a chance, too."

How memory brought back every word of that strange interview. Charles saw again the face of the dying man; heard again the stern, feeble voice, "Give yourself a chance."

He had given himself a chance. "Some natures, like comets, make strange orbits, and return from far." Charles had returned at last. The old man's investment had been a wise one. But, as Charles looked back, after three years, he saw that his friend had been right. His money debts had been the least part of what he owed. There were other long-standing accounts which he had paid in full during these three years, paid in the restless weariness and disappointment that underlay his life, in the loneliness in which he lived, in his contempt for all his former pursuits, which had left him at first devoid of any pursuits at all.

He had had, as was natural, very little happiness in his life, but all the bitterness of all his bitter past seemed as nothing to the agony of this moment. He had loved Evelyn with his imagination, but he loved Ruth with his whole heart and soul, and—he had lost her.

The night was far advanced. The dawn was already making faint bars over the tops of the shutters, was looking in at him as he sat motionless by his dim lamp and his dead fire. And, in spite of the growing dawn, it was a dark hour.

CHAPTER XX

Dare returned to Vandon in the highest spirits, with an enormous emerald engagement-ring in an inner waistcoat-pocket. He put it on Ruth's third finger a few days later, under the ancient cedar on the terrace at Vandon, a spot which, he informed her (for he was not without poetic flights at times), his inner consciousness associated with all the love scenes of his ancestors that were no more.

He was stricken to the heart when, after duly admiring it, Ruth gently explained to him that she could not wear his ring at present, until her engagement was given out.

"Let it then be given out," he said, impetuously. "Ah! why already is it not given out?"

She explained again, but it was difficult to make him understand, and she felt conscious that if he would have allowed her the temporary use of one hand to release a fly, which was losing all self-control inside her veil, she might have been more lucid. As it was, she at last made him realize the fact that, until Lord Polesworth's return from America in November, no further step was to be taken.

"But all is right," he urged with pride. "I have seen my lawyer; I make a settlement. I raise money on the property to make a settlement. There is nothing I will not do. I care for nothing only to marry you."

Ruth led him to talk of other things. She was very gentle with him, always attentive, always ready to be interested; but any one less self-centred than Dare would have had a misgiving about her feeling for him. He had none. Half his life he had spent in Paris, and, imbued with French ideas of betrothal and marriage, he thought her manner at once exceedingly becoming and natural. She was reserved, but reserve was charming. She did not care for him very much perhaps, as yet, but as much as she could care for any one. Most men think that if a woman does not attach herself to them she is by nature cold. Dare was no exception to the rule; and though he would have preferred that there should be less constraint in their present intercourse, that she would be a little more shy, and a little less calm, still he was supremely happy and proud, and only longed to proclaim the fortunate state of his affairs to the world.

One thing about Ruth puzzled him very much, and with a vague misgiving she saw it did so. Her interest in the Vandon cottages, and the schools, and the new pump, had been most natural up to this time. It had served to bring them together; but now the use of these things was past, and yet he observed, with incredulity at first and astonishment afterwards, that she clung to them more than ever.

What mattered it for the moment whether the pump was put up or not, or whether the cottages by the river were protected from the floods? Of course in time, for he had promised, a vague something would be done; but why in the golden season of love and plighted faith revert to prosaic subjects such as these?

Some men are quite unable to believe in any act of a woman being genuine. They always find out that it has something to do with them. If an angel came down from heaven to warn a man of this kind of wrath to come, he would think the real object of her journey was to make his acquaintance.

Ruth saw the incredulity in Dare's face when she questioned him, and her heart sank within her. It sank yet lower when she told him one day, with a faint smile, that she knew he was not rich, and that she wanted him to let her help in the rebuilding of certain cottages, the plans of which he had brought over in the summer, but which had not yet been begun, apparently for the want of funds.

"What you cannot do alone we can do together," she said.

He agreed with effusion. He was surprised, flattered, delighted, but entirely puzzled.

The cottages were begun immediately. They were near the river, which divided the Slumberleigh and Vandon properties. Ruth often went to look at them. It did her good to see them rising, strong and firm, though hideous to behold, on higher ground than the poor dilapidated hovels at the water's edge, where fever was always breaking out, which yet made, as they supported each other in their crookedness, and leaned over their own wavering reflections, such a picturesque sketch that it seemed a shame to supplant them by such brand new red brick, such blue tiling, such dreadful little porches.

Ruth drew the old condemned cottages, with the long lines of pollarded marshy meadow, and distant bridge and mill in the background, but it was a sketch she never cared to look at afterwards. She was constantly drawing now. There was a vague restlessness in her at this time that made her take refuge in the world of nature, where the mind can withdraw itself from itself for a time into a stronghold where misgiving and anxiety cannot corrupt, nor self break through and steal. In these days she shut out self steadfastly, and fixed her eyes firmly on the future, as she herself had made it with her own hands.

She had grown very grave of late. Dare's high spirits had the effect of depressing her more than she would allow, even to herself. She liked him. She told herself so every day, and it was a pleasure to her to see him so happy. But when she had accepted him he was so diffident, so quiet, so anxious, that she had not realized that he would return to his previous happy self-confidence, his volubility, his gray hats—in fact, his former gay self—directly his mind was at ease and he had got what he wanted. She saw at once that the change was natural, but she found it difficult to keep pace with, and the effort to do so was a constant strain.

She had yet to learn that it is hard to live for those who live for self. Between a nature which struggles, however feebly, towards a higher life, and one whose sole object is gracefully and good-naturedly, but persistently to enjoy itself, there is a great gulf fixed, of which often neither are aware, until they attempt a close relationship with each other, when the chasm reveals itself with appalling clearness to the higher nature of the two.

Ruth was glad when a long-standing engagement to sing at a private concert in one place, and sell modern knick-knacks in old English costume at another, took her from Slumberleigh for a week. She looked forward to the dreary dissipation in store for her with positive gladness; and when the week had passed, and she was returning once more, she wished the stations would not fly so quickly past, that the train would not hurry itself so unnecessarily to bring her back to Slumberleigh.

As the little local line passed Stoke Moreton station she looked out for a moment, but leaned back hurriedly as she caught a glimpse of the Danvers omnibus in the background, with its great black horses, and a footman with a bag standing on the platform. In another moment Mrs. Alwynn, followed by the footman, made a dart at Ruth's carriage, jumped in, seized the bag, repeated voluble thanks, pressed half her gayly dressed person out again through the window to ascertain that her boxes were put in the van, caught her veil in the ventilator as the train started, and finally precipitated herself into a seat on her bag, as the motion destroyed her equilibrium.

"Well, Aunt Fanny!" said Ruth.

"Why, goodness gracious, my dear, if it isn't you! And, now I think of it, you were to come home to-day. Well, how oddly things fall out, to be sure, me getting into your carriage like that. And you'll never guess, Ruth, though for that matter there's nothing so very astonishing about it, as I told Mrs. Thursby, you'll never guess where *I've* been visiting."

Ruth remembered seeing the Danvers omnibus at the station, and suddenly remembered, too, a certain request which she had once made of Charles.

"Where can it have been?" she said, with a great show of curiosity.

"You will never guess," said Mrs. Alwynn, in high glee. "I shall have to help you. You remember my sprained ankle? There! Now I have as good as told you."

But Ruth would not spoil her aunt's pleasure; and after numerous guesses, Mrs. Alwynn had the delight of taking her completely by surprise, when at last she leaned forward and said, with a rustle of pride, emphasizing each word with a pat on Ruth's knee:

"I've been to Stoke Moreton."

"How delightful!" ejaculated Ruth. "How astonished I am! Stoke Moreton!"

"You may well say that," said Mrs. Alwynn, nodding to her. "Mrs. Thursby would not believe it at first, and afterwards she said she was afraid there would not be any party; but there was, Ruth. There was a married couple, very nice people, of the name of Reynolds. I dare say, being London people, you may have known them. She had quite the London look about her, though not dressed low of an evening; and he was a clergyman, who had overworked himself, and had come down to Stoke Moreton to rest, and had soup at luncheon. And there was another person besides, a Colonel Middleton, a very clever man, who wrote a book that was printed, and had been in India, and was altogether most superior. We were three gentlemen and two ladies, but we had ices each night, Ruth, two kinds of ices; and the second night I wore my ruby satin, and the clergyman at Stoke Moreton, that nice young Mr. Brown, who comes to your uncle's chapter meetings, dined, with his sister, a very pleasing person indeed, Ruth, in black. In fact, it was a very pleasant little gathering, so nice and informal, and the footman did not wait at luncheon, just put the pudding and the hot plates down to the fire; and Sir Charles so chatty and so full of his jokes, and I always liked to hear him, though my scent of humor is not quite the same as his. Sir Charles has a feeling heart, Ruth. You should have heard Mr. Reynolds talk about him. But he looked very thin and pale, my dear, and he seemed to be always so tired, but still as pleasant as could be. And I told him he wanted a wife to look after him, and I advised him to have an egg beaten up in ever such a little drop of brandy at eleven o'clock, and he said he would think about it, he did indeed, Ruth; so I just went quietly to the house-keeper and asked her to see to it, and a very sensible person she was, Ruth, been in the family twenty years, and thinks all the world of Sir Charles, and showed me the damask table-cloths that were used for the prince's visit, and the white satin coverlet, embroidered with gold thistles, quite an heirloom, which had been worked by the ladies of the house when James I. slept there. Think of that, my dear!"

And so Mrs. Alwynn rambled on, recounting how Charles had shown her all the pictures himself, and the piazza where the orange and myrtle trees were, and how she and Mrs. Reynolds had gone for a drive together, "in a beautiful landau," etc., till they reached home.

As a rule Ruth rather shrank from travelling with Mrs. Alwynn, who always journeyed in her best clothes, "because you never know whom you may not meet." To stand on a platform with her was to be made conspicuous, and Ruth generally found herself unconsciously going into half mourning for the day, when she went anywhere by rail with her aunt. To-day Mrs. Alwynn was more gayly dressed than ever, but as Ruth looked at her beaming face she felt nothing but a strange pleasure in the fact that Charles had not forgotten the little request which later events had completely effaced from her own memory. He, it seemed, had remembered, and, in spite of what had passed, had done what she asked him. She wished that she could have told him she was grateful. Alas! there were other things that she wished she could have told him; that she was sorry she had misjudged him; that she understood him better now. But what did it matter? What did it matter? She was going to marry Dare, and *he* was the person whom she must try to understand for the remainder of her natural life. She thought a little wearily that she could understand *him* without trying.

CHAPTER XXI

The 18th of October had arrived. Slumberleigh Hall was filling. The pheasants, reprieved till then, supposed it was only for partridge shooting, and thinking no evil, ate Indian-corn, and took no thought for the annual St. Bartholomew of their race.

Mabel Thursby had met Ruth out walking that day, and had informed her that Charles was to be one of the guns, also Dare, though, as she remembered to add, suspecting Dare admired Ruth, the latter was a bad shot, and was only asked out of neighborly feeling.

After parting with Mabel, Ruth met, almost at her own gate, Ralph Danvers, who passed her on horseback, and then turned on recognizing her. Ralph's conversational powers were not great, and though he walked his horse beside her, he chiefly contented himself with assenting to Ruth's remarks until she asked after Molly.

He at once whistled and flicked a fly off his horse's neck.

"Sad business with Molly," he said; "and mother out for the day. Great grief in the nursery. Vic's dead!"

"Oh, poor Molly!"

"Died this morning. Fits. I say," with a sudden inspiration, "you wouldn't go over and cheer her up, would you? Mother's out. I'm out. Magistrates' meeting at D— —."

Ruth said she had nothing to do, and would go over at once, and Ralph nodded kindly at her, and rode on. He liked her, and it never occurred to him that it could be anything but a privilege to minister to any need of Molly's. He jogged on more happily after his meeting with Ruth, and only remembered half an hour later that he had completely forgotten to order the dog-cart to meet Charles, who was coming to Atherstone for a night before he went on to kill the Slumberleigh pheasants the following morning.

Ruth set out at once over the pale stubble fields, glad of an object for a walk.

Deep distress reigned meanwhile in the nursery at Atherstone. Vic, the much-beloved, the stoat pursuer, the would-be church-goer, Vic was dead, and Molly's soul refused comfort. In vain nurse conveyed a palpitating guinea-pig into the nursery in a bird-cage, on the narrow door of which remains of fur showed an unwilling entrance; Molly could derive no comfort from guinea-pigs.

In vain was the new horse, with leather hoofs, with real hair, and a horse-hair tail—in vain was that token of esteem from Uncle Charles brought out of its stable, and unevenly yoked with a dappled pony planted on a green, oval lawn, into Molly's own hay-cart. Molly's woe was beyond the reach of hay-carts or horse-hair tails, however realistic. Like Hezekiah, she turned her face to the nursery wall, on which trains and railroads were depicted; and even when cook herself rose up out of her kitchen to comfort her with material consolations, she refused the mockery of a gingerbread nut, which could not restore the friend with whom previous gingerbread nuts had always been equally divided.

Presently a step came along the passage, and Charles, who had found no one in the drawing-room, came in tired and dusty, and inclined to be annoyed at having had to walk up from the station.

Molly flew to him, and flung her arms tightly round his neck.

"Oh, Uncle Charles! Uncle Charles! Vic is dead!"

"I am so sorry, Molly," taking her on his knee.

Nurse and the nursery-maid and cook withdrew, leaving the two mourners alone together.

"He is *dead*, Uncle Charles. He was quite well, and eating Albert biscuits with the dolls this morning, and now—" The rest was too dreadful, and Molly burst into a flood of tears, and burrowed with her head against the faithful waistcoat of Uncle Charles—Uncle Charles, the friend, the consoler of all the ills that Molly had so far been heir to.

"Vic had a very happy life, Molly," said Charles, pressing the little brown head against his cheek, and vaguely wondering what it would be like to have any one to turn to in time of trouble.

"I always kept trouble from him except that time I shut him in the door," gasped Molly. "I never took him out in a string, and he only wore his collar—that collar you gave him, that made him scratch so—on Sundays."

"And he was not ill a long time. He did not suffer any pain?"

"No, Uncle Charles, not much; but, though he did not say anything, his face looked worse than screaming, and he passed away very stiff in his hind-legs. Oh!" (with a fresh outburst), "when cook told me that her sister that was in a decline had gone, I never thought," (sob, sob!) "poor Vic would be the next."

A step came along the passage, a firm light step that Charles knew, that made his heart beat violently.

The door opened and a familiar voice said:

"Molly! My poor Molly! I met father, and—"

Ruth stood in the door-way, and stopped short. A wave of color passed over her face, and left it paler than usual.

Charles looked at her over the mop of Molly's brown head against his breast. Their grave eyes met, and each thought how ill the other looked.

"I did not know—I thought you were going to Slumberleigh to-day," said Ruth.

"I go to-morrow morning," replied Charles. "I came here first."

There was an awkward silence, but Molly came to their relief by a sudden rush at Ruth, and a repetition of the details of the death-bed scene of poor Vic for her benefit, for which both were grateful.

"You ought to be thinking where he is to be buried, Molly," suggested Charles, when she had finished. "Let us go into the garden and find a place."

Molly revived somewhat at the prospect of a funeral, and though Ruth was anxious to leave her with her uncle, insisted on her remaining for the ceremony. They went out together, Molly holding a hand of each, to choose a suitable spot in the garden. By the time the grave had been dug by Charles, Molly was sufficiently recovered to take a lively interest in the proceedings, and to insist on the attendance of the stable-cat, in deep mourning, when the remains of poor Vic, arrayed in his best collar, were lowered into their long home.

By the time the last duties to the dead had been performed, and Charles, under Molly's direction, had planted a rose-tree on the grave, while Ruth surrounded the little mound with white pebbles, Molly's tea-time had arrived, and that young lady allowed herself to be led away by the nursery-maid, with the stable-cat in a close embrace, resigned, and even cheerful at the remembrance of those creature comforts of cook's, which earlier in the day she had refused so peremptorily.

When Molly left them, Ruth and Charles walked together in silence to the garden-gate which led to the foot-path over the fields by which she had come. Neither had a word to say, who formerly had so much.

"Good-bye," she said, without looking at him.

He seemed intent on the hasp of the gate.

There was a moment's pause.

"I should like," said Ruth, hating herself for the formality of her tone, "to thank you before I go for giving Mrs. Alwynn so much pleasure. She still talks of her visit to you. It was kind of you to remember it. So much seems to have happened since then, that I had not thought of it again."

At her last words Charles raised his eyes and looked at her with strange wistful intentness, but when Ruth had finished speaking he had no remark to make in answer; and as he stood, bareheaded by the gate, twirling the hasp and looking, as a hasty glance told her, so worn and jaded in the sunshine, she said "Good-bye" again, and turned hastily away.

And all along the empty harvested fields, and all along the lanes, where the hips and haws grew red and stiff among the ruddy hedge-rows, Ruth still saw Charles's grave, worn face.

That night she saw it still, as she sat in her own room, and listened to the whisper of the rain upon the roof, and the touch of its myriad fingers on the window-panes.

"I cannot bear to see him look like that. I cannot bear it," she said, suddenly, and the storm which had been gathering so long, the clouds of which had darkened the sky for so many days, broke at last, with a strong and mighty wind of swift emotion which carried all before it.

It was a relief to give way, to let the tempest do its worst, and remain passive. But when its force was spent at last, and it died away in gusts and flying showers, it left flood and wreckage and desolation behind. When Ruth raised her head and looked about her, all her landmarks were gone. There was a streaming glory in the heavens, but it shone on the ruin of all her little world below. She loved Charles, and she knew it. It seemed to her now as if, though she had not realized it, she must have loved him from the first; and with the knowledge came an overwhelming sense of utter misery that struck terror to her heart. She understood at last the meaning of the weariness and the restless misgivings of these last weeks. If heretofore they had spoken in riddles, they spoke plainly now. Every other feeling in the world seemed to have been swept away by a passion, the overwhelming strength of which she regarded panic-stricken. She seemed to have been asleep all her life, to have stirred restlessly once or twice of late, and now to have waked to consciousness and agony. Love, with women like Ruth, is a great happiness or a great calamity. It is with them indeed for better, for worse.

Those whose feelings lie below the surface escape the hundred rubs and scratches which superficial natures are heir to; but it is the nerve which is not easily reached which when touched gives forth the sharpest pang. Nature, when she gives intensity of feeling, mercifully covers it well with a certain superficial coldness. Ruth had sometimes wondered why the incidents, the books, which called forth emotion in others, passed her by. The vehement passion which once or twice in her life she had involuntarily awakened in others had met with no response from herself. The sight of the fire she had unwittingly kindled only made her shiver with cold. She believed herself to be cold—always a dangerous assumption on the part of a woman, and apt to prove a broken reed in emergency.

Charles knew her better than she knew herself. Her pride and unconscious humble-mindedness, her frankness with its underlying reserve, spoke of a strong nature, slow, perhaps, but earnest, constant, and, once roused, capable of deep attachment.

And now the common lot had befallen her, the common lot of man and womankind since Adam first met Eve in the Garden of Eden. Ruth was not exempt.

She loved Charles.

When the dawn came up pale and tearful to wake the birds, it found her still sitting by her window, sitting where she had sat all night, looking with blank eyes at nothing. Creep into bed, Ruth, for already the sparrows are all waking, and their cheerful greetings to the new day add weariness to your weariness. Creep into bed, for soon the servants will be stirring, and before long Martha, who has slept all night, and thinks your lines have fallen to you in pleasant places and late hours, will bring the hot water.

CHAPTER XXII

Reserved people pay dear for their reserve when they are in trouble, when the iron enters into their soul, and their eyes meet the eyes of the world tearless, unflinching, making no sign.

Enviable are those whose sorrows are only pen and ink deep, who take every one into their confidence, who are comforted by sympathy, and fly to those who will weep with them. There is an utter solitude, a silence in the grief of a proud, reserved nature, which adds a frightful weight to its intensity; and when the night comes, and the chamber door is shut, who shall say what agonies of prayers and tears, what prostrations of despair, pass like waves over the soul to make the balance even?

As a rule, the kindest and best of people seldom notice any alteration of appearance or manner in one of their own family. A stranger points it out, if ever it is pointed out, which, happily, is not often, unless, of course, in cases where advice has been disregarded, and the first symptom of ill health is jealously watched for and triumphantly hailed by those whose mission in life it is to say, "I told you so."

Mrs. Alwynn, whose own complaints were of so slight a nature that they had to be constantly referred to to give them any importance at all, was not likely to notice that Ruth's naturally pale complexion had become several degrees too pale during the last two days, or that she had dark rings under her eyes. Besides, only the day before, had not Mrs. Alwynn, in cutting out a child's shirt, cut out at the same time her best drawing-room table-cloth as well, which calamity had naturally driven out of her mind every other subject for the time?

Ruth had proved unsympathetic, and Mrs. Alwynn had felt her to be so. The next day, also, when Mrs. Alwynn had begun to talk over what she and Ruth were to wear that evening at a dinner-party at Slumberleigh Hall, Ruth had again shown a decided want of interest, and was not even to be roused by the various conjectures of her aunt, though repeated over and over again, as to who would most probably take her in to dinner, who would be assigned to Mr. Alwynn, and whether Ruth would be taken in by a married man or a single one. As it was quite impossible absolutely to settle these interesting points beforehand, Mrs. Alwynn's mind had a vast field for conjecture opened to her, in which she disported herself at will, varying the entertainment for herself and Ruth by speculating as to who would sit on the other side of each of them; "for," as she justly observed, "everybody has two sides, my dear; and though, for my part, I can talk to anybody— Members of Parliament, or bishops, or any one—still it is difficult for a young person, and if you feel dull, Ruth, you can always turn to the person on the other side with some easy little remark."

Ruth rose and went to the window. It had rained all yesterday; it had been raining all the morning to-day, but it was fair now; nay, the sun was sending out long burnished shafts from the broken gray and blue of the sky. She was possessed by an unreasoning longing to get out of the house into the open air—anywhere, no matter where, beyond the reach of Mrs. Alwynn's voice. She had been fairly patient with her for many months, but during these two last wet days, a sense of sudden miserable irritation would seize her on the slightest provocation, which filled her with remorse and compunction, but into which she would relapse at a moment's notice. Every morning since her arrival, nine months ago, had Mrs. Alwynn returned from her house-keeping with the same cheerful bustle, the same piece of information: "Well, Ruth, I've ordered dinner, my dear. First one duty, and then another."

Why had that innocent and not unfamiliar phrase become so intolerable when she heard it again this morning? And when Mrs. Alwynn wound up the musical-box, and the "Buffalo Girls" tinkled on the ear to relieve the monotony of a wet morning, why should Ruth have struggled wildly for a moment with a sudden inclination to laugh and cry at the same time, which resulted in two large tears falling unexpectedly, to her surprise and shame, upon her book.

She shut the book, and recovering herself with an effort, listened patiently to Mrs. Alwynn's remarks until, early in the afternoon, the sky cleared. Making some excuse about going to see her old nurse at the lodge at Arleigh, who was still ill, she at last effected her escape out of the room and out of the house.

The air was fresh and clear, though cold. The familiar fields and beaded hedge-rows, the red land, new ploughed, where the plovers hovered, the gray broken sky above, soothed Ruth like the presence of a friend, as Nature, even in her commonest moods, has ministered to many a one who has loved her before Ruth's time.

Our human loves partake always of the nature of speculations. We have no security for our capital (which, fortunately, is seldom so large as we suppose), but the love of Nature is a sure investment, which she repays a thousand-fold, which she repays most prodigally when the heart is bankrupt and full of bitterness, as Ruth's heart was that day. For in Nature, as Wordsworth says, "there is no bitterness," that worst sting of human grief. And as Ruth walked among the quiet fields, and up the yellow aisles of the autumn glades to Arleigh, Nature spoke of peace to her—not of joy or of happiness as in old days, for she never lies as human comforters do, and these had gone out of her life; but of the peace that duty steadfastly adhered to will bring at last—the peace that after much turmoil will come in the end to those who, amid a Babel of louder tongues, hear and obey the low-pitched voices of conscience and of principle.

For it never occurred to Ruth for a moment to throw over Dare and marry Charles. She had given her word to Dare, and her word was her bond. It was as much a matter of being true to herself as to him. It was very simple. There were no two ways about it in her mind. The idea of breaking off her engagement was not to be thought of. It would be dishonorable.

We often think that if we had been placed in the same difficulties which we see overwhelm others, we could have got out of them. Just so; we might have squeezed, or wriggled, or crept out of a position from which another who would not stoop could not have escaped. People are differently constituted. Most persons with common-sense can sink their principles temporarily at a pinch; but others there are who go through life prisoners on parole to their sense of honor or duty. If escape takes the form of a temptation, they do not escape. And Ruth, walking with bent head beneath the swaying trees, dreamed of no escape.

She soon reached the little lodge, the rusty gates of which barred the grass-grown drive to the shuttered, tenantless old house at a little distance. It was a small gray stone house of many gables, and low lines of windows, that if inhabited would have possessed but little charm, but which in its deserted state had a certain pathetic interest. The place had been to let for years, but no one had taken it; no one was likely to take it in the disrepair which was now fast sliding into ruin.

The garden-beds were almost grown over with weeds, but blots of nasturtium color showed here and there among the ragged green, and a Virginia-creeper had done its gorgeous red-and-yellow best to cheer the gray stone walls. But the place had a dreary appearance even in the present sunshine; and after looking at it for a moment, Ruth went in-doors to see her old nurse. After sitting with her, and reading the usual favorite chapter in the big Bible, and answering the usual question of "Any news of Master Raymond?" in the usual way, Ruth got up to go, and the old woman asked her if she wanted the drawing-block which she had left with her some time ago with an unfinished sketch on it of the stables. She got it out, and Ruth looked at it. It was a slight sketch of an octagonal building with wide arches all round it, roofing in a paved path, on which, in days gone by, it had evidently been the pernicious custom to exercise the horses, whose stalls and loose boxes formed the centre of the building. The stable had a certain quaintness, and the sketch was at that delightful point when no random stroke has as yet falsified the promise that a finished drawing, however clever, so seldom fulfils.

Ruth took it up, and looked out of the window. The sun was blazing out, ashamed of his absence for so long. She might as well finish it now. She was glad to be out of the way of meeting any one, especially the shooters, whose guns she had heard in the nearer Slumberleigh coverts several times that afternoon. The Arleigh woods she knew were to be kept till later in the month. She took her block and paint-box, and picking her way along the choked gravel walk and down the side drive to the stables, sat down on the bench for chopping wood which had been left in the place to which she had previously dragged it, and set to work. She was sitting under one of the arches out of the wind, and an obsequious yellow cat came out of the door of one of the nearest horse-boxes, in which wood was evidently stacked, and rubbed itself against her dress, with a reckless expenditure of hair.

As Ruth stopped a moment, bored but courteous, to return its well-meant attentions by friction behind the ears, she heard a slight crackling among the wood in the stable. Rats abounded in the place, and she was just about to recall the cat to its professional duties, when her own attention was also distracted. She started violently, and grasped the drawing-block in both hands.

Clear over the gravel, muffled but still distinct across the long wet grass, she could hear a firm step coming. Then it rang out sharply on the stone pavement. A tall man came suddenly round the corner, under the archway, and stood before her. It was Charles.

The yellow cat, which had a leaning towards the aristocracy, left Ruth, and, picking its way daintily over the round stones towards him, rubbed off some more of its wardrobe against his heather shooting-stockings.

"I hardly think it is worth while to say anything except the truth," said Charles at last. "I have followed you here."

As Ruth could say nothing in reply, it was fortunate that at the moment she had nothing to say. She continued to mix a little pool of Prussian blue and Italian pink without looking up.

"I hurt my gun hand after luncheon, and had to stop shooting at Croxton corner. As I went back to Slumberleigh, across the fields below the rectory, I thought I saw you in the distance, and followed you."

"Is your hand much hurt?" —with sudden anxiety.

"No," said Charles, reddening a little. "It will stop my shooting for a day or two, but that is all."

The colors were mixed again. Ruth, contrary to all previous conviction, added light red to the Italian pink. The sketch had gone rapidly from bad to worse, but the light red finished it off. It never, so to speak, held up its head again; but I believe she has it still somewhere, put away in a locked drawer in tissue-paper, as if it were very valuable.

"I did not come without a reason," said Charles, after a long pause, speaking with difficulty. "It is no good beating about the bush. I want to speak to you again about what I told you three weeks ago. Have you forgotten what that was?"

Ruth shook her head. *She had not forgotten.* Her hand began to tremble, and he sat down beside her on the bench, and, taking the brush out of her hand, laid it in its box.

"Ruth," he said, gently, "I have not been very happy during the last three weeks; but two days ago, when I saw you again, I thought you did not look as if you had been very happy either. Am I right? Are you happy in your engagement with—Quite content? Quite satisfied? Still silent. Am I to have no answer?"

"Some questions have no answers," said Ruth, steadily, looking away from him. "At least, the questions that ought not to be asked have none."

"I will not ask any more, then. Perhaps, as you say, I have no right. You won't tell me whether you are unhappy, but your face tells me so in spite of you. It told me so two days ago, and I have thought of it every hour of the day and night since."

She gathered herself together for a final effort to stop what she knew was coming, and said, desperately:

"I don't know how it is. I don't mean it, and yet everything I say to you seems so harsh and unkind; but I think it would have been better not to come here, and I think it would be better, better for us both, if you would go away now."

Charles's face became set and very white. Then he put his fortune to the touch.

"You are right," he said. "I will go away—for good; I will never trouble you again, when you have told me that you do not love me."

The color rushed into her face, and then died slowly away again, even out of the tightly compressed lips.

There was a long silence, in which he waited for a reply that did not come. At last she turned and looked him in the face. Who has said that light eyes cannot be impassioned? Her deep eyes, dark with the utter blankness of despair, fell before the intensity of his. He leaned towards her, and with gentle strength put his arm round her, and drew her to him. His voice came in a broken whisper of passionate entreaty close to her ear.

"Ruth, I love you, and you love me. We belong to each other. We were made for each other. Life is not possible apart. It must be together, Ruth, always together, always—" and his voice broke down entirely.

Surely he was right. A love such as theirs overrode all petty barriers of every-day right and wrong, and was a law unto itself. Surely it was vain to struggle against Fate, against the soft yet mighty current which was sweeping her away beyond all landmarks, beyond the sight of land itself, out towards an infinite sea.

And the eyes she loved looked into hers with an agony of entreaty, and the voice she loved spoke of love, spoke brokenly of unworthiness, and an unhappy past, and of a brighter future, a future with *her*.

Her brain reeled; her reason had gone. Let her yield now. Surely, if only she could think, if the power to think had not deserted her, it was right to yield. The current was taking her ever swifter whither she knew not. A moment more and there would be no going back.

She began to tremble, and, wrenching her hands out of his, pressed them before her eyes to shut out the sight of the earnest face so near her own. But she could not shut out his voice, and Charles's voice could be very gentle, very urgent.

But at the eleventh hour another voice broke in on his, and spoke as one having authority. Conscience, if accustomed to be disregarded on common occasions, will rarely come to the fore with any decision in emergency; but the weakest do not put him in a place of command all their lives without at least one result—that he has learned the habit of speaking up and making himself attended to in time of need. He spoke now, urgently, imperatively. Her judgment, her reason were alike gone for the time, but, when she had paced the solemn aisles of the woods an hour ago in possession of them, had she then even thought of doing what she was on the verge of doing now? What had happened during that hour to reverse the steadfast resolve which she had made then? What she had thought right an hour ago remained right now. What she would have put far from her as dishonorable then remained dishonorable now, though she might be too insane to see it.

Terror seized her, as of one in a dream who is conscious of impending danger, and struggles to awake before it is too late. She started to her feet, and, putting forcibly aside the hands that would have held her back, walked unsteadily towards the nearest pillar, and leaned against it, trembling violently.

"Do not tempt me," she said, hoarsely. "I cannot bear it."

He came and stood beside her.

"I do not tempt you," he said. "I want to save you and myself from a great calamity before it is too late."

"It is too late already."

"No," said Charles, in a low voice of intense determination. "It is not—yet. It will be soon. It is still possible to go back. You are not married to him, and it is no longer right that you should marry him. You must give him up. There is no other way."

"Yes," said Ruth, with vehemence. "There is another way. You have made me forget it; but before you came I saw it clearly. I can't think it out as I did then; but I know it is there. There is another way"—and her voice faltered—"to do what is right, and let everything else go."

Charles saw for the first time, with a sudden frightful contraction of the heart, that her will was as strong as his own. He had staked everything on one desperate appeal to her feelings; he had carried the outworks, and now another adversary—her conscience—rose up between him and her.

"A marriage without love is a sin," he said, quietly. "If you had lived in the world as long as I have, and had seen what marriage without love means, and what it generally comes to in the end, you would know that I am speaking the truth. You have no right to marry Dare if you care for me. Hesitate, and it will be too late! Break off your engagement now. Do you suppose," with sudden fire, "that we shall cease to love each other; that I shall be able to cease to love you for the rest of my life because you are Dare's wife? What is done can't be undone. Our love for each other can't. It is no good shutting your eyes to that. Look the facts in the face, and don't deceive yourself into thinking that the most difficult course is necessarily the right one."

He turned from her, and sat down on the bench again, his chin in his hands, his haggard eyes fastened on her face. He had said his last word, and she felt that when she spoke it would be her last word too. Neither could bear much more.

"All you say sounds right, *at first*," she said, after a long silence, and as she spoke Charles's hands dropped from his face and clinched themselves together; "but I cannot go by what any one thinks unless I think so myself as well. I can't take other people's judgments. When God gave us our own, he did not mean us to shirk using it. What you say is right, but there is something which after a little bit seems more right—at least, which seems so to me. I cannot look at the future. I can only see one thing distinctly, now in the present, and that is that I cannot break my word. I never have been able to see that a woman's word is less binding than a man's. When I said I would marry him, it was of my own free-will. I knew what I was doing, and it was not only for his sake I did it. It is not as if he believed I cared for him very much. Then, perhaps—but he knows I don't, and—he is different from other men—he does not seem to mind. I knew at the time that I accepted him for the sake of other things, which are just the same now as they were then: because he was poor and I had money; because I felt sure he would never do much by himself, and I thought I could help him, and my money would help too; because the people at Vandon are so wretched, and their cottages are tumbling down, and there is no one who lives among them and cares about them. I can't make it clear, and I did hesitate; but at the time it seemed wrong to hesitate. If it seemed so right then, it cannot be all wrong now, even if it has become hard. I cannot give it all up. He is building cottages that I am to pay for, that I asked to pay for. He cannot. And he has promised so many people their houses shall be put in order, and they all believe him. And he can't do it. If I don't, it will not be done; and some of them are very old—and—and the winter is coming." Ruth's voice had become almost inaudible. "Oh, Charles! Charles!" she said, brokenly, "I cannot bear to hurt you. God knows I love you. I think I shall always love you, though I shall try not. But I cannot go back now from what I have undertaken. I cannot break my word. I cannot do what is wrong, even for you. Oh, God! not even for you!"

She knelt down beside him, and took his clinched hands between her own; but he did not stir.

"Not even for you," she whispered, while two hot tears fell upon his hands. In another moment she had risen swiftly to her feet, and had left him.

CHAPTER XXIII

Charles sat quite still where Ruth had left him, looking straight in front of him. He had not thought for a moment of following her, of speaking to her again. Her decision was final, and he knew it. And now he also knew how much he had built upon the wild new hope of the last two days.

Presently a slight discreet cough broke upon his ear, apparently close at hand.

He started up, and, wheeling round in the direction of the sound, called out, in sudden anger, "Who is there?"

If there is a time when we feel that a fellow-creature is entirely out of harmony with ourselves, it is when we discover that he has overheard or overseen us at a moment when we imagined we were alone, or—almost alone.

Charles was furious.

"Come out!" he said, in a tone that would have made any ordinary creature stay as far *in* as it could. And hearing a slight crackling in the nearest horse-box, of which the door stood open, he shook the door violently.

"Come out," he repeated, "this instant!"

"Stop that noise, then," said a voice sharply from the inside, "and keep quiet. By — —, a violent temper, what a thing it is; always raising a dust, and kicking up a row, just when it's least wanted."

The voice made Charles start.

"Great God!" he said, "it's not—"

"Yes, it is," was the reply; "and when you have taken a seat on the farther end of that bench, and recovered your temper, I'll show, and not before."

Charles walked to the bench and sat down.

"You can come out," he said, in a carefully lowered voice, in which there was contempt as well as anger.

Accordingly there was a little more crackling among the fagots, and a slight, shabbily dressed man came to the door and peered warily out, shading his blinking eyes with his hand.

"If there is a thing I hate," he said, with a curious mixture of recklessness and anxiety, "it is a noise. Sit so that you face the left, will you, and I'll look after the right, and if you see any one coming you may as well mention it. I am only at home to old friends."

He took his hand from his eyes as they became more accustomed to the light, and showed a shrewd, dissipated face, that yet had a kind of ruined good looks about it, and, what was more hateful to Charles than anything else, a decided resemblance to Ruth. Though he was shabby in the extreme, his clothes sat upon him as they always and only do sit upon a gentleman; and, though his face and voice showed that he had severed himself effectually from the class in which he had been born, a certain unsuitability remained between his appearance and his evidently disreputable circumstances. When Charles looked at him he was somehow reminded of a broken-down thorough-bred in a hansom cab.

"It is a quiet spot," remarked Raymond Deyncourt, for he it was, standing in the door-way, his watchful eyes scanning the deserted court-yard and strip of green. "A retired and peaceful spot. I'm sorry if my cough annoyed you, coming when it did, but I thought you seemed before to be engaged in conversation which I felt a certain diffidence in interrupting."

"So you listened, I suppose?"

"Yes, I listened. I did not hear as much as I could have wished, but it was your best manner, Danvers. You certainly have a gift, though you dropped your voice unnecessarily once or twice, I thought. If I had had your talents, I should not be here now. Eh? Dear me! you can swear still, can you? How refreshing. I fancied you had quite reformed."

"Why are you here now?" asked Charles, sternly.

Raymond shrugged his shoulders.

"Why are you here?" continued Charles, bitterly, "when you swore to me in July that if I would pay your passage out again to America you would let her alone in future? Why are you here, when I wrote to tell you that she had promised me she would never give you money again without advice? But I might have known you could break a promise as easily as make one. I might have known you would only keep it as long as it suited yourself."

"Well, now, I'm glad to hear you say that," said Raymond, airily, "because it takes off any feeling of surprise I was afraid you might feel at seeing me back here. There's nothing like a good understanding between friends. I'm precious hard up, I can tell you, or I should not have come; and when a fellow has got into as tight a place as I have he has got to think of other things besides keeping promises. Have you seen to-day's papers?" with sudden eagerness.

"Yes."

"Any news about the 'Frisco forgery case?" and Raymond leaned forward through the door, and spoke in a whisper.

"Nothing much," said Charles, trying to recollect. "Nothing new to-day, I think. You know they got one of them two days ago, followed him down to Birmingham, and took him in the train."

Raymond drew in his breath.

"I don't hold with trains," he said, after a pause; "at least, not with passengers. I told him as much at the time. And the—the other one—Stephens? Any news of him?"

"Nothing more about him, as far as I can remember. They were both traced together from Boston to London, but there they parted company. Stephens is at large still."

"Is he?" said Raymond. "By George, I'm glad to hear it! I hope he'll keep so, that's all. I am glad I left that fool. He'd not my notions at all. We split two days ago, and I made tracks for the old diggings; got down as far as Tarbury under a tarpaulin in a goods train—there's some sense in a goods train—and then lay close by a weir of the canal, and got aboard a barge after dark. Nothing breaks a scent like a barge. And it went the right way for my business too, and travelled all night. I kept close all next day, and then struck across country for this place at night. If I hadn't known the lie of the land from a boy, when I used to spend the holidays with old Alwynn, I couldn't have done it, or if I'd been as dog lame as I was in July; but I was pushed for time, and I footed it up here, and got in just before dawn. And not too soon either, for I'm cleaned out, and food is precious hard to come by if you don't care to go shopping for it. I am only waiting till it's dark to go and get something from the old woman at the lodge. She looked after me before, but it wasn't so serious then as it is now."

"It will be penal servitude for life this time for—Stephens," said Charles.

"Yes," said Raymond, thoughtfully. "It's playing deuced high. I knew that at the time, but I thought it was worth it. It was a beautiful thing, and there was a mint of money in it if it had gone straight—a mint of money;" and he shook his head regretfully. "But the luck is bound to change in the end," he went on, after a moment of mournful retrospection. "You'll see, I shall make my pile yet, Danvers. One can't go on turning up tails all the time."

"You will turn them up once too often," said Charles, "and get your affairs wound up for you some day in a way you won't like. But I suppose it's no earthly use my saying anything."

"Not much," replied the other. "I guess I've heard it all before. Don't you remember how you held forth that night in the wood? You came out too strong. I felt as if I were in church; but you forked out handsomely at the collection afterwards. I will say that for you."

"And what are you going to do now you've got here?" interrupted Charles, sharply.

"Lie by."

"How long?"

"Perhaps a week, perhaps ten days. Can't say."

"And after that?"

"After that, some one, I don't say who, but some one will have to provide me with the 'ready' to nip across to France. I have friends in Paris where I can manage to scratch along for a bit till things have blown over."

Charles considered for a few moments, and then said:

"Are you going to dun your sister for money again, or give her another fright by lying in wait for her? Of course, if you broke your word about coming back, you might break it about trying to get money out of her."

"I might," assented Raymond; "in fact, I was on the point of making my presence known to her, and suggesting a pecuniary advance, when you came up. I don't know at present what I shall do, as I let that opportunity slip. It just depends."

Charles considered again.

"It's a pity to trouble her, isn't it?" said Raymond, his shrewd eyes watching him; "and women are best out of money-matters. Besides, if she has promised you she won't pay up without advice, she'll stick to it. Nothing will turn her when she once settles on anything, if she is at all like what she used to be. She has got dollars of her own. You had better settle with me, and pay yourself back when you are married. Dear me! There's no occasion to look so murderous. I suppose I'm at liberty to draw my own conclusions."

"You had better draw them a little more carefully in future," said Charles, savagely. "Your sister is engaged to be married to a man without a sixpence."

"By George," said Raymond, "that won't suit my book at all. I'd rather"—with another glance at Charles—"I'd rather she'd marry a man with money."

If Charles was of the same opinion he did not express it. He remained silent for a few minutes to give weight to his last remark, and then said, slowly:

"So you see you won't get anything more from that quarter. You had better make the most you can out of me."

Raymond nodded.

"The most you will get, in fact, I may say *all* you will get from me, is enough ready money to carry you to Paris, and a check for twenty pounds to follow, when I hear you have arrived there."

"It's mean," said Raymond; "it's cursed mean; and from a man like you, too, whom I feel for as a brother. I'd rather try my luck with Ruth. She's not married yet, anyway."

"You will do as you like," said Charles, getting up. "If I find you have been trying your luck with her, as you call it, you won't get a farthing from me afterwards. And you may remember, she can't help you without consulting her friends. And your complaint is one that requires absolute quiet, or I'm very much mistaken."

Raymond bit his finger, and looked irresolute.

"To-day is Wednesday," said Charles; "on Saturday I shall come back here in the afternoon, and if you have come to my terms by that time you can cough after I do. I shall have the money on me. If you make any attempt to write or speak to your sister, I shall take care to hear of it, and you need not expect me on Saturday. That is the last remark I have to make, so good-afternoon;" and, without waiting for a reply, Charles walked away, conscious that Raymond would not dare either to call or run after him.

He walked slowly along the grass-grown road that led into the carriage-drive, and was about to let himself out of the grounds by a crazy gate, which rather took away from the usefulness of the large iron locked ones at the lodge, when he perceived an old man with a pail of water fumbling at it. He did not turn as Charles drew near, and even when the latter came up with him, and said "Good-afternoon," he made no sign. Charles watched him groping for the hasp, and, when he had got the gate open, feel about for the pail of water, which when he found he struck against the gate-post as he carried it through. Charles looked after the old man as he shambled off in the direction of the lodge.

The Danvers Jewels And Sir Charles Danvers |

"Blind and deaf! He'll tell no tales, at any rate," he said to himself. "Raymond is in luck there."

It had turned very cold; and, suddenly remembering that his absence might be noticed, he set off through the woods to Slumberleigh at a good pace. His nearest way took him through the church-yard and across the adjoining high-road, on the farther side of which stood the little red-faced lodge, which belonged to the great new red-faced seat of the Thursbys at a short distance. He came rapidly round the corner of the old church tower, and was already swinging down the worn sandstone steps which led into the road, when he saw below him at the foot of the steps a little group of people standing talking. It was Mr. Alwynn and Ruth and Dare, who had evidently met them on his return from shooting, and who, standing at ease with one elegantly gaitered leg on the lowest step, and a cartridge-bag slung over his shoulders in a way that had aroused Charles's indignation earlier in the day, was recounting to them, with vivid action of the hands on an imaginary gun, his own performances to right and left at some particularly hot corner.

Mr. Alwynn was listening with a benignant smile. Charles saw that Ruth was leaning heavily against the low stone-wall. Before he had time to turn back, Mr. Alwynn had seen him, and had gone forward a step to meet him, holding out a welcoming hand. Charles was obliged to stop a moment while his hand was inquired after, and a new treatment, which Mr. Alwynn had found useful on a similar occasion, was enjoined upon him. As they stood together on the church steps a fly, heavily laden with luggage, came slowly up the road towards them.

"What," said Mr. Alwynn, "more visitors! I thought all the Slumberleigh party arrived yesterday."

The fly plodded past the Slumberleigh lodge, however, and as it reached the steps a shrill voice suddenly called to the driver to stop. As it came grinding to a stand-still, the glass was hastily put down, and a little woman with a very bold pair of black eyes, and a somewhat laced-in figure, got out and came towards them.

"Well, Mr. Dare!" she said, in a high distinct voice, with a strong American accent. "I guess you did not expect to see me riding up this way, or you'd have sent the carriage to bring your wife up from the station. But I'm not one to bear malice; so if you want a lift home to—what's the name of your fine new place?—you can get in, and ride up along with me."

Dare looked straight in front of him. No one spoke. Her quick eye glanced from one to another of the little group, and she gave a short constrained laugh.

"Well," she said, "if you ain't coming, you can stop with your friends. I've had a deal of travelling one way and another, and I'll go on without you." And, turning quickly away, she told the driver in the same distinct high key to go on to Vandon, and got into the fly again.

The grinning man chucked at the horse's bridle, and the fly rattled heavily away.

No one spoke as it drove away. Charles glanced once at Ruth; but her set white face told him nothing. As the fly disappeared up the road, Dare moved a step forward. His face under his brown skin was ashen gray. He took off his cap, and extending it at arm's-length, not towards the sky, but, like a good churchman, towards the church, outside of which, as he knew, his Maker was not to be found, he said, solemnly, "I swear before God what she says is one—great—*lie!*"

CHAPTER XXIV

If conformity to type is indeed the one great mark towards which humanity should press, Mrs. Thursby may honestly be said to have attained to it. Everything she said or did had been said or done before, or she would never have thought of saying or doing it. Her whole life was a feeble imitation of the imitative lives of others; in short, it was the life of the ordinary country gentlewoman, who lives on her husband's property, and who, as Augustus Hare says, "has never looked over the garden-wall."

We do not mean to insinuate for a moment that the utmost energy and culture are not occasionally to be met with in the female portion of that interesting mass of our fellow-creatures who swell the large volumes of the "Landed Gentry." Among their ranks are those who come boldly forward into the full glare of public life; and, conscious of a genius for enterprise, to which an unmarried condition perhaps affords ampler scope, and which a local paper is ready to immortalize, become secretaries of ladies' societies, patronesses of flower shows, breeders of choice poultry, or even associates of floral leagues of the highest political importance. That such women should and do exist among us, the conscious salt-cellars of otherwise flavorless communities, is a fact for which we cannot be too thankful; and if Mrs. Thursby was not one of these aspiring spirits, with a yearning after "the mystical better things," which one of the above pursuits alone can adequately satisfy, it was her misfortune and not her fault.

It was her nature, as we have said, servilely to copy others. Her conversation was all that she could remember of what she had heard from others, her present dinner-party, as regards food, was a cross between the two last dinner-parties she had been to. The dessert, however, conspicuous by its absence, conformed strictly to a type which she had seen in a London house in June.

Her dinner-party gave her complete satisfaction, which was fortunate, for to the greater number of the eighteen or twenty people who had been indiscriminately herded together to form it, it was (with the exception of Mrs. Alwynn) a dreary or at best an uninteresting ordeal; while to four people among the number, the four who had met last on the church steps, it was a period of slow torture, endured with varying degrees of patience by each, from the two soups in the beginning, to the peaches and grapes at the long-delayed and bitter end.

Ruth, whose self-possession never wholly deserted her, had reached a depth of exhausted stupor, in which the mind is perfectly oblivious of the impression it is producing on others. By an unceasing effort she listened and answered and smiled at intervals, and looked exceedingly distinguished in the pale red gown which she had put on to please her aunt; but the color of which only intensified the unnatural pallor of her complexion. The two men whom she sat between found her a disappointing companion, cold and formal in manner. At any other time she would have been humiliated and astonished to hear herself make such cut-and-dried remarks, such little trite observations. She was sitting opposite Charles, and she vaguely wondered once or twice, when she saw him making others laugh, and heard snatches of the flippant talk which was with him, as she knew now, a sort of defensive armor, how he could manage to produce it; while Charles, half wild with a mad surging hope that would not be kept down by any word of Dare's, looked across at her as often as he dared, and wondered in his turn at the tranquil dignity, the quiet ordered smile of the face which a few hours ago he had seen shaken with emotion.

Her eyes met his for a moment. Were they the same eyes that but now had met his, half blind with tears? He felt still the touch of those tears upon his hand. He hastily looked away again, and plunged headlong into an answer to something Mabel was saying to him on her favorite subject of evolution. All well-brought-up young ladies have a subject nowadays, which makes their conversation the delightful thing it is; and Mabel, of course, was not behind the fashion.

"Yes," Ruth heard Charles reply, "I believe with you we go through many lives, each being a higher state than the last, and nearer perfection. So a man passes gradually through all the various grades of the nobility, soaring from the lowly honorable upward into the duke, and thence by an easy transition into an angel. Courtesy titles, of course, present a difficulty to the more thoughtful; but, as I am sure you will have found, to be thoughtful always implies difficulty of some kind."

"It does, indeed," said Mabel, puzzled but not a little flattered. "I sometimes think one reads too much; one longs so for deep books—Korans, and things. I must confess,"—with a sigh—"I can't interest myself in the usual young lady's library that other girls read."

"Can't you?" replied Charles. "Now, I can. I study that department of literature whenever I have the chance, and I have generally found that the most interesting part of a young lady's library is to be found in that portion of the book-shelf which lies between the rows of books and the wall. Don't you think so, Lady Carmian?" (to the lady on his other side). "I assure you I have made the most delightful discoveries of this description. Cheap editions of Ouida, Balzac's works, yellow backs of the most advanced order, will, as a rule, reward the inquirer, who otherwise might have had to content himself with 'The Heir of Redclyffe,' the Lily Series, and Miss Strickland's 'Queens of England.'"

Charles's last speech had been made in a momentary silence, and directly it was finished every woman, old and young, except Lady Carmian and Ruth, simultaneously raised a disclaiming voice, which by its vehemence at once showed what an unfounded assertion Charles had made. Lady Carmian, a handsome young married woman, only smiled languidly, and, turning the bracelet on her arm, told Charles he was a cynic, and that for her own part, when in robust health, she liked what little she read "strong;" but in illness, or when Lord Carmian had been unusually trying, she always fell back on a milk-and-water diet. Mrs. Thursby, however, felt that Charles had struck a blow at the sanctity of home life, and (for she was one of those persons whose single talent is that of giving a personal turn to any remark) began a long monotonous recital of the books she allowed her own daughters to read, and how they were kept, which proved the extensive range of her library, not in book-shelves, but in a sliding book-stand, which contracted or expanded at will.

Long before she had finished, however, the conversation at the other end of the table had drifted away to the topic of the season among sporting men, namely the poachers, who, since their raid on Dare's property, had kept fairly quiet, but who were sure to start afresh now that the pheasant shooting had begun; and from thence to the recent forgery case in America, which was exciting every day greater attention in England, especially since one of the accomplices had been arrested the day before in Birmingham station, and the principal offender, though still at large, was, according to the papers, being traced "by means of a clew in the possession of the police."

Charles knew how little that sentence meant, but he found that it required an effort to listen unmoved to the various conjectures as to the whereabouts of Stephens, in which Ruth, as the conversation became general, also joined, volunteering a suggestion that perhaps he might be lurking somewhere in Slumberleigh woods, which were certainly very lonely in places, and where, as she said, she had been very much alarmed by a tramp in the summer.

Mrs. Thursby, like an echo, began from the other end of the table something vague about girls being allowed to walk alone, her own daughters, etc., and so the long dinner wore itself out. Dare was the only one of the little party who had met on the church steps who succumbed entirely. Mr. Alwynn, who looked at him and Ruth with pathetic interest from time to time, made laudable efforts, but Dare made none. He had taken in to dinner the younger Thursby girl, a meek creature, without form and void, not yet out, but trembling in a high muslin, on the verge, who kept her large and burning hands clutched together under the table-cloth, and whose conversation was upon bees. Dare pleaded a gun headache, and hardly spoke. His eyes constantly wandered to the other end of the table, where, far away on the opposite side, half hidden by ferns and flowers, he could catch a glimpse of Ruth. After dinner he did not come into the drawing-room, but went off to the smoking-room, where he paced by himself up and down, up and down, writhing under the torment of a horrible suspense.

Outside the moon shone clear and high, making a long picturesque shadow of the great prosaic house upon the wide gravel drive. Dare leaned against the window-sill and looked out. "Would she give him up?" he asked himself. Would she believe this vile calumny? Would she give him up? And as he stood the Alwynns' brougham came with two gleaming eyes along the drive and drew up before the door. He resolved to learn his fate at once. There had been no possibility of a word with Ruth on the church steps. Before he had known where he was, he and Charles had been walking up to the Hall together, Charles discoursing lengthily on the impropriety of wire fencing in a hunting country. But now he must and would see her. He rushed down-stairs into the hall, where young Thursby was wrapping Ruth in her white furs, while Mr. Thursby senior was encasing Mrs. Alwynn in a species of glorified ulster of red plush which she had lately acquired. Dare hastily drew Mr. Alwynn aside and spoke a few words to him. Mr. Alwynn turned to his wife, after one rueful glance at his thin shoes, and said:

"I will walk up. It is a fine night, and quite dry underfoot."

"And a very pleasant party it has been," said Mrs. Alwynn, as she and Ruth drove away together, "though Mrs. Thursby has not such a knack with her table as some. Not that I did not think the chrysanthemums and white china swans were nice, very nice; but, you see, as I told her, I had just been to Stoke Moreton, where things were very different. And you looked very well, my dear, though not so bright and chatty as Mabel; and Mrs. Thursby said she only hoped your waist was natural. The idea! And I saw Lady Carmian notice your gown particularly, and I heard her ask who you were, and Mrs. Thursby said—so like her—you were their clergyman's niece. And so, my dear, I was not going to have you spoken of like that, and a little later on I just went and sat down by Lady Carmian, just went across the room, you know, as if I wanted to be nearer the music, and we got talking, and she was rather silent at first, but presently, when I began to tell her all about you, and who you were, she became quite interested, and asked such funny questions, and laughed, and we had quite a nice talk."

And so Mrs. Alwynn chatted on, and Ruth, happily hearing nothing, leaned back in her corner and wondered whether the evening were ever going to end. Even when she had bidden her aunt "Good-night," and, having previously told her maid not to sit up for her, found herself alone in her own room at last—even then it seemed that this interminable day was not quite over. She was standing by the dim fire, trying to gather up sufficient energy to undress, when a quiet step came cautiously along the passage, followed by a low tap at her door. She opened it noiselessly, and found Mr. Alwynn standing without.

"Ruth," he said, "Dare has walked up with me. He is in the most dreadful state. I am sure I don't know what to think. He has said nothing further to me, but he is bent on seeing you for a moment. It's very late, but still—could you? He's in the drawing-room now. My poor child, how ill you look! Shall I tell him you are too tired to-night to see any one?"

"I would rather see him," said Ruth, her voice trembling a little; and they went down-stairs together. In the hall she hesitated a moment. She was going to learn her fate. Had her release come? Had it come at the eleventh hour? Her uncle looked at her with kind, compassionate eyes, and hers fell before his as she thought how different her suspense was to what he imagined. Suddenly—and such demonstrations were very rare with her— she put her arms round his neck and pressed her cheek against his.

"Oh, Uncle John! Uncle John!" she gasped, "it is not what you think."

"I pray God it may not be what I suppose," he said, sadly, stroking her head. "One is too ready to think evil, I know. God forgive me if I have judged him harshly. But go in, my dear;" and he pushed her gently towards the drawing-room.

She went in and closed the door quietly behind her.

Dare was leaning against the mantle-piece, which was draped in Mrs. Alwynn's best manner, with Oriental hangings having bits of glass woven in them. He was looking into the curtained fire, and did not turn when she entered. Even at that moment she noticed, as she went towards him, that his elbow had displaced the little family of china hares on a plush stand which Mrs. Alwynn had lately added to her other treasures.

"I think you wished to see me," she said, as calmly as she could.

He faced suddenly round, his eyes wild, his face quivering, and coming close up to her, caught her hand and grasped it so tightly that the pain was almost more than she could bear.

"Are you going to give me up?" he asked, hoarsely.

"I don't know," she said; "it depends on yourself, on what you are, and what you have been. You say she is not your wife?"

"I swear it."

"You need not do so. Your word is enough."

"I swear she is not my wife."

"One question remains," said Ruth, firmly, a flame of color mounting to her neck and face. "You say she is not your wife. Ought you to make her so?"

"No," said Dare, passionately; "I owe her nothing. She has no claim upon me. I swear—"

"Don't swear. I said your word was enough."

But Dare preferred to embellish his speech with divers weighty expressions, feeling that a simple affirmation would never carry so much conviction to his own mind, or, consequently, to another, as an oath.

A momentary silence followed.

"You believe what I say, Ruth?"

"Yes," with an effort.

"And you won't give me up because evil is spoken against me?"

"No."

"And all is the same as before between us?"

"Yes."

Dare burst into a torrent of gratitude, but she broke suddenly away from him, and went swiftly up-stairs again to her own room.

The release had not come. She laid her head down upon the table, and Hope, which had ventured back to her for one moment, took her lamp and went quite away, leaving the world very dark.

There are turning-points in life when a natural instinct is a surer guide than noble motive or high aspiration, and consequently the more thoughtful and introspective nature will sometimes fall just where a commonplace one would have passed in safety. Ruth had acted for the best. When for the first time in her life she had been brought into close contact with a life spent for others, its beauty had appealed to her with irresistible force, and she had willingly sacrificed herself to an ideal life of devotion to others.

"But we are punished for our purest deeds,
And chasten'd for our holiest thoughts."

And she saw now that if she had obeyed that simple law of human nature which forbids a marriage in which love is not the primary consideration, if she had followed that simple humble path, she would never have reached the arid wilderness towards which her own guidance had led her.

For her wilful self-sacrifice had suddenly paled and dwindled down before her eyes into a hideous mistake—a mistake which yet had its roots so firmly knit into the past that it was hopeless to think of pulling it up now. To abide by a mistake is sometimes all that an impetuous youth leaves an honorable middle age to do. Poor middle age, with its clear vision, that might do and be so much if it were not for the heavy burdens, grievous to be borne, which youth has bound upon its shoulders.

And worse than the dreary weight of personal unhappiness, harder to bear than the pang of disappointed love, was the aching sense of failure, of having misunderstood God's intention, and broken the purpose of her life. For some natures the cup of life holds no bitterer drop than this.

Ruth dimly saw the future, the future which she had chosen, stretching out waste and barren before her. The dry air of the desert was on her face. Her feet were already on its sandy verge. And the iron of a great despair entered into her soul.

CHAPTER XXV

Dare left Slumberleigh Hall early the following morning, and drove up to the rectory on his way to Vandon. After being closeted with Mr. Alwynn in the study for a short time, they both came out and drove away together. Ruth, invisible in her own room with a headache, her only means of defence against Mrs. Alwynn's society, heard the coming and the going, and was not far wrong in her surmise that Dare had come to beg Mr. Alwynn to accompany him to Vandon—being afraid to face alone the mysterious enemy intrenched there.

No conversation was possible in the dog-cart, with the groom on the back seat thirsting to hear any particulars of the news which had spread like wildfire from Vandon throughout the whole village the previous afternoon, and which was already miraculously flying from house to house in Slumberleigh this morning, as things discreditable do fly among a Christian population, which perhaps "thinks no evil," but repeats it nevertheless.

There was not a servant in Dare's modest establishment who was not on the lookout for him on his return. The gardener happened to be tying up a plant near the front door; the house-maids were watching unobserved from an upper casement; the portly form of Mrs. Smith, the house-keeper, was seen to glide from one of the unused bedroom windows; the butler must have been waiting in the hall, so prompt was his appearance when the dog-cart drew up before the door.

Another pair of keen black eyes was watching too, peering out through the chinks between the lowered Venetian blinds in the drawing-room; was observing Dare intently as he got out, and then resting anxiously on his companion. Then the owner of the eyes slipped away from the window, and went back noiselessly to the fire.

Dare ordered the dog-cart to remain at the door, flung down his hat on the hall-table, and, turning to the servant who was busying himself in folding his coat, said, sharply, "Where is the—the person who arrived here yesterday?"

The man replied that "she" was in the drawing-room. The drawing-room opened into the hall. Dare led the way, suppressed fury in his face, looking back to see whether Mr. Alwynn was following him. The two men went in together and shut the door.

The enemy was intrenched and prepared for action.

Mrs. Dare, as we must perforce call her for lack of any other designation rather than for any right of hers to the title, was seated on a yellow brocade ottoman, drawn up beside a roaring fire, her two smart little feet resting on the edge of the low brass fender, and a small work-table at her side, on which an elaborate medley of silks and wools was displayed. Her attitude was that of a person at home, aggressively at home. She was in the act of threading a needle when Dare and Mr. Alwynn came in, and she put down her work at once, carefully replacing the needle in safety, as she rose to receive them, and held out her hand, with a manner the assurance of which, if both men had not been too much frightened to notice it, was a little overdone.

Dare disregarded her gesture of welcome, and she sat down again, and returned to her work, with a laugh that was also a little overdone.

"What do you mean by coming here?" he said, his voice hoarse with a furious anger, which the sight of her seemed to have increased a hundred-fold.

"Because it is my proper place," she replied, tossing her head, and drawing out a long thread of green silk; "because I have a right to come."

"You lie!" said Dare, fiercely, showing his teeth.

"Lord, Alfred!" said Mrs. Dare, contemptuously, "don't make a scene before strangers. We've had our tiffs before now, and shall have again, I suppose. It's the natur' of married people to fall out; but there's no call to carry on before friends. Push up that lounge nearer the fire. Won't the other gentleman," turning to Mr. Alwynn, "come and warm himself? I'm sure it's cold enough."

Mr. Alwynn, who was a man of peace, devoutly wished he were at home again in his own study.

"It is a cold morning," he said; "but we are not here to discuss the weather."

He stopped short. He had been hurried here so much against his will, and so entirely without an explanation, that he was not quite sure what he had come to discuss, or how he could best support his friend.

"What do you want?" said Dare, in the same suppressed voice, without looking at her.

"My rights," she said, incisively; "and, what's more, I mean to have 'em. I've not come over from America for nothing, I can tell you that; and I've not come on a visit neither. I've come to stay."

"What are these rights you talk of?" asked Mr. Alwynn, signing to Dare to restrain himself.

"As his wife, sir. I am his wife, as I can prove. I didn't come without my lines to show. I didn't come on a speculation, to see if he'd a fancy to have me back. No, afore I set my foot down anywheres I look to see as it's solid walking."

"Show your proof," said Mr. Alwynn.

The woman ostentatiously got out a red morocco letter case, and produced a paper which she handed to Mr. Alwynn.

It was an authorized copy of a marriage register, drawn out in the usual manner, between Alfred Dare, bachelor, English subject, and Ellen, widow of the late Jaspar Carroll, of Neosho City, Kansas, U.S.A. The marriage was dated seven years back.

The names of Dare and Carroll swam before Mr. Alwynn's eyes. He glanced at the paper, but he could not read it.

"Is this a forgery, Dare?" he asked, holding it towards him.

"No," said Dare, without looking at it; "it is right. But that is not all. Now," turning to the woman, who was watching him triumphantly, "show the other paper—the divorce."

"I made inquiries about that," she replied, composedly. "I wasn't going to be fooled by that 'ere, so I made inquiries from one as knows. The divorce is all very well in America; but it don't count in England."

Dare's face turned livid. Mr. Alwynn's flushed a deep red. He sat with his eyes on the ground, the paper in his hand trembling a little. Indignation against Dare, pity for him, anxiety not to judge him harshly, struggled for precedence in his kind heart, still beating tumultuously with the shock of Dare's first admission. He felt rather than saw him take the paper out of his hand.

"I shall keep this," Dare said, putting it in his pocket-book; and then, turning to the woman again, he said, with an oath, "Will you go, or will you wait till you are turned out?"

"I'll wait," she replied, undauntedly. "I like the place well enough."

She laughed and took up her work, and, after looking at her for a moment, he flung out of the room, followed by Mr. Alwynn.

The defeat was complete; nay, it was a rout.

The dog-cart was still standing at the door. The butler was talking to the groom; the gardener was training some new shoots of ivy against the stone balustrade.

Dare caught up his hat and gloves, and ordered that his portmanteau, which had been taken into the hall, should be put back into the dog-cart. As it was being carried down he looked at his watch.

"I can catch the mid-day express for London," he said. "I can do it easily."

Mr. Alwynn made no reply.

"Get in," continued Dare, feverishly; "the portmanteau is in."

"I think I will walk home," said Mr. Alwynn, slowly. It gave him excruciating pain to say anything so severe as this; but he got out the words nevertheless.

Dare looked at him in astonishment.

"Get in," he said again, quickly. "I must speak to you. I will drive you home. I have something to say."

Mr. Alwynn never refused to hear what any one had to say. He went slowly down the steps, and got into the cart, looking straight in front of him, as his custom was when disturbed in mind. Dare followed.

"I shall not want you, James," he said to the groom, his foot on the step.

At this moment the form of Mrs. Smith, the house-keeper, appeared through the hall door, clothed in all the awful majesty of an upper servant whose dignity has been outraged.

"Sir," she said, in a clear not to say a high voice, "asking your pardon, sir, but am I, or am I not, to take my orders from—"

Goaded to frenzy, Dare poured forth a volley of horrible oaths French and English, and, seizing up the reins, drove off at a furious rate.

The servants remained standing about the steps, watching the dog-cart whirl rapidly away.

"He's been to church with her," said the gardener, at last. "I said all along she'd never have come, unless she had her lines to show. I ha'n't cut them white grapes she ordered yet; but I may as well go and do it."

"Well," said Mrs. Smith, "grapes or no grapes, I'll never give up the keys of the linen cupboards to the likes of her, and I'm not going to have any one poking about among my china. I've not been here twenty years to be asked for my lists in that way, and the winter curtains ordered out unbeknownst to me;" and Mrs. Smith retreated to the fastnesses of the house-keeper's room, whither even the audacious enemy had not yet ventured to follow her.

Meanwhile, Mr. Alwynn and Dare drove at moderated speed along the road to Slumberleigh. For some time neither spoke.

"I beg your pardon," said Dare at last. "I lost my head. I became enraged. Before a clergyman and a lady, I know well, it is not permitted to swear."

"I can overlook that," said Mr. Alwynn; "but," turning very red again, "other things I can't."

Dare began to flourish his whip, and become excited again.

"I will tell you all," he said with effusion—"every word. You have a kind heart. I will confide in you."

"I don't want confidences," said Mr. Alwynn. "I want straight-forward answers to a few simple questions."

"I will give them, these answers. I keep nothing back from a friend."

"Then, first. Did you marry that woman?"

"Yes," said Dare, shrugging his shoulders. "I married her, and often afterwards, almost at once, I regretted it; but *que voulez-vous*, I was young. I had no experience. I was but twenty-one."

Mr. Alwynn stared at him in astonishment at the ease with which the admission was made.

"How long afterwards was it that you were divorced from her?"

"Two years. Two long years."

"For what reason?"

"Temper. Ah! what a temper. Also because I left her for one year. It was in Kansas, and in Kansas it is very easy to marry, and also to be divorced."

"It is a disgraceful story," said Mr. Alwynn, in great indignation.

"Disgraceful!" echoed Dare, excitedly. "It is more than disgraceful. It is abominable. You do not know all yet. I will tell you. I was young; I was but a boy. I go to America when I am twenty-one, to travel, to see the world. I make acquaintances. I get into a bad set, what you call undesirable. I fall in love. I walk into a net. She was pretty, a pretty widow, all love, all soul; without friends. I protect her. I marry her. I have a little money. I have five thousand pounds. She knew that. She spent it. I was a fool. In a year it was gone." Dare's face had become white with rage. "And then she told me why she married me. I became enraged. There was a quarrel, and I left her. I had no more money. She left me alone, and a year after we are divorced. I never see her or hear of her again. I return to Europe. I live by my voice in Paris. It is five years ago. I have bought my experience. I put it from my mind. And now"—his hands trembled with anger—"now that she thinks I have money again, now, when in some way she hears how I have come to Vandon, she dares to came back and say she is my wife."

"Dare," said Mr. Alwynn, sternly, "what excuse have you for never mentioning this before—before you became engaged to Ruth?"

"What!" burst out Dare, "tell Ruth! Tell *her*! *Quelle idée*. I would never speak to her of what might give her pain. I would keep all from her that would cause her one moment's grief. Besides," he added, conclusively, "it is not always well to talk of what has gone before. It is not for her happiness or mine. She has been, one sees it well, brought up since a young child very strictly. About some things she has fixed ideas. If I had told her of these things which are passed away and gone, she might not,"—and Dare looked gravely at Mr. Alwynn—"she might not think so well of me."

This view of the case was quite a new one to Mr. Alwynn. He looked back at Dare with hopeless perplexity in his pained eyes. To one who throughout life has regarded the supremacy of certain truths and principles of actions as fixed, and recognized as a matter of course by all the world, however imperfectly obeyed by individuals, the discovery comes as a shock, which is at the moment overwhelming, when these same truths and principles are seen to be entirely set aside, and their very existence ignored by others.

Where there is no common ground on which to meet, speech is unavailing and mere waste of time. It is like shouting to a person at a distance whom it is impossible to approach. If he notices anything it will only be that, for some reasons of your own, you are making a disagreeable noise.

As Mr. Alwynn looked back at Dare his anger died away within him, and a dull pain of deep disappointment and sense of sudden loneliness took its place. Dare and he seemed many miles apart. He felt that it would be of no use to say anything; and so, being a man, he held his peace.

Dare continued talking volubly of how he would get a lawyer's opinion at once in London; of his certainty that the American wife had no claim upon him; of how he would go over to America, if necessary, to establish the validity of his divorce; but Mr. Alwynn heard little or nothing of what he said. He was thinking of Ruth with distress and self-upbraiding. He had been much to blame, of course.

Dare's mention of her name recalled his attention.

"She is all goodness," he was saying. "She believes in me. She has promised again that she will marry me—since yesterday. I trust her as myself; but it is a grief which as little as possible must trouble her. You will not say anything to her till I come back, till I return with proof that I am free, as I told her? You will say nothing?"

Dare had pulled up at the bottom of the drive to the rectory.

"Very well," said Mr. Alwynn, absently, getting slowly out. He seemed much shaken.

"I will be back perhaps to-night, perhaps to-morrow morning," called Dare after him.

But Mr. Alwynn did not answer.

Dare's business took him a shorter time than he expected, and the same night found him hurrying back by the last train to Slumberleigh. It was a wild night. He had watched the evening close in lurid and stormy across the chimneyed wastes of the black country, until the darkness covered all the land, and wiped out even the last memory of the dead day from the western sky.

Who, travelling alone at night, has not watched the glimmer of light through cottage windows as he hurries past; has not followed with keenest interest for one brief second the shadow of one who moves within, and imagination picturing a mysterious universal happiness gathered round these twinkling points of light, has not experienced a strange feeling of homelessness and loneliness?

Dare sat very still in the solitude of the empty railway carriage, and watched the little fleeting, mocking lights with a heavy heart. They meant *homes*, and he should never have a home now. Once he saw a door open in a squalid line of low houses, and the figure of a man with a child in his arms stand outlined in the door-way against the ruddy light within. Dare felt an unreasoning interest in that man. He found himself thinking of him as the train hurried on, wondering whether his wife was there waiting for him, and whether he had other children besides the one he was carrying. And all the time, through his idle musings, he could hear one sentence ringing in his ears, the last that his lawyer had said to him after the long consultation of the afternoon.

"I am sorry to tell you that you are incontestably a married man."

Everything repeated it. The hoofs of the cab-horse that took him to the station had hammered it out remorselessly all the way. The engine had caught it up, and repeated it with unvarying, endless iteration. The newspapers were full of it. When Dare turned to them in desperation he saw it written in large letters across the sham columns. There was nothing but that anywhere. It was the news of the day. Sick at heart, and giddy from want of food, he sat crouched up in the corner of his empty carriage, and vaguely wished the train would journey on for ever and ever, nervously dreading the time when he should have to get out and collect his wandering faculties once more.

The old lawyer had been very kind to the agitated, incoherent young man whose settlements he was already engaged in drawing up. At first, indeed, it had seemed that the marriage would not be legally binding—the marriage and divorce having both taken place in Kansas, where the marriage laws are particularly lax—and he seemed inclined to be hopeful; but as he informed himself about the particulars of the divorce his face became grave and graver. When at last Dare produced the copy of the marriage register, he shook his head.

"'Alfred Dare, bachelor and English subject,'" he said. "That 'English subject' makes a difficulty to start with. You had never, I believe, any intention of acquiring what in law we call an American domicil? and, although the technicalities of this subject are somewhat complicated, I am afraid that in your case there is little, if any, doubt. The English courts are very jealous of any interference by foreigners with the status of an Englishman; and though a divorce legally granted by a competent tribunal for an adequate cause might—I will not say would—be held binding everywhere, there can be no doubt that where in the eyes of our law the cause is *not* adequate, our courts would refuse to recognize it. Have you a copy of the register of divorce as well?"

"No."

"It is unfortunate; but no doubt you can remember the grounds on which it was granted."

"Incompatibility of temper, and she said I had deserted her. I had left her the year before. We both agreed to separate."

The lawyer shook his head.

"What's incompatibility?" he said. "What's a year's absence? Nothing in the eyes of an Englishman. Nothing in the law of this country."

"But the divorce was granted. It was legal. There was no question," said Dare, eagerly. "I was divorced in the same State as where I married. I had lived there more than a year, which was all that was necessary. No difficulty was made at the time."

"No. Marriage is slipped into and slipped out of again with gratifying facility in America, and Kansas is notorious for the laxity prevailing there as regards marriage and divorce. It will be advisable to take the opinion of counsel on the matter, but I can hold out very little hope that your divorce would hold good, even in America. You see, you are entered as a British subject on the marriage register, and I imagine these words must have been omitted in the divorce proceedings, or some difficulty would have been raised at the time, unless your residence in Kansas made it unnecessary. But, even supposing by American law you are free, that will be of no avail in England, for by the law of England, which alone concerns you, I regret to be obliged to tell you that you are incontestably a married man."

And in spite of frantic reiterations, of wild protests on the part of Dare, as if the compassionate old man represented the English law, and could mould it at his pleasure, the lawyer's last word remained in substance the same, though repeated many times.

"Whether you are at liberty or not to marry again in America, I am hardly prepared to say. I will look into the subject and let you know; but in England I regret to repeat that you are a married man."

Dare groaned in body and in spirit as the words came back to him; and his thoughts, shrinking from the despair and misery at home, wandered aimlessly away, anywhere, hither and thither, afraid to go back, afraid to face again the desolation that sat so grim and stern in solitary possession.

The train arrived at Slumberleigh at last, and he got out, and shivered as the driving wind swept across the platform. It surprised him that there was a wind, although at every station down the line he had seen people straining against it. He gave up his ticket mechanically, and walked aimlessly away into the darkness, turning with momentary curiosity to watch the train hurry on again, a pillar of fire by night, as it had been a pillar of smoke by day.

He passed the blinking station inn, forgetting that he had put up his dog-cart there to await his return, and, hardly knowing what he did, took from long habit the turn for Vandon.

It was a wild night. The wind was driving the clouds across the moon at a tremendous rate, and sweeping at each gust flights of spectre leaves from the swaying trees. It caught him in the open of the bare high-road, and would not let him go. It opposed him, and buffeted him at every turn; but he held listlessly on his way. His feet took him, and he let them take him whither they would. They led him stumbling along the dim road, the dust of which was just visible like a gray mist before him, until he reached the bridge by the mill. There his feet stopped of their own accord, and he went and leaned against the low stone-wall, looking down at the sudden glimpses of pale hurried water and trembling reed.

The moon came out full and strong in temporary victory, and made black shadows behind the idle millwheel and open mill-race, and black shadows, black as death, under the bridge itself. Dare leaned over the wall to watch the mysterious water and shadow run beneath. As he looked, he saw the reflection of a man in the water watching him. He shook his fist savagely at it, and it shook its fist amid a wavering of broken light and shadow back at him. But it did not go away; it remained watching him. There was something strange and unfamiliar about the river to-night. It had a voice, too, which allured and repelled him—a voice at the sound of which the grim despair within him stirred ominously at first, and then began slowly to rise up gaunt and terrible; began to move stealthily, but with ever-increasing swiftness through the deserted chambers of his heart.

No strong abiding principle was there to do battle with the enemy. The minor feelings, sensibilities, emotions, amiable impulses, those courtiers of our prosperous days, had all forsaken him and fled. Dare's house in his hour of need was left unto him desolate.

And the river spoke in a guilty whisper, which yet the quarrel of the wind and the trees could not drown, of deep places farther down, where the people were never found, people who—But there were shallows, too, he remembered, shallow places among the stones where the trout were. If anybody were drowned, Dare thought, gazing down at the pale shifting moon in the water, he would be found there, perhaps, or at any rate, his hat—he took his hat off, and held it tightly clinched in both his hands—his hat would tell the tale.

CHAPTER XXVI

Charles left Slumberleigh Hall a few hours later than Dare had done, but only to go back to Atherstone. He could not leave the neighborhood. This burning fever of suspense would be unbearable at any other place, and in any case he must return by Saturday, the day on which he had promised to meet Raymond. His hand was really slightly injured, and he made the most of it. He kept it bound up, telegraphed to put off his next shooting engagement on the strength of it, and returned to Atherstone, even though he was aware that Lady Mary had arrived there the day before, on her way home to her house in London.

Ralph and Evelyn were accustomed to sudden and erratic movements on the part of Charles, and to Molly he was a sort of archangel, who might arrive out of space at any moment, untrammelled by such details as distance, trains, time, or tide. But to Lady Mary his arrival was a significant fact, and his impatient refusal to have his hand investigated was another. Her cold gray eyes watched him narrowly, and, conscious that they did so, he kept out of her way as much as possible, and devoted himself to Molly more than ever.

He was sailing a mixed fleet of tin ducks and fishes across the tank by the tool shed, under her supervision, on the afternoon of the day he had arrived, when Ralph came to find him in great excitement. His keeper had just received private notice from the Thursbys' keeper that a raid on the part of a large gang of poachers was expected that night in the parts of the Slumberleigh coverts that had not yet been shot over, and which adjoined Ralph's own land.

"Whereabout will that be?" said Charles, inattentively, drawing his magnet slowly in front of the fleet.

"Where?" said Ralph, excitedly, "why, round by the old house, round by Arleigh, of course. Thursby and I have turned down hundreds of pheasants there. Don't you remember the hot corner by the coppice last year, below the house, where we got forty at one place, and how the wind took them as they came over?"

"Near *Arleigh*?" repeated Charles, with sudden interest.

"Uncle Charles," interposed Molly, reproachfully, "don't let all the ducks stick onto the magnet like that. I told you not before. Make it go on in front."

But Charles's attention had wandered from the ducks.

"Yes," continued Ralph, "near Arleigh. There was a gang of poachers there last year, and the keepers dared not attack them they were so strong, though they were shooting right and left. But we'll be even with them this year. My men are going, and I shall go with them. You had better come too, and join the fun. The more the better."

"Why should I go?" said Charles, listlessly. "Am I my brother's keeper, or even his underkeeper? Molly, don't splash your uncle's wardrobe. Besides, I expect it is a false alarm or a blind."

"False alarm!" retorted Ralph. "I tell you Thursby's head keeper, Shaw—you know Shaw—saw a man himself only last night in the Arleigh coverts; came upon him suddenly, reconnoitring, of course; for to-night, and would have collared him too if the moon had not gone in, and when it came out again he was gone."

"Of course, and he will warn off the rest to-night."

"Not a bit of it. He never saw Shaw. Shaw takes his oath he didn't see him. I'll lay any odds they will beat those coverts to-night, and, by George! we'll nail some of them, if we have an ounce of luck."

Ralph's sporting instinct, to which even the fleeting vision of a chance weasel never appealed in vain, was now thoroughly aroused, and even Charles shared somewhat in his excitement.

How could he warn Raymond to lie close? The more he thought of it the more impossible it seemed. It was already late in the afternoon. He could not, for Raymond's sake, risk being seen hanging about in the woods near Arleigh for no apparent reason, and Raymond was not expecting to see him in any case for two days to come, and would probably be impossible to find. He could do nothing but wait till the evening came, when he might have some opportunity, if the night were only dark enough, of helping or warning him.

The night was dark enough when it came; but it was unreliable. A tearing autumn wind drove armies of clouds across the moon, only to sweep them away again at a moment's notice. The wind itself rose and fell, dropped and struggled up again like a furious wounded animal.

"It will drop at midnight," said Ralph to Charles below his breath, as they walked in the darkness along the road towards Slumberleigh; "and the moon will come out when the wind goes. I have told Evans and Brooks to go by the fields, and meet us at the cross-roads in the low woods. It is a good night for us. We don't want light yet a while; and the more row the wind kicks up till we are in our places ready for them the better."

They walked on in silence, nearly missing in the dark the turn for Slumberleigh, where the road branched off to Vandon.

"We must be close upon the river by this time," said Ralph; "but I can't hear it for the wind."

The moon came out suddenly, and showed close on their right the mill blocking out the sky, and the dark sweep of the river below, between pale wastes of flooded meadow. Upon the bridge, leaning over the wall, stood the figure of a man, bareheaded, with his hat in his hands.

He could not see his face, but something in his attitude struck Charles with a sudden chill.

"By — —," he said, below his breath, plucking Ralph's arm, "there's mischief going on there!"

Ralph did not hear, and in another moment Charles was thankful he had not done so.

The man raised himself a little, and the light fell full on his white desperate face. He was feeling up and down the edge of the stone-parapet with his hands. As he moved, Charles recognized him, and drew in his breath sharply.

"Who is that?" said Ralph, his obtuser faculties perceiving the man for the first time.

Charles made no answer, but began to whistle loudly one of the tunes of the day. He saw Dare give a guilty start, and, catching at the wall for support, lean heavily against it as he looked wildly down the road, where the shadow of the trees had so far served to screen the approach of Charles and Ralph, who now emerged into the light, or at least would have done so, if the moonlight had not been snatched away at that moment.

"Holloa, Dare!" said Ralph, cheerfully, through the darkness, "I saw you. What are you up to standing on the bridge at midnight, with the clock striking the hour, and all that sort of thing; and what have you done with your hat—dropped it into the water?"

Dare muttered something unintelligible, and peered suspiciously through the darkness at Charles.

The moon made a feint at coming out again, which came to nothing, but which gave Charles a moment's glimpse of Dare's convulsed face. And the grave penetrating glance that met his own so fixedly told Dare in that moment that Charles had guessed his business on the bridge. Both men were glad of the returning darkness, and of the presence of Ralph.

"Come along with us," the latter was saying to Dare, explaining the errand on which they were bound; and Dare, stupefied with past emotion, and careless of what he did or where he went, agreed.

It was less trouble to agree than to find a reason for refusing. He mechanically put on his hat, which he had unconsciously crushed together a few minutes before, in a dreadful dream from which even now he had not thoroughly awaked. And, still walking like a man in a dream, he set off with the other two.

"There was suicide in his face," thought Charles, as he swung along beside his brother. "He would have done it if we had not come up. Good God! can it be that it is all over between him and Ruth?" The blood rushed to his head, and his heart began to beat wildly. He walked on in silence, seeing nothing, hearing nothing. Raymond and the poachers were alike forgotten.

It was not until a couple of men joined them silently in the woods, and others presently rose up out of the darkness, to whisper directions and sink down again, that Charles came to himself with a start, and pulled himself together.

The party had halted. It was pitch-dark, and he was conscious of something towering up above him, black and lowering. It was the ruined house of Arleigh.

"You and Brooks wait here, and keep well under the lea of the house," said Ralph, in a whisper. "If the moon comes out, get into the shadow of the wall. Don't shout till you're sure of them. Shaw is down by the stables. Dare and Evans you both come on with me. Shaw's got two men at the end of the glade, but it's the nearest coverts he is keenest on, because they can get a horse and cart up close to take the game, and get off sharp if they are surprised. They did last year. Don't stir if you hear wheels. Wait for them." And with this parting injunction Ralph disappeared noiselessly with Dare and the other keeper in the direction of the stables.

Ralph had been right. The wind was dropping. It came and went fitfully, returning as if from great distances, and hurrying past weak and impotent, leaving sudden silences behind. Charles and his companion, a strapping young underkeeper, evidently anxious to distinguish himself, waited, listening intently in the intervals of silence. The ivy on the old house shivered and whispered over their heads, and against one of the shuttered windows near the ground some climbing plant, torn loose by the wind, tapped incessantly, as if calling to the ghosts within. Charles glanced ever and anon at the sky. It showed no trace of clearing—as yet. He was getting cramped with standing. He wished he had gone on to the stables. His anxiety for Raymond was sharpened by this long inaction. He seemed to have been standing for ages. What were the others doing? Not a sound reached him between the lengthening pauses of the wind. His companion stood drawn up motionless beside him; and so they waited, straining eye and ear into the darkness, conscious that others were waiting and listening also.

At last in the distance came a faint sound of wheels. Charles and Brooks instinctively drew a long breath; and Charles for the first time believed the alarm of poachers had not been a false one after all. It was the faintest possible sound of wheels. It would hardly have been heard at all but for some newly broken stones over which it passed. Then, without coming nearer, it stopped.

Charles listened intently. The wind had dropped down dead at last, and in the stillness he felt as if he could have heard a mouse stir miles away. But all was quiet. There was no sound but the tremulous whisper of the ivy. The spray near the window had ceased its tapping against the shutter, and was listening too. Slowly the moon came out, and looked on.

And then suddenly, from the direction of the stables, came a roar of men's voices, a sound of bursting and crashing through the under-wood, a thundering of heavy feet, followed by a whirring of frightened birds into the air. Brooks leaned forward breathing hard, and tightening his newly moistened grip on his heavy knotted stick.

Another moment and a man's figure darted across the open, followed by a chorus of shouts, and Charles's heart turned sick within him. It was Raymond.

"Cut him off at the gate, Charles," roared Ralph from behind; "down to the left."

There was not a second for reflection. As Brooks rushed headlong forward, Charles hurriedly interposed his stick between his legs, and leaving him to flounder, started off in pursuit.

"Down to your left," cried a chorus of voices from behind, as he shot out of the shadow of the house; for Charles was some way ahead of the rest owing to his position.

He could hear Raymond crashing in front; then he saw him again for a moment in a strip of open, running as a man does who runs for his life, with a furious recklessness of all obstacles. Charles saw he was making for the rocky thickets below the house, where the uneven ground and the bracken would give him a better chance. Did he remember the deep sunken wall which, broken down in places, still separated the wilderness of the garden from the wilderness outside? Charles was lean and active, and he soon outdistanced the other pursuers, but a man is hard to overtake who has such reasons for not being overtaken as Raymond, and do what he would he could not get near him. He bore down to the left, but Raymond seemed to know it, and, edging away again, held for the woods a little higher up. Charles tacked, and then as he ran he saw that Raymond was making with headlong blindness through the shrubbery direct for the deep sunk wall which bounded the Arleigh grounds. Would he see it in the uncertain light? He must be close upon it now. He was running like a madman. As Charles looked he saw him pitch suddenly forward out of sight and heard a heavy fall. If Charles ever ran in his life, it was then. As he swiftly let himself drop over the wall, lower than Raymond had taken it, he saw Ralph and Dare, followed by the others, come streaming down the slope in the moonlight, spreading as they came. It was now or never. He rushed up the fosse under cover of the wall, and almost stumbled over a prostrate figure, which was helplessly trying to raise itself on its hands and knees.

"Danvers, it's me," gasped Raymond, turning a white tortured face feebly towards him. "Don't let those devils get me."

"Keep still," panted Charles, pushing him down among the bracken. "Lie close under the wall, and make for the house again when it's quiet;" And darting back under cover of the wall, to the place where he had dropped over it, he found Dare almost upon him, and rushed headlong down the steep rocky descent, roaring at the top of his voice, and calling wildly to the others. The pursuit swept away through the wood, down the hill, and up the sandy ascent on the other side; swept almost over the top of Charles, who had flung himself down, dead-beat and gasping for breath, at the bottom of the gully.

He heard the last of the heavy lumbering feet crash past him, and heard the shouting die away before he stiffly dragged himself up again, and began to struggle painfully back up the slippery hill-side, down which he had rushed with a whole regiment of loose and hopping stones ten minutes before. He regained the wall at last, and crept back to the place where he had left Raymond. It was with a sigh of relief that he found that he was gone. No doubt he had got into safety somewhere, perhaps in the cottage itself, where no one would dream of looking for him. He stumbled along among the loose stones by the wall till he came to the place by the gate where it was broken down, and clambering up, for the gate was locked, made his way back through the shrubberies, and desolate remains of garden, towards the point near the house where Raymond had first broken cover. As he came round a clump of bushes his heart gave a great leap, and then sank within him.

Three men were standing in the middle of the lawn in the moonlight, gathered round something on the ground. Seized by a horrible misgiving, he hurried towards them. At a little distance a dog-cart was being slowly led over the grass-grown drive towards the house.

"What is it? Any one hurt?" he asked, hoarsely, joining the little group; but as he looked he needed no answer. One glance told him that the prostrate, unconscious figure on the ground, with blood slowly oozing from the open mouth, was Raymond Deyncourt.

"Great God! the man's dying," he said, dropping on his knees beside him.

"He's all right, sir; he'll come to," said a little brisk man, in a complacent, peremptory tone. "It's only the young chap,"—pointing to the bashful but gratified Brooks—"as crocked him over the head a bit sharper than needful. Here, Esp,"—to the grinning Slumberleigh policeman, whom Charles now recognized, "tell the lad to bring up the 'orse and trap over the grass. We shall have a business to shift him as it is."

"Is he a poacher?" asked Charles. "He doesn't look like it."

"Lord! no, sir," replied the little man, and Charles's heart went straight down into his boots and stayed there. "I'm come down from Birmingham after him. He's no poacher. The police have wanted him very special for some time for the Francisco forgery case."

CHAPTER XXVII

Charles watched the detective and the policeman hoist Raymond into the dog-cart and drive away, supporting him between them. No doubt it had been the wheels of that dog-cart which they had heard in the distance. Then he turned to Brooks.

"How is it you remained behind?" he asked, sharply.

Brooks's face fell, and he explained that just as he was starting in the pursuit he had caught his legs on "Sir Chawles sir's" stick, and "barked hisself."

"I remember," said Charles. "You got in my way. You should look out where you are going. You may as well go and find my stick."

The poor victim of duplicity departed rather crestfallen, and at this moment Dare came up.

"We have lost him," he said, wiping his forehead. "I don't know what has become of him."

"He doubled back here," said Charles. "I followed, but you all went on. The police have got him. He was not a poacher after all, so they said."

"Ah!" said Dare. "They have him? I regret it. He ran well. I could wish he had escaped. I was in the door-way of a stable watching a long time, and all in a moment he rushed past me out of the door. The policeman was seeking within when he came out, but though he touched me I could not stop him. And now," with sudden weariness as his excitement evaporated, "all is, then, over for the night? And the others? Where are they? Do we wait for them here?"

"We should wait some time if we did," replied Charles. "Ralph is certain to go on to the other coverts. He has poachers on the brain. Probably the rumor that they were coming here was only a blind, and they are doing a good business somewhere else. I am going home. I have had enough enjoyment for one evening. I should advise you to do the same."

Dare winced, and did not answer, and Charles suddenly remembered that there were circumstances which might make it difficult for him to go back to Vandon.

They walked away together in silence. Dare, who had been wildly excited, was beginning to feel the reaction. He was becoming giddy and faint with exhaustion and want of food. He had eaten nothing all day. They had not gone far when Charles saw that he stumbled at every other step.

"Look out," he said once, as Dare stumbled more heavily than usual, "you'll twist your ankle on these loose stones if you're not more careful."

"It is so dark," said Dare, faintly.

The moon was shining brightly at the moment, and as Charles turned to look at him in surprise, Dare staggered forward, and would have collapsed altogether if he had not caught him by the arm.

"Sit down," he said, authoritatively. "Here, not on me, man, on the bank. Always sit down when you can't stand. You have had too much excitement. I felt the same after my first Christmas-tree. You will be better directly."

Charles spoke lightly, but he knew from what he had seen that Dare must have passed a miserable day. He had never liked him. It was impossible that he should have done so. But even his more active dislike of the last few months gave way to pity for him now, and he felt almost ashamed at the thought that his own happiness was only to be built on the ruin of poor Dare's.

He made him swallow the contents of his flask, and as Dare choked and gasped himself back into the fuller possession of his faculties, and experienced the benign influences of whiskey, entertained at first unawares, his heart, always easily touched, warmed to the owner of the silver flask, and of the strong arm that was supporting him with an unwillingness he little dreamed of. His momentary jealousy of Charles in the summer had long since been forgotten. He felt towards him now, as Charles helped him up, and he proceeded slowly on his arm, as a friend and a brother.

Charles, entirely unconscious of the noble sentiments which he and his flask had inspired, looked narrowly at his companion, as they neared the turn for Atherstone, and said with some anxiety:

"Where are you going to-night?"

Dare made no answer. He had no idea where he was going.

Charles hesitated. He could not let him walk back alone to Vandon— over the bridge. It was long past midnight. Dare's evident inability to think where to turn touched him.

"Can I be of any use to you?" he said, earnestly. "Is there anything I can do? Perhaps, at present, you would rather not go to Vandon."

"No, no," said Dare, shuddering; "I will not go there."

Charles felt more certain than ever that it would not be safe to leave him to his own devices, and his anxiety not to lose sight of him in his present state gave a kindness to his manner of which he was hardly aware.

"Come back to Atherstone with me," he said, "I will explain it to Ralph when he comes in. It will be all right."

Dare accepted the proposition with gratitude. It relieved him for the moment from coming to any decision. He thanked Charles with effusion, and then—his natural impulsiveness quickened by the quantity of raw spirits he had swallowed, by this mark of sympathy, by the moonlight, by Heaven knows what that loosens the facile tongue of unreticence—then suddenly, without a moment's preparation, he began to pour forth his troubles into Charles's astonished and reluctant ears. It was vain to try to stop him, and, after the first moment of instinctive recoil, Charles was seized by a burning curiosity to know all where he already knew so much, to put an end to this racking suspense.

"And that is not the worst," said Dare, when he had recounted how the woman he had seen on the church steps was in very deed the wife she claimed to be. "That is not the worst. I love another. We are affianced. We are as one. I bring sorrow upon her I love."

"She knows, then?" asked Charles, hoarsely, hating himself for being such a hypocrite, but unable to refrain from putting a leading question.

"She knows that some one—a person—is at Vandon," replied Dare, "who calls herself my wife, but I tell her it is not true and she, all goodness, all heavenly calm, she trusts me, and once again she promises to marry me if I am free, as I tell her, as I swear to her."

Charles listened in astonishment. He saw Dare was speaking the truth, but that Ruth could have given such a promise was difficult to believe. He did not know, what Dare even had not at all realized, that she had given it in the belief that Dare, from his answers to her questions, had never been married to the woman at all, in the belief that she was a mere adventuress seeking to make money out of him by threatening a scandalous libel, and without the faintest suspicion that she was his divorced wife, whether legally or illegally divorced.

Dare had understood the promise to depend on the legality or illegality of that divorce, and told Charles so in all good faith. With an extraordinary effort of reticence he withheld the name of his affianced, and pressing Charles's arm, begged him to ask no more. And Charles, half-sorry, half-contemptuous, wholly ashamed of having allowed such a confidence to be forced upon him, marched on in silence, now divided between mortal anxiety for Raymond and pity for Dare, now striving to keep down a certain climbing rapturous emotion which would not be suppressed.

One of the servants had waited up for their return, and, after getting Dare something to eat, Charles took him up to the room which had been prepared for himself, and then, feeling he had done his duty by him, and that he was safe for the present, went back to smoke by the smoking-room fire till Ralph came in, which was not till several hours later. When he did at last return it was in triumph. He was dead-beat, voiceless, and foot-sore; but a sense of glory sustained him. Four poachers had been taken red-handed in the coverts farthest from Arleigh. The rumor about Arleigh had, of course, been a blind; but he, Ralph, thank Heaven, was not to be taken in in such a hurry as all that! He could look after his interests as well as most men. In short, he was full of glorification to the brim, and it was only after hearing a hoarse and full account of the whole transaction several times over that Charles was able in a pause for breath to tell him that he had offered Dare a bed, as he was quite tired out, and was some distance from Vandon.

"All right. Quite right," said Ralph, unheeding; "but you and he missed the best part of the whole thing. Great Scot! when I saw them come dodging round under the Black Rock and—" He was off again; and Charles doubted afterwards, as he fell asleep in his arm-chair by the fire, whether Ralph, already slumbering peacefully opposite him, had paid the least attention to what he had told him, and would not have entirely forgotten it in the morning. And, in fact, he did, and it was not until Evelyn desired, with dignity, on the morrow, that another time unsuitable persons should not be brought at midnight to *her* house, that he remembered what had happened.

Charles, who was present, immediately took the blame upon himself, but Evelyn was not to be appeased. By this time the whole neighborhood was ringing with the news of the arrival of a foreign wife at Vandon, and Evelyn felt that Dare's presence in her blue bedroom, with crockery and crewel-work curtains to match, compromised that apartment and herself, and that he must incontinently depart out of it. It was in vain that Ralph and even Charles expostulated. She remained unmoved. It was not, she said, as if she had been unwilling to receive him, in the first instance, as a possible Roman Catholic, though many might have blamed her for that, and perhaps she *had* been to blame; but she had never, no, never, had any one to stay that anybody could say anything about. (This was a solemn fact which it was impossible to deny.) Ralph might remember her own cousin, Willie Best, and she had always liked Willie, had never been asked again after that time—Ralph chuckled—that time he knew of. She was very sorry, and she quite understood all Charles meant, and she quite saw the force of what he said; but she could not allow people to stay in the house who had foreign wives that had been kept secret. What was poor Willie, who had only— Ralph need not laugh; there was nothing to laugh at—what was Willie to this? She must be consistent. She could see Charles was very angry with her, but she could not encourage what was wrong, even if he was angry. In short, Dare must go.

But, when it came to the point, it was found that Dare could not go. Nothing short of force would have turned the unwelcome guest out of the bed in the blue bedroom, from which he made no attempt to rise, and on which he lay worn-out and feverish, in a stupor of sheer mental and physical exhaustion.

Charles and Ralph went and looked at him rather ruefully, with masculine helplessness, and the end of it was that Evelyn, in nowise softened, for she was a good woman, had to give way, and a doctor was sent for.

"Send for the man in D——. Don't have the Slumberleigh man," said Charles; "it will only make more talk;" and the doctor from D—— was accordingly sent for.

He did not arrive till the afternoon, and after he had seen Dare, and given him a sleeping draught, and had talked reassuringly of a mental shock and a feverish temperament he apologized for his delay in coming. He had been kept, he said, drawing on his gloves as he spoke, by a very serious case in the police-station at D——. A man had been arrested on suspicion the previous night, and he seemed to have sustained some fatal internal injury. He ought to have been taken to the infirmary at once; but it had been thought he was only shamming when first arrested, and once in the police-station he could not be moved, and—the doctor took up his hat—he would probably hardly outlive the day.

"By-the-way," he added, turning at the door, "he asked over and over again, while I was with him, to see you or Mr. Danvers. I'm sure I forget which, but I promised him I would mention it. Nearly slipped my memory, all the same. He said one of you had known him in his better days, at— Oxford, was it?"

"What name?" asked Charles.

"Stephens," replied the doctor. "He seemed to think you would remember him."

"Stephens," said Charles, reflectively. "Stephens! I once had a valet of that name, and a very good one he was, who left my service rather abruptly, taking with him numerous portable memorials of myself, including a set of diamond studs. I endeavored at the time to keep up my acquaintance with him; but he took measures effectually to close it. In fact, I have never heard of him from that day to this."

"That's the man, no doubt," replied the doctor. "He has—er—a sort of look about him as if he might have been in a gentleman's service once; seen-better-days-sort of look, you know."

Charles said he should be at D—— in the course of the afternoon, and would make a point of looking in at the police-station; and a quarter of an hour later he was driving as hard as he could tear in Ralph's high dog-cart along the road to D——. It was a six-mile drive, and he slackened as he reached the straggling suburbs of the little town, lying before him in a dim mist of fine rain and smoke.

Arrived at the dismal building which he knew to be the police-station, he was shown into a small room hung round with papers, where the warden was writing, and desired, with an authority so evidently accustomed to obedience that it invariably insured it, to see the prisoner. The prisoner, he said, at whose arrest he had been present, had expressed a wish to see him through the doctor; and as the warden demurred for the space of one second, Charles mentioned that he was a magistrate and justice of the peace, and sternly desired the confused official to show him the way at once. That functionary, awed by the stately manner which none knew better than Charles when to assume, led the way down a narrow stone passage, past numerous doors behind one of which a banging sound, accompanied by alcoholic oaths, suggested the presence of a freeborn Briton chafing under restraint.

"I had him put up-stairs, sir," said the warden, humbly. "We didn't know when he came in as it was a case for the infirmary; but seeing he was wanted for a big thing, and poorly in his 'ealth, I giv' him one of the superior cells, with a mattress and piller complete."

The man was evidently afraid that Charles had come as a magistrate to give him a reprimand of some kind, for, as he led the way up a narrow stone staircase, he continued to expatiate on the luxury of the "mattress and piller," on the superiority of the cell, and how a nurse had been sent for at once from the infirmary, when, owing to his own shrewdness, the prisoner was found to be "a hospital case."

"The doctor wouldn't have him moved," he said, opening a closed door in a long passage full of doors, the rest of which stood open. "It's not reg'lar to have him in here, sir, I know; but the doctor wouldn't have him moved."

Charles passed through the door, and found himself in a narrow whitewashed cell, with a bed at one side, over which an old woman in the dress of a hospital nurse was bending.

"You can come out, Martha," said the warden. "The gentleman's come to see 'im."

As the old woman disappeared, courtesying, he lingered to say, in a whisper, "Do you know him, sir?"

"Yes," said Charles, looking fixedly at the figure on the bed. "I remember him. I knew him years ago, in his better days. I dare say he will have something to tell me."

"If it should be anything as requires a witness," continued the man— "he's said a deal already, and it's all down in proper form—but if there's anything more——"

"I will let you know," said Charles, looking towards the door, and the warden took the hint and went out of it, closing it quietly.

Charles crossed the little room, and, sitting down in the crazy chair beside the bed, laid his hand gently on the listless hand lying palm upward on the rough gray counterpane.

"Raymond," he said; "it is I, Danvers."

The hand trembled a little, and made a faint attempt to clasp his. Charles took the cold, lifeless hand, and held it in his strong gentle grasp.

"It is Danvers," he said again.

The sick man turned his head slowly on the pillow, and looked fixedly at him. Death's own color, which imitation can never imitate, nor ignorance mistake, was stamped upon that rigid face.

"I'm done for," he said with a faint smile, which touched the lips but did not reach the solemn far-reaching eyes.

Charles could not speak.

"You said I should turn up tails once too often," continued Raymond, with slow halting utterance, "and I've done it. I knew it was all up when I pitched over that d——d wall onto the stones. I felt I'd killed myself."

"How did they get you?" said Charles.

"I don't know," replied Raymond, closing his eyes wearily, as if the subject had ceased to interest him. "I think I tried to creep along under the wall towards the place where it is broken down, when I fancy some one came over long after the others and knocked me on the head."

Charles reflected with sudden wrath that Brooks, no doubt, had been the man, and how much worse than useless his manœuvre with the stick had been.

"I did my best," he said, humbly.

"Yes," replied the other; "and I would not have forgotten it, either, if—if there had been any time to remember it in; but there won't be. I've owned up," he continued, in a labored whisper. "Stephens has made a full confession. You'll have it in all the papers to-morrow. And while I was at it I piled on some more I never did, which will get friends over the water out of trouble. Tom Flavell did me a good turn once, and he's been in hiding these two years for—well, it don't much matter what, but I've shoved that in with the rest, though it was never in my line—never. He'll be able to go home now."

"Have not you confessed under your own name?"

"No," replied Raymond, with a curious remnant of that pride of race at which it is the undisputed privilege of low birth and a plebeian temperament to sneer. "I won't have my own name dragged in. I dropped it years ago. I've confessed as Stephens, and I'll die and be buried as Stephens. I'm not going to disgrace the family."

There was a constrained silence of some minutes.

"Would you like to see your sister?" asked Charles; but Raymond shook his head with feeble decision.

"That man!" he said, suddenly, after a long pause. "That man in the door-way! How did he come there?"

"There is no man in the door-way," said Charles, reassuringly. "There is no one here but me."

"Last night," continued Raymond, "last night in the stables. I watched him stand in the door-way."

Charles remembered how Dare had said Raymond had bolted out past him.

"That was Dare," he said; "the man who was to have been your brother-in-law."

"Ah!" said Raymond with evident unconcern. "I thought I'd seen him before. But he's altered. He's grown into a man. So he is to marry Ruth, is he?"

"Not now. He was to have done, but a divorced wife from America has turned up. She arrived at Vandon the day before yesterday. It seems the divorce in America does not hold in England."

Raymond started.

"The old fox," he said, with feeble energy. "Tracked him out, has she? We used to call them fox and goose when she married him. By — —, she squeezed every dollar out of him before she let him go, and now she's got him again, has she? She always was a cool hand. The old fox," he continued, with contempt and admiration in his voice. "She's playing a bold game, and the luck is on her side, but she's no more his wife than I am, and she knows that perfectly well."

"Do you mean that the divorce was——"

"Divorce, bosh!" said Raymond, working himself up into a state of feeble excitement frightful to see. "I tell you she was never married to him legally. She called herself a widow when she married Dare, but she had a husband living, Jasper Carroll, serving his time at Baton Rouge Jail, down South, all the time. He died there a year afterwards, but hardly a soul knows it to this day; and those that do don't care about bringing themselves into public notice. They'll prefer hush-money, if they find out what she's up to now. The prison register would prove it directly. But Dare will never find it out. How should he?"

Raymond sank back speechless and panting. A strong shudder passed over him, and his breath seemed to fail.

"It's coming," he whispered, hoarsely. "That lying doctor said I had several hours, and I feel it coming already."

"Danvers," he continued, hurriedly, "are you still there?" Then, as Charles bent over him, "Closer; bend down. I want to see your face. Keep your own counsel about Dare. There's no one to tell if you don't. He's not fit for Ruth. You can marry her now. I saw what I saw. She'll take you. And some day—some day, when you have been married a long time, tell her I'm dead; and tell her—about Flavell, and how I owned to it—but that I did not do it. I never sank so low as that." His voice had dropped to a whisper which died imperceptibly away.

"I will tell her," said Charles; and Raymond turned his face to the wall, and spoke no more.

The struggle had passed, and for the moment death held aloof; but his shadow was there, lying heavy on the deepening twilight, and darkening all the little room. Raymond seemed to have sunk into a stupor, and at last Charles rose silently and went out.

He was dimly conscious of meeting some one in the passage, of answering some question in the negative, and then he found himself gathering up the reins, and driving through the narrow lighted streets of D— — in the dusk, and so away down the long flat high-road to Atherstone.

A white mist had risen up to meet the darkness, and had shrouded all the land. In sweeps and curves along the fields a gleaming pallor lay of heavy dew upon the grass, and on the road the long lines of dim water in the ruts reflected the dim sky.

Carts lumbered past him in the darkness once or twice, the men in them peering back at his reckless driving; and once a carriage with lamps came swiftly up the road towards him, and passed him with a flash, grazing his wheel. But he took no heed. Drive as quickly as he would through mist and darkness, a voice followed him, the voice of a pursuing devil close at his ear, whispering in the halting, feeble utterance of a dying man:

"Keep your own counsel about Dare. There is no one to tell if you don't."

Charles shivered and set his teeth. High on the hill among the trees the distant lights of Slumberleigh shone like glowworms through the mist. He looked at them with wild eyes. She was there, the woman who loved him, and whom he passionately loved. He could stretch forth his hand to take her if he would. His breath came hard and thick. A hand seemed clutching and tearing at his heart. And close at his ear the whisper came:

"There is no one to tell if you don't."

CHAPTER XXVIII

It was close on dressing-time when Charles came into the drawing-room, where Evelyn and Molly were building castles on the hearth-rug in the ruddy firelight. After changing his damp clothes, he had gone to the smoking-room, but he had found Dare sitting there in a vast dressing-gown of Ralph's, in a state of such utter dejection, with his head in his hands, that he had silently retreated again before he had been perceived. He did not want to see Dare just now. He wished he were not in the house.

Quite oblivious of the fact that he was not in Evelyn's good graces, he went and sat by the drawing-room fire, and absently watched Molly playing with her bricks. Presently, when the dressing-bell rang, Evelyn went away to dress, and Molly, tired of her castles, suggested that she might sit on his knee.

He let her climb up and wriggle and finally settle herself as it seemed good to her, but he did not speak; and so they sat in the firelight together, Molly's hand lovingly stroking his black velvet coat. But her talents lay in conversation, not in silence, and she soon broke it.

"You do look beautiful to-night, Uncle Charles."

"Do I?" without elation.

"Do you know, Uncle Charles, Ninny's sister with the wart on her cheek has been to tea? She's in the nursery now. Ninny says she's to have a bite of supper before she goes."

"You don't say so?"

"And we had buttered toast to tea, and she said you were the most splendid gentleman she ever saw."

Charles did not answer. He did not even seem to have heard this interesting tribute to his personal appearance. Molly felt that something must be gravely amiss, and, laying her soft cheek against his, she whispered, confidentially:

"Uncle Charles, are you uncomferable inside?"

There was a long pause.

"Yes, Molly," at last, pressing her to him.

"Is it there?" said Molly, sympathetically, laying her hand on the front portion of her amber sash.

"No, Molly; I only wish it were."

"It's not the little green pears, then," said Molly, with the sigh of experience, "because it's always *just* there, *always*, with them. It was again yesterday. They're nasty little pears," — with a touch of personal resentment.

Uncle Charles smiled at last, but it was not quite his usual smile.

"Miss Molly," said a voice from the door, "your mamma has sent for you."

"It's not bedtime yet."

"Your mamma says you are to come at once," was the reply.

Molly, knowing from experience that an appeal to Charles was useless on these occasions, wriggled down from her perch rather reluctantly, and bade her uncle "Good-night."

"Perhaps it will be better to-morrow," she said, consolingly.

"Perhaps," he said, nodding at her; and he took her little head between his hands, and kissed her. She rubbed his kiss off again, and walked gravely away. She could not be merry and ride in triumph up-stairs on kind curvetting Sarah's willing back, while her friend was "uncomferable inside." There was no galloping down the passage that night, no pleasantries with the sponge in Molly's tub, no last caperings in light attire. Molly went silently to bed, and as on a previous occasion when in great anxiety about Vic, who had thoughtlessly gone out in the twilight for a stroll, and had forgotten the lapse of time, she added a whispered clause to her little petitions which the ear of "Ninny" failed to catch.

Charles recognized, in the way Evelyn had taken Molly from him, that she was not yet appeased. It should be remembered, in order to do her justice, that a good woman's means of showing a proper resentment are so straitened and circumscribed by her conscience that she is obliged, from actual want of material, to resort occasionally to little acts of domestic tyranny, small in themselves as midge bites, but, fortunately for the cause of virtue, equally exasperating. Indeed, it is improbable that any really good woman would ever so far forget herself as to lose her temper, if she were once thoroughly aware how much more irritating in the long-run a judicious course of those small persecutions may be made, which the tenderest conscience need not scruple to inflict.

Charles was unreasonably annoyed at having Molly taken from him. As he sat by the fire alone, tired in mind and body, a hovering sense of cold, and an intense weariness of life took him; and a great longing came over him like a thirst—a longing for a little of the personal happiness which seemed to be the common lot of so many round him; for a home where he had now only a house; for love and warmth and companionship, and possibly some day a little Molly of his own, who would not be taken from him at the caprice of another.

The only barrier to the fulfilment of such a dream had been a conscientious scruple of Ruth's, to which at the time he had urged upon her that she did wrong to yield. That barrier was now broken down; but it ought never to have existed. Ruth and he belonged to each other by divine law, and she had no right to give herself to any one else to satisfy her own conscience. And now—all would be well. She was absolved from her promise. She had been wrong to persist in keeping it, in his opinion; but at any rate she was honorably released from it now. And she would marry him.

And that *second* promise, which she had made to Dare, that she would still marry him if he were free to marry?

Charles moved impatiently in his chair. From what exaggerated sense of duty she had made that promise he knew not; but he would save her from the effects of her own perverted judgment. He knew what Ruth's word meant, since he had tried to make her break it. He knew that she had promised to marry Dare if he were free. He knew that, having made that promise, she would keep it.

It would be mere sentimental folly on his part to say the word that would set Dare free. Even if the American woman were not his wife in the eye of the law, she had a moral claim upon him. The possibility of Ruth's still marrying Dare was too hideous to be thought of. If her judgment was so entirely perverted by a morbid conscientious fear of following her own inclination that she could actually give Dare that promise, directly after the arrival of the adventuress, Charles would take the decision out of her hands. As she could not judge fairly for herself, he would judge for her, and save her from herself.

For her sake as much as for his own he resolved to say nothing. He had only to keep silence.

"There's no one to tell if you don't."

The door opened, and Charles gave a start as Dare came into the room. He was taken aback by the sudden rush of jealous hatred that surged up within him at his appearance. It angered and shamed him, and Dare, much shattered but feebly cordial, found him very irresponsive and silent for the few minutes that remained before the dinner-bell rang, and the others came down.

It was not a pleasant meal. If Dare had been a shade less ill, he must have noticed the marked coldness of Evelyn's manner, and how Ralph good-naturedly endeavored to make up for it by double helpings of soup and fish, which he was quite unable to eat. Charles and Lady Mary were never congenial spirits at the best of times, and to-night was not the best. That lady, after feebly provoking the attack, as usual, sustained some crushing defeats, mainly couched in the language of Scripture, which was, as she felt with Christian indignation, turning her own favorite weapon against herself, as possibly Charles thought she deserved, for putting such a weapon to so despicable a use.

"I really don't know," she said, tremulously, afterwards in the drawing-room, "what Charles will come to if he goes on like this. I don't mind" — venomously—"his tone towards myself. That I do not regard; but his entire want of reverence for the Church and apostolic succession; his profane remarks about vestments; in short, his entire attitude towards religion gives me the gravest anxiety."

In the dining-room the conversation flagged, and Charles was beginning to wonder whether he could make some excuse and bolt, when a servant came in with a note for him. It was from the doctor in D— —, and ran as follows:

> "Dear Sir,
>
> "I have just seen (6.30 p.m.) Stephens again. I found him in a state of the wildest excitement, and he implored me to send you word that he wanted to see you again. He seemed so sure that you would go if you knew he wished it, that I have commissioned Sergeant Brown's boy to take this. He wished me to say 'there was something more.' If there is any further confession he desires to make, he has not much time to do it in. I did not expect he would have lasted till now. As it is, he is going fast. Indeed, I hardly think you will be in time to see him; but I promised to give you this message.
>
> Yours faithfully,
>
> R. White."

"I must go," Charles said, throwing the note across to Ralph. "Give the boy half a crown, will you? I suppose I may take Othello?" and before Ralph had mastered the contents of the note, and begun to fumble for a half-crown, Charles was saddling Othello himself, without waiting for the groom, and in a few minutes was clattering over the stones out of the yard.

There was just light enough to ride by, and he rode hard. What was it—what could it be that Raymond had still to tell him? He felt certain it had something to do with Ruth, and probably Dare. Should he arrive in time to hear it? There at last were the lights of D—— in front of him. Should he arrive in time? As he pulled up his steaming horse before the police-station his heart misgave him.

"Am I too late?" he asked of the man who came to the door.

He looked bewildered.

"Stephens! Is he dead?"

The man shook his head.

"They say he's a'most gone."

Charles threw the rein to him, and hurried in-doors. He met some one coming out, the doctor probably, he thought afterwards, who took him upstairs, and sent away the old woman who was in attendance.

"I can't do anything more," he said, opening the door for him. "Wanted elsewhere. Very good of you, I'm sure. Not much use, I'm afraid. Good-night. I'll tell the old woman to be about."

A dim lamp was burning on the little corner cupboard near the door, and, as Charles bent over the bed, he saw in a moment, even by that pale light, that he was too late.

Life was still there, if that feeble tossing could be called life; but all else was gone. Raymond's feet were already on the boundary of the land where all things are forgotten; and, at the sight of that dim country, memory, affrighted, had slipped away and left him.

Was it possible to recall him to himself even yet?

"Raymond," he said, in a low distinct voice, "what is it you wish to say? Tell me quickly what it is."

But the long agony of farewell between body and soul had begun, and the eyes that seemed to meet his with momentary recognition only looked at him in anguish, seeking help and finding none, and wandered away again, vainly searching for that which was not to be found.

Charles could do nothing, but he had not the heart to leave him to struggle with death entirely alone, and so, in awed and helpless compassion, he sat by him through one long hour after another, waiting for the end which still delayed, his eyes wandering ever and anon from the bed to the high grated window, or idly spelling out the different names and disparaging remarks that previous occupants had scratched and scrawled over the whitewashed walls.

And so the hours passed.

At last, all in a moment, the struggle ceased. The dying man vainly tried to raise himself to meet what was coming, and Charles put his strong arm round him and held him up. He knew that consciousness sometimes returns at the moment of death.

"Raymond," he whispered, earnestly. "Raymond."

A tremor passed over the face. The lips moved. The homeless, lingering soul came back, and looked for the last time fixedly and searchingly at him out of the dying eyes, and then—seeing no help for it—went hurriedly on its way, leaving the lips parted to speak, leaving the deserted eyes vacant and terrible, until after a time Charles closed them.

He had gone without speaking. Whatever he had wished to say would remain unsaid forever. Charles laid him down, and stood a long time looking at the set face. The likeness to Raymond seemed to be fading away under the touch of the Mighty Hand, but the look of Ruth, the better look, remained.

At last he turned away and went out, stopping to wake the old nurse, heavily asleep in the passage. His horse was brought round for him from somewhere, and he mounted and rode away. He had no idea how long he had been there. It must have been many hours, but he had quite lost sight of time. It was still dark, but the morning could not be far off. He rode mechanically, his horse, which knew the road, taking him at its own pace. The night was cold, but he did not feel it. All power of feeling anything seemed gone from him. The last two days and nights of suspense and high-strung emotion seemed to have left him incapable of any further sensation at present beyond that of an intense fatigue.

He rode slowly, and put up his horse with careful absence of mind. The eastern horizon was already growing pale and distinct as he found his way in-doors through the drawing-room window, the shutter of which had been left unhinged for him by Ralph, according to custom when either of them was out late. He went noiselessly up to his room, and sat down. After a time he started to find himself still sitting there; but he remained without stirring, too tired to move, his elbows on the table, his chin in his hands. He felt he could not sleep if he were to drag himself into bed. He might just as well stay where he was.

And as he sat watching the dawn his mind began to stir, to shake off its lethargy and stupor, to struggle into keener and keener consciousness.

There are times, often accompanying great physical prostration, when a veil seems to be lifted from our mental vision. As in the Mediterranean one may glance down suddenly on a calm day, and see in the blue depths with a strange surprise the sea-weed and the rocks and the fretted sands below, so also in rare hours we see the hidden depths of the soul, over which we have floated in heedless unconsciousness so long, and catch a glimpse of the hills and the valleys of those untravelled regions.

Charles sat very still with his chin in his hands. His mind did not work. It looked right down to the heart of things.

There is, perhaps, no time when mental vision is so clear, when the mind is so sane, as when death has come very near to us. There is a light which he brings with him, which he holds before the eyes of the dying, the stern light, seldom seen, of reality, before which self-deception and meanness, and that which maketh a lie, cower in their native deformity and slip away.

And death sheds at times a strange gleam from that same light upon the souls of those who stand within his shadow, and watch his kingdom coming. In an awful transfiguration all things stand for what they are. Evil is seen to be evil, and good to be good. Right and wrong sunder more far apart, and we cannot mistake them as we do at other times. The debatable land stretching between them—that favorite resort of undecided natures—disappears for a season, and offers no longer its false refuge. The mind is taken away from all artificial supports, and the knowledge comes home to the soul afresh, with strong conviction that "truth is our only armor in all passages of life," as with awed hearts we see it is the only armor in the hour of death, the only shield that we may bear away with us into the unknown country.

Charles shuddered involuntarily. His decision of the afternoon to keep secret what Raymond had told him was gradually but surely assuming a different aspect. What was it, after all, but a suppression of truth—a kind of lie? What was it but doing evil that good might come?

It was no use harping on the old string of consequences. He saw that he had resolved to commit a deliberate sin, to be false to that great principle of life—right for the sake of right, truth for the love of truth—by which of late he had been trying to live. So far it had not been difficult, for his nature was not one to do things by halves, but now—

Old voices out of the past, which he had thought long dead, rose out of forgotten graves to urge him on. What was he that he should stick at such a trifle? Why should a man with his past begin to split hairs?

And conscience said nothing, only pointed, only showed, with a clearness that allowed of no mistake, that he had come to a place where two roads met.

Charles's heart suffered then "the nature of an insurrection." The old lawless powers that had once held sway, and had been forced back into servitude under the new rule of the last few years of responsibility and honor, broke loose, and spread like wildfire throughout the kingdom of his heart.

The struggle deepened to a battle fierce and furious. His soul was rent with a frenzy of tumult, of victory and defeat ever changing sides, ever returning to the attack.

Can a kingdom divided against itself stand?

He sat motionless, gazing with absent eyes in front of him.

And across the shock of battle, and above the turmoil of conflicting passions, Ruth's voice came to him. He saw the pale spiritual face, the deep eyes so full of love and anguish, and yet so steadfast with a great resolve. He heard again her last words, "I cannot do what is wrong, even for you."

He stretched out his hands suddenly.

"You would not, Ruth," he said, half aloud; "you would not. Neither will I do what I know to be wrong for you, so help me God! not even for you."

The dawn was breaking, was breaking clear and cold, and infinitely far away; was coming up through unfathomable depths and distances, through gleaming caverns and fastnesses of light, like a new revelation fresh from God. But Charles did not see it, for his head was down on the table, and he was crying like a child.

CHAPTER XXIX

Dare was down early the following morning, much too early for the convenience of the house-maids, who were dusting the drawing-room when he appeared there. He was usually as late as any of the young and gilded unemployed who feel it incumbent on themselves to show by these public demonstrations their superiority to the rules and fixed hours of the working and thinking world, with whom, however, their fear of being identified is a groundless apprehension. But to-day Dare experienced a mournful satisfaction in being down so early. He felt the underlying pathos of such a marked departure from his usual habits. It was obvious that nothing but deep affliction or cub-hunting could have been the cause, and the cub-hunting was over. The inference was not one that could be missed by the meanest capacity.

He took up the newspaper with a sigh, and settled himself in front of the blazing fire, which was still young and leaping, with the enthusiasm of dry sticks not quite gone out of it.

Charles heard Dare go down just as he finished dressing, for he too was early that morning. There was more than half an hour before breakfast-time. He considered a moment, and then went down-stairs. Some resolutions once made cannot be carried out too quickly.

As he passed through the hall he looked out. The mist of the night before had sought out every twig and leaflet, and had silvered it to meet the sun. The rime on the grass looked cool and tempting. Charles's head ached, and he went out for a moment and stood in the crisp still air. The rooks were cawing high up. The face of the earth had not altered during the night. It shimmered and was glad, and smiled at his grave, care-worn face.

"Hallo!" called a voice; and Ralph's head, with his hair sticking straight out on every side, was thrust out of a window. "I say, Charles, early bird you are!"

"Yes," said Charles, looking up and leisurely going in-doors again; "you are the first worm I have seen."

He found Dare, as he expected, in the drawing-room, and proceeded at once to the business he had in hand.

"I am glad you are down early," he said. "You are the very man I want."

"Ah!" replied Dare, shaking his head, "when the heart is troubled there is no sleep, none. All the clocks are heard."

"Possibly. I should not wonder if you heard another in the course of half an hour, which will mean breakfast. In the mean time— —"

"I want no breakfast. A sole cup of— —"

"In the mean time," continued Charles, "I have some news for you." And, disregarding another interruption, he related as shortly as he could the story of Stephens's recognition of him in the door-way, and the subsequent revelations in the prison concerning Dare's marriage.

"Where is this man, this Stephens?" said Dare, jumping up. "I will go to him. I will hear from his own mouth. Where is he?"

"I don't know," replied Charles, curtly. "It is a matter of opinion. He is dead!"

Dare looked bewildered, and then sank back with a gasp of disappointment into his chair.

Charles, whose temper was singularly irritable this morning, repeated with suppressed annoyance the greater part of what he had just said, and proved to Dare that the fact that Stephens was dead would in no way prevent the illegality of his marriage being proved.

When Dare had grasped the full significance of that fact he was quite overcome.

"Am I, then," he gasped—"is it true?—am I free—to marry?"

"Quite free."

Dare burst into tears, and, partially veiling with one hand the manly emotion that had overtaken him, he extended the other to Charles, who did not know what to do with it when he had got it, and dropped it as soon as he could. But Dare, like many people whose feelings are all on the surface, and who are rather proud of displaying them, was slow to notice what was passing in the minds of others.

He sprang to his feet, and began to pace rapidly up and down.

"I will go after breakfast—at once—immediately after breakfast, to Slumberleigh Rectory."

"I suppose, in that case, Miss Deyncourt is the person whose name you would not mention the other day?"

"She is," said Dare. "You are right. It is she. We are betrothed. I will fly to her after breakfast."

"You know your own affairs best," said Charles, whose temper had not been improved by the free display of Dare's finer feelings; "but I am not sure you would not do well to fly to Vandon first. It is best to be off with the old love, I believe, before you are on with the new."

"She must at once go away from Vandon," said Dare, stopping short. "She is a scandal, the—the old one. But how to make her go away?"

It was in vain for Charles to repeat that Dare must turn her out. Dare had premonitory feelings that he was quite unequal to the task.

"I may tell her to go," he said, raising his eyebrows. "I may be firm as the rock, but I know her well; she is more obstinate than me. She will not go."

"She must," said Charles, with anger. "Her presence compromises Miss Deyncourt. Can't you see that?"

Dare raised his eyebrows. A light seemed to break in on him.

"Any fool can see that," said Charles, losing his temper.

Dare saw a great deal—many things besides that. He saw that if a friend, a trusted friend, were to manage her dismissal, it would be more easy for that friend than for one whose feelings at the moment might carry him away. In short, Charles was the friend who was evidently pointed out by Providence for that mission.

Charles considered a moment. He began to see that it would not be done without further delays and scandal unless he did it.

"She must and shall go at once, even if I have to do it," he said at last, looking at Dare with unconcealed contempt. "It is not my affair, but I will go, and you will be so good as to put off the flying over to Slumberleigh till I come back. I shall not return until she has left the house." And Charles marched out of the room, too indignant to trust himself a moment longer with the profusely grateful Dare.

"That man must go to-day," said Evelyn, after breakfast, to her husband, in the presence of Lady Mary and Charles. "While he was ill I overlooked his being in the house; but I will not suffer him to remain now he is well."

"You remove him from all chance of improvement," said Charles, "if you take him away from Aunt Mary, who can snatch brands from the burning, as we all know; but I am going over to Vandon this morning, and if you wish it I will ask him if he would like me to order his dog-cart to come for him. I don't suppose he is very happy here, without so much as a tooth-brush that he can call his own."

"You are going to Vandon?" asked both ladies in one voice.

"Yes. I am going on purpose to dislodge an impostor who has arrived there, who is actually believed by some people (who are not such exemplary Christians as ourselves, and ready to suppose the worst) to be his wife."

Lady Mary and Evelyn looked at each other in consternation, and Charles went off to see how Othello was after his night's work, and to order the dog-cart, Ralph calling after him, in perfect good-humor, that "a fellow's brother got more out of a fellow's horses than a fellow did himself."

Dare waylaid Charles on his return from the stables, and linked his arm in his. He felt the most enthusiastic admiration for the tall reserved Englishman who had done him such signal service. He longed for an opportunity of showing his gratitude to him. It was perhaps just as well that he was not aware how very differently Charles regarded himself.

"You are just going?" Dare asked.

"In five minutes."

Charles let his arm hang straight down, but Dare kept it.

"Tell me, my friend, one thing." Dare had evidently been turning over something in his mind. "This poor unfortunate, this Stephens, why did he not tell you all this the *first* time you went to see him in the afternoon?"

"He did."

"What?" said Dare, looking hard at him. "He *did*, and you only tell me this morning! You let me go all through the night first. Why was this?"

Charles did not answer.

"I ask one thing more," continued Dare. "Did you divine two nights ago, from what I said in a moment of confidence, that Miss Deyncourt was the—the—"

"Of course I did," said Charles, sharply. "You made it sufficiently obvious."

"Ah!" said Dare. "Ah!" and he shut his eyes and nodded his head several times.

"Anything more you would like to know?" asked Charles, inattentive and impatient, mainly occupied in trying to hide the nameless exasperation which invariably seized him when he looked at Dare, and to stifle the contemptuous voice which always whispered as he did so, "And you have given up Ruth to him—to *him*!"

"No, no, no!" said Dare, shaking his head gently, and regarding him the while with infinite interest through his half-closed eyelids.

The dog-cart was coming round, and Charles hastily turned from him, and, getting in, drove quickly away. Whatever Dare said or did seemed to set his teeth on edge, and he lashed up the horse till he was out of sight of the house.

Dare, with arms picturesquely folded, stood looking after him with mixed feelings of emotion and admiration.

"One sees it well," he said to himself. "One sees now the reason of many things. He kept silent at first, but he was too good, too noble. In the night he considered; in the morning he told all. I wondered that he went to Vandon; but he did it not for me. It was for her sake."

Dare's feelings were touched to the quick.

How beautiful! how pathetic was this *dénouement*! His former admiration for Charles was increased a thousand-fold. *He also loved!* Ah! (Dare felt he was becoming agitated.) How sublime, how touching was his self-sacrifice in the cause of honor! He had been gradually working himself up to the highest pitch of pleasurable excitement and emotion; and now, seeing Ralph the prosaic approaching, he fled precipitately into the house, caught up his hat and stick, hardly glancing at himself in the hall-glass, and, entirely forgetting his promise to Charles to remain at Atherstone till the latter returned from Vandon, followed the impulse of the moment, and struck across the fields in the direction of Slumberleigh.

Charles, meanwhile, drove on to Vandon. The stable clock, still partially paralyzed from long disuse, was laboriously striking eleven as he drew up before the door. His resounding peal at the bell startled the household, and put the servants into a flutter of anxious expectation, while the sound made some one else, breakfasting late in the dining-room, pause with her cup midway to her lips and listen.

"There is a train which leaves Slumberleigh station for London a little after twelve, is not there?" asked Charles, with great distinctness, of the butler as he entered the hall. He had observed as he came in that the dining-room door was ajar.

"There is, Sir Charles. Twelve fifteen," replied the man, who recognized him instantly, for everybody knew Charles.

"I am here as Mr. Dare's friend, at his wish. Tell Mr. Dare's coachman to bring round his dog-cart to the door in good time to catch that train. Will it take luggage?"

"Yes, Sir Charles," with respectful alacrity.

"Good! And when the dog-cart appears you will see that the boxes are brought down belonging to the person who is staying here, who will leave by that train."

"Yes, Sir Charles."

"If the policeman from Slumberleigh should arrive while I am here, ask him to wait."

"I will, Sir Charles."

"I don't suppose," thought Charles, "he will arrive, as I have not sent for him; but, as the dining-room door happens to be ajar, it is just as well to add a few artistic touches."

"Is this person in the drawing-room?" he continued aloud.

The man replied that she was in the dining-room, and Charles walked in unannounced, and closed the door behind him.

He had at times, when any action of importance was on hand, a certain cool decision of manner that seemed absolutely to ignore the possibility of opposition, which formed a curious contrast with his usual careless demeanor.

"Good-morning," he said, advancing to the fire. "I have no doubt that my appearance at this early hour cannot be a surprise to you. You have, of course, anticipated some visit of this kind for the last few days. Pray finish your coffee. I am Sir Charles Danvers. I need hardly add that I am justice of the peace in this county, and that I am here officially on behalf of my friend, Mr. Dare."

The little woman, who had risen, and had then sat down again at his entrance, eyed him steadily. There was a look in her dark bead-like eyes which showed Charles why Dare had been unable to face her. The look, determined, cunning, watchful, put him on his guard, and his manner became a shade more unconcerned.

"Any friend of my husband's is welcome," she said.

"There is no question for the moment about your husband, though no doubt a subject of peculiar interest to yourself. I was speaking of Mr. Dare."

She rose to her feet, as if unable to sit while he was standing.

"Mr. Dare is my husband," she said, with a little gesture of defiance, tapping sharply on the table with a teaspoon she held in her hand.

Charles smiled blandly, and looked out of the window.

"There is evidently some misapprehension on that point," he observed, "which I am here to remove. Mr. Dare is at present unmarried."

"I am his wife," reiterated the woman, her color rising under her rouge. "I am, and I won't go. He dared not come himself, a poor coward that he is, to turn his wife out-of-doors. He sent you; but it's no manner of use, so you may as well know it first as last. I tell you nothing shall induce me to stir from this house, from my home, and you needn't think you can come it over me with fine talk. I don't care a red cent what you say. I'll have my rights."

"I am here," said Charles, "to see that you get them, Mrs.—*Carroll.*"

There was a pause. He did not look at her. He was occupied in taking a white thread off his coat.

"Carroll's dead," she said, sharply.

"He is. And your regret at his loss was no doubt deepened by the unhappy circumstances in which it took place. He died in jail."

"Well, and if he did—"

"Died," continued Charles, suddenly fixing his keen glance upon her, "nearly a year after your so-called marriage with Mr. Dare."

"It's a lie," she said, faintly; but she had turned very white.

"No, I *think* not. My information is on reliable authority. A slight exertion of memory on your part will no doubt recall the date of your bereavement."

"You can't prove it."

"Excuse me. You have yourself kindly furnished us with a copy of the marriage register, with the date attached, without which I must own we might have been momentarily at a loss. I need now only apply for a copy of the register of the decease of Jasper Carroll, who, as you do not deny, died under personal restraint in jail; in Baton Rouge Jail in Louisiana, I have no doubt you intended to add."

She glared at him in silence.

"Some dates acquire a peculiar interest when compared," continued Charles, "but I will not detain you any longer with business details of this kind, as I have no doubt that you will wish to superintend your packing."

"I won't go."

"On the contrary, you will leave this house in half an hour. The dog-cart is ordered to take you to the station."

"What if I refuse to go?"

"Extreme measures are always to be regretted, especially with a lady," said Charles. "Nothing, in short, would be more repugnant to me; but I fear, as a magistrate, it would be my duty to—" And he shrugged his shoulders, wondering what on earth could be done for the moment if she persisted. "But," he continued, "motives of self-interest suggest the advisability of withdrawing, even if I were not here to enforce it. When I take into consideration the trouble and expense you have incurred in coming here, and the subsequent disappointment of the affections, a widow's affections, I feel justified in offering, though without my friend's permission, to pay your journey back to America, an offer which any further unpleasantness or delay would of course oblige me to retract."

She hesitated, and he saw his advantage and kept it.

"You have not much time to lose," he said, laying his watch on the table, "unless you would prefer the house-keeper to do your packing for you. No? I agree with you. On a sea voyage especially, one likes to know where one's things are. If I give you a check for your return journey, I shall, of course, expect you to sign a paper to the effect that you have no claim on Mr. Dare, that you never were his legal wife, and that you will not trouble him in future. You would like a few moments for reflection? Good! I will write out the form while you consider, as there is no time to be lost."

He looked about for writing materials, and, finding only an ancient inkstand and pen, took a note from his pocket-book and tore a blank half-sheet off it. His quiet deliberate movements awed her as he intended they should. She glanced first at him writing, then at the gold watch on the table between them, the hours of which were marked on the half-hunting face by alternate diamonds and rubies, each stone being the memorial of a past success in shooting-matches. The watch impressed her; to her practised eye it meant a very large sum of money, and she knew the power of money; but the cool, unconcerned manner of this tall, keen-eyed Englishman impressed her still more. As she looked at him he ceased writing, got out a check, and began to fill it in.

"What Christian name?" he asked, suddenly.

"Ellen," she replied, taken aback.

"Payable to order or bearer?"

"Bearer," she said, confused by the way he took her decision for granted.

"Now," he said, authoritatively, "sign your name there;" and he pushed the form he had drawn up towards her. "I am sorry I cannot offer you a better pen."

She took the pen mechanically and signed her name—*Ellen Carroll*. Charles's light eyes gave a flash as she did it.

"Manner is everything," he said to himself. "I believe the mention of that imaginary policeman may have helped, but a little stage effect did the business."

"Thank you," he said, taking the paper, and, after glancing at the signature, putting it in his pocket-book. "Allow me to give you this"— handing her the check. "And now I will ring for the house-keeper, for you will barely have time to make the arrangements for your journey. I can allow you only twenty minutes." He rang the bell as he spoke.

She started up as if unaware how far she had yielded. A rush of angry color flooded her face.

"I won't have that impertinent woman touching my things."

"That is as you like," said Charles, shrugging his shoulders; "but she will be in the room when you pack. It is my wish that she should be present." Then turning to the butler, who had already answered the bell, "Desire the house-keeper to go to Mrs. Carroll's rooms at once, and to give Mrs. Carroll any help she may require."

Mrs. Carroll looked from the butler to Charles with baffled hatred in her eyes. But she knew the game was lost, and she walked out of the room and up-stairs without another word, but with a bitter consciousness in her heart that she had not played her cards well, that, though her downfall was unavoidable, she might have stood out for better terms for her departure. She hated Dare, as she threw her clothes together into her trunks, and she hated Mrs. Smith, who watched her do so with folded hands and with a lofty smile; but most of all she hated Charles, whose voice came up to the open window as he talked to Dare's coachman, already at the door, about splints and sore backs.

Charles felt a momentary pity for the little woman when she came down at last with compressed lips, casting lightning glances at the grinning servants in the background, whom she had bullied and hectored over in the manner of people unaccustomed to servants, and who were rejoicing in the ignomiy of her downfall.

Her boxes were put in—not carefully.

Charles came forward and lifted his cap, but she would not look at him. Grasping a little hand-bag convulsively, she went down the steps, and got up, unassisted, into the dog-cart.

"You have left nothing behind, I hope?" said Charles, civilly, for the sake of saying something.

"She have left nothing," said Mrs. Smith, swimming forward with dignity, "and she have also took nothing. I have seen to that, Sir Charles."

"Good-bye, then," said Charles. "Right, coachman."

Mrs. Carroll's eyes had been wandering upward to the old house rising above her with its sunny windows and its pointed gables. Perhaps, after all the sordid shifts and schemes of her previous existence, she had imagined she might lead an easier and a more respectable life within those walls. Then she looked towards the long green terraces, the valley, and the forest beyond. Her lip trembled, and turning suddenly, she fixed her eyes with burning hatred on the man who had ousted her from this pleasant place.

Then the coachman whipped up his horse, the dog-cart spun over the smooth gravel between the lines of stiff, clipped yews, and she was gone.

CHAPTER XXX

Mr. Alwynn had returned from his eventful morning call at Vandon very grave and silent. He shook his head when Ruth came to him in the study to ask what the result had been, and said Dare would tell her himself on his return from London, whither he had gone on business.

Ruth went back to the drawing-room. She had not strength or energy to try to escape from Mrs. Alwynn. Indeed it was a relief not to be alone with her own thoughts, and to allow her exhausted mind to be towed along by Mrs. Alwynn's, the bent of whose mind resembled one of those mechanical toy animals which, when wound up, will run very fast in any direction, but if adroitly turned, will hurry equally fast the opposite way. Ruth turned the toy at intervals, and the morning was dragged through, Mrs. Alwynn in the course of it exploring every realm—known to her—of human thought, now dipping into the future, and speculating on spring fashions, now commenting on the present, now dwelling fondly on the past, the gayly dressed, officer-adorned past of her youth.

There was a meal, and after that it was the afternoon. Ruth supposed that some time there would be another meal, and then it would be evening, but it was no good thinking of what was so far away. She brought her mind back to the present. Mrs. Alwynn had just finished a detailed account of a difference of opinion between herself and the curate's wife on the previous day.

"And she had not a word to say, my dear, not a word—quite *hors de combat*—so I let the matter drop. And you remember that beautiful pig we killed last week? You should have gone to look at it hanging up, Ruth, rolling in fat, it was. Well, it is better to give than to receive, so I shall send her one of the pork-pies. And if you will get me one of those round baskets which I took the dolls down to the school-feast in—they are in the lowest shelf of the oak chest in the hall—I'll send it down to her at once."

Ruth fetched the basket and put it down by her aunt. Reminiscences of the school-feast still remained in it, in the shape of ends of ribbon and lace, and Mrs. Alwynn began to empty them out, talking all the time, when she suddenly stopped short, with an exclamation of surprise.

"Goodness! Well, now! I'm sure! Ruth!"

"What is it, Aunt Fanny?"

"Why, my dear, if there isn't a letter for you under the odds and ends," holding it up and gazing resentfully at it; "and now I remember, a letter came for you on the morning of the school-feast, and I said to John, 'I sha'n't forward it, because I shall see Ruth this afternoon,' and, dear me! I just popped it into the basket, for I thought you would like to have it, and you know how busy I was, Ruth, that day, first one thing and then another, so much to think of—and—*there it is*."

"I dare say it is of no importance," said Ruth, taking it from her, while Mrs. Alwynn, repeatedly wondering how such a thing could have happened to a person so careful as herself, went off with her basket to the cook.

When she returned in a few minutes she found Ruth standing by the window, the letter open in her hand, her face without a vestige of color.

"Why, Ruth," she said, actually noticing the alteration in her appearance, "is your head bad again?"

Ruth started violently.

"Yes—no. I mean—I think I will go out. The fresh air—"

She could not finish the sentence.

"And that tiresome letter—did it want an answer?"

"None," said Ruth, crushing it up unconsciously.

"Well, now," said Mrs. Alwynn, "that's a good thing, for I'm sure I shall never forget the way your uncle was in once, when I put a letter of his in my pocket to give him (it was a plum-colored silk, Ruth, done with gold beads in front), and then I went into mourning for my poor dear Uncle James—such an out-of-the-common person he was, Ruth, and such a beautiful talker—and it was not till six months later—niece's mourning, you know—that I had the dress on again—and a business I had to meet it, for all my gowns seem to shrink when they are put by—and I put my hand in the pocket, and—"

But Ruth had disappeared.

Mrs. Alwynn was perfectly certain at last that something must be wrong with her niece. Earlier in the day she had had a headache. Reasoning by analogy, she decided that Ruth must have eaten something at Mrs. Thursby's dinner-party which had disagreed with her. If any one was ill, she always attributed it to indigestion. If Mr. Alwynn coughed, or if she read in the papers that royalty had been unavoidably prevented attending some function at which its presence had been expected, she instantly put down both mishaps to the same cause; and when Mrs. Alwynn had come to a conclusion it was not her habit to keep it to herself.

She told Lady Mary the exact state in which, reasoning always by analogy, she knew Ruth's health must be, when that lady drove over that afternoon in the hope of seeing Ruth, partly from curiosity, or, rather, a Christian anxiety respecting the welfare of others, and partly, too, from a real feeling of affection for Ruth herself. Mrs. Alwynn bored her intensely; but she sat on and on in the hope of Ruth's return, who had gone out, Mrs. Alwynn agreeing with every remark she made, and treating her with that pleased deference of manner which some middle-class people, not otherwise vulgar, invariably drop into in the presence of rank; a Scylla which is only one degree better than the Charybdis of would-be ease of manner into which others fall. If ever the enormous advantages of noble birth and ancient family, with all their attendant heirlooms and hereditary instincts of refinement, chivalrous feeling, and honor, become in future years a mark for scorn (as already they are a mark for the envy that calls itself scorn), it will be partly the fault of the vulgar adoration of the middle classes. Mrs. Alwynn being, as may possibly have already transpired in the course of this narrative, a middle-class woman herself, stuck to the hereditary instincts of *her* class with a vengeance, and when Ruth at last came in Lady Mary was thankful.

Her cold, pale eyes lighted up a little as she greeted Ruth, and looked searchingly at her. She saw by the colorless lips and nervous contraction of the forehead, and by the bright, restless fever of the eyes that had formerly been so calm and clear, that something was amiss—terribly amiss.

"I've been telling Lady Mary how poorly you've been, Ruth, ever since Mrs. Thursby's dinner-party," said Mrs. Alwynn, by way of opening the conversation.

But in spite of so auspicious a beginning the conversation flagged. Lady Mary made a few conventional remarks to Ruth, which she answered, and Mrs. Alwynn also; but there was a constraint which every moment threatened a silence. Lady Mary proceeded to comment on the poaching affray of the previous night, and the arrest of a man who had been seriously injured; but at her mention of the subject Ruth became so silent, and Mrs. Alwynn so voluble, that she felt it was useless to stay any longer, and had to take her leave without a word with Ruth.

"Something is wrong with that girl," she said to herself, as she drove back to Atherstone. "I know what it is. Charles has been behaving in his usual manner, and as there is no one else to point out to him how infamous such conduct is, I shall have to do it myself. Shameful! That charming, interesting girl! And yet, and yet, there was a look in her face more like some great anxiety than disappointment. If she had had a disappointment, I do not think she would have let any one see it. Those Deyncourts are all too proud to show their feelings, though they have got them, too, somewhere. Perhaps, on the whole, considering how excessively disagreeable and scriptural Charles can be, and what unexpected turns he can give to things, I had better say nothing to him at present."

The moment Lady Mary had left the house, Ruth hurried to her uncle's study. He was not there. He had not yet come in. She gave a gesture of despair, and flung herself down in the old leather chair opposite to his own, on which many a one had sat who had come to him for help or consolation. All the buttons had been gradually worn off that chair by restless or heavy visitors. Some had been lost, but others—the greater part, I am glad to say—Mr. Alwynn had found and had deposited in a Sèvres cup on the mantle-piece, till the wet afternoon should come when he and his long packing-needle should restore them to their home.

The room was very quiet. On the mantle-piece the little conscientious silver clock ticked, orderly, gently (till Ruth could hardly bear the sound), then hesitated, and struck a soft, low tone. She started to her feet, and paced up and down, up and down. Would he never come in? She dared not go out to look for him for fear of missing him. Why did not he come back when she wanted him so terribly? She sat down again. She tried to be patient. It was no good. Would he never come?

She heard a sound, rushed out to meet him in the passage, and pulled him into the study.

"Uncle John," she gasped, holding out a letter in her shaking hand. "That man who was taken up last night was—Raymond. He is in prison. He is ill. Let us go to him," and she explained as best she could that a letter had only just been found written to her by Raymond in July, warning her he was in the neighborhood of Arleigh, near the old nurse's cottage, and that she might see him at any moment, and must have money in readiness. The instant she had read the letter she rushed up to Arleigh, to see her old nurse, and met her coming down, in great agitation, to tell her that Raymond, whom she had shielded once before under promise of secrecy, had been arrested the night before.

In a quarter of an hour Mr. Alwynn and Ruth were driving swiftly through the dusk, in a close carriage, in the direction of D——. On their way they met a dog-cart driving as quickly in the opposite direction which grazed their wheel as it passed; and Ruth, looking out, caught a glimpse, by the flash of their lamps, of Charles's face, with a look upon it so fierce and haggard that she shivered in nameless foreboding of evil, wondering what could have happened to make him look like that.

CHAPTER XXXI

It was still early on the following morning that Dare, forgetting, as we have seen, his promise to Charles, arrived at Slumberleigh Rectory—so early that Mrs. Alwynn was still ordering dinner, or, in other words, was dashing from larder to scullery, from kitchen to dairy, with her usual energy. He was shown into the empty drawing-room, where, after pacing up and down, he was reduced to the society of a photograph album, which, in his present excited condition, could do little to soothe the tumult of his mind. Not that any discredit should be thrown on Mrs. Alwynn's album, a gorgeous concern with a golden "Fanny" embossed on it, which afforded her infinite satisfaction, inside which her friends' portraits appeared to the greatest advantage, surrounded by birds and nests and blossoms of the most vivid and life-like coloring. Mr. Alwynn was encompassed on every side by kingfishers and elaborate bone nests, while Ruth's clear-cut face looked out from among long-tailed tomtits, arranged one on each side of a nest crowded with eggs, on which a strong light had been thrown.

Dare was still looking at Ruth's photograph, when Mr. Alwynn came in.

"Do you wish to speak to Ruth?" he asked, gravely.

"Now, at once." Dare was surprised that Mr. Alwynn, with whom he had been so open, should be so cold and unsympathetic in manner. The alteration and alienation of friends is certainly one of the saddest and most inexplicable experiences of this vale of tears.

"You will find her in the study," continued Mr. Alwynn. "She is expecting you. I have told her nothing, according to your wish. I hope you will explain everything to her in full, that you will keep nothing back."

"I will explain," said Dare; and he went, trembling with excitement, into the study. Fired by Charles's example, he had made a sublime resolve as he skimmed across the fields, made it in a hurry, in a moment of ecstasy, as all his resolutions were made. He felt he had never acted such a noble part before. He only feared the agitation of the moment might prevent him doing himself justice.

Ruth rose as he came in, but did not speak. A swift spasm passed over her face, leaving it very stern, very fixed, as he had never seen it, as he had never thought of seeing it. An overwhelming suspense burned in the dark, lustreless eyes which met his own. He felt awed.

"Well?" she said, pressing her hands together, and speaking in a low voice.

"Ruth," said Dare, solemnly, laying his outspread hand upon his breast and then extending it in the air, "I am free."

· Ruth's eyes watched him like one in torture.

"How?" she said, speaking with difficulty. "You said you were free before."

"Ah!" replied Dare, raising his forefinger, "I said so, but it was an error. I go to Vandon, and she will not go away. I go to London to my lawyer, and he says she is my wife."

"You told me she was not."

"It was an error," repeated Dare. "I had formerly been a husband to her, but we had been divorced; it was finished, wound up, and I thought she was no more my wife. There is in the English law something extraordinary which I do not comprehend, which makes an American divorce to remain a marriage in England."

"Go on," said Ruth, shading her eyes with her hand.

"I come back to Vandon," continued Dare, in a suppressed voice, "I come back overwhelmed, broken down, crushed under feet; and then," — he was becoming dramatic, he felt the fire kindling — "I meet a friend, a noble heart, I confide in him. I tell all to Sir Charles Danvers," — Ruth's hand was trembling — "and last night he finds out by a chance that she was not a true widow when I marry her, that her first husband was yet alive, that I am free. This morning he tells me all, and I am here."

Ruth pressed her hands before her face, and fairly burst into tears.

He looked at her in astonishment. He was surprised that she had any feelings. Never having shown them to the public in general, like himself, he had supposed she was entirely devoid of them. She now appeared quite *émue*. She was sobbing passionately. Tears came into his own eyes as he watched her, and then a light dawned upon him for the second time that day. Those tears were not for him. He folded his arms and waited. How suggestive in itself is a noble attitude!

After a few minutes Ruth overcame her tears with a great effort, and, raising her head, looked at him, as if she expected him to speak. The suspense was gone out of her dimmed eyes, the tension of her face was relaxed.

"I am free," repeated Dare, "and I have your promise that if I am free you will still marry me."

Ruth looked up with a pained but resolute expression, and she would have spoken if he had not stopped her by a gesture.

"I have your promise," he repeated. "I tell my friend, Sir Charles Danvers, I have it. He also loves. He does not tell me so; he is not open with me, as I with him, but I see his heart. And yet—figure to yourself—he has but to keep silence, and I must go away, I must give up all. I am still married—*Ou!*—while he—But he is noble, he is sublime. He sacrifices love on the altar of honor, of truth. He tells all to me, his rival. He shows me I am free. He thinks I do not know his heart. But it is not only he who can be noble." (Dare smote himself upon the breast.) "I also can lay my heart upon the altar. Ruth,"—with great solemnity—"do you love him even as he loves you?"

There was a moment's pause.

"I do," she said, firmly, "with my whole heart."

"I knew it. I divined it. I sacrifice myself. I give you back your promise. I say farewell, and voyage in the distance. I return no more to Vandon. There is no longer a home for me in England. I leave only behind with you the poor heart you have possessed so long!"

Dare was so much affected by the beauty of this last sentence that he could say no more, but even at that moment, as he glanced at Ruth to see what effect his eloquence had upon her, she looked so pallid and thin (her beauty was so entirely eclipsed) that the sacrifice did not seem quite so overwhelming, after all.

She struggled to speak, but words failed her.

He took her hands and kissed them, pressed them to his heart (it was a pity there was no one there to see), endeavored to say something more, and then rushed out of the room.

She stood like one stunned after he had left her. She saw him a moment later cross the garden, and flee away across the fields. She knew she had seen that gray figure and jaunty gray hat for the last time; but she hardly thought of him. She felt she might be sorry for him presently, but not now.

The suspense was over. The sense of relief was too overwhelming to admit of any other feeling at first. She dropped on her knees beside the writing-table, and locked her hands together.

"*He told,*" she whispered to herself. "Thank God! Thank God!"

Two happy tears dropped onto Mr. Alwynn's old leather blotting-book, that worn cradle of many sermons.

Was this the same world? Was this the same sun which was shining in upon her? What new songs were the birds practising outside? A strange wonderful joy seemed to pervade the very air she breathed, to flood her inmost soul. She had faced her troubles fairly well, but at this new great happiness she did not dare to look; and with a sudden involuntary gesture she hid her face in her hands.

It would be rash to speculate too deeply on the nature of Dare's reflections as he hurried back to Atherstone; but perhaps, under the very real pang of parting with Ruth, he was sustained by a sense of the magnanimity of what, had he put it into words, he would have called his attitude, and possibly also by a lurking conviction, which had assisted his determination to resign her that life at Vandon, after the episode of the American wife's arrival, would be a social impossibility, especially to one anxious and suited to shine in society. Be that how it may, whatever had happened to influence him most of the chance emotion of the moment, it would be tolerably certain that in a few hours he would be sorry for what he had done. He was still, however, in a state of mental exaltation when he reached Atherstone, and began fumbling nervously with the garden-gate. Charles, who had been stalking up and down the bowling-green, went slowly towards him.

"What on earth do you mean by going off in that way?" he asked, coldly.

"Ah!" said Dare, perceiving him, "and she—the—is she gone?"

"Yes, half an hour ago. Your dog-cart has come back from taking her to the station, and is here now."

Dare nodded his head several times, and stood looking at him.

"I have been to Slumberleigh," he said.

"Yes, contrary to agreement."

"My friend," Dare said, seizing the friend's limp, unresponsive hand and pressing it, "I know now why you keep silence last night. I reason with myself. I see you love her. Do not turn away. I have seen her. I have given her back her promise. I give her up to you whom she loves; and now—I go away, not to return."

And then, in the full view of the Atherstone windows, of the butler, and of the dog-cart at the front door, Dare embraced him, kissing the blushing and disconcerted Charles on both cheeks. Then, in a moment, before the latter had recovered his self-possession, Dare had darted to the dog-cart, and was driving away.

Charles looked after him in mixed annoyance and astonishment, until he noticed the butler's eye upon him, when he hastily retreated, with a heightened complexion, to the shrubberies.

CONCLUSION

It was the last day of October, about a week after a certain very quiet little funeral had taken place in the D— — Cemetery. The death of Raymond Deyncourt had appeared in the papers a day or two afterwards, without mention of date or place, and it was generally supposed that it had taken place some considerable time previously, without the knowledge of his friends.

Charles had been sitting for a long time with Mr. Alwynn, and after he left the rectory he took the path over the fields in the direction of the Slumberleigh woods.

The low sun was shining redly through a golden haze, was sending long burning shafts across the glade where Charles was pacing. He sat down at last upon a fallen tree to wait for one who should presently come by that way.

It was a still, clear afternoon, with a solemn stillness that speaks of coming change. Winter was at hand, and the woods were transfigured with a passing glory, like the faces of those who depart in peace when death draws nigh.

Far and wide in the forest the bracken was all aflame—aflame beneath the glowing trees. The great beeches had turned to bronze and ruddy gold, and had strewed the path with carpets glorious and rare, which the first wind would sweep away. Upon the limes the amber leaves still hung, faint yet loath to go, but the horse-chestnut had already dropped its garment of green and yellow at its feet.

A young robin was singing at intervals in the silence, telling how the secrets of the nests had been laid bare, singing a requiem on the dying leaves and the widowed branches, a song new to him, but with the old plaintive rapture in it that his fathers had been taught before him since the world began.

She came towards him down the yellow glade through the sunshine and the shadow, with a spray of briony in her hand. Neither spoke. She put her hands into the hands that were held out for them, and their eyes met, grave and steadfast, with the light in them of an unalterable love. So long they had looked at each other across a gulf. So long they had stood apart. And now, at last—at last—they were together. He drew her close and closer yet. They had no words. There was no need of words. And in the silence of the hushed woods, and in the silence of a joy too deep for speech, the robin's song came sweet and sad.

"Charles!"

"Ruth!"

"I should like to tell you something."

"And I should like to hear it."

"I know what Raymond told you to conceal. I went to him just after you did. We passed you coming back. He did not know me at first. He thought I was you, and he kept repeating that you must keep your own counsel, and that, unless you showed Mr. Dare's marriage was illegal, he would never find it out. At last, when he suddenly recognized me, he seemed horror-struck, and the doctor came in and sent me away."

Charles knew now why Raymond had sent for him the second time.

There was a long pause.

"Ruth, did you think I should tell?"

"I hoped and prayed you would, but I knew it would be hard, because I do believe you actually thought at the time I should still consider it my duty to marry Mr. Dare. I never should have done such a thing after what had happened. I was just going to tell him so when he began to give me up, and it evidently gave him so much pleasure to renounce me nobly in your favor that I let him have it his own way, as the result was the same. My great dread, until he came, was that you had not spoken. I had been expecting him all the previous evening. Oh, Charles, Charles! I waited and watched for his coming as I had never done before. Your silence was the only thing I feared, because it was the only thing that could have come between us."

"God forgive me! I meant at first to say nothing."

"Only at first," said Ruth, gently; and they walked on in silence.

The sun had set. A slender moon had climbed unnoticed into the southern sky amid the shafts of paling fire which stretched out across the whole heaven from the burning fiery furnace in the west. Across the gray dim fields voices were calling the cattle home.

Charles spoke again at last in his usual tone.

"You quite understand, Ruth, though I have not mentioned it so far, that you are engaged to marry me?"

The Danvers Jewels And Sir Charles Danvers | 319

"I do. I will make a note of it if you wish."

"It is unnecessary. I shall be happy, when I am at leisure to remind you myself. Indeed, I may say I shall make a point of doing so. There does not happen to be any one else whom you feel it would be your duty to marry?"

"I can't think of any one at the moment. Charles, you never *could* have believed I would marry *him*, after all?"

"Indeed, I did believe it. Don't I know the stubbornness of your heart? You see, you are but young, and I make excuses for you; but, after you have been the object of my special and judicious training for a few years, I quite hope your judgment may improve considerably."

"I trust it will, as I see from your remarks—it will certainly be all we shall have to guide us both."

Postscript.—Lady Mary would not allow even Providence any of the credit of Charles's engagement; she claimed the whole herself. She called Evelyn to witness that from the first it had been her work entirely. She only allowed Charles himself a very secondary part in the great event, to which she was apt to point in later years as the crowning work of a life devoted—under Church direction—to the temporal and spiritual welfare of her fellow-creatures; and Charles avers that a mention of it in the long list of her virtues will some day adorn the tombstone which she has long since ordered to be in readiness.

Molly was disconsolate for many days, but work, that panacea of grief, came to the rescue, and it was not long before she was secretly and busily engaged on a large kettle-holder, with kettle and motto entwined, for Charles's exclusive use, without which she had been led to understand his establishment would be incomplete. When this work of art was finished her feelings had become so far modified towards Ruth that she consented to begin another very small and inferior one—merely a kettle on a red ground—for that interloper, but whether it was ever presented is not on record.

Vandon is to let. The grass has grown up again through the niches of the stone steps. The place looks wild and deserted. Mr. Alwynn comes sometimes, and looks up at its shuttered windows and trailing, neglected ivy, but not often, for it gives him a strange pang at the heart. And as he goes home the people come out of the dilapidated cottages, and ask wistfully when the new squire is coming back.

But Mr. Alwynn does not know.